The Counterfeit Madam

Pat McIntosh

Constable • London

Constable & Robinson Ltd
55–56 Russell Square
London WC1B 4HP
www.constablerobinson.com

First published in the UK by Robinson,
an imprint of Constable & Robinson, 2012

A copy of the British Library Cataloguing in Publication
Data is available from the British Library

ISBN: 978-1-78033-161-4

Printed and bound in the UK

1 3 5 7 9 10 8 6 4 2

Born and brought up in Lanarkshire, PAT MCINTOSH lived and worked in Glasgow before settling on Scotland's west coast, where she lives with her husband and three cats.

Also by Pat McIntosh

The Harper's Quine
The Nicholas Feast
The Merchant's Mark
St Mungo's Robin
The Rough Collier
The Stolen Voice
A Pig of Cold Poison

For all the people who taught me geology,
in propriam memoriam KAGS and JDL
and also for Imogen, copy-editor without equal

Students of the geology of the West of Scotland will recognise that I have taken serious liberties with Campsie Glen. In fact, I have borrowed a section of the Ochils, which are also Carboniferous lava flows, and transplanted it to the Campsies. I am indebted to *Bonanzas and Jacobites: the Story of the Silver Glen*, by Stephen Moreton (National Museums of Scotland, 2007) for the details of geology and setting.

Ever since it became a kingdom, Scotland has had two native languages, Gaelic (which in the fifteenth century was called Ersche) and Scots, both of which you will find used in the Gil Cunningham books. I have translated the Gaelic where needful, and those who have trouble with the Scots could consult the Dictionary of the Scots Language, to be found at http://www.dsl.ac.uk/dsl/

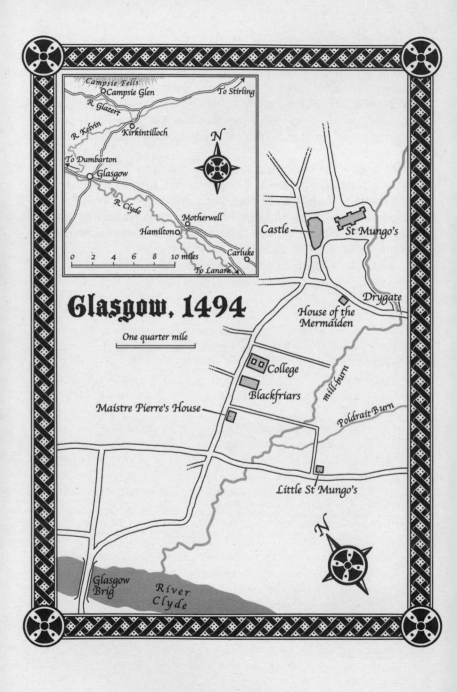

Campsie Fells
Campsie Glen
R. Glazert
To Stirling
R. Kelvin
Kirkintilloch
N
To Dumbarton
Glasgow
R. Clyde
Motherwell
Hamilton
Carluke
0 2 4 6 8 10 miles
To Lanark

Castle
St Mungo's
Drygate

Glasgow, 1494

One quarter mile

House of the Mermaiden

College
Blackfriars

Maistre Pierre's House

mill burn

Poldrait Burn

Little St Mungo's

N

Glasgow Brig
River Clyde

Chapter One

Gil Cunningham had hoped that the first time he set foot in the whorehouse on the Drygate would also be the last; but by the time all was settled he felt quite at home within its artful painted chambers.

The first inkling he had of the matter came one day in late April, in the form of a loud knocking at the door of his father-in-law's house as family and servants were eating their midday meal in the hall. Conversation at the long board ceased and heads turned towards the sound; Gil and Alys exchanged a surprised glance, Alys's aged French duenna Catherine paused in her absorption of sops-in-wine. The wolfhound Socrates was already on his feet, the hackles standing up on his narrow back. A stranger, Gil concluded.

'Who calls at the dinner-hour?' wondered Maistre Pierre, pushing back his great chair. He rose with caution, muttering darkly about his knees, but his young journeyman Luke was before him, opening the big planked door to reveal a serving-man in unfamiliar blue-grey livery bowing on the doorstep, felt bonnet in hand.

'My mistress, Dame Isabella Torrance, seeks Maister Gil Cunningham,' he said. 'Is this where he dwells?'

'Isabella Torrance?' Gil repeated in some surprise, going forward as Luke turned to relay the message. 'She's still alive, then?'

'She's at the gate, maister,' said the man.

Gil looked down at his wife as she joined him in the doorway. 'Godmother to my sister Tib,' he explained.

'Dwells over by Stirling, I think. I wonder if it's about Tib's marriage?'

'Stirling?' repeated Alys. 'Whatever is she doing in Glasgow?'

The servant shrugged his shoulders.

'Likely she'll tell you hersel,' he offered. 'Will I bid her come in?'

'Aye, bid her enter,' said Maistre Pierre from the head of the table. 'We are still at meat, man, ask her if she will join us.'

'She doesny eat in the middle of the day,' the man said, shaking his head regretfully.

There was a commotion in the pend which led out to the street, and a number of people emerged into the courtyard, headed by a short, stout, loud individual with a stick. Their guest had not waited to be invited in. Alys exclaimed briefly and hurried down the steps past Gil to offer a welcome. Her curtsy was spurned with a brief nod, her arm was ignored, and the small dark figure ploughed across the yard to the foot of the steps where it stopped, scowling up at Gil with eyes like jet rosary beads.

Dame Isabella was probably five feet high and the same around, though this girth also engrossed a vast furred brocade gown which hung open over several layers of different, equally expensive, black fabrics. Beneath a black silk Flemish hood with extravagantly long foreparts, finely pleated linen framed her small padded face, heightening its colour unbecomingly; she had a dab of a nose, separated by a dark wispy moustache from a mouthful of very large, improbably white teeth. She seemed to have brought her entire household visiting; at her back were four sturdy grooms, including the man who had come to the door, and two waiting-women.

'So you're Gelis Muirhead's laddie, are you?' she said in deep, disparaging tones. 'Aye, you've a look of her, though you're more like your faither.' This was clearly not a compliment. 'At least you've more sense than get yoursel slain the way he did. And both your brothers, was it?'

'Dame Isabella,' Gil said, very politely, and bowed.

'Welcome to my house. Will you enter, madame?' offered Maistre Pierre over Gil's shoulder.

'Aye, I'll come in. You're the good-father I take it. I hope ye've a seat for me. I want a word wi young Gilbert, afore that gowk Sempill gets involved. Here, you fools, get me up these steps.'

'Sempill? John Sempill of Muirend?' Gil repeated, but the servants who surrounded Dame Isabella had begun the considerable task of hoisting her up the fore-stair, which she endured with much shouting and brandishing of her stick. In his ear his father-in-law said,

'What does she want with Sempill? Why should he come here?'

'No idea,' said Gil, stepping back to allow the nearest manservant elbowroom. 'When did we see him last?' He counted on his fingers. 'It must have been August last year. It's been the gallowglass – Euan Campbell – who brought me the money for the boy's keep at both the quarter-days since then.' He met Maistre Pierre's eye. 'If it's about the boy, it's likely no good.'

'So I think,' agreed the mason. They both turned to look inside the hall, where Maistre Pierre's foster-child, small John McIan, bastard son of John Sempill's runaway wife and her lover the harper, was perched on his nurse's knee at the long table addressing a large crust of bread.

'Sempill still needs an heir, surely?' said Maistre Pierre doubtfully. 'That was why he acknowledged John. What is he about now?'

'We'll find out soon enough,' said Gil.

'Parcel of fools!' announced Dame Isabella. Achieving the topmost step, she paused long enough to adjust her grasp on her stick and surged forward, shaking off her gasping servants and ignoring Maistre Pierre's courtesies as she had ignored Alys's. Behind her, Alys slipped up the fore-stair and into the hall, with a brief touch on Gil's hand as she went.

3

'You're at meat, are you?' continued their guest, staring at the household arranged round the long board. Small John waved his crust and shouted something unintelligible. 'I hope you've all had your bowels open at stool the day. It's no good to eat on a full bowel.'

'Will you not join us, madame?' Alys offered, gesturing at the head of the table. 'There is good broth, and fresh oatcakes and cheese—'

'No.' The black beads considered her. 'I suppose you're the French wife. Christ aid us, you've a nose on you like a papingo's. I see he's no bairned you yet. Has he bedded you? Is your bowels regular? You'll no take if your bowel's full, it unbalances the humours.'

Alys stared at the old woman, amazement outweighing her natural courtesy. Gil moved to intervene, but Catherine had already risen and now forestalled him.

'*Vraiment, madame,*' she said in her elegant French, 'you do right to concern yourself with such matters. It is important to keep the humours of the body balanced, but I find the young are often careless of their internal economy.'

'And who are you?' demanded Dame Isabella in the same language. 'You speak French uncommonly well, even if you have not kept your teeth as I have.'

Over the two black-draped heads Alys caught Gil's eye, her expression carefully neutral. Catherine closed her toothless mouth on whatever reply came first, and Gil said hastily,

'This is Madame Catherine Calvin, who keeps my wife company. Will you sit in by the hearth, madam, while they clear the board?'

'Aye, and watch all,' said Dame Isabella, 'so I can tell Gelis Muirhead what kind of household you're wedded into. No, I'll ha no refreshment. It's no my hour for it.'

'Lady Cunningham was with us for a week at Yule,' observed Catherine. 'She is a most cultured lady, and speaks excellent French.'

4

Dame Isabella ignored this shaft, and seated herself nearest the hearth, staring about her. The household, taking the hint, began the process of dismantling the long table, stacking up platters and bowls and sweeping the cloth into a bundle to be shaken into the courtyard. By the time board and trestles were in place against the wall, Dame Isabella's entourage had been dismissed to the kitchen, save for a man with a huge leather satchel and one waiting-woman who studied Maistre Pierre with intent dark eyes, and the two old ladies were deep in a conversation involving the humours, the elements, and the zodiac. Gil, standing awkwardly by, was aware of his wife conferring with her father, and of the mason's two journeymen leaving the house, but his mind was occupied with possible reasons for this sudden visitation.

He had met Dame Isabella once or twice as a boy, and felt she had not improved. She had been a member of Margaret of Denmark's household alongside his mother, which was presumably why she had been invited to stand godmother to his youngest sister. Lady Cunningham had mentioned her occasionally over the years; he vaguely recalled that she had been wedded at least twice since the death of her royal mistress, though to judge by her black garb and the pleated linen barbe pinned below her chin she was currently a widow. Small wonder, he thought.

As Tib's godmother, it would be appropriate for her to do something for the girl before her approaching marriage, whether it embraced coin or a gift of land or jewels, and as Tib's nearest male relative he could expect to be consulted in the transaction. But she had mentioned John Sempill's involvement. There was no connection between Sempill and Tib that he knew of.

'*Maistre le notaire* awaits your convenience, *madame*,' said Catherine by the hearth. 'We should not keep him waiting, perhaps.'

'He's got little enough to do,' pronounced Dame Isabella, but she turned to stare at Gil. 'Like my servants, the useless troop. Come here, Gilbert. Is that the brat?' She

5

nodded towards small John, who was just being led towards the kitchen stair by his quiet nurse.

'That's John Sempill's heir,' agreed Gil, repressing anger. 'Does this concern the boy? My good-father should be present if so.'

'Why? What's it to do wi him?'

'The boy is in my care,' said Maistre Pierre, coming forward from the door. Dame Isabella glared at him, grunted, and gestured at the bench opposite her.

'You may as well sit down and all, then, and listen.' Catherine rose at this point with a murmured farewell, which was ignored, and Alys moved quietly towards one of the far windows, where she had left her needlework. 'Now, Gilbert. You'll ken I've two goddaughters, your sister Isobel and a lassie Magdalen Boyd, who's some kin of yours so Gelis your mother tells me.'

'Boyd.' Gil sat down obediently beside his father-in-law, searching his memory of the kindred. 'Aye, she is. Third or fourth cousin, I'd say. There was a brother too, name of – name of – was it Alexander? They were about penniless, I think.'

'That was their faither's doing,' she said dismissively. 'Any road, Magdalen has wedded John Sempill for her second husband.' She looked with satisfaction at his astonished face. 'Aye, a good match, for the both of them, and I was right glad to support it.'

'I'd not wed my worst enemy's daughter to John Sempill,' said Gil. Beside him Maistre Pierre rumbled agreement.

'He's done better than you have, mewed up here in a town wi a barren foreigner. Maidie has no trouble wi him. But the point is, she's in a likely way.' Sweet St Giles, when were they wedded, Gil wondered grimly, not looking at Alys. 'So she's no wanting another man's get to be Sempill's heir, no when she's in a way to provide him wi one. Sempill's in full agreement, so they're proposing that he'll no recognize the brat as his heir any longer, and in consideration they're offering it a bit land here in Glasgow where it's handy.'

Gil stared at her, preserving his expression as best he might. After a moment Maistre Pierre said,

'But does the man Sempill have anything left to offer? I thought he was hard pressed.'

'He was,' Gil said. 'He was in Glasgow to deal with that when his wife – his first wife,' he corrected himself, 'was killed, and left her son motherless. That was why he took the boy for his heir, so old Canon Murray would leave him his fortune, though I think the old man still lives.' He eyed Dame Isabella, hoping his dislike did not show. 'I take it his circumstances have changed with the new marriage?'

She gave a bark of laughter.

'Aye, they've changed, and for the better. So will you accept the offer?'

'We can't say,' said Gil without pausing to consult with Maistre Pierre, 'until we know what the offer might be.'

'That's a pity,' said Dame Isabella, 'for once that's dealt wi I've a couple of plots to dispose of and all. There's one of them out Carluke way, been in my family for years, and one in Strathblane, they bring in much the same rent, and we'll can see about which goes to Maidie and which to your sister Isobel.'

'It would surely be more convenient,' said Maistre Pierre reasonably, 'that the Lanarkshire property go to the Lanarkshire lassie, unless your other goddaughter dwells there also. No, she must be in Renfrewshire,' he corrected himself.

'We'll can see,' Dame Isabella repeated. Gil sat still, wondering how his mother had ever liked this woman enough to invite her to be Tib's godmother. The bargain was clear enough: if he agreed to Sempill's proposal for young John McIan and accepted the offered property in exchange for the boy's present status as Sempill's heir, Tib would get the land close to where she would be settled; if not, it was likely she would find herself in possession of a patch of Strathblane, a full day's ride from her new home, with the

7

attendant difficulties of administering the rent and overseeing the tenants.

'We need to know more, madam,' he said as politely
as he could, 'and we'll need time to consider. As the
boy's tutor and foster-father we should take it all in
advisement—'

'You've an hour to think on it,' she retorted. 'We're to
meet at your uncle the Canon's house. He made a right to-
do about having no time, this was the only moment in the
week he could spare us, as if he didny dwell and work in
the burgh, so you'd best no be late.'

It was hardly worth trying to explain, Gil thought, that
the Official of Glasgow, the senior judge of the diocese,
had a caseload that would tax an elephant and regularly
worked all the hours he was not sleeping. Sempill had
been fortunate to find a moment when Canon Cunningham could see them. As for the papers he himself had to
complete for the next day's taking of sasines in Rottenrow,
that would clearly have to wait until later.

'Will we convoy you up the road?' he suggested.

'No, you'll no. If you need to consult, you'll consult, for
I want a decision the day, else the whole goes to Maidie.'
She turned her head. 'Here, Attie scatterwit, where are
ye? And you, you worthless frivol. Call the men, and send
out to see if Sproat's waited like I bade him. Time I was on
the road.'

When Maistre Pierre returned from seeing their unwelcome guest to the street he found Gil discussing the
interview with Alys.

'*Mon Dieu!*' he said, shutting the house door and leaning on it. '*Quelle horreur de femme! Ma mie*, your nose does
not in the least resemble a parrot's, it is the image of that
of your sainted mother.'

Gil had already reassured his wife on this point, though
she did not seem to be concerned; now he said in Scots,

'*Christ never such another bought That ever I saw.* I've aye thought it was little wonder Margaret of Denmark died young, given her household. So do we accept?'

'It depends what the offer is,' said his father-in-law.

'I would be glad for John to be clear of Sempill,' Alys observed, 'but should we not consult his father?'

'McIan? Do we know where McIan is?' Gil wondered.

'They were to be in Stirling, and then they are coming here, so Ealasaidh sent me the other day.'

'We'll not get a reply from Stirling within an hour.'

'No, I fear not,' said Maistre Pierre. 'But if we are both to go up the road, there is another matter to see to.' He crossed to the hearth and reached up onto the carved hood of the chimney-breast. 'We may take this counterfeit silver to the Sheriff while we are there.'

'More false coin,' said Andrew Otterburn glumly.

'It looks like it,' said Gil.

The present depute Provost of Glasgow was a lanky Borderer in his forties with a long gloomy face. Gil suspected his mother must have been a Chisholm, to judge by the deep, close set of his eyes, but had never quite liked to ask. The man had a difficult task; Sir Thomas Stewart, Provost of Glasgow for eight or ten years, had demitted office at Yule and Archbishop Robert Blacader had installed Maister Otterburn to take care of his burgh until the election of a new provost at the Town Meeting in the autumn. Sir Thomas had been accepted and respected, and his successor did not meet with unanimous approval. It did not help that Glasgow and the surrounding area was plagued by an outbreak of false coin, of which the first specimens had come to light in the burgh coffers themselves less than a month after Otterburn was put in post.

Now, discovered in the Provost's lodgings in the Castle, he scrutinized the handful of coins Maistre Pierre offered him as if they were personal bad tidings.

'Aye,' he said at length. 'I'd say they were out of the same workshop. See, these are all the same plack wi James Third on it, and that's the silver threepenny piece wi four mullets on the back. I've had two o these brought me from the bawdy-house. The madam wasny best pleased, I can tell you.' He turned the coin to the light, then bit it reflectively and shook his head. 'My lord's right keen to learn the source of these, but I've not found yet where they come fro', though it seems there are more entering through Dumbarton out of the Isles. How did you come by these, maister?'

'The placks came back from the market yesterday,' said Maistre Pierre. 'The maidservant who brought them thought they came from more than one trader. The silver piece I had from Daniel Hutchison, in a bag of coin.'

'Hutchison,' Otterburn repeated. 'Oh, aye, he's putting a new wing to his house, is that right? Over in the Gorbals. Outside the burgh, strictly,' he added, spinning one of the placks. It twirled once or twice and fell over.

'But the coin has come into the burgh,' Gil pointed out.

'Oh, I'm not arguing.'

'You say they come from the Isles?' Maistre Pierre said. 'Who should make false coin in the Isles? Is there any source of metal?'

'None that I ken,' admitted Otterburn. 'I'd not say the coin was being struck out yonder, just that it comes back in from there.'

'So someone is taking it there,' Gil said thoughtfully. 'Where from, and why?'

'Good questions.' Otterburn spun the plack again. 'As to where from, likely the same place as these came from, which my lord would like fine to ken as I say, but why's another matter.'

'To alter the balance of wealth out there?' suggested Maistre Pierre. 'Is there any suddenly rich?'

'The Islesmen set less store by coin than we do,' said Gil. 'It's a world of barter and payment in kind, wi little call for money within factions. I suppose if one kinship was

10

buying the friendship of another, or buying in gallow-glasses – hired fighting men, like the Campbell brothers, from Ireland or another part of the Isles – they might need coin. Is there any word of that kind of thing?'

'When is there no?' said Otterburn, making a long face. 'The King didny settle matters out there, for all he took John of the Isles prisoner last year. Indeed, matters are worse, for they're all at each other's throats now to determine who has his place. Word is the King's Grace is planning to go out again this spring.' He stacked the coins neatly, considering them. 'Would this come within your writ, Maister Cunningham? As Blacader's quaestor? I'm thinking it's about time we did something about it, other than wringing our hands and passing resolutions in the burgh council.'

'It would,' Gil said cautiously, 'if my lord so instructed me. If you were to suggest to him that I look into it, I'd be glad to—'

'It's as good as done, man,' said Otterburn. He hitched up the shoulders of his fur-lined gown, swept the coins off the table-carpet into his hand and moved to the cabinet beside the tall window. 'Walter can scribe me a note of where these came from and I'll put them wi the others, and then he can write to my lord. The day's despatch has yet to go. And when that's done and we've had my lord's agreement,' he added, 'I'll let you hear all I ken of the things. It's no a lot, I confess.'

'Pursuing false moneyers would make a change from pursuing murderers,' observed Maistre Pierre as they made their way up Rottenrow.

Gil nodded, thinking about the conversation. Otterburn's slow manner and gloomy speech had convinced most of the burgesses of Glasgow that he was a fool, but more than once he had shown a deeper knowledge of what was afoot in his burgh than one might expect after less than four months in post. Sir Thomas's clerk Walter served him willingly and well, always a good sign. If Otterburn had not yet tracked down the source of the counterfeit money, it must be well hidden.

'I do not understand what goes on in the Isles,' Maistre Pierre went on. 'I had thought all was settled last year, but by what the Provost says—'

Gil eyed his father-in-law, a man in accurate touch with the politics of Scotland and most of Europe.

'John MacDonald, Lord of the Isles, was forfeit this time last year,' he said, 'and did penance for all his crimes in January there, and resigned his lands into the King's hands.'

'That part I know. Your uncle tells me he is now the King's pensioner somewhere in Stirling. But who is in his shoes? Someone must hold his lands and command the wild Ersche.'

'That's the problem, as Otterburn said. More than one possible heir, all with influence, none with authority to command the whole of the region.'

'Has he no direct heir?'

'He had.' Gil paused to enumerate. 'His son Angus Og, which I think means Young Angus, was the obvious successor—'

'Was,' repeated the mason.

'Aye. Angus Og was murdered by his harper in '90. He was wedded to yet another of old Argyll's daughters – a sister of the present earl—'

'So there are Campbells in it. I might have known.'

'Indeed. There's a posthumous son, now in this earl's care—'

'Ah!'

'—and John's two nephews are bickering with Argyll and with McIan of Ardnamurchan about who has *de facto* control of the Isles. It's hardly simple at best, but it's not easy to understand if you're not from the Isles yourself.'

'That I agree with.'

The front door of Canon Cunningham's house was standing open as they approached. There seemed to be

12

a commotion on the stairs within, and a familiar voice reached them shouting abuse from the midst of a group of struggling servants. They strode on without hesitation, to enter the house by the kitchen door, and found Canon Cunningham's housekeeper Maggie, stout and red-faced, setting the leather beakers on a tray while a jug of buttered ale warmed at the hearth. Clearly Sempill and his party were not the most esteemed clients; those got the glasses from the cupboard in the hall, with wine, white or red, or even the Dutch spirits.

Maggie looked round as they stepped into the vaulted chamber, and nodded to the mason.

'Good day to ye, maister, and how are ye? Maister Gil, he's asking where you are. Oh, get off wi you,' she added, as Gil came to kiss her broad cheek. 'Are you well? How does Mistress Alys do?'

'Well enough.' Gil inspected the rack of little cakes left to cool on the broad scrubbed table. 'She sends her greetings. These are good, Maggie. There's nothing comes out of our kitchen quite like them. Try one, Pierre.'

Maggie looked gratified, but smacked his hand away as he reached for a second cake. 'Away up the stair wi you, Maister Gil, I tellt you he was asking for you and they're all up there waiting. You can get another of these after.'

'Who's waiting? Who did Sempill bring for witnesses?'

'Oh, a great crowd. Sempill himsel,' she counted on her work-worn fingers, 'and that cousin that's aye wi him – Philip, is it? Him that swore to revenge Bess Stewart on him and hasny done it yet, that I ever heard. Sempill's new wife, a couple more fellows, and that Dame Isabella wi a hantle of servants, still heaving her up the stair like a barrel in a sling by the sound of it. No, maister, the cakes is for after, one's all you're getting. I better put them by afore they all come down to my kitchen to wait while she gets her business seen to.'

'Aye, this new wife,' said Gil. 'Had you heard of the marriage? Did anyone warn the lassie's kin?'

13

'That's what I wondered,' she agreed, with satisfaction. 'No, I'd not heard, and nor had the old man. He's right put out about that. I wonder your lady mother never mentioned it, seeing the lassie must be cousins wi her. Maybe she's too taen up wi Lady Tib's marriage.'

'Who was the first husband?' asked Maistre Pierre. 'I take it he was a wealthy man.'

'That I've not heard,' Maggie said regretfully, 'but likely you're right, maister, and he left her better off than he got her. That Sempill wouldny take her without something to sweeten the match. Or maybe this land that Dame Isabella's to settle on them was the attraction.'

Gil nodded. He had set eyes only once or twice on either Sempill cousin since the episode, almost two years since, when Sempill's runaway wife Bess Stewart had been discovered dead in the half-built addition to the cathedral. Gil had been directed to find her killer, and in doing so had made the closer acquaintance of Pierre Mason and his daughter Alys; by the time the matter was solved he was betrothed to Alys, his intended career in the church abandoned, and Pierre had agreed to foster Bess's baby son, with Gil as the boy's guardian. John Sempill's interest in the child was solely financial, which in Sempill's case, he thought now, would be a more powerful attraction than parenthood, and if the man's financial position had changed then his attitude to the boy had probably changed too.

'And that Dame Isabella,' Maggie pursued, 'I opened the door to her manservant, and the maister cam down the stair to greet her himsel. So she asks him a gey intrusive question and tells him he's looking his age. As for the names she calls her folk! I'll keep out her road while I can. And then,' she went on, setting her hand on the jug of ale to test its temperature, 'there's her two nephews, and you'll never guess who one of them is.'

'Go on, then,' he invited as she paused.

'That lad Lowrie Livingstone,' she said triumphantly,

and lifted the jug. 'Here, you might as well make yoursel useful.'

The company Maggie had detailed was seated in a half-circle on the new carved backstools, Dame Isabella just taking her seat at the centre beside another lady. To one side were Sempill and his cousin, on the other was the lanky fair-haired Lowrie Livingstone with a man who must be his kinsman. Facing them Canon David Cunningham, senior judge of the diocese, was ensconced in one of the window spaces, surrounded by stools, a succession of documents spread on top of each. His balding head was covered by a black felt coif and round legal bonnet, and his furred gown was drawn up about his ears against the chill of the spring afternoon.

Dame Isabella's men retired to the door of the other stair, and one of her waiting-women began fanning her with a painted leather fan. As Gil stepped in off the kitchen stair with the tray of buttered ale in his hands, John Sempill, stocky and sandy-haired in a suit of cherry velvet clothes Gil had seen before, leaned round the back of his chair and glowered at him.

'So there you are, Gil Cunningham. Took your time, did you no?'

'And God's greeting to you too, John,' said Gil with extreme politeness.

'Gilbert,' said Canon Cunningham, removing his spectacles. 'And Peter. Dame Isabella, you mind Gelis's third son. Mistress Boyd, my nephew. And his good-father, Maister Peter Mason. Gilbert, I think you know all here but Maister Alexander Livingstone.' He indicated the stranger, who had risen. Beside him Lowrie also leapt to his feet and came to take the tray from Gil, freeing him to raise his hat in a general greeting. 'And you've brought a refreshment. A wee cup of hot ale, friends. Peter, come and be seated.'

'Get away from me wi that thing, Annot, it's more harm than good,' pronounced Dame Isabella in her gruff bark. 'You two trollops get over by the wall out my road. So

15

you're Gelis Muirhead's laddie, are you? And have you had your bowels open at stool the day?'

So that's how we play this hand, Gil thought. He bowed without answering and turned to help Lowrie who had set the tray on the cupboard.

'Maister Gil.' The young man's ears were flying scarlet. 'I'm right glad to see you again.'

'Lowrie.' Gil nodded to him and began pouring the steaming ale. 'What brings you back to Glasgow? I thought you had won your degree.'

'Aye, I determined last autumn.' Lowrie gave him an embarrassed grin. 'I'm attending my aunt. Dame Isabella. She was wedded to my great-uncle Thomas the year afore he died,' he divulged quietly, lifting the first two beakers. 'And my uncle Eckie's here to represent the family interest.'

Gil took in all that was not said in this brief speech, noting with approval that there was no attempt to apologize for the old woman, as his uncle said,

'We'll drink to a successful settlement, friends, and then we can get to work.'

'It's simple enough,' began Sempill, but was overridden by Dame Isabella.

'Have you nothing stronger than this, David Cunningham?' she demanded in that deep bark. 'Ale doesny suit me, it disagrees wi the bowel and rots the teeth. A wee tait spirits would be more acceptable, it's my hour for a bit cordial.'

'Madam, we'll not expect Canon Cunningham to offer us spirits when it's hardly past noon,' objected Maister Livingstone. He was a thin-faced man with the typical nondescript hair and mid-coloured eyes of the Lowland Scot, and a strong family resemblance to the taller, fairer, handsomer Lowrie; he was dressed with ostentation in yellow velvet trimmed with squirrel, neither colour flattering to him. Dame Isabella glared at him and thumped the floor with her stick.

16

'You can expect what you like, Eckie, I'm an old woman—' she began.

'I believe you're of an age with Canon Cunningham, madam,' observed Philip Sempill quietly.

'Never mind that,' said Sempill irritably, 'let's get on wi the matter at hand. It's simple enough, like I said. See, we want to disinherit the harper's brat, and Maidie here will gie it a property in Glasgow in exchange, and then Dame Isabella yonder wants to gie Maidie and me some land somewhere in joint feu—'

'John.' His new wife spoke gently, but he was instantly silent, turning to her. She put a hand on his wrist. 'Will I explain it, John?'

'I'll explain it, Maidie,' Dame Isabella announced, handing her empty beaker to Lowrie.

'Christ aid, woman, you ken nothing about it!' objected Sempill.

'You be quiet!' she ordered. 'It's all as I had Eckie here write it down, David. The harper's brat would have nothing to complain of, Maidie's offering it land that brings in a good rent, and we've all the papers here wi us,' she gestured at the men at the door and one of them looked alert, a hand going to his satchel of documents, 'so we can get it all agreed now. Then when that's done we'll see about which of these two properties goes to Maidie and which to this laddie's sister Isabel.'

'It would surely be more convenient,' said Canon Cunningham reasonably, as Maistre Pierre had done, 'for the Lanarkshire property to go to the Lanarkshire lassie, and the one in Strathblane to go to the lady wi a house in Glasgow, which is that much closer.'

'We'll get the other business sorted first,' she said. 'Then we'll see. If you've no aquavit' you can gie me some more o that buttered ale, though I've no doubt I'll regret it. Here's my beaker, Lowrence.'

'I'd ha welcomed a chance to think about this ahead of the time, John,' Gil said, as civilly as he might. 'As the boy's tutor I should take it all in advisement.'

'It would have been more usual,' commented Philip Sempill from beyond his cousin. Always the voice of reason, thought Gil, but Sempill snarled at him.

'You keep out of this. Aye, give you warning, Gil Cunningham and let you think up a list of reasons to turn it down! That's why we—'

'John.' Again that quiet voice. Sempill stopped speaking, and Magdalen Boyd smiled at him, then at Canon Cunningham. 'Sir, my husband has told me the whole tale.'

I'll wager he hasn't, thought Gil, studying her. She was a pale creature in her early thirties, a year or two older than Sempill, neither pretty nor plain, dressed decently but without display in a well-cut gown of the natural grey of the wool. Her eyes were a very light blue, even lighter than her husband's, with pale brows and lashes; her whole face seemed like a faint sketch, silverpoint on white paper, framed by the bands of her linen undercap. The plain black woollen veil pinned over all emphasized her pallor. Her smile, on the other hand, was gentle and without dissimulation, and her voice was low and slightly husky, very attractive to hear.

'I ken fine the bairn's none of his get,' she went on. 'It seems to me the boy and his well-wishers can hardly complain if we offer him a property wi a good income now as an exchange for a dubious heirship.' She turned to face Gil. 'I think we are kin in some degree, Maister Gilbert,' she went on. 'I hope we can come to an agreement.'

'I hope so.' Gil returned the smile, comparing her in some amazement to the showy, expensive mistress he had encountered in Sempill's company two years since.

'We'll drink to a successful outcome, maisters,' said Canon Cunningham again, asserting control over the gathering, 'and then we'll see whose interests can be served by all these transactions. I'll say this, John,' he added reprovingly, 'it's away less simple than you let me understand.'

'He hadny seen half the argument,' pronounced Dame Isabella, emerging from her beaker. 'And I've another

18

thing to settle wi you, Gilbert,' she added ominously, 'but we'll get the disponement agreed first.'

Drawing up a backstool beside his father-in-law, Gil was aware of Lowrie flinching at this statement. What was the old carline planning, he wondered.

'Saint Peter's balls! It's perfectly simple,' objected Sempill. '*He*,' he jerked his thumb at Gil, 'signs the papers as the bairn's tutor and accepts the two tofts on the Drygate, we tear up all the copies of the agreement about it being my heir, and all's done. Then you can sort out what comes to us and what goes to his sister.'

'*Two* tofts on the Drygate?' Gil repeated.

'Are you deaf, man? That's what I said.'

'Which two? Are they contiguous? What's built on them? You mentioned a good income, but what's the figure?' Sempill rolled his eyes. 'John, you wouldny accept a tract of land for yoursel without checking all these things, you can hardly object if I make certain for the boy.'

'Indeed not, Maister Gil.' Lady Magdalen gestured to the man still standing against the wall, and he came forward with his bag of documents. She ignored the rolled parchments, dipped into the bag and selected a folded docket with several seals dangling from it in their little pouches, and then another, and leaned forward to hand these to Canon Cunningham. 'Here's the titles, sir. I've no knowledge o the Drygate, but they both go into some detail about the boundaries.'

Gil moved to look over his uncle's shoulder as the older man replaced his spectacles and spread out the first parchment. There was no plan, but as Mistress Boyd had said a wordy description of the boundaries made it clear which toft was discussed and what was built on it.

'Clerk's Land. A common boundary to the west with the toft belonging to the altar of the Holy Rood,' said Canon Cunningham reflectively. 'That would be – aye, I can place it, a good property, should bring in a substantial rent, Gilbert. Four, no three houses and two workshops built on it. A generous offer.'

19

'It's that, all right,' said Sempill resentfully. 'And all good craftsmen, disobliging though they—' He bit off what he was about to say.

'And the other?' Gil said. They must really want rid of any claim wee John might have, he thought. His uncle lifted the other docket and began unfolding it.

'Is there more o that buttered ale, Lowrence?' demanded Dame Isabella. 'As for you, Gilbert, come here beside me and tell me o your sister Isobel. Who is it she's to wed, anyhow? And what about your own wife? How have ye no bairns yet? Have you no bedded her?'

'Maister Gilbert is occupied about his pupil's interests, godmother,' said Mistress Boyd in her quiet voice.

'I was lady-in-waiting to the late queen, I think I take precedence over a harper's bastard,' pronounced Dame Isabella, and thumped her stick on the floor again. 'Gilbert! Do as I bid you!'

Gil straightened up and eyed the old woman, trying again to conceal his dislike.

'I will, madam,' he acknowledged, 'as soon as you explain to me why you are so urgent that we accept the property with the bawdy-house built on it.'

There were several reactions in the room. Maistre Pierre's eyebrows went up; Philip Sempill and both the Livingstone men were startled, some of the servants hid smiles. Sempill himself scowled, his wife looked down in what seemed like a modest woman's response, and Dame Isabella gave a bark of laughter.

'I tellt you Gelis Muirhead's laddie would never miss that!' She leaned forward and prodded Sempill in the thigh with the stick. 'But you would aye ken better than your elders.'

'Is that the new house?' said Maister Livingstone with interest. 'The lassies all has strange foreign names to go by, Cleone and the like, and it's all painted inside, quite remarkable, wi pictures. Or so they say,' he added, going scarlet as he found everyone looking at him. 'You'd think

Long Mina's place would ha been enough for a town the size of Glasgow.'

'That's the house,' agreed Dame Isabella, with another bark. Gil, who had heard much the same from one or two of his friends among the songmen, kept silent.

'You were aware of it,' Canon Cunningham stated.

'Aye, we were aware of it,' said Sempill belligerently. 'What's amiss? It's only been there six month or so. It brings in a good rent, it's no trouble. What's your objection?'

'Just how good is the rent?' asked Maistre Pierre.

'It's no a tenant everyone would welcome,' said the Official. 'Gilbert is the boy's tutor, and has his reputation to consider, as a man of law in this burgh and as the Archbishop's man.'

Dame Isabella snorted. 'I could tell ye a tale or two o Robert Blacader, Archbishop or no. Why should a harper's brat turn up its nose at what an archbishop doesny mind?'

If you have to ask, thought Gil, little point in trying to explain. He looked down at his uncle, who was tracing the description of the boundaries with a long forefinger, and then at Sempill's wife.

'The house called the Mermaiden,' he said. 'A pleasure-garden, a kaleyard, stables, other offices. It's quite a property, madam. Are you certain you want to offer it to the boy, with or without the sitting tenant?'

Magdalen Boyd raised her head to look him in the eye.

'I am quite certain,' she said. 'I don't go back on my word.'

'I'll swear to it and all,' said Sempill. 'The brat can have both the properties, so long as his keepers accept that he's no my heir any longer. Name me any relics you please, I'll swear.'

'John.' His wife turned to him. He glanced at her, went red, and muttered some apology. Gil registered this exchange and set it aside to consider later.

'We need time to think about your proposal,' he said. 'The harper ought to be present, and Pierre and I should consult—'

'They've naught to do wi it!' said Sempill. 'It was you that signed the last time as the brat's tutor, you'll do this time!'

'I am agreed wi my nephew,' said the Official, lifting his tablets. He found a suitable leaf, and began to smooth out the previous notes in the wax with the blunt end of his stylus. 'This is no simple conveyancing matter, John, the conditions you set need a bit thought. At the least,' he paused, deciphering a word in the document, 'the boy's well-wishers have to inspect the properties.'

'We could do that now,' suggested Philip Sempill.

'They're exactly as it says there!' said his cousin indignantly. 'I'm no trying to—'

'John.'

'Maidie drives an honest bargain,' said Dame Isabella as Sempill fell silent. 'You've no need to worry. So how long will you want to think it over, Gilbert? Will you sort it afore your sister's marriage, d'ye think?'

Gil met her gaze again. The black beads glittered at him, and he said politely,

'Oh, sooner than that, madam. Give me two days.'

'Right,' began Sempill.

'But before we depart,' Gil pursued, 'maybe you'd let me have a sight of the documents for the two properties you're planning to gift your goddaughters, madam.'

Maister Alexander Livingstone straightened up, paying attention at that.

'Aye,' said Dame Isabella after a moment. 'No such a bad notion. Attie, you scatterwit, bring me those documents again. And a course there's the other matter and all,' she added, delving in the bag as her goddaughter had done and passing two wads of parchment across. Beside her Lowrie fidgeted, clearly embarrassed.

'Two mile from Carluke,' Canon Cunningham read, unfolding one docket. 'Banks of the Clyde – oh, aye, I ken the property. A generous gift, madam.' He removed his spectacles to peer at Dame Isabella. 'My niece is fortunate in her godmother.'

'Aye, but she hasn't got the land yet,' the old woman pointed out. 'It's that or the other. I've yet to make up my mind.'

'The house of Ballencleroch, together wi the whole Clachan of Campsie.' Gil had reached the description of the boundaries on the second document. 'Stretching up the Campsie Burn to the edge of the muirland.'

'What?' Sempill straightened up sharply, and his back-stool tilted on its carved legs. He caught himself before all went flying, and stared from Gil to his wife. 'Up the Campsie Burn? I thought that was yours already! You said – your man said—'

'No, John. That was never mine.'

'What's this?' demanded Dame Isabella. 'Aye, Ballencleroch's mine. What ails ye, John?'

He frowned at her, chewing his lip, and clearly trying to recall something.

'I thought it was Maidie's,' he repeated.

'Balgrochan is mine, that lies next to it, east along Strathblane,' said hs wife gently.

'Balgrochan,' Sempill repeated. 'No Ballencleroch?'

'I gied Balgrochan to Maidie when you were wedded,' pronounced Dame Isabella in her harsh deep voice. 'As you ken well, you light-fingered hempie. I'll get a word wi you later, John Sempill.'

'Aye, we will, madam,' he retorted, scowling at her.

'When did you come by Ballencleroch, madam?' asked Maister Livingstone. Dame Isabella did not look at him.

'Thomas gave it me outright,' she stated. 'As a marriage-gift.'

'Well, he shouldny ha done that,' said Maister Livingstone. He reached into his sleeve to produce a fat wad of parchment, unfolded it, and leaned forward to hand it to Canon Cunningham. 'I have the title here, handed me by my brother Archie. It never belonged to Thomas.'

'What?' John Sempill leapt to his feet. This time his back-stool clattered to the floor behind him, but he ignored it, lunging forward to snatch at the document. Canon Cunningham held it out of his reach, and Dame Isabella prodded him again with her stick.

'Sit down and behave, John,' she ordered him. 'Eckie, what are ye about? It's mine, I tell ye, Thomas and me signed the papers. They're there, David, under the other.'

'Aye. indeed. Here are two sets of titles to the land,' Canon Cunningham said, looking disapprovingly from one document to the other, 'with quite different names on them, conveyed in different hands, and at dates four year apart. This is highly irregular.'

'Thomas should never have alienated the land,' said Maister Livingstone firmly, sitting back. 'It's a part of the heritable portion, held from the Earl of Lennox and his forebears these fifty year. It went to my faither and now to Archie. Thomas never had a say in it.'

'You said you'd already—' Sempill began, glaring at Dame Isabella. Lowrie had quietly assisted Lady Magdalen to set his backstool on its legs; now she thanked him with a smile, put a hand on her husband's wrist and drew him back to sit again.

'We need to look at this again, that much is clear,' she said. 'Canon Cunningham, I'm right sorry that we've taken up your time wi such a guddle. We'll away now and—'

'We'll do nothing of the sort!' Dame Isabella's stick thumped again. 'I tell ye it's mine, Eckie, and I'll hear no different! As for you, you great fool,' she added, baring her large white teeth at Sempill, 'we'll need to sort out which of Maidie's properties it is you've been neglecting.'

'At the very least, Isabella,' said Canon Cunningham, 'your possession is questionable and the matter must be replait till it can be studied carefully. No, your good-daughter is right, we can make no decision the day.'

'Can you look into it, sir?' asked Lady Magdalen.

'There's no need of looking into it!' declared the old woman.

'I'd be grateful,' began Maister Livingstone.

Canon Cunningham shook his head.

'I haveny the time,' he said. 'I've a caseload this week would try a team of oxen. This was the only—' His voice trailed off as he looked at Gil, one eyebrow raised.

'But what about the other matter?' demanded Sempill.

'I'll take it on,' Gil said to his uncle, with resignation. 'If you think it proper, sir. But it will take me longer than the two days I promised you,' he added, turning to Dame Isabella. 'I'll need to talk to a few folk, and I have work o my own to see to.'

'You're all in a league against me!' she declared, thumping the stick again. 'I'm an old woman, and I—' She broke off, clutching at her massive chest. One of the waiting-women exclaimed and hurried forward to bend over her anxiously, patting the plump red cheeks, then pulling at her own skirts to reach her purse.

'Oh, madam! Oh, where have I put your drops? Forveleth, do you have them?' She tugged at the purse-strings, rummaged in the laden depths without result. The other woman dragged her dark gaze from Maistre Pierre and came forward quietly, producing a tiny flask which Annot unstopped and waved under her stricken mistress's nose. 'There, now, no need to go upsetting yourself.'

'It aye upsets me,' croaked Dame Isabella, with less than her usual force, 'when folk crosses me. Don't let them cross me, Annot.'

'How your woman's to prevent it,' said Sempill angrily, 'is more than I can see. You've crossed the rest of us the day, madam, and I'll see you—'

'John.'

'And I want a word wi you, Sempill,' added Dame Isabella, suddenly regaining vigour. 'There's a matter needs discussion. You'll attend me this afternoon, or I'll ken the reason.'

25

Canon Cunningham glanced over his shoulder at the April sunshine.

'I must away,' he said, without visible regret. 'Richie will have two sets of witnesses and their men of law waiting for me. I'll leave it in your hands then, Gilbert.'

Chapter Two

'What is your kinsman about, making such an offer?' asked Maistre Pierre, and hitched the collar of his big cloak higher. 'Confound this wind. It would bite through plate mail.'

'I've no notion,' admitted Philip Sempill, closing the gate of his town house behind them. 'If John was acting alone I'd assume he was up to no great good, but Maidie Boyd is a different matter. She'll deal honestly.'

'If I hadn't recognized the house, she would never have pointed it out to me,' Gil observed.

'*Caveat emptor*,' said Maistre Pierre. 'She is not obliged to do so, after all.'

'How did John come to wed her? Was it you promoted the match, Philip?' Gil asked, setting off down Rottenrow towards the Wyndhead.

'It was,' the other man agreed, falling into step beside him.

Gil turned to catch his eye.

'So that was your revenge,' he said, grinning. 'And a good one, too.'

'Revenge?' Philip repeated, his expression innocent. 'I proposed a match I thought would suit my kinsman, is all.'

'But why the whorehouse?' persisted Maistre Pierre. 'I should have thought, if it brings in so good a rent, they would sooner hold onto it.'

'I think Maidie's embarrassed by it,' said Philip.

'I'm flattered,' said Gil obliquely.

They made their way down the slope of Rottenrow and into the busy Drygate, walking fast in the chill wind. Here the sound of hammers, of shuttle and loom, of wood and metal tools, was all round them. Glass-workers, wax-pourers, metalworkers of many kinds, embroiderers and makers of images, occupied the smaller buildings on the back-lands, practising all the amazing variety of trades which supported the life of a cathedral church. Further down the Drygate itself, past the narrow wynd which led to the tennis-court, a row of shops such as those of the burgh stationer and Forrest the apothecary gave way to houses of stone and then of wood. There were fewer passers-by, and the slope levelled out. Gil stopped beside a gable-end of wattle and daub, looking along the muddy alley which led past the house door.

'That's the toft belongs to Holy Rood altar there,' he said, gesturing at the building they had just passed, 'so this and the next one are the ones that concern us. This must be Clerk's Land, where we have three houses and two workshops—' He craned from the end of the alleyway, counting. 'There are more buildings than that, we'd need a closer look. What do you think, Philip?'

'There is a hammerman in this nearest shop,' observed Maistre Pierre over Philip's agreement. 'Smallwares, I think,' he added, listening to the metallic beating. 'Perhaps a pewterer. And there is a lorimer yonder, to judge by the leather scraps on the midden.'

'We can check that later,' said Gil. 'For now, I'd be well in favour of accepting this toft on John's behalf, subject to closer inspection. Would you agree?'

'Oh, certainly.' His father-in-law braced himself. 'Now do we visit this bawdy-house? They will be disappointed when they find we are not customers.'

'It's the paintings that interest me,' said Philip, grinning. 'Eckie told me more about them.'

The house fronting the street on the next toft was rather more impressive, a wooden-clad structure of three storeys whose doorframe and the beams of the overhanging upper floors were carved and painted with foliage and flowers. The street door bore an incised and brightly-coloured image of a mermaid, well-known symbol of sexual licence.

'Well, that should attract the passing trade,' said Gil, surveying this. 'Was it done for the madam? Did she change the name of the house when she moved in here?'

'I've no a notion,' said Philip.

Gil rattled the ring up and down its twisted pin. The shutter nearest the door swung open and a maidservant in a headdress of good linen leaned out, gave them one swift assessing glance, and said,

'We're closed another hour or more, maisters.'

'I'd like a word with your mistress on a matter of business,' Gil said. The woman studied them again, and nodded.

'Come away in. I'll fetch the mistress down to ye.' She drew her head back in and appeared shortly at the door. 'Come up out the cold and be seated. Madam willny be long.'

She was a pudding-faced woman of forty or so, confident and discreet in her bearing, clad like an upper servant in a gown of good cloth with its skirts pinned up over a checked kirtle. She led them up a newel stair to a wide, brightly painted hall, set padded backstools for them by the warm hearth, and vanished up a further stair. There were footsteps overhead, and women's quiet voices and laughter. Someone began tuning a lute. Gil, who had been in Long Mina's establishment once or twice on legal business, recognized that this house was in a different category.

'I fear we cannot afford their prices,' said Maistre Pierre, echoing his thought. 'They must ask enough to recover the cost of these walls.'

'It was never a local man painted this,' said Philip, turning about to stare. 'It's been someone that studied overseas, surely.'

'In High Germany,' said Maistre Pierre confidently. 'I have seen a St Barbara from Cologne with just such waving gold hair.' He went over to look closely at a lady clad in nothing but the hair, depicted in a niche of greenery in the company of an armed man. 'Also that helm is German work.'

'The colours certainly aren't local,' Gil said.

'Well, now,' said a husky voice behind them. 'Three new guests, and I can see you all appreciate the arts. That's a day to put a nock in the bedpost!'

The woman who came forward from the stair was tall, nearly as tall as Gil, and lean. She was richly gowned and jewelled, and her face was painted in a way the women of Glasgow did not use, the pale blue eyes darkly outlined and the strong mouth tinted a deep red which showed up sharply against her white skin. An elaborate headdress concealed her hair completely, but Gil found himself wondering if her brows were really that dark. Behind her the maidservant slipped past and down to the lower floor.

'Good day, maisters all,' she went on, curtsying, and looked from one to the other. 'I've met none of you, but I think I can place you all three. *Je crois que vous êtes monsieur le maçon français,*' she said to Maistre Pierre. 'Which means you must be his good-son, I think, Maister Cunningham, and you,' she paused, considering, 'you're no Sempill of Muirend, but you're gey like him. Sempill of Knockmade.'

'You're well informed, madam,' said Gil. 'And you?'

'Oh!' She touched her chin with a lean forefinger and tipped her head sideways in a parody of coyness. 'You can call me Madam Xanthe,' she said after a moment. 'Seat yourselves, maisters. Agrippina will bring us a refreshment, and you can tell me what fetches you here, for I can see it's no a matter of the usual business of the house.'

Xanthe and Agrippina, forsooth, thought Gil. Maister Livingstone had heard right.

'Does living in Glasgow agree with you?' he asked in Latin. His father-in-law shot him a sharp glance; Madam Xanthe drew breath as if to answer, then tittered improbably and batted the question away with a long white hand.

'Oh, you'll ha to excuse me, maister! French I can manage, and I've a few words o High Dutch, but Latin's beyond my skills.'

'Forgive me,' he said. 'I took it a lady like yoursel would read in the Classics. How do you like living in Glasgow, then?'

'It makes a change.' She turned as the same woman returned with a tray of glasses and a jug of wine. 'Set it there, lass, and I'll serve. Aye, a change,' she continued as Agrippina withdrew quietly. 'And yoursels, maisters? Does Glasgow agree wi you?'

'Well enough, seeing I was born here,' said Philip Sempill. 'Where were you before you came here?'

'Ah, where was any of us afore we came here?' she responded, handing him a brimming glass. 'That's too deep for me and all.' She handed wine to Maistre Pierre and to Gil, and sat back, raising her own glass. 'Your good health, maisters. Now, what can a poor woman do for three burgesses of Glasgow? Is it about the counterfeit coin we had?'

'Ah!' said Gil. 'I took it it was Long Mina who'd had that. Tell me about it.'

She spread her free hand. 'What's to tell? Counting the takings the eve of Thomas Sunday, I recognized two false silver threepenny pieces, and took them to the Provost as my duty is.'

'That's more than most burgesses would do,' observed Maistre Pierre. 'It's a loss of six silver pennies, after all, not to be accepted lightly.'

She tipped her head back, and looked sideways at him beneath the pleated gold gauze of her undercap.

'This is a house of honest dealing, *maistre*. I'll no give out false coin even in taxes. So once it's in my hands it's a loss any way, the Provost might as well have it. Besides, I hadny his acquaintance yet, the chance was no to be missed.'

'You recognized them?' Gil said. 'How? What showed you they were false?'

'No balls,' she said, and tittered. 'Four wee mullets about the cross, instead of two mullets and two balls. Oh no, I mind Eckie Livingstone called them pellets,' she added reflectively, 'and he ought to ken, wi his experience.'

'What, is he that Livingstone?' asked Gil in surprise. 'I hadn't realized. Alexander Livingstone was moneyer to James Third,' he explained to his father-in-law. 'It must be twenty year since, but I mind my father talking of him. If this is the same man I must get a word wi him about the process, we need to know what to look for, whether it's like to be hidden in Glasgow. I've no idea what size of a workshop we'd be seeking.'

'No hope, I suppose,' said Maistre Pierre, 'that you would tell us where the false coin came from, madame?'

'Never dream o't, *maistre*!' she said. 'Mind you, if you were to attend here on an evening, you'd be one of the society, and could learn all sorts o secrets and mysteries.'

'Is that right?' said Gil, turning his glass in his hand. 'Such as where you get this wine, madam? It's uncommon good.'

'Oh, some secrets are no for sharing!'

'What do you mean by the society?' asked Philip. 'Are your customers all in a league, or something?'

'That's it exact,' she agreed. 'But we call them guests, maister. Once a man's called here of an evening, taken part in our entertainment, which is music and singing and the like, whether he stays late or goes home to his own household, he's a member of the society. You'd be surprised at some of the names I've got writ down,' she added, then looked away, hand over her crimson mouth, in a play of realizing she had said too much.

'And the false coin came from one or more of your – guests,' said Gil, 'rather than from the market.'

'Two silver threepenny pieces? No from the market, sir, and I've had no dealings wi the merchant houses lately that would leave me wi coin to that value in my hand.'

Gil nodded, recognizing the slight stress on *houses*. It was possible she could be persuaded to give him more precise information, but not in front of two other people. He did not relish the thought of a more intimate conversation; something about Madam Xanthe repelled him, and it was nothing to do with her striking appearance and arch manner, which reminded him of a bawd-mistress he had encountered in Paris.

'In fact,' said Philip Sempill, 'we're no here about the false coin, though I've no doubt Maister Cunningham welcomes what you've tellt him.' She looked sharply, briefly, at Gil then turned to face Philip, opening her eyes very wide. 'I'm here to represent Mistress Magdalen Boyd, who I believe is your landlord.'

'Mistress Boyd?' she repeated. 'Aye, she is, maister. What's she at? I do trust she's well?'

'She has offered this toft and the next one to my foster-son,' said Maistre Pierre, 'as severance, I suppose you might say, in recognition of the boy no longer being John Sempill's heir.'

'John Sempill? The new husband?' The arch manner had vanished.

'The same,' agreed Gil.

'Maybe you should explain it from the start,' she said. 'Who is the heir, then? What's it about? If I've to pay over a heriot fee to a new superior, I'd as soon know why.'

Gil, with a glance at Philip, set out the history of the offer. Madam Xanthe listened without interrupting him, and finally nodded.

'She's within her rights, I suppose, if she wishes her own bairn to be the legitimate heir. And you'll accept the offer?'

'We have not yet decided,' said Maistre Pierre. 'We thought to inspect the property, to clarify the decision.'

'Oh, I'd advise you to accept,' she said, with a return to her former manner. 'I pay a good rent, *maistre*, and it's a handsome house; once we move on and it's right fumigated you'll find another tenant easy enough.' That titter again. 'You might even be able to leave the image on the door.'

'Once you move on,' Gil repeated. 'So you don't see staying in Glasgow, madam?'

'Our Lady save us, no,' she said. 'We leave afore folks get bored.'

'I do not think folk would so soon tire of you, mistress,' said Maistre Pierre.

'Oh, you'd be amazed,' she responded, looking at him sideways. 'You'd be amazed. So I suppose you'll wish to view us, maisters? A wee tour of the fixed assets?' She turned her head, not waiting for an answer, and called, 'Agrippina! Send Cato to me. The laddie will show you about,' she went on. 'I'll leave you wi him, for there's matters to see to above stair. My lassies need to keep abreast of the news, you might say, and we open for business in an hour or so.'

Cato proved to be a gangling boy of sixteen or so, who emerged from the stair dragging on a velvet jerkin and grinning nervously. Madam Xanthe exclaimed in exasperation and rose, towering over the boy, her fur-lined brocade swinging, to cuff him briskly about the ear.

'I've tellt you often enough, you fasten the jerkin out-by, you don't come in here dressing yoursel!' He rubbed the ear, looking sulky, and she went on, 'Put yoursel straight, you're trussed all awry, and then show these maisters about the outhouses and the kaleyard.'

'All o them? And the wee pleasance and all?' asked Cato. She sighed.

'Aye, the wee pleasance and all, and the kitchen if Strephon allows it. All but the house.' She turned to her guests again with a coy crimson smile, and curtsied. 'If you'll forgive me then, maisters. And I hope to see you all again some evening.'

'I should wish to see the house as well,' said Maistre Pierre, rising.

'Oh, no, maister, I couldny allow that,' said Madam Xanthe. 'That's a privilege has to be earned, you might say.'

'Nevertheless—' began Philip.

'An account of what offices it contains would be enough for now,' Gil said. 'How many chambers, madam? And closets?'

'Seven chambers,' she returned promptly. 'Including this we're standing in. One, two—' She counted visibly. 'Three closets. Four hearths. That's under this roof, and then under their own roofs there's the kitchen, the washhouse, the stores – Cato can show you those. I'd hope he's able for that,' she added, looking sourly down at the boy, who gave her a deprecating grin. 'I'll bid you good day, maisters. And if you're to look into the matter of the false coin, Maister Cunningham,' she digressed again, with another sideways glance from the painted eyes, 'I'm right glad to hear it, for I'm sure we'll all rest easier in our beds for knowing you're on the hue and cry.'

Leading them down the stair and across a chamber where the woman Agrippina was mending linen, the boy called Cato led them out by the back door of the house and across a paved yard. Early flowers in tubs shivered in the wind on either side of the doorsill.

'The flowers are bonnie. Do you tend them?' Gil asked.

'No me, maister, I've a black thumb,' confessed Cato. 'A'thing I tend to dies. No, that's Kit– Cleone,' he corrected himself, 'that sees to the plants. She says it makes a nice change, raising up something that stays up.'

Gil looked sharply at the boy, aware of Philip Sempill on his other side reacting in the same way, but Cato, apparently oblivious to the double meaning in his words, went on,

'This is the kitchen, maisters. Are you wanting to see in? Only that Ste– Strephon isny in a good mood the day, and if the supper spoils—'

'It's a good kitchen,' Gil said, assessing the little building. 'Two doors and plenty windows. You'd get out easy enough if it caught fire.'

'That's what Strephon says,' agreed Cato. 'And yonder's the privy, and the coal house, and the lime house, and the feed store, and—' He led them onwards, telling off all the buildings as they passed them.

'When did Madam Xanthe move in here?' asked Maistre Pierre, looking about him.

'A month afore Martinmas last,' said Cato promptly.

'Early October, so more than six month since,' observed the mason. 'And I would say no maintenance done in that time and longer.' He nodded at the row of storehouses. 'Two broken hinges, peeling paint, the limewash not renewed this winter. The window-frames are dry, they need a coat of linseed. The bawdy-house may pay a good rent, but it is not a good tenant. These houses of timber must be groomed like a horse, daily.'

'I hardly think maintenance was in the lease,' said Philip Sempill.

'I've never been tellt to do aught about that,' said Cato, equally defensive. 'Madam aye has other tasks for me. And Hercules,' he mangled the name badly, 'is aye waking nights, in case of trouble, so he has to sleep daytimes.'

Gil nodded. It had seemed likely there was some more impressive guardian about the place than this lad. He wondered what Hercules might own for his baptismal name.

They followed Cato past the storehouses, across a second small courtyard, and through a gap in a wicker fence into a garden which sloped down towards the Molendinar and a further sturdy outhouse by the distant gate. To left and right more wicker fencing marked the edges of the property. The hammering from the next toft was clearly audible.

'That's the pleasance,' the boy said unnecessarily, waving at the low bristles of box hedging. 'It was right bonnie when we came here, but I've no notion how to keep it, and nor's Kit. And yonder's the washhouse, where the lassies has a bath every month and washes all their hairs. They've a right merry time of it,' he said wistfully, 'I'd like fine to join them, for they take in cakes and ale and all sorts, and bar the door. But that's when madam has me empty the privy and the garderobe, and stands over me to see I do it right.'

'There is a garderobe?' enquired Maistre Pierre with professional interest. 'Where is it? Where does it drop?'

Cato turned, grinning, and pointed back at the house. It rose above the cluster of outhouses, much plainer on this side, with a row of small upper windows which engendered regular waves in the thatch, and a high stone chimney with four octagonal pots.

'You see the upstairs windows, maister? That's Cleone and Daphne's chamber at this end, and then the next one's Armerella's and Calypso, and then Galatea and Clymene.' He was stumbling over these names too; it took Gil a little while to recognize Amaryllis. 'And at that end it's the two windows of madam's chamber and closet, see, and the garderobe's atween them and it drops down the outside of the house next the privy.'

'Typical,' said Maistre Pierre, shaking his head. 'It need not be so, there are ways to keep the soil from the house walls, but local wrights never make use of them.'

'It's no so bad,' said Cato. 'The rain washes the most o't down. Stinks a bit when it's a dry spell.'

'So have you seen enough to make a decision?' enquired Philip Sempill over the boy's head.

'We'd like a bit time to consider,' said Gil promptly. 'I told the old – dame it would be longer than two days, after all.' He moved towards the house, saying to Cato, 'Are the neighbours any trouble? There's a good many folk working on the toft on this side that we passed. Who dwells on the other side?'

'That's Maister Fleming,' said Cato. 'He's the weaver, ye ken, has his weaving-shed out the back there. He's no bother, no since madam bought all the blankets for the house off him and cleared his warehouse. This side's more trouble, they's aye a din ower the fence. See, there's Adkin Saunders the pewterer for a start, a short temper he has, him and his wife's aye arguing and their weans screaming—' This was patently true, the children could be heard screaming now. 'And then there's Noll Campbell the whitesmith, he's a good craftsman, we've some o his tin-wares in the hall, but he's a right grumphy fellow. Madam says the two o them has a competition to see who can work longest, and then they has great arguments and shouting and their wives joining in and all.'

'A pewterer, a whitesmith – who else is there?' asked Philip Sempill.

'Danny Bell the lorimer,' supplied Cato, counting carefully on his fingers, 'Dod Muir the image-maker, that took a stick to me when I went to fetch Ki– Cleone's shift when it blew ower the fence. And thingmy wi his donkey-cart. That's all five.'

'So you have to disentangle the ownership,' said Alys, 'and then make certain Dame Isabella gives the right piece of land to Tib. How can you do that? Does your uncle expect you to cast a horoscope, or raise an incantation over a brazier of herbs, or something?'

'The Canon has confidence in his nephew,' said Catherine in faint reproof.

'Rather too much confidence,' Gil said. 'I'll go up in the morning and get a word with him.'

'And with Sempill or his wife, I suppose,' offered Maistre Pierre.

The supper was over and the table dismantled. They had given a brief account of their afternoon over the meal, but now Gil was describing in more detail what had been said and what they had seen.

'And these two tofts on the Drygate,' Alys went on. 'You said one of them is the new brothel. What does a two-year-old want with a brothel? Do you mean to accept it?'

'It's a valuable property,' Gil said, 'and the madam says she plans to move on soon. I'd be in favour, so long as we had that in writing.'

'Mm.' Alys shook out the bundle of linen in her lap

and hunted for the needle in the seam. 'And the other property?'

'Busy. Four craftsmen and Danny Sproat with his donkey-cart. Again, a good rent-roll, probably we'd get as much as Sempill sends us each quarter from that one alone.'

'A wise investment, then. How will you proceed?'

'Maister Livingstone is to come here,' Gil said, glancing at the fading light from the windows, 'about now, indeed, and tomorrow I'll wait on Dame Isabella, and as Pierre says I must get a word with Magdalen Boyd, though I suppose Sempill will be present. Likely the rest of the day's my own.'

'And this question of the false money,' Alys said, and bit off her thread. She selected a second needle from the row stuck ready-threaded into the cushion of the bench beside her, drew the candles closer and began another row of neat stitches. 'When will you have time to look into that?'

'When I've sorted the other thing.' Gil grimaced. 'Though if my lord orders me to see to it, it ought to take precedence.'

'Is there any person in Glasgow who is suddenly wealthy?' asked Catherine. 'I have heard nothing, *maistre*, but you speak to many people in a day's work.'

Gil glanced at her in surprise. This small, aged, devout woman knew an amazing amount about what went on in Glasgow despite her lack of any spoken Scots; it was unusual for her to admit ignorance.

'Nor have I,' he admitted, 'but that's no help. We don't know that the coiners are in Glasgow, and in any case it wouldn't be wise to spend all the coin you had forged in the one place. Most folk know exactly how well off their neighbours are. A handful here, a couple of placks there, would be easier to pass off.'

'As in the Isles,' observed Maistre Pierre.

'How noisy is the work?' asked Alys. 'I suppose if one must strike each coin the hammering would be heard.'

'Noisy enough. Hard to keep it secret in the country-side,' said Gil thoughtfully, 'unless the workshop was very isolated, and yet in a town the neighbours are just as alert.'

Alys raised her head, listening.

'Not hammering,' she said, 'but someone in the court-yard. Could it be Maister Livingstone?'

'I'll take him up to our lodging,' said Gil, rising as the sound of feet on the fore-stair reached them. 'We can sit in my closet.'

'You see,' said Alexander Livingstone finally, contemplating the array of documents on the bench cushions, 'we've the whole chain here, from when my grandsire Archibald took sasine from Albany's steward in '35, down to my brother Archie's payment of the heriot fee ten year since when he inherited.' He turned to lift his glass of wine from the window-ledge where he had set it, and drank appreciatively.

'It's very clear,' observed Alys. 'Is it unusual to find so complete a record?'

'Not particularly,' said Gil. 'My father had a set of papers very like this, the record of sasine from the Hamil-tons, with all the succession from his grandsire.' He bent to the nearest, to reintroduce its crumbling seal into the little linen bag which protected it.

'I mind *my* grandsire telling me,' offered Lowrie, 'how his faither, that's old Archibald, had to go to take sasine all over again and get that first instrument given in his hand, only because the King wanted all writ down so it would be clear at law. He aye said there was no need of papers until the King started meddling.'

'Ah!' said Alys. 'So all Scotland suddenly had to get all written down.' She looked at Gil, her eyes dancing. 'Notar-ies' wives must have come out in new gowns that year.'

'Those that were wedded,' said Maister Livingstone seriously, hitching his yellow velvet round his shoulders. 'Notaries were mostly churchmen at that day.'

40

Gil's closet at the end of the short enfilade of chambers was barely big enough for two guests, let alone the armful of documents the Livingstone men had brought. They had abandoned his writing-desk and returned to the outermost room just as Alys arrived with the wine; she had stayed to watch fascinated while Maister Livingstone spread out the succession of parchments under the two candles on the pricket-stand, with a brief comment about each, like a fortune-teller laying out cards.

'So that's the original,' he went on now, gesturing again at the first document with its crumbling seal. 'Then it passed from Albany to Alan Stewart as feu superior, and then to the present man, John Stewart, that's now titled Earl of Lennox—'

'All very clear,' Gil agreed. 'And here's the record of renewal of sasine at your grandsire's death in '62, and then at your father's death ten year since, with the sasine-oxen duly noted.'

'I like this one,' said Alys, bending to one of the papers. *'Twa oxin, gra hornit and white checkit.* They must have been handsome beasts.'

'They were,' said Maister Livingstone sourly. 'I mind those. Best plough-team on the lands, they were.'

'Where are these usually kept?' Gil asked, nodding at the array of documents.

'The strongbox at Craigannet,' said Lowrie. 'My faither and me sorted them out afore we set out for Glasgow, all that seemed germane to the auld body's plans. You should see what we kept back,' he added, brushing dust from his person.

'Why?' asked Gil. Both men looked at him a little blankly, but Alys nodded. 'Why did your father think the sasines might be needed?'

There was a pause, into which Lowrie said,

'Ah. Well.'

'She's done something of the sort afore,' said his uncle with reluctance. 'Archie said, take these along in case, and no to lose them.'

'Are you saying, in fact, Thomas may not have alienated the lands we're dealing wi today? That her claim is false?'

'I'd be surprised if he did,' said Maister Livingstone, hitching up his yellow velvet again.

'Tell me about it. When did she wed your uncle? Why did they wed? They must ha been both well up in their age.'

'For mutual comfort of each other's possessions,' muttered Lowrie. Alys suppressed a giggle. 'He once tellt me he'd known her when they were both young,' he added. 'I think they both knew Elizabeth Livingstone. Her that was wedded to John of the Isles,' he elucidated, 'she and Thomas, and I suppose my grandsire, were second cousins or thereabouts.' He found his uncle staring at him, and subsided.

'Isabella and Thomas was wedded in '90,' said Maister Livingstone, returning to the point. 'I think Thomas had his eye on some lands she had in Strathblane at the time, which would sit nicely alongside these two Livingstone holdings that we're at odds about now. But she kept a tight grip on their management, no joint feus for her, and yet somehow Thomas's own property all turned out to have been held in joint feu after he died.'

'Were they fond?'

'Doted, more like,' said Lowrie.

'In fairness, no,' said his uncle to that. 'Thomas was deaf as an adder by then,' he explained to Gil, 'which you can see would be an advantage, and the old carline would pat his hand, order his favourite dinner, and go her own way. They were easy enough together. Mostly.'

'There were some rare brulzies,' said Lowrie, 'if he crossed her, but mostly he did as she pleased.'

'So she's changed little in the time.'

'Changed not at all. She's aye been like that, an arglebarglous steering old attercap, fit to tramp on any man's toes, or woman besides.'

'She's made my mother's life a misery,' Lowrie

contributed, 'since ever Thomas died, two year ago at Yule, and why her woman Annot stays wi her I've no notion.'

'Or any of them,' said his uncle. 'I'd think shame, to miscall honest workers the way she does, let alone the way she speaks to her equals.'

'Is she lodged wi you just now? Has she said anything more about the Strathblane portions? What makes her so certain they're hers, for instance?'

Lowrie covered his eyes with one hand, and his uncle groaned.

'Cold tongue pie wi bitter sauce, we had for supper this night,' he admitted. 'We're all of us lodged in Canon Aiken's house, seeing he's away to preach at his benefice, and he's left us some of the servants. It's a right good cook he keeps, but it was all wasted this evening, I couldny taste a morsel of it for the old dame haranguing us both. Ingratitude, enmity, lack of respect—'

'Jealousy, bitterness,' Lowrie supplied. 'Oh, and ill manners. She's aye been one to judge others by herself. She maintains that Thomas held everything in joint fee wi her, but when my uncle asked her for proof and the documents to it she began drumming her heels, and then—' He paused, looking awkward, but his uncle took up the tale again with no qualms.

'Then she announced that she would go to stool, and left the board. Her women went wi her, poor souls, Annot and the other one, but I'd had about all I could take o her nonsense and could face no more o the supper, good as it was. And then,' he pursued, indignation warming his tone, 'John Sempill turns up, saying she wanted a word wi him, as I recall her telling him in Canon Cunningham's house, and she kept him waiting in her antechamber, then they had a roaring tulzie, I'm surprised you never heard it down here, and she dismissed him, and we had to listen to him raging about her manners and offer him a drink afore he'd leave us. Just afore we came out, that was.'

'Well, it was an entertainment,' said Lowrie.

'So she has not offered any proof,' said Alys.

'What else has she given away?' Gil asked. 'And who did she give it to? Has she issue of her own?'

'No bairns that we know of,' said Maister Livingstone. 'She's right fond of Magdalen Boyd, we've met the lady a time or two in her company, and she's mentioned your sister, maister. Thomas had no issue neither.'

'I reckon Holy Kirk will be the ultimate beneficiary,' said Lowrie.

'As to what she's alienated,' pursued Maister Livingstone, 'we aye suspicioned this other stretch of Strathblane, the next property, Balgrochan that Mistress Boyd mentioned, was rightly part of the heriot, but Archie could never prove it. She gave that to Mistress Boyd at her second marriage, whenever that was.'

'There was the lands in Teviotdale she sold to the Maitlands,' observed Lowrie. 'My faither was certain he'd seen the names on something in the great kist, but there was nothing to be found when he searched, and the superior had nothing either.'

Gil nodded. The Livingstone family obviously held to the same custom as his own father, and most other landowners. The documents which embodied their right to occupy this or that portion of the realm of Scotland were kept in one place, protected with the rest of the family's valuables. The overlord, the feu superior, would have a copy; the man of law who had drawn up the original document might or might not hold a third copy, but he would certainly have a record of the transaction written into his protocol book, his formal record of all the legal proceedings he had witnessed.

'Who conveyed these portions for her?' he asked. 'How did she convince him the lands were hers to convey? *An instrument of sasine granted to any man is not sufficient proof that his wife was seized in the same lands.*'

Maister Livingstone blinked at the Latin, but both Lowrie and Alys murmured in agreement.

'My faither might recall who handled the sale to the Maitlands. Whoever it was, if she just said they were hers, likely he'd accept it. It would take a better man than most to argue wi her,' said Lowrie frankly. 'She's like a runaway cart when she gets going. What's more,' he went on, thinking aloud, 'Thomas might never have had a paper for all that was his anyway, not everyone gets a new document drawn up when they inherit. Why pay for something you might never need?'

Gil nodded again, studying the spread of crabbed writing and looping signatures before him.

'It's clear enough by these,' he said to Maister Livingstone, 'that the lands of Ballencleroch with the Clachan of Campsie are rightly part of the inheritance, and therefore are now held by Livingstone of Craigannet – by your brother. I'll proceed on that assumption for now, until the old dame can show me any different. I wonder where she had the Lanarkshire lands from?'

'She said those had been in her family,' said Alys. 'Where would you go to confirm that?'

'My uncle might ken who I should ask,' Gil said. 'And I should speak to your brother's own man of law, maybe, maister. Who is he? Would he have dealt wi Dame Isabella? No, surely he'd have recognized the properties.'

'Mm.' Maister Livingstone's face grew longer, and he crossed himself. 'That was our kinsman George. A third or fourth cousin, practising in Stirling. Dee'd last Martinmas, he did. Archie's had no call to replace him yet.'

'His house went on fire,' supplied Lowrie. 'His papers went up in flames and all.'

'Our Lady receive him,' said Alys, and crossed herself. Gil sighed. This was not a simple trail, that was becoming obvious.

'We need to ask your brother if he recalls who acted for the old dame,' he said, counting off the points, 'I need to ask my uncle what he knows about the Lanarkshire lands, and I need to get a closer look at the papers for the two properties again. Dame Isabella took them back, I think.'

'We can send our man Jock Russell out to Craigannet,' offered Lowrie, 'he can fetch back word from my faither.'

'That would help,' Gil said. He turned away from the spread of papers and lifted the jug of Malvoisie which Ays had brought. 'Time for another mouthful, I'd say. And while we drink it, what can you tell me, Maister Livingstone, about how coins are struck?'

'What can I tell you?' repeated Maister Livingstone, startled. 'Why, about all you'd wish to ken, I dare say, for I was moneyer to James Third, along wi Tammas Todd, and oversaw the whole process for five year. What brings that into your mind? Is it this counterfeit coin you have in Glasgow? The auld carline's never tried to pass you a false plack, has she!'

He chuckled at his joke. Gil smiled politely and refilled his glass with the dark gold wine.

'Have a seat,' he suggested, handing it over, 'and tell me the process. How does it begin?'

In fact there was rather more than he wished to know. Maister Livingstone's memory was excellent, but indiscriminate, and before long Gil's head was whirling in a cloud of details, of the distinctions between different royal portraits on the one side of a coin and the decoration round the cross on the other, of different inscriptions and values, weights of silver and fineness of the alloy.

'But the coining itself,' he prompted. 'How does that go?'

'Oh, in the assay, as I'm just telling you.' Livingstone sipped appreciatively. 'Then when your metal's been made equal to the fineness laid down by contract—' His speech tumbled off again like a flight of pigeons, describing casting the ingots, finger-thick and a foot long, the annealing, beating flat, annealing again, the cutting into coin-sized squares which were stacked and beaten circular.

'Then they're cast into a vat of argol and boiled,' he related, 'and then they're struck.'

'Argol?' questioned Alys. 'What is that, maister?'

'Er – it's what you'd call tartar of wine, likely—'

'The same as I'd use to make sponge-cakes rise?' she said in amazement. 'What does that do to them?'

46

'I wouldny ken, mistress.' Livingstone tasted the Malvoisie again. 'It makes the blanks more ready to take the impress, softens the metal I suppose. Anyway then they're struck, like I said. You've your pile, that's a column of iron,' he curved thumb and middle finger of his free hand to demonstrate the breadth, 'wi a spike at the base to hold it secure in the block, and your trussel, that's another column. And each of them has one face of the coin engraved on the flat end, so when you put your blank between the two and strike it a few times wi a mell, there's your coin. Your groat or whatever you set out to strike.'

'It seems a great deal of work to make a groat,' she said dubiously.

'Oh, it's that,' he agreed, 'but you don't make just the one groat. A good man working wi a basket of blanks can strike twenty or thirty in an hour.'

'So it is a noisy process,' said Gil.

'Aye, it's noisy. Your moneyer has to strike hard and straight every time, and the pile and trussel ring out, being iron, and then there's the beater and the shear-man. Plenty o noise in a Mint, there is.'

'Do the dies have to be iron?' Gil asked. 'Would a softer metal do?'

'Oh, it would *do*,' agreed Livingstone, 'but it wouldny last. You'd need a fresh die afore the six month was out, and you never get them quite the same, no matter how good your craftsman is. You'd get the Mint accused o making false coin!' He laughed at that.

'And how about waste?' asked Gil. 'Things go wrong in any craft.'

'They do,' Maister Livingstone nodded solemnly. 'You've to make certain each groat's worth a groat, that there's as many coins out of a pound of siller as there should be, no more and no less. You need to be sure both images are struck clean and single, wi no double strikes or part strikes, and you need to weigh it all in and all out again to make sure none of it's walked out in your moneyer's shoon. And the dies has to be locked up at the day's end and given out again the next morning.'

'The dies? So they never go missing?' said Gil. Maister Livingstone grinned.

'What do you think, maister? But they're generally found again. There's no that many folks can dispose of them, a wee session all round wi the torturer uncovers what happened quick enough.'

'But surely,' said Lowrie, and stopped as they all looked at him. 'Surely an engraver could make you a die if you wanted one? No need to risk stealing what would be missed, just get the man to copy a coin for you – you might even get the same engraver that made the originals, if you paid him enough.'

'Aye, you could,' said his uncle with scepticism, 'but you've still to get the siller, which is one of the scarcest things in all Scotland, I've no need to tell you, laddie, as well as finding the other craftsmen you need.'

'How much room does the coiner use for working?' asked Alys. 'The Mint must be a good size, I suppose, but if you need not have the assay-house and the strongroom and so forth, could a man work by his own hearth?'

'Aye, or in an outhouse,' agreed Livingstone. He considered. 'The other work has to be done somewhere, a course. I'd agree wi you, a counterfeiter likely won't trouble himsel wi the assaying, but the metal still has to be cast and cut and annealed.'

'Somewhere wi space for metalworking, then,' said Gil. 'Even if they clear it all away when they're not at the task. A fire or a furnace, tongs and a crucible and ladle—'

'Furnace,' said Livingstone. 'You'll not melt siller on a kitchen fire.' He set down his glass, and looked at the dark window. 'We'd best away up the road, maister. The auld wife has to be watched, or she's up to all sorts. I'll not weep at her funeral, I can tell you. Have I tellt you all you need for now?'

Chapter Three

'We were wedded just before Martinmas,' said Magdalen
Boyd. Gil eyed her, wondering how to put his next
question. She saw his expression and smiled faintly. 'John
and I deal excellently well,' she said. 'I'll not deny it was
a matter of convenience for both of us, but I've found great
good in him.'

'You have?' said Gil before he could help it. 'I mean –
I'm glad to hear that.'

It was probably not yet Terce, but he had begun the day
before Prime recording an exchange of sasines on a muddy
toft away along Rottenrow. After a short but frustrating
interview with Canon Cunningham, which the older man
had ended by claiming an early appointment at his chamber in the Consistory Tower, he had crossed the street to the
gates of the town house which had once belonged to John
Sempill and was now the property of his cousin Philip.
Lady Magdalen had greeted him pleasantly, sent out to
find her husband, and sat down to talk to her guest; a tray
with small ale and little cakes had appeared immediately.

'He's that attentive,' she went on, 'far more than my first
man, and he manages my estates for me, which is something I found a great burden, for I've no understanding o
these things.'

Gil stared at her in fascination, trying to reconcile this
image of John Sempill with the man he knew. After a
moment he abandoned the attempt and said,

'Tell me more about these two tofts on the Drygate. How
did you come by them?'

'They were a part of my tocher when I was first wedded,' she said. 'My brother purchased them in '89. There's no need for you to worry about them, they're mine to dispose of as I please, wi John's consent, and you can see I have that.'

So the feu superior was either the Archbishop or the burgh, he thought, and the records should be in Glasgow. That simplified that.

'Did you ken who were the tenants?'

She nodded, going faintly pink across the cheekbones.

'The wester toft, the one where there's all the workshops, we took on wi the most of those tenants in place. The other one, the house—' She bit her lip. 'My brother purchased that from one of the Walkinshaws. I think it was where their mother dwelt afore she founded the almshouse. We had one tenant or another in it for a year or two, and then this – woman and her business offered me a good rent, and my brother thought I should accept.'

'You've had no dealings direct with her?'

She shook her head.

'My brother dealt wi't first, and then John since we were wedded, and I think he's had no need o speaking wi the woman, she's sent the rent in good time each quarter-day. To tell truth, maister, I've never been in the house. I was right concerned, what Maister Livingstone said about the paintings. Are they – are they—?'

'The ones I saw were seemly enough,' he assured her, 'though the subjects themselves were a touch wanton. A few painted drapes and they'd be fit for anyone's een.'

'Hmm.' She did not sound convinced. 'Or maybe a good coat o limewash. So have you come to a decision, maister?'

'Not yet,' said Gil. 'I'd like a closer look at all the workshops, and a wee while wi the accounts. But it's beginning to look like a right generous offer.'

She gave him another gentle smile.

'It's only right that John's heir should be his own get,' she said, 'but I'd not want to see the other bairn lose by it. His mother was gently bred, after all.'

50

So is his father, in his own country, thought Gil, but said nothing. She nudged the plate of little cakes towards him, but anything she might have said was drowned out by the arrival of John Sempill, flinging wide the house door and exclaiming,

'There you are, Gil Cunningham! I was out in the town looking for you.'

'I sent word I'd meet you here,' Gil said mildly, rising. Sempill snorted angrily, but slammed the door behind him and came forward to salute his wife, his belligerent expression softening as he looked at her.

'Did you get a word wi Dame Isabella, John?' she asked. 'Is all clear now?'

'Aye,' he said airily. 'She's – showed me how it happened. Likely there's more to discuss,' he added, 'I'll need another word wi her. What's ado here?'

'We've been talking o the two tofts on the Drygate,' said his wife. 'Maister Gil would like to see the rent-rolls.'

He dragged another backstool beside hers and sat down.

'Aye, I suppose,' he said ungraciously. 'I've got them in the kist in our chamber. Is that what you're here for?'

'Part of it,' Gil said. 'I've to find out the history of these lands out in Strathblane and all, and I hoped you might help me there. Did I hear you say you'd taken the one Dame Isabella named to be Lady Magdalen's property already?'

Sempill scowled at that.

'Aye,' he said. 'But I've just said, I was mistaken. It's never been Maidie's. I'd mixed up the two names. See, they're too much alike,' he went on more fluently, 'Balgrochan and Ballencleroch, and it's Balgrochan that's been Maidie's all along. She showed me that last night, and the old – woman's confirmed it now, may she—'

'John.'

'I think you had that from Dame Isabella too,' Gil said, looking at Lady Magdalen. She nodded. 'Was there ever any thought that it might no ha been hers to dispone?'

51

'We've got the dispositions,' said Sempill before his wife could speak, 'all sealed and witnessed. The lands o Balgrochan are Maidie's own, I tell you.'

'John.' She put a calming hand on his wrist. He subsided, and she said direct to Gil,'To tell truth, my godmother's Livingstone kin by marriage put up some tale o it being part of the heriot land at the time, but I took it she would ken what she'd a right to. I set it down to them no wishing to see the land go out o the family. I'm beginning to wonder, now, if she's maybe been mistaken. She's well up in her age, after all, she might be getting – for all she's so vigorous, you ken—'

'Childish? A course she is!' said Sempill. 'And has been for years, at that.'

Lady Magdalen bit her lip, and Gil nodded understandingly.

'Might I see the documents?' he prompted. Husband and wife exchanged another look.

'If you would, John,' she said. He rose obediently. 'Best to fetch them down here, I think, the light's better here.'

Does she put something in his meat? Gil wondered as Sempill left the hall. Lady Magdalen watched him go, with what seemed like genuine fondness, then turned to Gil again.

'I think you're no long wedded yoursel, maister?' she said. 'And to a French lady, am I right? You speak French, then?'

'I was four years at Paris,' he replied.

'Paris! My brother studied there and all. Did you like it?'

'I did,' he said briefly, images of the city and the university drifting in his head. The raucous narrow streets of the Latin quarter, the stationers, the book dealers, and the great church of Our Lady on its island in the river, looming over all. He blinked, and found Lady Magdalen offering him another of the small cakes.

'So did my brother,' she said, nodding. 'Travel is a wonderful thing, though the food can be strange, so I've heard.'

'They eat bread and meat, just as we do.'

'But snails as well, so they say, and garlic in everything. Oh, John, you were quick, that was clever.'

'Aye, well, they were to hand.' Sempill thrust the bundle of documents at Gil and went to sit down beside his wife, who gave him another of those encouraging smiles. Gil set the rent-rolls to one side and lifted the third item, the title-deed, to inspect it before Sempill changed his mind.

'This is the wrong docket,' he said after a moment.

'It's the one I put back in the kist last night,' said Sempill aggressively. 'It canny be the wrong one.'

'None the less,' Gil said, 'it's the title to Ballencleroch, no Balgrochan. The one the Livingstones dispute.'

'What? Let me see!'

'John.' Lady Magdalen put one hand on his wrist, and stretched out the other to Gil. 'May I see, sir?' She took the crimped and pleated parchment and looked briefly at the heading, then at the seals at its foot, and nodded. 'Aye, I'm agreed. My godmother must have given us back the wrong document yestreen. She must have the other still in Attie's bag.'

'Aye, you're right,' said Sempill in faint surprise, peering over her shoulder. 'The auld – woman must have been mistook in that and all. We'll ha to get the right one off her.'

'Might I see that one?' Gil accepted it back and spread it flat, studying the peripheral wording. It seemed clear enough and perfectly in order; Thomas Livingstone and Isabella Torrance his wife had taken sasine of the lands detailed, in joint possession, on a date in 1490. He drew out his tablets and found a clean leaf.

'What are you writing?' demanded Sempill suspiciously.

'The names of the witnesses,' Gil replied. 'And the factor who acted for the Earl of Lennox. One of them might recall the name of the man of law, if Dame Isabella won't tell me. I need to establish who has the right to this land before my sister's marriage.'

'I'd as soon it was put straight too,' agreed Magdalen Boyd. 'She'd not hear my questions yestreen, grew angry when I tried to persist, so I left the matter, but—'

'Here's her man Attie now,' said Sempill, straightening up to stare at the window. 'Just crossing the yard.'

'Maybe she's sent the other deed,' said his wife. Sempill snorted, and turned to watch one of his cousin's servants make her way across the hall in response to the knocking at the door. Gil finished making notes and checked carefully again that the name of the man who had drawn up the document was not recorded, and suddenly realized that both Sempill and his wife were exclaiming in surprise and shock.

'But what can have happened?' Lady Magdalen said. 'She was in good health yesterday. John, did you see her just now? Was she well?'

'Just – oh, just the now? Same as she was yesterday – in full voice,' said Sempill, 'calling me for all sorts over nothing. I'd no ha looked for her to drop down dead either. What happened, man?'

'We're no certain,' said the man Attie, his livery bonnet held against his chest. 'She was well enow when Annot left her to – to her prayers, but when she returned there she was—' He crossed himself, and Sempill did likewise, pale blue eyes round with astonishment. Lady Magdalen bent her head and murmured something. 'We're thinking maybe she took an apoplexy, or her heart failed her, or the like. Maister Livingstone's sent for a priest, but—'

Gil looked round the dismayed faces and pulled off his own hat.

'Are you saying Dame Isabella's dead? This morning?'

'Aye,' said Sempill sourly. 'So the man says. Trust the auld woman to thwart me in her last deed. So you can just fold that up and let me have it back,' he added, pointing at the document Gil still held.

'John,' said his wife reprovingly. 'There's none of us can ken the moment of our death.'

'But how?' Gil asked. 'What came to her?' His mind was working rapidly as he spoke. Lady Magdalen's transaction would probably be unaffected, but Tib's marriage gift would almost certainly not reach her now, so the question of whether the lands in Strathblane were Dame Isabella's to dispose of was a matter for the Livingstone family and not for him. He began to fold the crackling parchment. 'What came to her?' he repeated.

Attie shook his head.

'We're no certain,' he said again. 'Annot left her in her chamber, like I said, and when she gaed back in, there she was on the floor, and stone dead.'

'Did you fetch a priest to her?'demanded Sempill.

'Maister Livingstone has sent for one, Attie says,' Lady Magdalen reminded him.

'Has anyone else seen her?' Gil asked. 'You're certain she's dead, no just fallen in a stupor? An apoplexy can be—'

'I'm no sure,' admitted Attie, 'for I never saw her, but Annot's in the hysterics and Maister Livingstone tellt the household she was dead, bade me bring word here and then go for the layer-out. Will you wish to see her afore she's washed and made decent, mem?'

'N-no,' said Lady Magdalen doubtfully. 'No, I'd sooner wait till she's in her dignity. Send my condolences to Maister Livingstone on the death of his kinswoman, Attie, and say I'll come down afore suppertime.' She seemed even paler than usual; Gil, suddenly recalling her condition, and certain her husband would never think of doing so, reached for the ale-jug and filled her beaker.

'You should drink a little,' he said. 'You'll feel steadier.'

'Aye.' She took the beaker from him. 'My thanks, maister. Attie, will you go down to the kitchen, tell them the news, bid them see you right. I – I—' She put her other hand to her head, and smiled weakly. 'I canny believe it. She's aye been so robust, I'd ha thought she'd go on for ever.'

'Do you need to lie down?' said Sempill, belatedly recognizing her distress. 'Attie, send her woman up to her! And you'll have to leave,' he added to Gil. 'We canny be looking at all this stuff the now.'

'I've questions yet,' Gil said mildly, reaching for the nearer rent-roll as the man Attie bowed and retreated to the kitchen door. 'See your wife right, man, and then we'll talk.'

The craftsmen of Clerk's Land were hard at work, to judge by the hammering sounds from the several houses. Armed with the details from the rent-roll and Sempill's sour comments on each tenant, Gil made his way along the muddy path, identifying the buildings and their occupants, making a note of necessary repairs and at the same time turning over in his mind the likely effects of Dame Isabella's death on her various schemes. It seemed hard to believe, given the old woman's forceful presence in Maistre Pierre's house and then in Canon Cunningham's only the day before, but sudden death could take anybody. He knew Canon Aiken's house where the Livingstones were lodged, further down the Drygate; he could call on them later to condole, if that was the right word in the circumstances.

The children he had heard yesterday were wailing again inside the house nearest the road, though a man's voice shouted at them from time to time. 'That's Adkin Saunders, pewterer,' Sempill had said, 'an ill-mannered dyvour, and his wife's a great Ersche bairdie wi no respect for her betters. They pay their rent, but,' he had added with reluctance. The pewterer was seated by the window, intent on shaping some vessel over a mould, his hammer tapping busily, though he cast a sideways glance at the intruder. Further down the toft two women were talking shrilly in Ersche; presumably one of them was the man's wife. What had she said to Sempill, Gil wondered.

56

'There's Danny Bell, that's a lorimer, he doesny dwell on the toft but come in to his workshop by the day. Has a dog as ill favoured as himsel, but at least he's taught it to do his bidding.' That was complimentary, by Sempill's low standards; the man was a stringent judge of dogs. 'And Dod Muir, that's an image-maker, works in wood and metal and all sorts, wee hurb of a niffnaff. Both of them pays their rent right enough and all.'

At least, he reflected, peering into a low ramshackle shed and finding an assortment of barrels and a stock of small pieces of wood, at least Dame Isabella did not seem to have died by violence. This must be the image-maker's woodstore, and yonder was certainly the lorimer's workshop, with the scraps of leather round the door and pieces of horse-harness hung in the window; the lorimer himself, a young man with startling red hair, was visible at his bench working with leather-punch and hammer. His dog, a small shaggy creature with sharp ears, lay in the doorway and watched Gil suspiciously.

Two of the children from the pewterer's house ran past him as he moved on, heads down as if fearing pursuit. He hoped they had got out to play for a while. The image-maker was not at home, his house shuttered and silent; the man sounded inoffensive, to judge by Sempill's contemptuous description.

He moved on down the path, past another long low house with an open barn at its further end.

'Then there's Noll Campbell,' Sempill had said, tapping the rent-roll. 'I've had more trouble wi him than the whole – It's another hallirakit Erscheman, a right sliddery scruff, wi a mouthful o abuse for any that speaks wi him, one that would sell his granny for dog's meat. Makes enough to keep a prentice, but will he ever ha the rent together for the quarter-day? No him! I wish you well o him.' There was a vindictive tone in his voice; clearly this Campbell and Sempill had crossed more than once.

In the barn, the whitesmith straightened up and stared at him under black scowling brows, tongs in hand; behind him in the shadows another man turnèd to look. That must be the apprentice. Gil nodded at them, and the smith bent to his work again, tap-tapping at what seemed likely to become a lantern.

Beyond the building was a kaleyard with a drying-green, where the women were still arguing in Ersche over a piece of linen. The children ran back up the path, and the two women paused as he came into sight, gazing open-mouthed at him, two Highland women with brows as dark as the smith's, one young and slender, the other older and heavier. Both were clad in brown linen aprons tied on over loose checked gowns, whiter linen folded and pinned on their heads.

'Good day to you,' he said, raising his hat to them. 'Is that Danny Sproat's stable down yonder?'

One of them nodded. The older one said civilly enough, in accented Scots,

'Aye. Aye, it is. But you will not be finding Danny the now. He iss out with the cart and the donkey, just, and not back before tomorrow so he was saying.'

'I'm only wanting a look inside the stable,' he said reassuringly. They looked at each other, and the one who had spoken gathered up the disputed washing.

'Bethag will show you,' she said, turning towards the houses. 'There is a way of opening the door, to be keeping the donkey in, you ken.' She added something in Ersche; the other woman gave her a sharp look, then smiled awkwardly at Gil and gestured towards the small building at the foot of the toft. He followed her, looking about. The kaleyard seemed to be divided up; none of the households would get a living from it, but it would provide all with some green vegetables for most of the year, assuming the donkey did not get through the woven hazel fence.

The door was well secured, though he could probably have opened it without difficulty. Bethag dragged one leaf open and nodded at the shadowed interior; he peered in, identifying stall and manger for the donkey and the standing for the little cart it pulled. The woman spoke in Ersche, pointing at the far wall.

'What is it?' he asked. She gave him that awkward smile again and crossed to open a shutter above the cart standing, and by its light showed him a place where the planking was splintered and gnawed. Something scurried over their heads in the low rafters, and she looked up apprehensively. 'Aye, you get rats in a stable. You need a dog here. Can Danny Bell not bring his dog down to sort matters?'

She nodded, and moved to the door, pointing at the feed sack with a sour, unintelligible comment. He looked about again, comparing the small building with the rent he knew Sproat paid and finding it reasonable, and turned to follow her out.

Pain stabbed savagely at his head, and the world went dark.

The next thing he was fully aware of was of lying face-down on grass, soaking wet and shivering, with an upheaval in his stomach which became a paroxysm of vomiting. As it passed off and he collapsed shuddering on one elbow again, a pair of booted feet came into his field of view, followed by a swirl of dark red broadcloth.

'You see, madam, there he's, just like I said! And he's lost his hat!'

He knew the voice. Who was it?

'Aye, just like you said. Good laddie, Cato, you did very well here. Now gie me a hand to lift him.' Strong hands seized him, dragged him upright. Pain knifed through his head, the world swung around, and a face came close to his, a bright mouth, painted eyes, gold-edged veil. 'Well, he's no been drinking. Come away, son, we'll get you indoors. Can you walk?'

'I seen them put him in the burn!' Cato was at his other side, urging him on. One foot in front of the other, teeth chattering, an expert grip on his elbow holding him up, he moved forward. Grass, a muddy path, more grass. Steps, a gate. A gravel path with weeds. Cato still prattling about the burn. Who had been in the burn? Was that why he was so wet? They were in a house now. The bawdy-house. What was it called? Why did his head hurt? The bawd-mistress was talking too.

'Cato, I said you're a good laddie, but you can be quiet the now. Come away in, son, we'll have you in here by the brazier. There, you can lie down a bit. Cato, send Agrippina to me wi the good cordial, and bid Strephon put some broth to heat, and then fetch me some towels, two o the big ones, I'd say, till we get him dried off.'

Expert fingers were working at his clothes. He tried to push the hands away, mumbling an objection, and there was a firm grip on his chin.

'Look at me. Look at me, Gil Cunningham.' He opened his eyes, and found Madam Xanthe's painted face close to his. 'You're wringing wet, we have to get you out those clothes and dry afore you take your death. I'm no threat to your wee wife, man.' She moved back a little. 'Ah, Agrippina. See me a glass o that stuff. Come up a wee bit, laddie.'

The cordial was fiery and sweet, bit his throat on the way down but sent warmth through him and seemed to clear his head. He looked about him, as Madam Xanthe dragged his jerkin off and started on the points which fastened hose to doublet. He was half-lying on a padded bench, in a chamber he had not seen before, well lit and full of women's gear, a basket of spinning and another of sewing on the windowsill. It seemed odd to find such a thing in a bawdy-house.

'What happened?' he asked. 'Did the boy say I was in the burn?'

'I seen you!' Cato arrived with an armful of linen towels. 'It was some o them next door, they carried you out the back gate and threw you into the mill-burn.'

He stared at the boy, trying to work out what this could mean.

'And it was me got you out,' Cato continued proudly, 'for I saw you wereny right awake, and I thought maybe you'd not get out afore you got to the millwheels, so I ran down the bank and I got you out! I never got your hat, but,' he added deprecatingly.

'I was in the stable,' Gil said after a moment. 'Oh, my head!'

'And then I came and fetched madam. Right lucky you was back, madam, so it was!'

'Here,' said Madam Xanthe, pausing in her activities, and felt round his skull with gentle hands. 'Is your head broke?' He flinched as she touched a tender spot. 'No, the skin's whole, but there's a lump like a hen's egg below the crown here. You've had a right dunt, I'd say. What were you at in the stable, that they took exception? No stealing a ride on the donkey, I hope, I'd hate to think o the sight.'

He shook his head, and immediately regretted it.

'I don't recall.' He braced himself as she bent to haul one of his boots off. 'I was. I was talking to.' He paused, and the faces swam up in his memory. 'Sempill and his wife. And then,' he shivered again, and Agrippina came forward and began loosening the strings of his shirt. 'Aye, she's dead.'

'Who's dead?' Madam Xanthe said sharply, staring up at him, the red paint on her lips suddenly stark against her white skin. He swallowed.

'Dame – Dame Isabella. The man came to tell us. So I needny concern myself wi her lands.'

'Dame Isabella,' repeated Madam Xanthe, as Agrippina dragged his shirt over his head and began rubbing at his back and chest with one of the towels. 'Aye, well, small loss her. Now we'll ha your small-clothes off. Never fret, we've all seen one of those afore. Will you have me send to your wife for dry clothing, or will you borrow what we can find round the place?' She tittered, with a brief return of her usual manner. 'It all depends, I suppose, whether you want her to know you're here.'

61

That was easy. He must be late for dinner already. Let them know now, explain the situation later. And it would take some explaining, he felt.

'Send home, if you would,' he said, giving up one arm to Agrippina's ministrations. 'Does the laddie ken where—'

'I ken where!' said Cato. 'It's the big house right by the Blackfriars.'

By the time the boy returned Gil felt much more human. A bowl of hot broth and a hunk of bread had warmed him and steadied his stomach, only his hair was still damp, and he was beginning to remember what had led up to the moment when someone must have struck him on the head.

'I stepped out of the stable,' he said. 'The woman was ahead of me, it wasn't her—'

'I'm glad to hear it,' observed Madam Xanthe with irony from her seat by the window. He looked up, startled, and she met his gaze directly for a moment before the arch smile spread to her eyes. 'I'd not like to think she'd felt the need to strike you down. You've a name in this town, Maister Cunningham.'

That seemed too difficult to work out. He went back to his ruminations.

'It must ha been someone behind the door. What did the boy see?'

'All he said to me was that he'd seen them next door throw you into the burn. If he'd seen you struck down he'd ha let us all know.'

'I suppose nobody else was looking out,' he said without much hope.

'Ah, now, there's a thought. Bide here.'

Draped like an antique statue and without his boots, he was hardly likely to go anywhere, but he said nothing, merely put his aching head back against the panelling behind him and considered what to do next. He had a good case against the tenants of Clerk's Land, and it seemed he had at least one witness, though how good the boy Cato would be before the bailies was another matter. His immediate instinct was to accept the property on small John's behalf and evict all the tenants, pausing only to double the rent, but the due process of the law might be a better weapon, and in any case there remained the question of why they had treated him like this. All he had done was look at the premises, make a few notes, and speak civilly to two of the women. Were they hiding something, he wondered, and if so what?

Shortly Madam Xanthe reappeared, followed by a tow-headed girl in a low-cut dress who trailed a strong scent of musk and violets and paused inside the door, eyeing Gil speculatively.

'Cleone was at her practice by the window,' announced Madam Xanthe, 'like a good lassie. Though it's all good lassies in this house, a course,' she added with another sly, sideways glance. 'Tell Maister Cunningham what you saw, my dear.'

'Aye, well,' observed Cleone pertly, 'I wouldny ha been at my practice if I could ha been sleeping, but what wi her snoring—'

'What, again? She'll have to go at the quarter if she canny stop that, it's no attraction. Go on, what did you see? Was this the man?'

Cleone eyed Gil again. Her eyes were blue, with dark rings round them.

'The one I saw was wearing black.'

'Aye, and his black is all wet and hung up in the kitchen. He doesn't go about draped in sheets for every day. Get on wi't, girl.'

Cleone shrugged, causing an interesting change in the scenery of her low neckline.

'There was those two next door, squabbling away in Ersche, and this man or one like him, clad all in black, came down the path and spoke to them. Then one of them, I think it was the Barabal one, went off up among the houses and the other one took him down to look at the donkey's stable.'

Gil nodded in spite of himself, and winced as pain stabbed in his head.

'And then what?' he asked. 'What did you see?'

'I was studying the tablature a wee while,' Cleone admitted, 'but when I looked up there was a man ahint the door of the stable, and when you stepped out he struck you on the head wi his mell. And then they took and carried you out the gate, and dropped you in the water, and then I saw Cato running down our path. So I went back to my practice.'

'Could you identify him?' Gil asked. 'Could you say who he was?'

She looked at him with those blue eyes, smiling earnestly.

'It was Dod Muir,' she said. 'I'm right certain.'

'The image-maker,' Gil said, and she nodded.

'Why did you not go out to help Cato?' demanded her mistress.

'Because I wasny dressed. You're aye telling us no to show off our—'

'Aye, that'll do. You're certain o what you saw?'

Cleone shrugged again.

'It wasny Campbell nor Saunders. It wasny Danny Bell, he's easy enough to make out, wi his hair. It wasny Sproat the donkey man, for he's no in Glasgow. Who else would it be?'

'You tell me, girl,' said Madam Xanthe in exasperation. 'Was it Dod Muir or no?'

'Aye, it was,' said Cleone.

'Aye, well. So there you are, Maister Cunningham. Dod Muir the image-maker it was, if this lassie's to be trusted, and if I was you I'd take him to law and double his rent as well.'

'You could be right.' He managed a smile for Cleone, who said with sympathy,

'Is your head right sore? Ag– Agrippina's got a rare bottle for a sore head.'

'Aye, that's a good thought, lass. You get back to your practice,' said her mistress briskly, 'see if you can master *I long for thy virginitie* for the night, and I'll—' Her head turned, and she peered out of the window. 'Is that the laddie back? Who's he brought wi him?'

With him? Not Alys or Pierre, surely, Gil thought in alarm. Though Alys, he acknowledged to himself, would probably find the visit both interesting and entertaining.

It was neither Alys nor Pierre; it was Lowrie Livingstone, even more embarrassed than Gil to discover him in such a situation.

'I'm right sorry to trouble you,' he said, backing into a corner of the chamber and knocking over the basket of spinning, 'just we really needed to find you, but if you're no feeling up to it we can maybe—'

'No, we can't,' said Gil, emerging from the neck of his shirt. 'Tell me again. Mally Bowen said—'

'She says she's no willing to lay the old – dame out until you've looked at her. It was you she named, no her husband the Serjeant. So I'm sent out to find you, and I'd just come to your house when this fellow,' he nodded towards Cato, who was now grinning speechlessly at Cleone, 'fetched up at the door saying you were here at the bawdyhouse and needed your clothes.'

Gil covered his eyes.

'Is that what he said?'

'He did explain,' Lowrie assured him. 'Though I don't think he mentioned you'd been struck on the head.'

'That's no worry. I'd sooner my wife was annoyed than anxious,' Gil said, cautiously resuming the process of dressing. Alys had sent the old doublet and the summer gown; it did seem likely she was annoyed. But she had remembered boots, a hat, and his old purse. 'So Dame Isabella's still waiting to be laid out. She'll have to wait a bit longer now, she must have begun to set. Did Mally Bowen say what was troubling her?'

'No.'

Madam Xanthe swept back into the chamber, shooed Cato and Cleone out and handed Gil a glass of something dark.

'Drink that,' she ordered him, 'it should help your head. Your clothes are nowhere near dry, Strephon tells me. I'll send them back the morn, if you can manage without till then.'

'I'll find something to put on my back, I've no doubt,' said Gil. He swallowed the mixture cautiously, recognizing the familiar tang of willow-bark, and returned to the task of fastening his points. 'We'll send to fetch them. One of the men would be glad of the errand, no need to take Cato from his work.'

Lowrie gave a crack of laughter at this, and went red as Madam Xanthe looked more closely at him.

'Well, here's a likely young gentleman,' she said, approaching him. He backed into his corner again, looking alarmed, and she put out a long finger and tipped his chin up. 'Oh, aye, you'd get a free entry any evening you care, young sir,' she pronounced, relishing the ambiguity. Gil, deliberately looking away to find his way into the summer gown, said in French,

'Are you sure he's up to your weight?'

'Oh!' Madam Xanthe tittered, but released Lowrie and said in the same language, 'He's your steed, is he? I'd not thought that of you, *maistre*.'

Gil turned to meet her eyes directly.

'I'm in your debt and Cato's,' he said, 'for this morning's support, but that doesn't give you the right to affront me or my friends. Nor does it come well from you to do so,' he went on, with a slight emphasis on the *vous*.

The arch gaze sharpened slightly, then she looked away, with that annoying titter.

'Oh, get on wi you,' she said in Scots. 'Away and get about your business, and then go and comfort your wee wife. Or deal wi Isabella Torrance, if that's what's needed.'

* * *

66

'She's still in her chamber,' said Maister Livingstone.

They had found him in the first-floor hall of Canon Aiken's substantial house, pacing anxiously before the hearth, though scattered documents on a nearby bench suggested he had been trying to deal with legal matters. 'We'll no get her laid out now till she softens,' he went on. 'I've sent for Mistress Bowen to come back, she can let you know what troubles her about the corp. She wouldny tell me, and she'd said naught to Annot.'

'And you've no idea?' Gil prompted. The other man shook his head.

'She shut the door,' Lowrie said, 'shut herself and Annot in, and then, oh, barely a *Te Deum* later she's back out with her basin and towel, hustles Annot out by the arm, saying she had to talk to you first.'

'But is there some doubt about how Dame Isabella died?'

Livingstone shrugged.

'I'd not have said so. Her woman came wailing to me first thing, *Oh, she's deid, my lady's deid*, and I went wi her to see, and there's the old carline on the floor of the chamber like she'd just fallen there, lying there in her shift, eyes open, mouth open, you'd think she's seen a ghost. No doubt that she was dead, but I saw no sign of any injury or the like, no signs that suggested poison to me, save a wee bit blood at her nose, which I take to mean an apoplexy.'

'It sounds like it,' Gil agreed. 'Has the corp been touched since Mistress Bowen left? Has anyone been into the chamber?'

'I wouldny cross a layer-out. I ordered it left alone. Annot made some outcry about prayers for her mistress, but I bade her stand at the door wi her beads, and set two of our men on to keep the rest away. The priest said he'd send a couple of bidders up from St Agnes, but he took little persuasion himself to go away meantime.' Gil looked startled, and both Livingstone men grimaced. 'She'd loosed her bowels,' the elder explained, and put a hand to his nose. 'It's a bit—'

'There's Mistress Bowen now,' said Lowrie as a hinge creaked outside. 'Will we go down to meet her?'

The house stood round three sides of a courtyard, so that the hall windows looked out over the knot-garden and the little fountain at its centre, as well as the gate opposite. To judge by the ladders and stacked timber there were carpenters working on one of the shorter wings, though they did not appear to be active today. Dame Isabella and her entourage were lodged in the other wing, where a set of three linked chambers at ground level had been made comfortable with hangings and padded furniture. The first of these seemed full of people, though this resolved into the man Attie and two grooms in green livery talking about crossbows, several elderly women in the dark habit of St Agnes' almshouse praying industriously for the departed, and Mistress Bowen, a spare body in middle age bundled in a blue striped plaid, the long ends of her white linen headdress tied up on the top of her head for a day's work, her towel and basin in her arms.

'Good day to ye, maister,' she said, and bobbed a curtsy to all three men impartially. 'I'll be glad to get this sorted and get the poor soul her rights.'

'Aye, well, it might ha been easier if you'd tellt me what was wrong at the first,' said Maister Livingstone sourly, but she ignored him and led the way into the second chamber. By the far door a tearful Annot looked up as they entered, and hauled herself up from her knees, folding her beads into her hand.

'And time too!' she said. 'She'll be set by now, no hope of making her decent afore evening, it'll be the morn afore she—'

'You'll not tell me my job,' said Mistress Bowen, and laid a hand to the door. 'Has she been disturbed since I left, maister?'

'Only if Annot's been in,' said Livingstone.

'No! No!' disclaimed Annot. 'At least,' she bit her lip, and they all looked at her. 'I couldny bear to think of her staring like that, I laid a cloth to her face!'

'I tellt you to leave her alone,' said Livingstone in annoyance. Gil ignored them and followed Mistress Bowen into the chamber.

The first thing one noticed was the stink, which caught at the throat and made one gag. The next was Dame Isabella herself, sprawled in her filthy shift like a stranded porpoise, half on her side. The cloth Annot had mentioned covered her face, long locks of grey hair snaking from under it across the polished floorboards. A pantofle of scuffed embroidered velvet had fallen off and lay a yard or so away; the other was still wedged on the plump foot over its defiled stocking. Gil closed his eyes briefly, muttering a prayer for the dead, thinking again how death stripped all dignity from a human being.

'Amen,' said Mistress Bowen, crossing herself.

'Is she just as you left her?' he asked. 'What was it you wanted to show me?'

'Aye.' She had shed the plaid and tied on an apron. Beneath it she wore a working woman's short-sleeved gown of grey wool; now she began to roll up the sleeves of kirtle and shift, baring wiry forearms. 'In this calling, maister, you get to ken the signs of a death. Heart trouble, apoplexy, old age. Poverty.' Gil nodded, wondering if his belly would hold out against the smell in the chamber. 'Whether a death's been expected or no.' She bent, feeling one of the outstretched arms with a professional air. 'Aye, aye, she's progressing well. Now, poverty's no been a problem here,' she measured the girth of the arm with a wry smile, 'but just the same it didny seem right to me. So I'd a good look at the corp. There's no saying what more I'll uncover when I get her right washed, but to start wi I found,' she twitched the linen cloth away, 'here's what I found.'

The face was hideous, as Maister Livingstone had implied, staring eyes and open mouth giving the impression

69

of someone gazing into Hell, the trickle of blackened blood caked in the wispy moustache adding to the horror. Gil, unable to help himself, reached out and tried to close the eyelids, and discovered they were set wide as they were.

'See here,' said Mistress Bowen, and he realized she had put back a handful of the thinning hair and was pointing at the old woman's ear. It was delicately whorled, pink, quite incongruously pretty and scrupulously clean. It was a pity when convention demanded that women had to hide attractive features, he reflected, thinking of Alys's long honey-coloured hair which now he only saw at night.

'Look closer,' prompted Mistress Bowen. 'Someone's stoppit her lug.'

He looked obediently, and looked again. Half-hidden within the hollow of the ear was a black dot, like the ticks he had to extract from Socrates' coat if they went out onto the Dow Hill.

'It's no a tick,' said Mistress Bowen when he mentioned this. 'Touch it.'

He got down on one knee and inspected the mark. It was raised, roughly square, and not black as he had first thought but dark as iron, with flecks of rust-red which –

'Sweet St Giles!' he said, and crossed himself. 'It's a nail.'

He put out a finger to test the thing. It was iron, cold iron. No, not cold, he recognized, nearer lukewarm, cooling with the corpse.

'Aye,' said Mistress Bowen grimly. 'Now how did that get there?'

'Murder,' he said. 'We need to send for the Serjeant.'

Chapter Four

'What are you saying?' demanded Maister Livingstone from the doorway. 'A nail? How has the old witch got a nail in her lug? That makes no sense!'

'It does if someone put it there,' said Lowrie. 'Will I send Attie out for the Serjeant, uncle?'

'But in here? She was at her prayers, Annot said. Here, Annot, woman, tell him!'

Annot, grasping what was being said, collapsed onto her knees again wailing incoherently. The men in the outermost chamber could be heard asking what ailed her. Gil ignored all, covered up the corpse's hideous face and sat back on his heels, gazing round the chamber.

The door from the courtyard into the set of chambers was in the angle of the two wings, so this furthest chamber was at the outermost end of the wing and had windows in three walls, the door in the fourth. It was light, therefore, and contained a great number of items. He counted a free-standing box bed, set up so as to protect its occupants from most of the draughts, several kists which seemed to be Dame Isabella's baggage, two settles, a folding table, a prayer-desk. The hangings lay in folds round the wall-foot as if they had been bought for a room with higher tenterhooks; they would surely impede anyone who hid behind them and hoped to step out quickly grasping hammer and –

'What did he use to strike it home?' he said aloud. Mistress Bowen, on her way to attend to Annot, gave him an approving look. 'Is there a mell in the chamber? Anything that could be used for one?'

'The wrights has mells in the other wing, all different sizes,' said Livingstone, but his nephew had begun casting about, peering behind and under the furniture. 'Are you saying – are you saying someone cam in here and struck a nail into her lug while she was at her prayers? And killed her? But how wad she ever let that come to pass? Did she no call for help, for her servants? It doesny make sense.'

'Done and dunted,' Lowrie muttered from under the nearer settle. 'No, maister, I see nothing that's like to be used for the purpose that wouldny show the marks or break in two when you tried it. That pewter basin, or her jewel-box, for instance.' He lifted the basin, looking at its unblemished base. 'Likely he took it away wi him.'

'Aye, that would be too easy,' said Gil. He got to his feet and looked down at the corpse. 'Tell me, Mistress Bowen, is this how you found her lying when you first saw her?'

She paused in her soothing of Annot, considered the body, and said,

'Aye, more or less. Her shift was up about her hurdies, I pullt it down for decency, but I've heard the Serjeant on about moving a corp too often to make that mistake. As soon as I jaloused it wasny natural, I took care I never changed anything else.'

'She's just the way she was when I saw her,' said Livingstone. He bit at a knuckle. 'It was maybe no right to leave her there on the floor in her dirt, but to be honest I didny fancy handling her, the state she's in, and anyway no sense in more of us getting fouled than need be.' Mistress Bowen glanced at him, but said nothing. 'Will I send the boy out to find the Serjeant, then? Is that what—?'

'Attie's away to find him already,' said Lowrie, returning from the outer room.

'And I'll need a word with Attie when he gets back,' said Gil, 'with all her servants indeed, and this one in particular.' He looked at Annot, now sobbing on Mistress Bowen's shoulder. 'As soon as she's fit for it,' he added.

'Give her a bit longer,' said Mistress Bowen. 'If there's another lassie about the place maybe she could give me a hand, we'll get the departed made clean at least. I'll not ask the St Agnes women, they're full old to be heaving the likes of her around, the souls.' She looked down at Annot and patted her back soothingly. 'Thanks be to Our Lady, we had her shroud out of her baggage when I was first here.'

'Then we can clean up the chamber,' muttered Livingstone. 'What Canon Aiken's going to say – violent death in his house, and the state the chamber's in, and all! But this doesny make sense, Maister Cunningham, why would an ill-tempered old attercap like her let a man close enough to drive a nail into her head?'

'Someone she trusted,' said his nephew, 'someone she'd no reason to be suspicious of? Mind you, she'd suspect the Archbishop himself,' he added.

'It makes no sense,' repeated Livingstone.

By the time Annot had been led away by one of the kitchen-maids for a nice sit-down and maybe a cup of buttered ale with honey in it, Gil had managed to get a good look around him.

There was a grey woollen bedgown lying on top of the counterpane, a black velvet gown with embroidered sleeves hung on a peg on the wall, more armfuls of black cloth on top of a kist must be the other garments Dame Isabella had discarded last night. A second kist had been opened, and a bundle of folded linen lay on top of the contents: the shroud Mistress Bowen had mentioned, without which no provident person would travel.

A set of rosary beads of carved ivory with jet gauds lay coiled beside a worn velvet-covered book on the prayer-desk by one of the windows. On the nearer settle a bowl of water, still faintly warm to the hand, and a pile of towels suggested the morning routine. The jewel-box Lowrie had noticed, of wood covered in leather and fastened by a stout brass strap, lay on the further settle, a silver cross on a chain dangling from beneath its lid; a close-stool covered in blue velvet to match the prayer-book stood half-hidden beyond the settle, and added its contribution to the appalling atmosphere in the room.

Livingstone, with a muttered excuse, had retreated to the outer chamber to wait for the Serjeant, but Lowrie remained, prowling about and looking awkwardly from time to time at the corpse.

'Maybe we'll can get her made decent,' said Mistress Bowen, returning with a jug of water. 'Did you see enough, maister, can I move her now?'

'In a moment,' Gil said. 'I'd as soon leave her for the Serjeant to see as well. Mistress, what would you say happened here?'

'Oh, she was at stool,' the woman said, 'that's for certain. It's all down her legs and her hose, you can see, but there's little enough on the boards.'

He nodded. This had been his reading too.

'What made you look for – for what you found, mistress?' Lowrie asked suddenly. She turned to him, and her thin face softened a little.

'Violent death's never a bonnie sight,' she said obliquely. 'What made me look? The sight o her, maister. Her eyes starting out like that, the blood at her nose, yet her face is pale and there's no other signs o an apoplexy. I mind my mother, that had the same calling, telling me the tale o just such a death she attended, oh,' she paused to reckon, 'forty year syne or more. Only there the nail was easier to find, not being driv' home the same way.'

'I never heard that tale,' Gil said. And what other stories would a layer-out have to tell, he wondered.

'Aye, well, you wouldny. My mother never tellt any but me. The corp was a foul-tempered fellow, she said, and had broke all his wife's limbs in turn and started on his daughters.' She closed her mouth firmly on that subject and turned to the corpse. 'I'd as soon tend to her now, maister, never mind waiting for Serjeant Anderson. I've one of the kitchen lassies out-by, ready to give a hand.'

'Not just yet,' said Gil. 'I'm still trying to work this out. She was seated over yonder, then,' he nodded towards the close-stool, 'and someone struck a nail into her ear.' He drew back the cloth and considered the black dot of the nail-head again, and put his fingers to his own ear to match the place. 'He must have moved fast, to strike home before she was aware of it. Or she,' he added scrupulously.

'If the stool's not been moved,' said Lowrie.

'No by me,' said Mistress Bowen.

'It's where I last saw it,' the young man agreed. 'Then someone could have approached her round the settle, whichever way she was facing.'

'Someone she knew,' said Gil, 'someone she trusted, someone she'd no objection to having in the chamber while she was occupied like that.'

'Anyone in the house, then,' said Lowrie. 'Not that she trusted any of us, as I said, but she'd summon any or all and sit there enthroned, giving out her orders for the day. Her women, her grooms, me or my uncle.'

'Well, they aye say the wealthy has no need of good manners,' said Mistress Bowen disapprovingly.

'At that rate, mistress, Isabella Torrance could ha bought and sold Scotland,' said Lowrie.

'So how did she come to be lying here?' wondered Gil. 'Did she move herself?'

'Maybe it didn't kill her immediately,' said Lowrie slowly. 'Head wounds are orra things, I know that.'

'It's possible. I've seen stranger,' said Mistress Bowen.

Gil looked down at the sprawled figure, half on its side, plump limbs part-flexed.

'Aye, I suppose. She rose up and came forward—'

'Maybe she thought to go after whoever it was as they left.' Lowrie was prowling round the bed, and now leaned forward to sniff cautiously at its woodwork. 'I'd say she's laid her hand to this end panel, maybe to steady herself.' He turned to open the shutters of the window over the prayer-desk, doubling the light that fell on the area he indicated. 'Aye, it's smeared like her shift.'

'Her hands are foul.' Gil considered this. 'And then she collapsed where we see her. That would work. She looks as if she fell rather than being carried or dragged.'

A loud, confident voice rose in the outermost room, with a commotion of several people. Maister Livingstone could be heard trying to explain what had happened, but the new voice overrode his.

'No, no, I'll just hae a look mysel afore you explain all. Ben here, is she? And Maister Cunningham's here already, you say.'

There was a heavy tread, and Serjeant Anderson proceeded into the chamber, a well-built man in the long blue gown of a burgh servant with the embroidered badge on the breast. He nodded to Gil, then stopped just inside the door, his hand halfway to his head.

'Your bonnet, Serjeant,' said Mistress Bowen, her tone nicely combining formality and wifely reproof. He completed the gesture and removed his felt hat, staring at the corpse. His constable peered round his arm and stepped back, grimacing, but the Serjeant came forward, bent ponderously to look under the linen cloth, and retreated.

'Our Lady's garters, Mally, have ye no washed her yet? It's no decent leaving her like that. And what's this about murder, any road? She looks more like an apoplexy to me.'

'Aye, so I thought at first,' said his wife, 'but see here.'

Shown the evidence of misdoing, the Serjeant surveyed it for a long moment, tested the rigidity of Dame Isabella's neck and jaw, then straightened up and looked at Gil.

'Aye, Maister Cunningham,' he pronounced. 'So you've time to spare from your researches about the burgh, I see. How far have ye got, then?'

'John!' said Mistress Bowen, reminding Gil irresistibly of Magdalen Boyd. The Serjeant threw his spouse a quick glance and continued more civilly,

'See, if it was me, I'd ha questioned all her servants by now. She's been lying there a good while, by the feel of her. How long was it known she was dead?'

'Aye, well, small chance of that,' said Maister Livingstone from behind the constable. He stepped into the chamber, dragging the man Attie by the arm. 'Here's this lad only the now telling me, her own folk has run, Serjeant, all but two of them. Lifted their bundles and vanished.'

'I couldny stop them,' said Attie miserably. 'It was that Marion started it, said she wasny staying here to get the blame o the old wife taking an apoplexy, and the other lads saw it the same way and up and left. I tried to tell them you'd never charge them wi it, maister,' he said to Maister Livingstone, 'but they wouldny hear me.'

'Aye, well,' said the Serjeant. 'I'll ha their names off yir maister and we'll get the constables after them. If I cry them from the Cross we'll run them to ground soon enough.'

'That's if they've stayed in Glasgow,' Gil said, considering the situation. If only one servant had run, he might have read it as an admission of guilt, but four fugitives confused the picture. 'Maybe you should ask at the gates, too.'

'I ken my job, Maister Cunningham,' said the Serjeant.

They had repaired to the outermost chamber of the set, to allow Mistress Bowen and her assistant to resume work. While Livingstone dismissed the two men in green livery with a long list of people to call on with news of Dame Isabella's death, Lowrie had quietly set up a table, and now, to the Serjeant's evident gratification, he and Gil were seated behind it like a miniature court, Attie standing before them mangling his velvet bonnet, with Lowrie himself and the scrawny constable at either end making notes. The old women of St Agnes' were still at their task in the corner, but their soft ancient voices were more soothing than distracting.

'Why did Marion think she would get the blame, Attie?' Gil asked now.

77

'I don't know.' Attie spread his hands, the bonnet dangling from one like a dead bird. 'She wasny making sense.'

'Tell me what happened,' Gil said. The man looked blank. 'What was the first you knew of your mistress's death?'

'First we all knew,' said Livingstone, striding the length of the chamber and back. One of the bedeswomen looked up at him, but did not break off her murmured recital. 'When Annot came running out crying that she was dead. Is that right, lad?' he flung at the servant.

'Where were you at the time, maister?' Gil asked him. 'You said Annot came to you – where was that?'

'We were in the hall,' Lowrie contributed. His uncle nodded.

'Aye, so we were.'

'Let's hear how the day started,' said the Serjeant. 'Was the departed just as usual? Who dealt wi her first?'

'That would be her women,' said Attie, working his bonnet between his hands. He was a lean, dark-haired fellow in his early twenties, Gil guessed, with a frightened air which was probably natural in the circumstances. 'They're her bedfellows, see.'

'And you men slept where?' asked the Serjeant.

'Yonder in the mid chamber, see, on a couple straw pletts, which you'll find stowed in ahint the big kist.'

Gil sat back and listened while the Serjeant led Attie competently through the beginning of the day. The grooms had risen first, naturally, though they had heard the women stirring soon after. One of the men had fetched bread and ale from the kitchen and all four had broken fast. The two waiting-women had also eaten in snatches as they moved back and forth through the set of chambers.

'Your mistress ate nothing?' Gil asked.

'She'd not eat first thing,' said Lowrie at his elbow, 'not till she'd—'

'Not till she'd been to stool,' confirmed Attie awkwardly. 'You never – you never – Nicol, that's had several places afore this, he said he never seen anyone like the old carline

78

neither for concern wi her belly. So they got her up, and fetched her the glass hot water she likes, and we heard her shouting about her bedgown, and then she summoned us in wi orders for the day.'

'What, before she was dressed? Why should her women not carry the orders out to you?' Gil asked.

Attie shook his head. 'She never trusted a one of us to carry a sensible word to the others.'

'Same wi the rest of the household,' contributed Livingstone. 'If she wanted to say a thing she'd summon you afore her, even Archie or my good-sister under their own roof.'

'So what were the orders?' demanded the Serjeant. 'What would she have you all do?'

Attie shut his eyes, the better to remember, while the old women switched in unison from *Pater noster* to *Ave Maria*.

'Nicol and Billy was to go find out when the Campbells would be back,' he produced, 'I think they'd a word for the place they lodge in, and Alan and me was to go an errand to the potyngar she favoured, which you'd ken wouldny be the nearest, and fetch a list o things, and straight back here.'

'And did you?' asked the Serjeant.

'Aye, we did,' Attie assured them, 'for it wasny worth the beating if we'd dawdled.'

'And the women?'

'Likely they'd be set to getting her dressed,' suggested Livingstone.

'Aye, that was it,' agreed the groom. 'That was the usual. Takes an hour or two, what wi lacing her up and getting all the points tied and dressing her head, and her changing her mind, and she's right particular how you comb her head, or so Forveleth aye says.'

'Forveleth?' questioned Gil.

'Forveleth,' Lowrie said. 'It's her right name. An Erschewoman, she is. Dame Isabella would aye call her Marion.'

'Said she couldny abide these heathen names,' supplied Attie. 'A bonnie enough lass, but away wi the fairy half the time, full of ravery about one or another ill-wishing her.' This must refer to the missing woman, Gil assumed, rather than her mistress. 'I tried to stop her running off,' he added, 'but she said she'd seen a corp laid out in the middle chamber there whenever we set foot in it. Daft, I call it, for it was in the inmost one the auld carline died.'

'And how long was ye about your errand?' demanded the Serjeant impatiently. 'When did ye get back from the potyngar's? Which was it, any road?'

'It was Jimmy Syme's, away down the High Street,' said Attie earnestly. Gil looked at the man, reckoning in his mind how long it might take to walk down to the apothecary shop of Syme & Renfrew in the High Street, and what short cuts might be possible. 'And we were no that long,' Attie went on, 'straight there and back like we were told to, quicker than the other two any road, and then we just sat here in this chamber. They cry us waiting-men, after all,' he said sourly.

'Here? Could you see the door to your mistress's chamber?' Gil asked.

'Oh, aye,' said Attie. He waved a hand at the corner where the bedeswomen sat, from which Gil reckoned the doorway would be hidden. 'We were yonder, waiting for the auld carline to send out for us, only the first thing that happened was Annot going in to her, and she screamed,' he went on more fluently, 'and started up saying *My lady's dead!* and when we went to see, well, you ken what we saw.'

'So when you and – Alan, was it?' said Gil, 'left, she was alive, and the first you saw of her after you got back, she was dead. Is that right?'

Attie looked at him for a moment, turning this over in his mind, and then nodded.

'That's it, maister,' he said in some relief. 'That's it exact.'

'And the two of you were together the whole time?'

'Oh, aye, maister,' Attie assured him. 'The whole time. Never took our een off one anither.'

80

'Then why did Alan run off?' demanded Maister Livingstone.

'Aye, that's the nub o it,' agreed the Serjeant. 'If the two o ye could speak for one another, he'd no need to run off and cast suspicion on hissel, and the same for the two other lads.'

'He never said,' said Attie doubtfully. 'But him and Nicol's brothers, see, maybe he wouldny want to stay here on his lone.'

'What had the two of ye to fetch from the potyngar?' asked Livingstone. Lowrie looked up from his notes, and nodded. 'Was it paid, or do we have to take it back and get it struck off the slate?'

'Alan had it by heart,' said Attie, 'five or six different – all on the slate, maister – and he put them all in the breast o his jerkin, and I'm thinking he never took them out when we got back here.' He looked uneasily at Livingstone's expression, and counted on his fingers. 'An ounce o root ginger, an ounce o cloves. Flowers o sulphur two ounce – that's all I recall, maister, but I ken there was more. Was it a nutmeg, maybe? Or senna-pods?'

'Oh, if he's got that lot on him we'll smell him out readily enough,' said the Serjeant, laughing heartily. 'You'll can set that great dog o yourn after him, Maister Cunningham.' He tilted his chair back, then forward again with a thump. 'Right, I'd say that's all I want from you the now, lad, we'll hear what the woman has to say that's no run away. Tammas, away and find her, I think she was to be in the kitchen.'

His scrawny constable left obediently. Livingstone said rather sharply to Attie,

'And you can get about the tasks I gave you, my lad. We'll need the mortcloth, and the hatchments have to go up at the door.'

'But where do I get them all, maister? It's no our house, I've never a—'

'Ask at the kitchen, you great gowk! St Peter's bones, the old beldam was right enough calling you scatterwits.'

81

Attie turned to go, and checked as a shadow darkened the door to the courtyard.

'Here you all are!' said John Sempill. 'There's never a soul answering your door at the house, Eckie, and I want the title to Balgrochan back, for the old dame never gave us the right papers. What's afoot, then, what's come to the old carline? They're saying out in the town it's murder.'

'Aye, maister, it is that,' pronounced the Serjeant with relish. 'Were you acquaint wi the corp, then?'

'Aye,' said Sempill, scowling at him. 'She's – she was my wife's godmother. So what's come to her? Have you no taken whoever it was yet?'

'Just gie it time, maister,' said the Serjeant. 'Ah, here's the woman. Sit there, lass, and tell me your name.'

Annot, tearstained and tremulous, halted on the threshold at sight of Sempill; he stared back at her with round pale eyes, then abruptly turned away saying to Gil,

'Are you in this and all? What's ado? What came to her, then, if it wasny an apoplexy?'

'Someone drove a nail in her head,' reported Livingstone before Gil could speak. 'She's done and dunted, John, and quite a bargain for some of us.'

'When?'

'That's what we're trying to find out,' Gil said. 'When did you see her?'

Sempill paused a moment, like a man trying to reckon times. Behind him the women of St Agnes' embarked on another round of the rosary.

'I'm no right sure,' he said finally. 'But she was well enough when I saw her,' he added aggressively, 'it was never me that nailed her down. How could you—' He stopped again, looked from one hand to another with small gestures as if holding nail and hammer, looked at Annot and the bedeswomen. 'What, right through her veil and cap and that? Must ha been a mighty dunt! Can I see her? Will she be fit for my wife to view?'

'No just yet,' said Livingstone, 'they're still washing her.

82

Come away, John, and let the Serjeant get questioning folk, though he'll maybe want a word wi you—'

'No, no,' said the Serjeant, waving grandly. 'That's no a bother, her own folk'll tell me all I need.'

Sempill was persuaded away with a mutter of Malvoisie, the two note-takers picked up their instruments, and the Serjeant drew a deep breath and began.

It was clear almost immediately that Annot was not going to be a helpful witness. Asked her name she stumbled and stammered over the formal Ann, the everyday Annot, and two forms of her surname, which was either Hutchie or Hutchison.

'What do you usually get?' the Serjeant asked her. 'What does most folk call you?'

'Annot,' she said miserably. 'Save for my mistress, that calls me – called me Sparflin Annie.'

'That's a good one!' said the Serjeant. 'And are you a sparfler, then, Annot?'

She shook her head, blinking away more tears, and Lowrie put in,

'Her mistress had names for all her servants, Serjeant, none of them very complimentary. Attie Scatterwit, Marion Frivol, Billy Blate.'

'And none of them true,' said Annot, with a faint flicker of old indignation.

Gil studied her. She was a small, well-rounded woman, probably past thirty, and would be comely when her face was not puffed with weeping. She was dressed well but without show as fitted her station, in a gown of dark blue broadcloth, good linen on her head, her only jewellery a cross on a cord and the beads at her girdle. Why her mistress would call her a spendthrift was not immediately clear.

She was now attempting to deal with the beginning of the day, stopping and starting and muddling herself. The Serjeant was showing signs of irritation; with an effort, Gil pulled himself together and applied himself to his duties.

83

'Mistress Annot,' he said. She turned her eyes on him. 'Attie tells us your mistress called the men in to give them their orders before she was dressed. Is that right?'

'Oh, yes, yes, that's – well, no afore she was dressed, exactly, for we'd – she'd never ha sat there in her shift, we'd to—'

'That was her usual way,' said Lowrie.

'How was she clad?' Gil persevered.

'Her bedgown about her and yesterday's cap over her hair,' Annot said with a sudden access of coherence, 'for we'd combed her and washed her hands and face, and she'd drunk her glass o hot water, though it wasny to her liking—'

'What's no to like in a glass o hot water?' demanded the Serjeant. 'Daft way to start the day, to my thinking. No nourishment in it.'

'It was – it wasny – she said it wasny hot,' Annot stammered, 'though it burned my fingers.'

'Humph!' said the Serjeant.

'What happened next?' Gil asked. 'After the men went away, what did you and Marion have to do for your mistress?'

'She'd go to her prayers,' Annot bit her lip, then nodded. 'Aye, that was – for she aye – so she dismissed us, bid us return in an hour.'

'An hour!' repeated the Serjeant. 'Was she praying for the whole o Scotland by name? So you left her an hour. Was she well when you went back?'

'Oh aye. Well, she must ha been, for she called us in herself – and then we – she would have us wash her – and we'd barely – as soon as her clean shift was on her she would go to – she would—'

'Go to stool,' Gil prompted when she hesitated. She nodded at that. He frowned, trying to concentrate. 'She needed a stick to walk, or else support. So you had to help her across the room?' She nodded again. 'And were you and Marion both still present?'

She stared at him, puzzled.

84

'We were both washing her. Oh I see, yes, the both of us was getting out her clean cap and her comb and that while she sat there, until – for she shouted at us, *Get out my sight you pair o* – so we went, I went out to the kitchen to get anither bite o food—'

'Why had you not had a bite when she was at her prayers?' Gil asked.

'I wasny hungry at the time,' she said simply.

'So you went straight to the kitchen,' said the Serjeant. She nodded, sniffling. 'And where did the other woman go, this Marion? Was she at hand all the time you were away? Never tell me you leave your mistress unattended?'

'Aye, for she'd – if she bade us – I reckoned a quarter-hour would be—' Annot swallowed, glanced at Lowrie, and said, more coherently, 'My mistress sent the both o us from her, so we went.'

'But where was the other one? Tell me that!' demanded the Serjeant.

'Was she about the house?' Lowrie suggested. 'Or did she step out for a bit?'

At that Annot's face crumpled.

'I canny say,' she wailed, 'for I've no a notion, only it canny have been Marion that – she never – I canny tell where she was! And then she came to the kitchen, and we – we got talking, so we did, and it was longer than I meant to leave her! And then when I came back she was, she was,' she scrubbed at her eyes with her sleeve. 'I'll see her face afore me the rest o my days, I'm certain o't.'

'Mistress Annot,' said Gil. 'The man that came in just now.'

She blinked at him, trying to follow his thoughts.

'Sempill of Muirend, aye,' she said after a moment.

'When was he last here? Did he have word with your mistress this morning?'

She shook her head in surprise.

'Oh, no, maister. No this morning. He was here yestreen, right enough, and they had a word.' Lowrie grunted, but did not comment. 'Through the window, and all,' she added.

'What about?' Gil asked.

'I wasny listening. I couldny hear.'

'So this Marion was about the house for a while on her own,' said the Serjeant, returning to the immediate issue. 'How long for, would you say? How far could she get in the time?'

The constable looked up and offered, 'Maybe she was at the privy hersel.'

The Serjeant guffawed.

'More than likely,' he said, 'by the way this death stinks.' He laughed loudly again at his joke, sat back in his chair and went on, 'Did you get all that writ down, Tammas? Good lad. Well, young maister, if you'll can give us a note of the names of all these that's gone missing, and a description, we'll away and let you get on. I'll get them cried at the Cross and through the town, and one o them will turn out to be the guilty party, most likely this woman wi the two names, that's as clear as day to me.' Lowrie looked doubtfully at Gil, and the Serjeant followed his gaze. 'You're agreed, I take it, Maister Cunningham?'

Gil shrugged, being careful not to move his head more than necessary.

'I'm agreed we need to talk to the servants that have run off,' he said, 'but I'd say there's a lot more to learn. We haven't got the whole story here.'

'We've enough of it for my purpose,' said the Serjeant, rising. 'I'll report all to the Provost if you like, maister, no need for you to go up the hill as well. No, no, Maister Cunningham, it's clear as day to me, like I said. One of her servants has slain her, and small wonder, wicked crime though it is, from the way she's treated them.'

'No, surely no,' protested Annot, sniffling, while Lowrie looked hard at his notes. 'None of us would never do a thing like that – it's been some wicked fellow passing that's come in off the street and found her unattended—'

86

'And stole nothing? Those velvet gowns would sell for a good sum down the rag market,' said Serjeant Anderson, 'let alone her beads and the silver cross I saw ben there. No, no, lass, you'll no tell me. One o them that's run has taken their chance, finding her unattended and no others in sight, and lifted a mell and nail from the carpenters' work across the yard. Is there no someone in Holy Writ that got slain that way, maister?' he asked Gil, who blinked at him and answered almost automatically,

'Sisera the man of Canaan. In the Book of Judges.'

'Aye, I thought that,' said the Serjeant with satisfaction. 'And where's Maister Livingstone to be found? In the hall, you say? Right, then. I'll see you in good time, maisters.' He gathered up his constable and sailed out. Gil sat back against the wall, put a cautious hand to his aching head and sighed. Lowrie raised his eyes from his tablets.

'What would you wish to do now, Maister Gil?' he asked. 'Have you more questions for Annot here or Attie, or do you want to seek out the mell, or what?'

'If the women have finished,' Gil said reluctantly, 'I'd as soon get another look at the bedchamber. Little chance of any sign anyway, but by the afternoon you'll have all Glasgow tramping through it to pay their respects and destroying whatever there is.'

'I'll go and ask, maister,' volunteered Annot timidly. He nodded, and she braced herself and set off into the other chamber. Lowrie looked down at his notes again.

'Do you want to take a copy of this, or should I write it out for you? There's one or two things they said—'

'There were, weren't there,' Gil agreed. 'Give me a read of it if you will.'

Although Mistress Bowen was just completing her task when Annot tapped at the door, it was some time before Gil got access to the chamber. The process of locating Attie, the laying-out board and four stools of equal height was a lengthy one; then both Gil and Lowrie had to lend a hand in moving the body onto the board and the board into the middle chamber to rest on the stools. Annot, Mistress

Bowen and the kitchen-maid who had helped her saw to the decent disposition of the linen shroud, and stood back. Lowrie reached for his purse, and Gil went to stand in the chamber door, surveying the scene. The two women had obviously turned their attention to the chamber itself when they had dealt with the corpse; the place smelled much fresher than when he had first seen it.

'Here, what's this?' said Mistress Bowen sharply behind him. He turned, to find her looking indignantly at her palm. 'I'll no be bought, maister—'

'Indeed no!' said Lowrie hastily, his neck reddening. 'I hope you'll tell the Sheriff what you found and no other, when the time comes. No, no, it's in consideration of a dirty task, mistress, and there's a shroud-penny to Kirstie as well.'

Mollified, the two departed and the bedeswomen from St Agnes' were installed beside their client. Annot, clearly feeling more settled now that the ordeal of her questioning was over, knelt beside them. Gil moved carefully into the bedchamber, looking about him.

'Tell me a bit more,' he said as Lowrie joined him.

'There's a fair bit more to tell,' the younger man agreed.

'John Sempill, for a start. You've something to add to Annot's tale? When was he here?'

'Last night after dinner, as she said. The old woman kept him standing, and then refused to see him privately. A roaring row in the antechamber.'

'Your uncle said the same,' Gil recalled. 'So not this morning?'

'Not that I know,' Lowrie said warily.

'But he got a word wi her anyway.' Gil frowned, trying to think of what Sempill had said earlier.

'Aye. After he left us he stopped by this window,' he nodded at the one opposite the bed-foot, which gave onto the courtyard, 'and shouted through it at her, and they'd another roaring argument you could hear in Partick, till he flung off out the gate bawling threats—' Lowrie stopped, suddenly aware of what he was saying. 'He said,' he continued more slowly, 'he'd see her in Hell afore he did whatever it was she'd ordered him to do. She was looking out at the window, and asked what his wife would say if she kent what he'd been at, and he, he went closer and said something quiet, and she laughed at him. So he stormed off out the gate.'

'Where were you?' Gil asked. 'Where were her servants, at that?'

'I've no notion where her servants were,' Lowrie admitted, 'though I'd not believe Annot heard none of it, but I was hanging out the upstairs window listening for all I was worth. I've not had such entertainment all week. Is the man aye so birsie?'

'He's much improved since this marriage, if you'll believe me,' Gil said. And where had Sempill been this morning, he wondered, when he told his wife he was talking to Dame Isabella? 'Now, do you see aught amiss here? Aught that's out of place or missing?'

'I'd not know.' Lowrie looked about him. 'She was right persnickety, I'd guess her kists are all packed just so, but you want Annot for that. I'll fetch her in.' He turned to go, then hesitated. 'Maister, I'd say I was wi my uncle from the time the two o us came down for our porridge till Annot came running to say she was dead, for we were going back over all the documents and debating what to do about the Strathblane lands.'

'I'm glad to hear it.'

'So am I,' Lowrie admitted. 'But the thing is, we were at the back o the hall, looking onto the garden, so we neither of us saw nor heard anything from this side the house. And a course the kitchen's out that way and all, so she was right unattended, nobody within call in any direction, if what Annot says is right.'

'Except her murderer.' Gil sighed. 'It's not an easy one to piece together. She was enthroned yonder, and to judge by the sign she was in no position to move. Unless her bowels were loosed as she died,' he added thoughtfully. He stepped into the room and looked about him.

'Someone entered the chamber, and lifted something to use as a hammer, or else brought one in, then went around the settle and behind her,' he did so as he spoke, finding to his relief that the cover was down on the close-stool, 'and drove the nail into her ear.'

'Into the far side of her head.' Lowrie put his hand up to his own skull. 'She'd be facing the window, with the settle at her left side. Does that work? Nail in the left hand, mell in the right, reach across over the top of her head – why? Why no strike it in at the back or the crown?'

'So that she didn't see the blow coming,' Gil guessed. 'The left hand over her head, as you said, and the right striking from behind her. It's odd, just the same, you'd think the wall would cramp your movement. Unless,' he stooped, looking at the shutters in the lower portion of the window, 'unless she was looking out of the window. This is just ajar, there's a good view of the street.'

'She was right nosy,' Lowrie said. 'That would be like her, to sit there looking up the Drygate, however she was occupied.'

'Aye, I like that better. And then whoever it was left, and took the mell with them.'

'And she tried to follow.' Lowrie grimaced. 'Maybe she was a cantankerous old attercap, but nobody deserves a death like that.'

Annot, summoned from her prayers, seemed likely to start weeping again, and was not reassured by Lowrie saying,

'We're still trying to find out what happened.'

'It wasny me,' she protested, 'I wasny here, I've never a notion what can have come to her, save it was some wicked soul off the street!'

'Look about you,' Gil said, 'and see if you can tell me what's changed from,' he paused, considering. 'From the time the men were in to get their orders this morning.'

'The men?' She stared at him, then applied herself to this idea. 'Oh, maister, all's different.'

'Where was your mistress seated?'

90

'Here on the settle,' she pointed, 'and that bowl and towels wasny there on the bench, for we'd washed her hands and face afore she rose and set the bowl on the wee table by the bed-foot.'

'How was she clad?'

'Her good bedgown that's lying on the bed now, wrapped all about her and tied decent.'

'What about her feet?'

'Her pantofles. She aye wears her pantofles in the mornings, blue velvet wi stitch-work on them, and her hose under them for warmth. Her head? Just her cap, to cover her hair decent.'

'What else is different?' Gil persisted. 'Has anything been moved? Are her kists all as they should be?'

'I, I think so. Save that someone's opened up her jewel-kist,' she said, with sudden indignation. 'Who's been prying?'

'Is aught missing?' Lowrie asked. She looked at him, then crossed the chamber to where the leather-clad box lay on the settle. Setting back the lid she inspected the multiplicity of little bags of velvet or brocade it contained.

'Her silver cross,' she murmured, lifting it, 'the great chain, the two small chains, the jet from St Hilda's, the pearl rope, the pearl chain—'

Sweet St Giles, thought Gil, what an inventory. The woman could have funded a Crusade.

'There's just the one thing missing,' said Annot finally, looking up at them. 'And Christ be my witness, Maister Lowrie, it was here when I last looked in this kist. It's a purse of silver coin, maister, that she never touched or would let us touch. It should be at the bottom of the kist and it's no there, look, you can see where it ought to be.'

'And you've a witness,' said Andrew Otterburn. 'No a very reliable one, by all I hear, but he kens what he saw, I suppose.'

'I'd say so,' agreed Gil.

91

'And they struck you down so that you lost your senses. Aye, I've got that. Pity it wasny to the effusion of your blood, maister, but we canny have everything.'

'I'll contrive to do without it,' Gil said, touching the back of his head gingerly. Otterburn acknowledged this with a flick of his eyebrows. 'And likely Madam Xanthe will swear to what she knows, taking me in near senseless and drying me off.'

'Aye, so I hear,' agreed Otterburn drily. 'Well, well, we'll get it writ up in due process and serve them wi't as a summons, but will we do aught afore that? Would you wish any other action? We canny have the Archbishop's man struck down all anyhow. *Per exemplum*, I'd be happy enough to send Andro and two-three men to search the place, take the man Muir's workshop apart, gie them a bit fright.' Gil nodded. 'Walter, man, see to that, would you? They've plenty time afore supper.'

The clerk left the chamber, and Otterburn sat back.

'Now, this matter of murder and maybe robbery at Canon Aiken's house,' he went on. 'You're saying you're no right convinced by John Anderson's version?'

'I'm saying,' Gil replied carefully, 'there are more questions to be asked. It might be that the Serjeant's right, but it might not. I'm not clear about a few things.' He pinched the bridge of his nose, trying to call some of them to mind. 'For one, all her people said she wore her cap to give the men orders, but when she lay dead she was bareheaded and there was no cap to be seen. For another, it was a right sharp morning, but she had only her shift on her, nothing round her shoulders. And now this matter of the missing purse of coin.'

'You think these things matter?'

'The coin matters, for certain, and I think the others might.'

Otterburn nodded, making small squares with the little stylus in the wax of his tablets. After a moment he said,

'Well, no harm if Anderson pursues these servants he's cried at the Cross, for we'll need to speak to them whatever else we jalouse. And this bag o siller has to be found and all. You'll make your own enquiries, I take it? Aye. Well, call on me if you need help, man. There's a whole troop o armed men eating their heads off out there, we need to gie them occupation.' He threw Gil another look. 'But no the day, I hope. You look to me as if you're about done.'

'I'm for home,' Gil agreed. 'I've a few things to discuss wi my wife.'

'I'll wager you have,' said Otterburn, grinning.

Chapter Five

Alys was not speaking to him.

He could see that she was distressed; her face was pinched and drawn back from the high narrow bridge of her nose, the delicate feature to which Dame Isabella had taken such exception. If he spoke she glanced at him, but did not react. He had seen her apply the same treatment to her father when he had displeased her. What did I say to Lowrie? he thought. I should have kept my mouth shut. Socrates, apparently feeling he was also in disgrace, leaned against his knee shivering.

It did not help that the hall of Maistre Pierre's house was full of music and people. As well as the mason himself, the harper McIan and his sister Ealasaidh, a fiddler, a drummer, and Catherine improbably tapping a foot to *The Battle of Harlaw* were gathered round the hearth; in various corners of the big chamber the McIans' two servants (Two? he thought, they must be doing well just now) and the company of musicians which somehow condensed about them wherever they went, not to mention small John and his nurse Nancy and all their own servants, seemed to be dancing to the infectious rhythms. The dinner would be burning. No, it was long past dinnertime, but the supper would definitely be afflicted, and all he wanted to do was sit down quietly and talk his day through with Alys, who could always help him to think more clearly.

The battle came to an end. Alys began shooing the women back to their work in the kitchen, and McIan set his harp aside, making certain it was standing firmly beside the arm of his host's great chair.

'God's greeting to you, Maister Cunningham,' he said, turning his white eyes towards Gil.

'Ah, Gilbert.' Maistre Pierre beckoned. 'See who has blown in off the High Street. Come from Stirling the day, they tell me.'

'How are you, sir?' Gil came forward with Socrates at his heel. The harper rose to his majestic height and bowed, long silver hair falling over his brow, the white beard settling back on his chest as he straightened up again. 'And Mistress Ealasaidh?'

'We are both well, maister, by God's grace. And so is that bonnie wee skellum yonder, that is growing like a weed.' The blank gaze swung to small John, who was still dancing though the music had stopped, and the austere mouth softened. 'You take good care of him in this house. I think he is well loved.'

'Indeed yes!' said Maistre Pierre.

'He brightens the place,' Gil said simply. The fiddler and drummer had retreated to the other end of the hall and now struck up a court dance, the sharp drumbeats striking pain in his head. Two recorders and a still shawm joined in on the second phrase, and one of the singers began showing John the steps. 'Have you heard him sing?'

'He sings like a lintie,' offered Ealasaidh McIan, seated beside the mason on one of the two long settles. Not much past thirty, nearly as tall as her brother, she was clad for travel in the loose checked gown of an Erschewoman, her dark hair curling down her back. She looked hard at Gil, but went on, 'His mammy was full of music, Our Lady call her from Purgatory, so small wonder if he has it too. Did I hear the man Sempill has taken another woman?'

'He has,' Gil agreed. 'And she leads him as if she had a ring through his – his nose. I'd say the boy's mammy is well avenged.'

Her eyes glittered, but her brother said,

'Leave that the now, woman. Maister Cunningham, I have a word for you from the Archbishop.'

'Sir?' Gil removed his hat carefully, as if his master was present. The harper bent his head a moment, then said in a startling imitation of Robert Blacader's ponderous speech,

'My greetings and blessing to Maister Cunningham, and let him ken this. The matter of the false coin is in hand, it's my will he shouldny involve himself. If I need his help I'll send to him.' Across the hall Alys looked up sharply, but said nothing. Gil felt himself reddening.

'*Mon Dieu!*' said Maistre Pierre. 'But who else should deal with it in Glasgow? You or Otterburn should take it on, I would think, and he has asked you, so it cannot be him.'

The harper, reverting to his own manner, said, 'Best to let it lie the now. You will be caught up in it soon enough, maister. There is much unknown, and more hidden.'

Used to this kind of gnomic utterance, Gil did not question the man, but replaced his hat with care, sat down beside Catherine on the other settle, and applied himself to repressing anger. His master the Archbishop had just snubbed him before his ward's father and the entire household, and he could do nothing about it.

'The Isles are full of the stuff,' observed Ealasaidh.

'We will not speak of that,' said her brother, sitting down again. She slid him a dark look, but said no more. 'And you, maister. What have you been at the day? There is death about you, and it links to the boy.'

'Indirectly,' Gil agreed, wishing he could leave the conversation, leave the hall, go and sit peacefully in their own apartment. The dog nudged his knee with his long nose, and he stroked the soft ears.

'Indeed it does,' agreed Maistre Pierre. 'What are all these tales I hear, Gilbert? Is that dreadful old woman dead in truth?'

'It is news of the most distressing,' observed Catherine in French.

'Tell it,' prompted McIan. His sister put a cup of ale into his hand. 'Who is slain?'

The musicians had all gathered about the plate-cupboard at the far end of the hall, where someone had propped a new piece of music against the larger of the two salts. This one did not involve the drum. Over an argument about where the repeats should fall Gil identified Dame Isabella, with interpolations from Maistre Pierre, explained her connection with small John, described her death. Alys listened, quietly pouring more ale or handing little cakes; he was aware of her attention, though she did not look at him. Ealasaidh sat by her brother and exclaimed at each turn of the tale, but the harper was as silent as Alys.

'To be rid of the man Sempill!' Ealasaidh burst out as he finished. 'Angus, we accept the offer, surely!'

'If it still stands,' Gil cautioned her. 'Lady Magdalen may change her mind, now her godmother is dead.'

'If it still stands,' agreed her brother, 'I am in favour.'

'The rents would keep the boy easily,' supplied Maistre Pierre, 'and we may put some aside for his education as well.'

'But this woman who is dead.' McIan shook his head. 'There is darkness and betrayal there.'

'If it was her servant slew her, that is betrayal enough,' observed Ealasaidh.

'And the violence to yourself, Maister Cunningham.' Gil, who had slid over that part, did not look at Alys. 'Have you taken hurt?'

'A headache, a wetting, no more than that.'

'Hmm.' Maistre Pierre rose, removed Gil's hat, felt carefully at his skull with large gentle hands. 'No, I think your skull is hard enough,' he said at length, as Gil flinched. 'A lump like a goose-egg, but nothing worse. Continue your tale. What were they concealing, do you suppose?'

'If I knew, it wouldny be concealed,' he said wearily. 'All I did was look into Danny Sproat's stable and frighten the rats. I saw nothing untoward there.'

'No, you need to look elsewhere,' agreed the harper.

'I should like to search the toft, nevertheless,' said Maistre Pierre.

'Otterburn's men are doing that,' Gil said.

'Drink this.' Alys was at his elbow – when had she left the hall? – handing him a small beaker of something. He swallowed it obediently, tasting willow-bark tea, honey, something else familiar. He looked up warily and smiled his thanks, and she met his eye, though she did not return the smile. Was he forgiven or not? he wondered.

The band by the plate-cupboard embarked on another piece of music, passing this one by ear, laughing as the sweet-sharp phrases modulated in different hands. Ealasaidh, with a glance at her brother, rose and drew Alys away to talk to John, who was inclined to be a little shy of his tall aunt. The harper sat back and said,

'I have a favour to ask of this house.'

'Ask it,' said Maistre Pierre largely.

'I am bound for the West, for Ardnamurchan. I had as soon not take my sister, for I think the journey is not easy. Is it possible—'

'Pooh! No need to ask,' said Maistre Pierre. 'You and Mistress Ealasaidh both are welcome under my roof, sir, for as long as you wish it. What takes you into the West?'

'I think we should not ask,' said Gil quietly.

'Resentment, enmity, tipping of the scales of power.'

'That is true all over Scotland,' said Maistre Pierre.

'Oh, aye,' said McIan, 'and of this death here in Glasgow, but I spoke of the Isles. The false coin breeds enmity, and the rest. That is its purpose.'

'To whose advantage?' asked the mason.

'Always a good question, with always the same answer.'

The Campbells, thought Gil. The Earl of Argyll. People keep mentioning the Campbells today.

'With good reason,' said McIan, and he realized he had spoken aloud. 'The young one, the new earl, may not be the match of his sire, but he has the same nature. Tell me, maisters, has that pair of Campbell brothers been seen in Glasgow lately? Eoghan and Niall, you recall them?'

'Them!' said Maistre Pierre.

'Euan and Neil,' Gil agreed. 'I saw Euan at the quarter-day when he brought the money for John's keep from Sempill, but I've heard nothing of them in the last month. Why, have you? Who are they working for now? Not Sempill, then?'

'For MacIain. No, not myself, but the greatest of the name, the man that holds Ardnamurchan of the King.' He fell silent. Gil leaned back against the settle and stared at nothing, while the musicians started on yet another tune.

It seemed to have been a very long day already, and it was not over yet. The sasine transaction which had begun it was unlikely to come back at him, but everything else seemed to have questions attached which would lead him in all kinds of directions, and he was feeling unbelievably weary. Perhaps that was the dunt on the head, he thought. Begin at the beginning: where is the title to Balgrochan? Is it important that the old woman kept it back? Where was Sempill this morning if he didn't see Dame Isabella?

'Well, Gilbert,' said Maistre Pierre beside him, sounding amused. 'And was that the whole tale, son-in-law?'

He opened his eyes with a start. The hall was much emptier and much darker than it had been a moment ago. The musicians had vanished.

'I wasn't asleep,' he said hastily.

'No, of course not. But what have you been about, that the whole town is talking of you being rescued naked from the bawdy-house?'

'What?' he exclaimed, and put a hand involuntarily to his head as pain stabbed. 'Sweet St Giles, no wonder Alys is displeased. It was nothing of the sort – indeed they saved my life, I think.'

'As strong as that?' The mason sat down. 'Tell me again. We have time before supper, I think.'

'Where is McIan gone?'

Maistre Pierre waved a large hand towards the courtyard.

'They are gone to settle in, or perhaps to see John in his cradle. Now tell me about the bawdy-house.'

'We'll set up the table shortly,' said Alys from the other end of the hall. She came forward, still unsmiling. 'Go over the first part, at least. They took you in and warmed you, sent here for dry clothing. What did they give you for your hurt?'

'Some sort of cordial, and a bowl of broth.' He looked up at her. 'We owe them a debt, sweetheart.'

'For certain,' agreed Maistre Pierre.

She nodded.

'I suppose we do,' she agreed, with what seemed like reluctance. 'I'd sooner have you live, and spoken of all over the town, than otherwise.' She considered the hand he extended to her, and put her own in it. The world seemed to straighten round him. 'So how did it happen?'

McIan and his manservant departed after supper for some engagement in the burgh. The harper was his usual dignified self, clad in a blue velvet gown with his hair combed down over his shoulders, but his sister watched them leave and said,

'The Deil alone knows when himself will be home. It might be before the dawn. By what Whistling Tam was saying it will be a wild night of it.'

'You do not go with him?' asked Maistre Pierre curiously. She shook her head.

'I've no notion where he gets the strength. There is ower many years on me for riding all day and then playing all night after it. I had sooner be here, where the bairn is.' She looked round their faces as they stood by the hearth. 'But I think you have things to discuss. I should go to my rest, maybe.'

Alys and her father both exclaimed against this, and Gil said, concealing reluctance, 'You've heard the half of it

100

already, and I could do with the woman's view of what I saw. You and Alys will see things I never noticed.' And a pity that Catherine always retires immediately supper is cleared, he thought.

'Come and sit down,' said Alys. 'We have no usquebae in the house, but there is wine.'

In fact Ealasaidh was little help. Gil went over the morning again, detailing what he had seen and learned, and she exclaimed over every turn of the tale as she had done earlier, with shocked comments about the customs of Dame Isabella and her household. Alys listened quietly, and said as he finished,

'Scatology not eschatology, despite her age.' He glanced at her, acknowledging the play on words, and she went on, 'I think you are right, Gil, there are things which do not make sense.'

'The whole thing makes no sense!' declared her father. 'More wine, mistress?'

'But to permit someone to come close enough with a hammer and nail!' said Ealasaidh, accepting her refilled glass. 'And occupied like that, the shameless woman!'

'How well did she hear, do you know?' asked Alys.

'A good point,' said Gil. 'Certainly her voice was like a deaf woman's.'

'I thought she had no trouble when we saw her yesterday,' objected Maistre Pierre.

'There's many can hear well enough if they know they're addressed,' said Ealasaidh.

Gil frowned, trying to fit this into the sequence he had assembled.

'She'd have seen him – or her,' he added scrupulously, 'over the back of the settle.' He rose and paced about the hearth, gesturing to place the furniture of the chamber where Dame Isabella died. 'A settle much like that one, perhaps a little lower, near the window. The close-stool behind it. The bed about here, in the midst of the chamber, so one must approach round one side of it or the other. No chance of creeping up on her.'

'So someone she trusted,' said Alys. 'Gil, did you say her head was bare when she lay dead? Could one of her women have been combing out her hair?'

'That would fit,' he agreed. 'It was all about her head in locks. Not Annot, I think, she mentioned combing her earlier but not just before she was sent out. Perhaps it was the other one.'

'So you seek the woman who is gone missing,' said Ealasaidh. 'Do you think the Serjeant will find her?'

'Not necessarily,' said Alys. 'We need to speak to her, but she may not have the answer. Even if she had returned, the woman might have left her mistress again for some reason, and the killer took advantage of the moment.'

'I do not think the Serjeant will find her easily,' said Maistre Pierre. 'All his shouting of names at the Cross does is tell the pursued he must go to ground.'

'Ah. And if she has kin in Glasgow, they will not give her up. You are right, maister,' said Ealasaidh. 'But she has also robbed her mistress.'

'She or another.' Gil put a hand to his head. 'I wish I knew how long it was before Annot discovered her, and when the men came back and sat watching the door.'

'You suspect more than one person is involved?' Maistre Pierre deduced.

'I don't know.' He leaned back against the settle, wishing he could think clearly. Alys looked at him anxiously, but before she could speak Socrates scrambled up from where he lay sprawled before the hearth, and stood glaring at the door, head down and hackles up. Maistre Pierre rose, feet sounded on the fore-stair outside, someone knocked loudly.

There were two of the Provost's men on the step, wearing triumphant grins and bearing a message.

'Oh, aye,' agreed the senior man, 'we went through the toft like ripe fruit, me and a couple lads from the top, four more at the back gate wi their arms open, and we got a few things that was well worth it, one suspicion o theft, one fine for a fire too close to the thatch. We never got into the man's workshop that we was to search, he wasny present, there was no key to his house and no sufficient reason for breaking down the door. But the best of the catch, maister, was the woman that's wanted by the Serjeant for this matter in the Drygate.'

'What, already?' said Gil in amazement. 'She was on the toft you searched? What was she doing there? Who was she hiding wi?'

'Now that, maister,' admitted the man, 'I've no notion o. Dickon, you took her up, did she say aught in your hearing?'

'No to say a useful word,' said his companion. 'She'd a bundle wi her, and a bit roastit cheese in her hand, and cam running out the back gate like a roe deer, right into my arms.' He rubbed his ear. 'Gied me a good bang on the lug wi her bundle, she did, right heavy it was, and I was one o the lucky ones, and calling us for everything, so we searched the bundle, and here was this bag o siller. We've got her for theft any road, whatever else she's done.'

'Aye,' said the other man, 'and the Provost says, if you'd wish to see her questioned afore she gets handed to the Serjeant, come by first thing the morn's morn and you can ask her what you will, and he's sent the same word to Maister Livingstone that's her maister.'

'She will have kin there,' said Ealasaidh from the background. 'There will be someone on the toft that is out of the Highlands, I have no doubt.'

'At least two of the women,' agreed Gil. 'Tell Maister Otterburn I'll be at the Castle at Prime, man.'

'If the woman,' said Maistre Pierre, closing the great door behind the two men, 'is a speaker of Ersche, you need an interpreter.'

'She speaks Scots well enough to be employed,' Alys said.

'None the less.' Maistre Pierre looked at Ealasaidh. 'It might be wise to take another speaker of the language with you.'

'Och, yes,' she agreed, 'I would be happy to help. I can find out for you why she killed her mistress, no trouble.'

'Why did your father do that?' Gil asked. 'I've no need of help to question the woman, and if I do, I've no doubt Otterburn can put his hand on an Ersche-speaker.'

Alys, shaking her hair out of its long braid, lifted the comb and said,

'Perhaps she will be useful.' He grunted, and she looked intently at him in the candlelight. 'How is your head?'

'Sore. I'll live. I am *soo ful of knyghthode that knyghtly I endure the payne.*' He unlaced his doublet and drew it off. 'I suppose I can hardly take you as well now, it would look—'

'As if I really couldn't trust you,' she finished, and gave him an enigmatic stare. 'No, not after today's work.'

'That's not what I was going to say,' he said ruefully. 'Sweetheart, I'm sorry if you're to be embarrassed by it.'

'I can deal with it,' she said. 'I sent Luke to the apothecary's when he came in, with a list of sweetmeats and delicacies. Tomorrow by daylight he will take them round to the bawdy-house in a basket with ribbons, to the front door, as a gift from me. Oh, and a purse for the laddie. Cato, did you say he was called?'

'*The wisdom of an heap of learned men,*' he quoted. 'Alys, that is true cunning.'

She looked at him sideways, round the honey-gold curtain of her hair. Her mouth twitched as if she was repressing a smile.

'And what is it worth,' she asked, 'if I promise not to tell your mother?'

'Fights like a wildcat,' Otterburn said succinctly. 'One man wi a hot ear, two more wi scratches, and wee Allie wi a bitten thumb, and we'll all pray that doesny infect.'

'Annot's saying she's aye had a temper,' said Maister Livingstone sourly.

'That's the first I've heard of that,' objected Lowrie beside him. 'She's aye seemed to me one that took what life threw at her, and stayed calm about it.'

'So she'll stay in chains, maister,' continued Otterburn, ignoring this, 'but apart fro that you can all ask her what you please. And Mistress McIan to be interpreter, I take it?'

'What was in her bundle?' Gil asked. 'The men said something about coin.'

'Oh, aye.' Otterburn looked slightly less gloomy, and indicated the rack of shelves behind him, where a swathe of checked cloth suggested a plaid knotted round a collection of objects. 'That's a rare piece of good fortune. Well, I think it is. She'd a leather bag o coin about her, which I take to be the one that's missing from the dead woman's kist, according to her other waiting-woman, as you reported to me last night. Where's that note, Walter? It's quite a sum, and the interesting thing about it, maister,' he accepted a sheet from his clerk and turned it towards Gil, 'is that it's all false money, every piece.'

'False?' Livingstone repeated, startled. 'How would the old – woman come by false coin?'

'All of it?' Gil stared at the Provost, then looked down at the inventory of Forveleth's bundle. Walter's neat clerk-hand listed a few personal items, and beneath them quantities of coin, line upon line, the totals adding up to a magnificent amount.

'All false coin,' repeated Otterburn, 'the most o't these James Third placks and the threepenny piece wi the four mullets, same as we've been finding all about Glasgow. Now what do you make of that, maister? I,' he said in faint triumph, 'think you're in the matter now whatever my lord says. And I'd like it if you'd cast an eye over the coins themselves, Maister Livingstone,' he added, 'now we've as many of them gathered in the one place, and see what you can tell us.'

'Aye, gladly,' agreed Livingstone.

'Was she maybe collecting it?' offered Ealasaidh from beside Gil. 'Maybe she would take it out of use.'

'Hardly,' said Gil. 'It's near five hundred merks' worth. Even Blacader couldny spare that easily out of a year's income.' He looked at Otterburn, and back at the notes. 'Have you questioned the woman about it at all?'

'No a word. I wanted my supper, and I reckoned she'd keep. Will we have her up here, or go down to her? It's warmer here.'

The woman Marion or Forveleth was somewhat battered by her experiences, but her spirit was not affected. Dragged struggling into the little panelled chamber by two of Otterburn's men she halted before his desk, glared at him, and spat something in Ersche which made Ealasaidh's mouth tighten.

'You speak civil to the Provost!' ordered one of her escort, with a blow to her shoulder. She turned on him, manacled hands aiming for his crotch in a rising hammer-blow which he avoided expertly. His companion seized and flung her to the floor, where she knelt hissing more virulent Ersche.

'Compose yoursel, woman!' said Livingstone. Otterburn looked down at her, then over to where Gil and Ealasaidh sat near the window.

'Do we want to ken what she's saying, mistress?' he asked.

'No, I would say not,' agreed Ealasaidh disapprovingly. 'You should think shame, a decent woman, using language the like,' she added to the prisoner. Forveleth turned her head to see who spoke, and froze, her mouth open, staring.

'You!' she said after a moment. The men in the chamber looked at one another.

'Do you know her?' asked Otterburn. Ealasaidh shook her head.

'No,' she said firmly. 'I was never seeing her in my life. She speaks the Gaelic of the Lennox, we have not travelled there much.'

106

'She seems to know you,' said Gil warily. Forveleth glanced at him, then addressed Ealasaidh in Ersche. There was a brisk exchange of what seemed to be repeated assertion and denial, before Otterburn broke in with,

'Enough of this. Speak Scots, woman, or we'll ha what you say put into the Scots, one or the other. What's it about, mistress?'

Ealasaidh shook her head again, reddening.

'She claims she was seeing me, here in Glasgow two days since, when I was still at Stirling and witnesses to say so. Nonsense, it is. What do you wish to ask her, maister?'

'How could she do that?' Otterburn asked. 'If you've witnesses, why did she persist? When was this, anyway?'

'I never saw you in Glasgow before, mistress,' said Livingstone, 'and I'd say this woman's been nowhere I haveny been mysel in the last two days.'

Not quite true, thought Gil.

'It is nothing, nothing at all,' said Ealasaidh, the scarlet sweeping down her neck under the black woollen veil of her formal hood. 'She is babbling.'

'I am not, and you know it,' said the prisoner in her accented Scots. 'If it isny true now, it will be, I tell you that. You were always at the man's shoulder, him that is man of the house where this one,' she nodded at Gil, 'is good-son. A better gown, you were wearing. Red brocade and velvet sleeves,' she added thoughtfully.

'Never mind this now,' said Otterburn, losing patience. 'There's as much to go over afore she gets handed to the Serjeant. You, woman, what's your name?'

Her name was Forveleth nic Iain nic Muirteach, which caused Walter some trouble, and she was born in Balloch in the Lennox. She had served Dame Isabella five years now, before and after her marriage to Thomas Livingstone, and the old carline's temper was getting worse, she'd have left anyway at the quarter-day –

'That's enough o that,' said Otterburn. 'Why did you run off when you found her dead?'

'Did she find her dead?' Gil asked. 'I'd as soon go over yesterday from the start, maister, if you'll allow it.'

Otterburn glanced at him, and sat back. Gil came forward from his seat by the window and stood looking down at the prisoner. She looked back at him hardily, despite the split lip and the bruises on her face. Her decent worsted gown was stained and filthy from her night in the cells, and scraps of damp straw clung to sleeve and hem.

'Your mistress is dead,' he said after a moment. She nodded, and waited for him to continue. 'Do you know how she died?'

'No.' She paused to consider. 'I was thinking maybe it was – it was—' She threw a few words of Ersche at Ealasaidh, who said sulkily,

'She was thinking it was an apoplexy, the same as you were saying, Maister Cunningham.'

'So you did see her after she was dead,' Gil said. 'Tell me about the morning. You and Annot got her up, I think, and then called the men in so she could give them orders.' Forveleth nodded at that. 'What happened next?'

She closed her dark eyes to think.

'We washed her,' she said. 'Och, no, she would be saying her prayers first. A good hour, that took her. Then she would, she would,' she hesitated, 'attend to something private, you understand.'

'I understand,' said Gil. 'I also understand that the two of you, Annot and yoursel, were in and out for a space while she was occupied.'

Forveleth tightened her swollen mouth, winced, but nodded agreement. 'Until she ordered us away,' she said. '*Out of my sight*, she said, and called us a pair of worthless trollops. Forever bad-wording us, she was. So we left.'

'What did you do then?' Gil asked.

For the first time, Forveleth looked uneasy.

'I'd maybe no mind,' she said.

'You've been clear enough up to now,' Otterburn said.

'You went to the kitchen eventually, we ken that,' Gil

108

said. 'Where were you between the time you were dismissed and the time you reached the kitchen?'

'About. It's a fair walk out to the kitchen.'

'Annot got there long before you did.' Gil studied her, thinking about Alys's comments last night. 'Did you go back in to your mistress? You were combing her, I think. What did you do with her cap?'

'Her *cap*?' the woman repeated.

'A cap?' said Otterburn, interested. 'Now there's one in your bundle, lassie. How did that get there?'

'Is that you stolen your mistress's linen as well as the rest?' demanded Livingstone.

'I never!' she said sharply, as Walter rose and quietly fetched the bundle. 'Here, that's mine, those are my things—'

'What, all of it?' Otterburn untied the heavy woollen stuff and spread it out. 'Two shifts, a kirtle,' he glanced at the prisoner still kneeling before him, 'aye, yours rather than hers to judge by the quality, a comb, some good linen,' he patted the folded wad, checking that nothing nestled among the layers, 'two holy pictures and your Sunday beads. This cap,' he turned it, put both hands inside it to mould it out, and looked at the prisoner again. 'Yours or hers, woman?'

Ealasaidh came forward with her hand out. Otterburn gave her the item, raising his eyebrows, and she sniffed at it, then bent to sniff at the kneeling woman, moving her linen veil aside despite Forveleth's objections.

'Hers,' she said, in a tone which invited no discussion. Gil and Otterburn exchanged startled glances.

'So where,' Gil said, recovering first, 'is the cap your mistress was wearing when Annot last saw her? When she went to stool?'

'I'd maybe no mind. And keep her off me!' said the prisoner indignantly.

'Forveleth,' Gil said, hunkering down beside her. 'Look at me.' She turned the dark eyes on him, wary as a cornered animal. 'You're in trouble here, you must see that.

109

You and Annot were the last to see your mistress alive, and Annot has witnesses for where she was till Dame Isabella was found dead. Then you ran off, and you were lifted yestreen fleeing from the Provost's men, wi a great bag of false coin about you—'

'I never!' she said hotly. 'I never did! I never had any such thing—' She turned to Ealasaidh and burst into impassioned Ersche.

'Be quiet, woman!' ordered Otterburn. He gestured at his clerk, who moved to open the great kist by the wall. 'What about this, then? Five hundred merk of false coin, found in your bundle.' He put his hand on the leather sack as Walter deposited it on the table.

'Is that the bag?' said Lowrie. Otterburn flicked him a glance, and went on,

'You touched that, I'd say, and to some purpose.'

She stared at the object, looked at Otterburn, back at the leather bag.

'I never saw that in my life,' she said firmly. 'I have no knowledge of whose it might be, but it is never my mistress's purse. That is blue velvet and gold braid. You may ask at Annot if you are not believing me.'

'Is it, now, maister?' Otterburn asked Livingstone, who shook his head.

'I'm no her tirewoman. Ask at Annot, like she says, she'll let you ken.'

Forveleth looked alarmed, and turned to Ealasaidh again, with more of the Ersche, shaking her head repeatedly. Ealasaidh answered, there was a longer exchange. Gil got to his feet, easing cramped muscles.

'She is telling me a great story,' said Ealasaidh eventually, and looked from Otterburn to Gil. 'She says, she waited in the next chamber, the one where she was seeing a laid-out corp, and the old woman was calling her back in after a while, to comb her hair and listen while she abused her for a thieving Erschewoman. Then she says her mistress suddenly ordered that she bring her this purse of blue velvet and leave her, so she put the comb by and went out to the kitchen, and talked with the other women. She says they will be swearing to it if you ask them.'

'Now that's all foolery!' exclaimed Otterburn, but Gil nodded, watching Forveleth's face as Ealasaidh recounted her tale.

'What did you do with the cap?' he asked. The woman stared at him, then suddenly put a hand to the breast of her gown, delved briefly within its low square neckline, and drew out a crumpled handful of linen.

'I mind now, I was putting it down my busk while I combed her hair,' she said, 'and then she was sending me away, so I forgot it.'

'Like I said,' exclaimed Livingstone, 'thieving her mistress's linen and all!'

Ealasaidh took the little bundle from her, sniffed it, inspected it briefly, handed it on.

'This one is not hers,' she said. Gil, shaking it out, had to agree. This cap was made in a different style, of much better linen, and though it smelled faintly of Forveleth there was a strong, sour undernote of unwashed hair about it. He stood looking down at it, watching the scene Ealasaidh had described play out in his head.

'Why did she send you away the second time?' he asked.

'She's making it up,' said Livingstone. 'I don't believe a word o this.'

'No, it makes sense, uncle,' said Lowric.

'For modesty, maybe?' said Ealasaidh. Forveleth snorted.

'Her? She'd not know the word, for all she was flyting at Annot and me for immodest trollops. She never said why I was to leave,' she added, 'nor I would not be knowing what her reason was. She was looking out of the window while I stood beside her and combed at her hair, and then in the midst of that she bid me fetch her blue velvet purse and be gone.' She paused, closing her eyes for a moment. 'I think it was – it was—' She groped for the Scots, then said something to Ealasaidh, who nodded slowly and translated:

111

'She is thinking her mistress acted on a sudden, in haste maybe, for she would not take the time to miscall her the way she was doing in general, only she was bidding her leave her immediate.' She looked earnestly at Gil. 'I think that is a wise thing she says.'

'You never looked out of the window yourself?' Gil asked. The woman shrugged.

'I was looking, but I was not seeing whatever it was caused her to send me away. Nor she was not giving me time to stand and stare,' she added, her bruised mouth twisting.

'And what about this sack o coin?' demanded Otterburn. 'How d'you account for it being in your bundle, woman? We've only your word for it that it's no the purse missing from Isabella Torrance's kist.'

'I swear it's no! Ask at Annot,' protested Forveleth. 'And no more it is not the purse she kept at her belt, that all her household has seen. I never saw this leather one in my life!'

'No, it's no the purse the old dame usually had by her,' agreed Lowrie.

'There would never be room in the kist for a bag that size,' said Gil.

Otterburn glanced at him, and grunted.

'So where did it come from?' he repeated. 'It was tied in your plaid wi the rest, woman, no sense in denying it—'

'I never put it there!' The manacles clinked again as Forveleth spread her hands. 'I was never seeing it afore, I wouldny ken who had it nor who put it in my things, I am not wanting anything to do with it.'

'That's fortunate,' said Otterburn, 'for you'll no see it again, save when it's produced as evidence.' He hefted the thing in his hand, and nodded to Livingstone. 'Walter, where's the counting-cloth? If you'd take the lot over to the window, maister, I'd be glad of anything you can tell me about it.'

'Whose house were you sheltering in on Clerk's Land?' Gil asked Forveleth. He trawled through his memory for the names, and listed them. 'Is someone there kin to you? Saunders the pewterer wi the screaming weans, Danny Bell the lorimer, Campbell the ill-tempered whitesmith, Dod Muir, Danny Sproat.' He watched her carefully, but her expression did not alter. 'I'd guess it was Campbell's house. A kinsman, is he?'

'He is not!' she said quickly. 'And nor his wife neither. There is no Campbells kin to me!'

'That makes a change,' said Gil. 'So is that where you were sheltering? What took you there?'

'I was not sheltering, I was just passing through the toft,' she retorted, 'when all on a sudden it was full of soldiers. Any decent woman would run from men of that kind.' She spat in Gaelic again and glared at the two men who had escorted her in, who still stood on either side of her. One of them kneed her shoulder.

'Less of that, you,' he said sharply.

'Marion,' said Lowrie. Recovering her balance, she glanced up at him. 'Why did you run? And the three men? Why did you all go off? You never thought we'd blame you for the old dame's death, did you?'

'Three men?' she said, and bent her head.

'Where are the men?' Gil asked. She shrugged her shoulders, not looking up.

'I've not saw them. I'm no their keeper.'

'I've had enough of this,' said Otterburn impatiently. 'Maister Cunningham, she's to be turned over to the Serjeant, so if you want to ask her any more, ask at him.' Gil nodded. 'He might get some more out of her wi the pilliwinks, but I'd say we'd enough to charge her wi a good few things already.' He watched as the prisoner was hauled to her feet, protesting. 'Theft, possession of false coin, fleeing a murder scene, and probably murder as well. Take her away, lads. Right, Maister Livingstone, have you anything to tell us off these coins?'

Lowrie met Gil's eye across the chamber, but did not speak. His uncle, who had spread the contents of the leather sack out across the squared counting-cloth on a

113

stool by the window, and was sliding the thin coins about into different groups, did not reply at first; when Otterburn repeated the question he looked up and said,

'Aye, aye, they've plenty to tell me. Bide a bittie till I – ah!' He turned a coin over and back again, tilted it to the light, and put it carefully between two others. 'That's it, I'd say.' He was still turning coins over, adding them to one pile or another. 'These are struck wi two different sets of dies, Provost.'

'Different coiners?' asked Otterburn. 'Are we looking for two workshops?'

'No, no, I'd say not, for some of them—' he turned another coin. 'These threepenny pieces, some of them have one pattern on the reverse and some another, but the same head on them.'

'One die has worn out?' Gil suggested.

'Aye, more like.' The man's fingers danced over the little heaps of coin. 'See, here we've this head, a good copy of the second portrait of James Third, and on the reverse a cross and four mullets, where it should be a cross wi two mullets and two pellets. Now these ones are the same, and these, save that the die's wearing away, you can scarce see one o the mullets and the head could be Queen Margaret for all you can discern.'

'Is it no just the coin that's worn?' Otterburn asked.

'It's no worn. It's as thick as the others.' Livingstone tapped the offending coin with his fingernail. 'I'd say the die wasny steel. Maybe brass or the like, something softer any road. Now here,' he lifted four or five coins, which slithered in his hand like fish-scales. 'Here we've a fresh head, wi ringlets, which the other never had, and the worn mullet on the reverse, and here we've the new head and a new reverse wi all showing clear.'

'So what does that let me know?' Otterburn asked, peering at the late king on one of the coins. Livingstone looked blankly at him for a moment, then assembled his thoughts.

'Well. They've cut a set o dies, and used them to make all these,' he waved a hand above the greater part of the heaped coins, 'and then when they wore out they've cut a new set, first the head and then the cross. I'm no sure it—'

'Cut?' said Gil. 'Not cast?'

'No, that's likely why they're using brass,' Livingstone said. 'You can engrave it, see. It's an easier process for your counterfeiter, you just need to draw the image on the end o the die and engrave it, no need to play about wi casting in iron and impressing on steel. If you've a man wi a good ee and a steady hand, it's no great trouble.'

'How easy is it to find sic a one?' asked Otterburn. Livingstone shrugged.

'Easy enough. When I'd charge o the Mint for the late king I could ha laid my hand on five or six in Edinburgh, within easy walk o the Mint, and likely the same again further about the town.'

'Gets us nowhere much,' said Otterburn. He tossed the coin in the air, caught it on the back of his hand. 'Heads or crosses, maister?'

'Heads,' said Lowrie promptly. The Provost looked at him, half-smiling, and uncovered the coin. The cross with its four mullets greeted their gaze.

'It was never her,' said Ealasaidh, striding down the High Street beside Gil.

'I'm agreed,' said Lowrie, on her other side, 'but what makes you say that?'

Gil dragged his mind from an unsatisfactory interview with the Serjeant. The man had been at pains to tell him that the carpenters at work in Canon Aiken's house had left no mell or other such implement lying about, something Gil should have thought to check for himself, and had made clear his expectation of getting a confession out of Forveleth before noon. Torture was a valuable method of interrogation, Gil knew, but he disliked the thought of it applied to a woman.

'She thought it was an apoplexy. Nor she never robbed the old woman of the blue velvet purse.'

'She could be lying,' Gil offered.

'She could.' Her tone made it clear she thought it unlikely.

'Why did she say she had seen you before?' Lowrie asked.

'Och, that.' She reddened again. 'Foolishness. There is those that see things, and it means little. What will you do now, Maister Cunningham? Who will you question next?'

'Sempill,' said Gil, his heart sinking at the thought. Ealasaidh snorted. 'And I should speak to your uncle's household again, Lowrie.'

'That should be easy enough arranged,' said the young man. He drew a breath and went on, rather hesitantly, 'Maister Gil, did Dame Isabella – when she spoke wi you – did she, did she say aught about me?'

'About you?' Gil paused, staring at him and trying to recall the conversation he had had with the deceased. 'No, I'd say not. Should she have?'

'No,' said Lowrie hastily, reddening. Gil turned to move on, but Ealasaidh took hold of his arm.

'Is that no Maister Mason's boy?' she asked, craning her neck to see through the groups of people in the busy street. 'A good laddie, that. He is seeking someone.'

'Maister Gil!' said Luke, dodging round a group of women with baskets, their plaids bright in a sudden blink of sunshine. 'Mistress.' He doffed his cap to Ealasaidh and then to Gil, acknowledged Lowrie politely and stood in front of them, catching his breath. 'The maister said I should tell you, Maister Gil.'

'Tell me what?' Gil gestured down the street, and they moved on.

'About yestreen,' Luke said earnestly. 'See when the mistress sent me to the 'pothecary shop, and I got a great list o things, and she bade me ask for a sweetie myself, and I had one of the marchpane cherries—' Gil repressed a shudder. He would never feel the same about marchpane cherries since last autumn. 'Oh, and Jennet and me took the basket to the house wi the mermaiden on the door

116

afore I started work the day, and they were right pleased wi the gift, said how it was awfy generous o the mistress. I never saw any lassies in their stays, but,' he added with regret.

'Is that what you were to tell me?' Gil prompted.

'No, no, it was this. When I told the maister of it he said you should hear it. I was talking wi Maister Syme, see, and I mentioned how strange it was that two o that old carline's men should ha been in his shop right at the time she was killed—' How did the boy know that? Gil wondered. Information seemed to travel round the burgh on the wind. 'And Maister Syme said *No, no, it was just the one*. And the maister said I was to let you hear it. And another thing,' Luke went on. 'Lady Kate sent to say she'd be glad of your company a wee while the day, one of the wee lassies has something she wants to tell you.' He judged Gil's expression correctly, and added, 'The mistress bade me say she thought it was something to the point.'

Chapter Six

'Just the one,' confirmed James Syme.

'Can you describe him?' Gil studied the apothecary across his workbench, aware of Lowrie at his side doing the same. Syme was a handsome young man with golden hair and an irritating way of speaking, as if he was confiding a secret. Married to his partner's elder daughter, on the older man's death he had found himself in charge of the flourishing business and was managing it well and methodically. Any observations he had made were likely to be accurate.

Now Syme set down the pestle with which he was reducing dandelion leaves to a green paste, and turned to lift a ledger from the shelf behind him. Across the shop his assistant looked up, and returned to a similar task.

'Yesterday,' he murmured. 'Early. Aye, here it is, Maister Cunningham. Root ginger, cloves, flowers of sulphur, a bottle of the restorative for the hair, senna-pods, rhubarb, and a wee box of the anise laxative. Suffered badly wi her belly, the poor lady.' Gil forbore to comment. 'Fourpence, another fourpence, two pence for the ginger and again for the cloves, the bottle, the other matters, that came to three shillings and a penny, and the lad handed it to me in silver—' He gazed briefly out of the window. 'Aye, he was alone. Taller than me, near your height I'd say, well-set-up fellow wi brown hair, big ears, very civil.'

'Alan,' said Lowrie confidently. Gil nodded. It certainly did not sound like Attie.

'And no sign of the other man, maybe waiting outside?' he prompted.

'Not that I saw.'

'Have you checked the coin the lad gave you?'

'Checked it?' Syme stared at him, then looked at the pyne-pig on the shelf beside the ledger. 'No – no, I – I never thought. We've no much trouble wi false coin here, Nanty has more down by the Tolbooth, one or two a day he gets or so he says.'

Only one of the handful of silver threepenny pieces in the tin box was false. Syme looked at it, biting his lip.

'There was more,' he said. 'Like I said, maister, the lad gave me three shillings in silver. Three groats,' he poked through the thin coins, which slid away from his finger, 'and eight threepennies, and two ha'pennies. I hope we've no given out false coin in change. I've a reputation to consider.' He caught up the counterfeit and held it out to Gil. 'Maister, I'm assuming you're looking into the business, since you've asked me about it, or at least that you can gie this to the Provost. I'd as soon it was out of my hands.'

'I'll pass it to the Provost,' Gil said resignedly.

'There was an odd thing, though,' Syme went on, fastening the box down. 'Yestreen, when we'd a gathering, the three apothecary houses in the burgh, as we do, we were speaking o this. Aye, I'd best let you hear what Nanty had to say.'

'She wanted to tell you herself,' Kate said, 'and it's a day or two since I saw you, I thought this was the best way.' She peered across the window space at Gil. 'Are you well? There's all sorts o tales about the town.'

'Oh, is that it?' Gil grinned at his favourite sister.

They were in the hall of the house at Morison's Yard, where Kate's husband Augie Morison ran his business, a few doors down the High Street from Maistre Pierre's dwelling. Kate herself spent a lot of time in this big, light

119

window-bay, seated in her carved wooden chair with her crutches propped close at hand.

They had already discussed the health and amazing development of Kate's baby son, godson to Gil and Alys, who it seemed was asleep upstairs. Now Gil set his beaker of ale down on the tray beside him and sat back, leaning against the pale oak panelling. 'You want the tale from the horse's mouth? You should ask at Lowrie here, he rescued me out of the place.'

'The bawdy-house? I thought you were well in charge, maister,' offered Lowrie, palming another of Ursel's little cakes. 'Sending out for your clothes and all.'

'No, Alys came by this morning to see Edward and tellt me the gist of it,' Kate said, 'and since she was here when Nan and the girls came back she heard their tale too and went off saying she'd send to you to look in. So what like are these paintings?'

'No as bad as they're reputed. Naked goddesses and the like, all very tasteful.'

'I never saw them,' said Lowrie regretfully. 'The back o the house is quite plain.'

'Magdalen Boyd wants to cover them in limewash.'

'She would,' said Kate. There were light hasty feet on the stair leading down into the hall, and her stepdaughters burst into the room, followed by their nurse making chiding noises about their behaviour. Both girls checked at sight of a stranger, but Kate smiled, and held out a hand. 'Here, my lassies, come and make your curtsies.'

The older girl came obediently, smiling shyly at the guests, and curtsied as directed. The younger flung herself across the chamber, ended up at Gil's knee, fixed him with a penetrating grey stare and said,

'Uncle Gil, we found the man that's making the bad pennies.'

'I'll tell him!' said her sister indignantly. 'It was me that found him!'

'Now, lassies,' said their nurse. 'That's no way to—'

'It's Uncle Gil,' said the younger girl, 'don't have to be *polite.*'

'Ysonde!' said Kate. 'Come here! Wynliane, go and tell your uncle what you saw.'

Wynliane, almost eight, with her father's blue eyes and soft fair hair, came to Gil's side, glancing doubtfully at Lowrie. Her new front teeth had come in, and she looked more like Augie than ever. Gil introduced them, and Lowrie doffed his hat, making the child blush. Her nurse said bracingly,

'Tell Maister Gil about it, like your mammy bids you. Good day to you, maister,' she added. 'I hope you're well? We went to the market this morning, me and the lassies,' she explained, 'for they've a penny or two for spending.' She glanced significantly at Kate, now occupied in explaining to Ysonde just why a young lady should be polite to everyone, and Gil recalled that his sister's birthday was approaching. He nodded his understanding, and stout Nan smiled and gestured to Wynliane.

'Me and Nan and Ysonde,' the child agreed, 'and we went to all the stalls, and bought Ursel a col– colandrain—'

'Colander,' prompted Nan, her black brows rising in amusement.

'Yes, for the kitchen, and we bought – I bought—'

'Something,' Gil supplied. 'And did you get pennies back?'

Wynliane nodded gratefully. At Kate's side, Ysonde drew herself up, fixed her stepmother with a direct grey stare and said dramatically,

'*Is this sothe, my moder dere?*'

Gil suppressed a grin as he recognized the quotation, and concentrated on Wynliane. 'And one of them was a false coin, was it?'

The older girl nodded again.

'Do you still have it?' Nod. 'Will you show me it?'

She held out her hand. Sticking to her palm was another of the threepenny pieces, cross side uppermost.

121

'I saw it was false first!' proclaimed Ysonde. She crossed to them in a sort of travelling curtsy, bobbed another one at Lowrie, and gabbled, 'I ask your pardons, Maister Gil, Maister Lowrie, for my discourtesy. I saw it was false first,' she repeated, duty done. 'For I asked Da how he knew when it was false coins and he showed me how to look.' She grabbed at the coin, her sister snatched it out of reach, and Nan separated the two children expertly. 'Look, it's easy seen. Let me *show* them!'

'Let me hold the coin,' said Gil, 'and then you can show me. Which stall was it this came from?'

'I'll show you first,' said Ysonde. She bent her curly head over Gil's hand, pointing out the distinctions and obscuring the coin, while Wynliane in her soft voice said,

'The man was rude.' She bit her lip, leaning her head against Nan's broad waist. 'He shouted at Nan. When we told him it was false coin.'

'And then he was in the chapel,' supplied Ysonde. 'And he fighted with the other man, and they knocked each other down and rugged them down in inches.'

Recognizing a line from the Hallowe'en play which had taken place here in this hall, Gil repressed a grimace. Kate said,

'Now, Ysonde. Let Wynliane tell it to your uncle the way you both told it to me this morning.'

'Ysonde, will you show me the coin?' suggested Lowrie, holding his hand out. Gil passed him the slip of silver and Ysonde followed it importantly. Wynliane began to explain the tale, with help from Nan.

They had told the man on the stall that the coin was false, but he had been angry, and accused Nan of trying to pass false coin back to him out of her own purse. Ysonde had been certain the coin was one the man had given her sister, but Nan was less sure.

'So we just left it,' she said, 'and I wish now I'd argued the matter.'

'What stall was this?' Gil asked. Kate, at the other side

122

of the wide window space, looked elaborately out at the men stacking huge yellow-glazed crocks in the yard.

'A sweetmeat seller,' Nan mouthed. He nodded understanding.

'And then we went to St Mungo's,' Wynliane continued.

'That's Little St Mungo's out the Gallowgate,' Nan amended. 'I've a fondness for the wee place, seeing I grew up next it.' Gil knew the little chapel, a crumbling structure outside the eastward yett of the burgh in which his uncle took an interest; small as it was it contained three or four altars to different saints, screened off with hangings of mouse-nibbled brocade. 'We went to say our prayers, did we no, my lass?'

Wynliane nodded.

'And the man was there,' said Ysonde from where she stood beside Lowrie. 'Him and the other man was fighting.'

'They were arguing,' Nan corrected. 'We were saying our prayers to Our Lady, all quiet in her wee chapel, and these two came in, and that busy arguing they never heard us.'

'They were shouting,' agreed Wynliane, burrowing against Nan's apron.

'The sweetie man said it was a cheat,' said Ysonde, 'and trying to get him in trouble, and then they fighted, and fell down battling each other. And then the priest came and stopped them,' she said regretfully.

'There was all blood,' said Wynliane.

'You never told me that, lass,' said Kate.

'Naught but a bloody nose, mem,' said Nan reassuringly.

'So one of them blamed the other for passing him false coin,' Gil interpreted, 'and there was a fight. Did you learn any more? Who were they?'

Nan shook her head.

'I'd say they were maybe neighbours,' she said. 'They wereny kin, they wereny alike at all, but they seemed to ken one another right well. The one we'd spoke to, I never heard his name, but the other one,' she paused, frowning. 'Sir Tammas cried him, was it Miller?'

'Miller?' Gil repeated. 'You're sure of that?'

'No.' She shook her head again. 'I was a wee bit taigled, you'll understand,' she glanced significantly at Wynliane, 'and no paying that much mind. Miller or a name like it, Wright or Carter or the like.'

'And I said,' said Ysonde importantly, 'we had to tell you, cos Mammy Kate said you was asking all about the false coins in Glasgow.'

'Very right,' said Lowrie. She gave him one of her rare smiles, accepting the praise as her due.

'Then what?' asked Gil. 'Did they hear you? Did they go on talking?'

'The dusty man said,' Ysonde recalled with a sudden attack of accuracy, 'the priest was an interfering auld ruddoch, and the sweetie man was a greetin-faced wantwit, and then he stamped out—'

'Ysonde!' said Kate.

'You swored,' said Wynliane, equally shocked.

'Did not!' retorted her sister, going red.

'Did so!'

'You'd never use words like that yoursel, would you?' said Lowrie encouragingly. 'You were just telling us what the man said.'

'Well, it was what he said,' she iterated, lower lip stuck out 'And the sweetie man told the priest the dusty man was getting him in trouble, and then he went away too.'

'That's about it, Maister Gil,' agreed Nan. 'I'm hoping it was worth dragging you down here for, but it doesny seem like much to me.'

'What did they look like?' Gil asked. 'What were they wearing?'

'The sweetie man had a belt,' said Wynliane. 'With a namel buckle.'

'Aye, that's right, lassie,' agreed Nan. 'A pretty thing, it was, save the enamel was chipped. Otherwise,' she thought briefly, and shrugged. 'He was clad like any working man in Glasgow, I'd say, a leather doublet, a blue jerkin under it. I never noticed his hose, they were maybe hodden grey or the like, but he'd a blue bonnet on his head. He was a young fellow, maybe five-and-twenty, no so much as thirty. I never took much of a look at the other, but,' she paused to think again. 'I'd ha thought him a wee bittie younger by the way he spoke.'

'Why did you call one of them the dusty man?' Lowrie asked Ysonde. She looked up at him, scowling, from where she stood within his arm. 'Was he dusty?'

'Don't know. That's what the sweetie man called him.'

'I think I'll take a walk down to St Mungo's,' Gil said. 'Can you come wi me, Lowrie?'

The young man nodded, and removed his arm from about Ysonde, saying,

'I have to go now.'

There was a brief argument, but Ysonde was eventually persuaded that the two men could find the chapel by themselves. Wynliane put up her face to be kissed, saying,

'Will you come back and tell us?'

'Maister Gil will tell you, I expect,' said Lowrie.

'No, you're to come,' ordered Ysonde. 'Say you'll come.'

'If I'm permitted,' Lowrie said. Gil exchanged startled glances with Kate, but Ysonde accepted this reluctantly, and they took their leave.

Out in the street, glancing at the sky, Gil said, 'We've likely time to go by Little St Mungo's now. Then I could do wi a word wi your man Attie.'

'So could I,' said Lowrie absently. 'That's a lively wee lassie of your sister's. How old is she? The two o them are her stepdaughters, you said?'

'Ysonde? She's five or six, I think. She's a wildcat,' Gil said, 'and about as ready to gentle.'

'But sharp as a,' Lowrie paused, swallowed, and visibly changed what came next, 'sharp as a new pin. Quoting from *Floris and Blanchflour* at six!'

'It's one of their father's favourites. He's likely read it to them a few times.'

125

'Oh, is that it?' Lowrie stepped aside to avoid a marauding pig. 'If she grows up aught like madam your sister she'll be a rare gem.'

Sir Tammas Dubbs, priest of Little St Mungo's, was a worn elderly man in worn elderly garments, with a long knitted scarf wound round his neck. He was about to say Nones with the clerk who was shuffling about in the chancel waiting for him, and was unwilling at first to listen to Gil's questions.

'There's a many fights atween folk in this parish,' he said brusquely. 'I pay no mind, other than try to stop them killing one another.'

'These two wereny killing one another,' Gil said. 'They were arguing because one said the other had got him into some trouble over some coin.'

There was a resonant thump on the end wall of the little building. The clerk, to Gil's astonishment, erupted from the chancel and hurried to the door, trailing a muttering stream of curses. Sir Tammas turned to watch him go, and said over his shoulder,

'Aye, well. And half my parish wi him, I've no doubt.'

'One of them might be called Miller.' Sir Tammas turned abruptly and stared at Gil, then looked away again. 'And the other sells sweetmeats along the Gallowgate, and has an enamel buckle to his belt.'

Outside the clerk was shouting indignantly. Impudent young voices answered him, and a taunting chant began. The priest clicked his tongue in annoyance, and shook his head.

'I've no idea who it might ha been,' he said. 'Like I tell ye, there's fights all the time.'

'What, in here and all?' Lowrie asked. Sir Tammas glanced at him, but did not answer.

'Have you had any trouble wi false coin?' Gil moved casually so that light fell on the priest's face.

126

'None. Now I must go, my sons, you're holding back the Office.' Sir Tammas raised his hand, muttered a perfunctory blessing, and strode to the door, the ends of his scarf flying. As soon as he stepped outside the mockery stopped, and after a moment priest and clerk returned and crossed to the chancel without looking at Gil. They were barely within the dark archway, and the priest's cracked elderly voice had just risen in the first words of the Office, when there was another thump on the wall. Sir Tammas checked, then continued. The Office should not be interrupted.

Gil, grinning at Lowrie, went quietly to the door and stepped out. He was just in time to surprise the next boy swinging on the knotted rope hung from the eaves. Distracted, the youngster misjudged his timing, and instead of kicking off from the gable he thumped into the stonework, let go the rope, and fell in a winded heap at the foot of the wall.

'Ah, ye bausy juffler, Dod Armstrang!' said the lad next in line, without sympathy, and leapt for the swinging rope. Clinging with both hands he kicked expertly at the stonework and twirled away in a circle, grinning widely and back-heeling the recumbent boy's shoulder as he spun past. 'See, that's how ye dae't. No, it's no auld Dubbsie, it's a pair o fine daft chiels fro the town.'

Seeing the truth of this, three or four more boys came back to their game, staring at the strangers. Gil raised his hat to them, at which they giggled, and nudged one another. They were a ragged crew, barefoot and clad in handed-down hose and jerkins, one or two lacking a shirt, all very dirty.

'I'm looking for two men that were here earlier,' he said. 'Maybe you saw them?'

The boys looked sideways at one another, and the fallen one pulled himself to his feet. The lad in possession of the rope jumped down, staggering slightly, and said,

'Maybe. Maybe no. What's it to you?'

127

'It might be worth something,' Gil said, reaching for his purse. All their eyes followed the movement.

'Who was it you were looking for?' demanded the spokesman.

'A man that sells sweetmeats from a stall, and has an enamel buckle to his belt,' Gil said hopefully.

'That's—' began one of the smaller boys, and was elbowed by his neighbour.

'And who else?'

'Aye, but that's—'

'The other one might be called Miller.'

'Miller? Naw,' said the spokesman quickly, 'we never seen neither o them.'

'Aye, but Jamsie,' protested the smaller boy who had spoken. Jamsie turned and seized him by the ear.

'Shut yer gub! Come on, the lot o yez, we're away out o here. We never seen them, maister,' he added to Gil, 'and if you're wise, you never seen him neither.'

'Well!' said Lowrie behind Gil, as the boys scattered. 'That's interesting.'

'It is,' agreed Gil. He looked about him. St Mungo's stood a short way from the East Port, beside the road which led out to Bothwell and Cadzow, surrounded by the undisciplined huddle of small houses which lurked at the gates of any sizeable burgh. Those who could not afford to live in the burgh lived outside it, as did a few tradesmen wealthy enough to ignore the rules about indwelling of burgesses, their bigger properties set back from the road and the middens. Off to their left a track ran past the west end of the chapel, down to cross the Poldrait Burn. 'If we cut through here, we come out at the back of—'

'At the back of the College,' Lowrie agreed, 'or we could go on up the mill-burn to the Drygate.'

There was a great deal of coming and going at Canon Aiken's house, but Maister Livingstone came down to the door himself as they crossed the yard.

'How far have ye got?' he asked without preamble. 'Lowrie, where ha ye been all the morning? They're saying now we canny put her in the ground till there's been a quest on her, and her murderer named.'

'Till there's been a quest, at least,' Gil agreed. 'Has Otterburn told you when it might be?'

'The morn's morn, he said, and he'd his men here asking all kind o questions. What like was this purse that's missing, and where was her comb, and the like. I'm no her tirewoman, I said, ask at her women. If Marion canny tell them, Annot will.'

'And did she?'

'Did she what? Oh, tell them? I've no idea, they spoke wi her in yonder,' Livingstone nodded towards the black-draped range where Dame Isabella was clearly still lodged, 'but they went away satisfied, I suppose she had something to say. I was dealing wi Andrew Hamilton for a coffin.'

'Greyfriars will take her, sir,' Lowrie put in.

'First time in her life she's been welcome, I'd say,' said the older man. 'Come up and have a glass of Malvoisie, maister, if you've the time.'

'Gladly,' said Gil, with a feeling that the day might improve slightly now, 'but I want a word wi your man Attie. Is he about? And maybe Annot and all.'

'Oh, he's about,' said Livingstone, 'for all the use he is, and the house going like St Mungo's Fair, what wi folk coming to pay their respects and see what she died o. Come away up and I'll see if they can find him.'

One of Livingstone's green-liveried servants bore a tray with a jug of Malvoisie and three glasses into the hall. Attie followed him, looking like one going to his execution, and while Livingstone served out the wine and waved Gil to a seat by the hearth the man stood against the wall, mangling his velvet bonnet and trying to be invisible. He came forward reluctantly when ordered.

'Attie, I've spoken to Maister Syme,' Gil said bluntly.

'How long were you and Alan together yesterday morning, in truth?'

'Well,' Attie licked his lips. 'Well. Aye, well, no very long, to say right, maister. We went – we gaed – see, there's this lassie serves Fleming the weaver, and, and, and her and me had got talking the day we cam into Glasgow, and I seen her again the other nicht, and here she was at their back gate in the morning, so, well, Alan went on by the path to the High Street, see, and I stayed daffing wi the lassie, and it wasny but a moment afore Alan came back,' he assured them earnestly, 'for we'd no more than tellt each other where we came from and who we served, and then I had to go back along wi Alan.' He ground to a halt and looked in apprehension from Gil to Livingstone, who was inflating slowly with anger.

From the door Lowrie said, 'What's the lassie's name, Attie?'

The man turned towards the calm voice with relief.

'Bess Wilkie, Maister Lowrie, and she's eighteen year old and comes fro Partick, and she likes serving Maister Fleming in cause of she's learning all sorts of weaving and how to work wi wool and all sorts, and he's a good maister,' the words tumbled out. 'She'd tell you hersel, maister, I'm sure, or Maister Cunningham, you've only to ask the lassie!'

Further questioning gained little more information. Attie had stood at the gate talking to the girl Bess for what had seemed to him a short time, while Alan went to the High Street along the path by the mill-burn and returned with the apothecary's package tucked in the folds of his plaid.

'I'm right sure it was the package,' he said earnestly, 'you ken the way a potyngar wraps things, that way they have o folding the paper.'

Returning to Canon Aiken's house they had taken up their position in the outer chamber of their mistress's apartment, to wait until she should call for them. But the next to enter her chamber had been Annot, and she had found the old woman dead.

'I'd swear to that,' he assured them, wringing his bonnet in sweating hands, 'I'd swear on any bones you set afore me, and the True Cross, and you could take me into St Mungo's and I'd swear it afore the saint hissel. It's the truth, maisters.'

'But why should we believe you now,' Lowrie asked, 'when you've lied already?'

'No to mention the delay you've caused to learning who killed your mistress,' said Livingstone, 'so we canny get her in her coffin. Here, what's the right story about the other two lads? Where did Billy and Nicol go, tell me that?'

'I wouldny ken, maister,' said Attie miserably, 'for I never saw them till they cam back here and waited along wi Alan and me.'

'Were you talking about where you'd been?' Gil asked. 'Did they say aught about their errand?'

The man stared at him, obviously applying some thought to the question.

'Aye,' he said after a moment. 'They did.'

'Well?' prompted Gil.

'They said it hadny been a pleasure. I mind now,' he produced, 'they were saying one they cried Dusty was a right cross-grained fellow, Billy had naught but a sweering off him when he took some word to him, and Nicol said, Aye, the man Campbell was the same.'

Lowrie met Gil's eyes across the hearth, and said to the servant,

'That sounds as if they were separate errands.'

'Aye, it does,' agreed Attie, in faint surprise.

'You told us yesterday,' said Gil, 'that these men, Nicol and Billy, had been sent to ask when the Campbells would be home.'

'I did that, maister,' agreed Attie. 'That was what she bade them do.'

'What Campbells are these? Are they the same as the man Campbell that Nicol spoke to?'

Attie shook his head warily.

131

'I wouldny ken, maister, it wasny my errand, see, and they never said aught about that, just what I recalled the now. But it seemed to me,' he added thoughtfully, 'as if they kent a bit more about it all than I did, when the mistress gied them their orders.'

'Can you mind what her words were?' Lowrie asked. 'Was there any sign they were to go different ways?'

Attie applied more thought, but shook his head.

'I canny mind, Maister Lowrie,' he said. 'All I mind her saying was, You two, go and find out when the Campbells will be back in Glasgow. And she called them a few names and all.'

'What did she call them?' Gil asked, wondering if the names might be significant. A signal of some kind, an indication of where the men should go?

Attie looked anxious.

'Just the same as ever, maister. Billy Blate, Nicol Runsch, ca'd Nicol a useless weed of a fellow and Billy a spiritless fool. None of it true, neither.'

'I've heard her use both those by-names,' Lowrie said. Gil nodded, discarding the idea, and gestured to Livingstone, who set down his glass and led Attie from the chamber, his expression grim. 'Where will you go next,' he asked diffidently.

'I need a word wi John Sempill,' said Gil with resignation.

'Is Eck Livingstone finished wi that parchment yet?' demanded Sempill. 'I need it back, Maidie needs to show she's—'

'John.' Magdalen Boyd turned to Gil, closing her book and laying it in her lap. Today she was wearing another gown of undyed wool, this one of light soft brown; it gave her pale skin some warmth. 'Maister, I'm sure you'll see, I'd sooner that parchment was back in our keeping, so long as we can be certain the land's mine.'

'It's yours all right, no question!'

132

'I've no knowledge of the matter,' Gil said truthfully. 'I'm here about your godmother's death.'

'Nothing to do wi us,' said Sempill. 'And if the Livingstones couldny keep the old termagant safe, why should that concern us?' He glanced at his wife's expression and swiftly changed attitude. 'Mind, it's vexed Maidie. If it's no an apoplexy, like Eck says, then the sooner you get someone taken up for it the better we'll like it.'

'Then someone's to hang for it,' said Lady Magdalen quietly. 'How should that please me, John?'

He looked at her, baffled, and Gil seized the opportunity.

'Did either of you ever set eyes on her purse of silver?' he asked.

'Purse of silver?' repeated Sempill. 'What purse? Where did she keep it? No, I never saw sic a thing,' he added belatedly.

'Never,' said Lady Magdalen simply. 'I knew she was well to do, but we never spake of money, only of land. Is it missing, sir?'

'It is. What's more, it's missing out of her jewel-box, and the rest of the contents left untouched.'

'That's all Maidie's now,' said Sempill, possessive and inaccurate.

'Perhaps she gave it to someone herself,' suggested his wife.

'Who could she have given it to?'

'How would we ken what the old beldam was up to in Glasgow?'

'John.'

Does he know it went missing in Glasgow, thought Gil, or is he simply making an assumption?

'Maister,' said Lady Magdalen, turning her gentle smile on Gil, 'I wasny close to my godmother, but I held her in regard. She met a sorry end, and I'd like to ken why, and see the miscreant given time to repent. We'll help any way we can, the both of us.'

'It would help if I could speak wi the two of you separately,' Gil said. She looked at him attentively, but said,

133

'I've no secrets from my husband, sir. Ask what you will of me, then I'll leave you and John thegither.'

'I've no secrets either,' began Sempill. She put a hand on his wrist.

'You can speak plainer without me, I've no doubt,' she said.

Nor have I, thought Gil. In fact he had little to ask Lady Magdalen, and she had less to tell him. They had met in Glasgow three days since at Dame Isabella's instigation, and the old woman had learned only then of the plan to disinherit small John in exchange for the two plots on the Drygate.

'I think she only thought of bargaining with you after that,' said Lady Magdalen. 'She'd promised me the other property in Strathblane more than once.'

'Aye, she had,' muttered Sempill.

'I think she aye intended I'd get that and your sister would get the one by Carluke. I suppose she's maybe settled it all in her will.'

'Have you inspected either property?' Gil asked. She shook her head, the dark wool of her veil swinging by her jaw.

'The rents come in on time, no need to worry the tenants. John sees to all for me.'

Gil glanced at Sempill, who tucked his thumbs in the armholes of his leather doublet and looked back rather defiantly.

'And one other thing. Yesterday after I left you, when I was inspecting the toft on the Drygate, I was struck down and thrown in the Molendinar.'

Sempill guffawed.

'I heard about that. And rescued birk-naked fro the bawdy-house, weren't you!'

'A dreadful thing,' said Lady Magdalen, and her husband subsided. 'I hope you took no lasting harm, maister?'

'I'll live,' he said. 'Have you any idea what they might be up to, that they took exception to a stranger?'

'They're half of them wild Ersche on that toft,' said Sempill. 'No saying what they'll take exception to. Was you robbed? I'd take it on and double the rents if I was you.'

'I don't know why they would attack you, maister,' said Lady Magdalen. 'I was shocked when I heard of it. Young Lowrie, that was waiting on my godmother, he told me of it when we,' she bent her head, 'when we went to pay our respects.'

Sempill crossed himself in a perfunctory way, then looked quickly at his wife. She was smiling sadly at Gil.

'If that's all you've to ask me, sir,' she prompted. He rose politely, and she made her farewells and left, her feet sounding lightly on the stair. Gil sat down again and looked at Sempill, who had not moved.

'Well, John,' he said. The other man eyed him warily. 'Tell me where you went yesterday morning, then.'

'I went to see,' began Sempill, and stopped as the thought quite visibly reached him that Gil must have spoken to the Livingstone household. 'Nothing to do wi you,' he finished.

'Well,' said Gil, 'you said you went to see Dame Isabella, you didny see her that morning, and now she's dead. What's more,' he persisted as Sempill opened his mouth, 'I ken fine you had words wi her the night before through her window, and she threatened you. So where did you go yesterday? Did you set out to find someone who'd nail her for you?'

'If you ken so much,' said Sempill, 'you can find out for – no, I never did!'

'You'd not rather tell me your version first?' Gil suggested.

'It's none o your business. What's it to do wi the matter, any road?'

'So it was you that hired someone to kill her, then?'

'I never said any such thing!'

'And what was it she threatened to tell your wife? What have you been at, John?'

'I've done naught against the law!' Sempill said, bristling. 'Just because I disobliged the old witch, she was threatening to tattle to – any road, it's naught to do wi her death, I tell you!'

'So where were you, if it's that harmless?'

'Nowhere you need to ken.'

'The bawdy-house?'

'No! I've no need to frequent sic places now,' said Sempill, making a recovery, 'no like some of us.'

'And Lady Magdalen kens all about Euphemia, does she?' Two could play that game.

'Aye, she does!'

'Well, was it the other toft, the next one?' Gil persisted, unconvinced.

'What would I go there for?'

'And what about these two properties in Strathblane? What are they like, anyway?'

'As to that,' said Sempill disobligingly, 'you can ask at Eck Livingstone, seeing he made claim to them both. Likely he kens the tenants' birthdays and all.'

'I'll do that,' said Gil. 'And I'll be back, when I've other questions. You've been a great help, John.' He got to his feet, enjoying the faint look of alarm on Sempill's face. 'Oh, one other thing. You mind those two gallowglasses you had working for you? Neil and Euan Campbell, I think their names were. Have you seen aught of them lately?'

'Them?' Sempill studied the question with suspicion.

'Them. It was Euan brought me the boy's keep at the quarter-day, so I ken you've seen him at least this year.'

'Aye, so he did. No, I haveny seen them since then. They're not working for me, any road, just I saw Euan and I kent he would find you. He was glad enough for a bit extra work.'

'What were they doing when you saw Euan? Who are they working for, if it's not yoursel?'

Sempill shrugged.

'I didny ask,' he said.

'You'd no need to,' said his cousin Philip, coming into

the hall from the screens passage. 'They were under your hand, coming and going for Dame Isabella.'

'Oh, so they were,' said Sempill, glaring at him. 'But mostly they were going, which is why I'd forgot.'

'For Dame Isabella?' Gil repeated in surprise. So were those the Campbells that her men were to ask after, he wondered. And yet Attie did not seem to know them. 'Going where?'

'No idea,' said Sempill. 'And now if you're about done, Gil Cunningham, I'll see you out of my cousin's house.'

'No need to trouble,' said Philip, 'I'll do that.' He waited politely for Gil to step out of the front door and followed him down the fore-stair. Pausing at its foot he said conventionally, 'A bad business this.'

'Very,' said Gil.

'You won't have had a chance to look at the land in Strathblane? The one that might go to your sister?' Gil looked at him, startled, and Philip caught himself up and went on, 'No, that's daft, it'll never happen now. Unless the old lady made a will, I suppose.'

'Not the portion out by Carluke?'

'There's no argument about Isabella's right to that,' Philip said, 'no other interest in it, and it's been in her family for years, or so she said. Whereas the other patch, well . . .'

'You think an inspection would be worthwhile. Why?'

'I just wondered about it. It seems to be gey profitable, it's remarkable that the old dame would let it out her hands.'

Their eyes met. Then Philip glanced away, up at the sky, and shook himself.

'No point standing out here in the drizzle,' he said. 'Will you be at the quest? It's called for the morn after Terce.'

'I suspect he is right,' said Alys, her eyes on Jennet and Nancy who were were folding the cloth from the long board. 'How far is it? Can you be back in a day?'

137

'No more than twelve miles,' Gil answered, 'and sixteen hours of daylight. I should think so, unless I find something untoward out there.' He dipped his hands in the basin placed ready near the door, and reached for the towel. 'I could go tomorrow, rather than hear the quest on Dame Isabella, but there are still questions I need to ask in Glasgow. The morning's lasted longer than I intended.'

'I'll be at the quest, never fear,' announced Ealasaidh from the hearth, where she was watching small John playing with his wooden horse. 'I can bring you word of what's said, and maybe I can be translating for Forveleth nic Muirteach, too, if need be. Will you be going to hear it, lassie?' she asked Alys.

'I will.' Alys stepped back as another maidservant emerged from the kitchen stair with a laden tray. 'Set it yonder on the small table, Annis. He can serve himself.' She lifted the small salt down from the cupboard, checked to see how full it was, and gestured at the stool drawn up to the table. 'Come and eat, Gil. The Provost will not reveal all he knows, I suspect, though the Serjeant might. Did you speak to the woman Annot?'

'I did,' he said, seating himself obediently, 'before I left Livingstone's house. She described the missing purse for me, blue velvet with gold braid and a tassel. I asked her how she kent it was silver in it, if she wasny allowed to touch it, and she admitted to having looked one time.'

'Did she count it?'

'Near twenty-eight merks, all in threepenny pieces.'

'That was a good look,' said Ealasaidh darkly. Alys threw her a quick smile, but said,

'More of the false coin, do you think?'

'I'd be surprised if it wasn't, at this rate,' Gil agreed. 'What puzzles me is, where was she getting it? Sweetheart, this is more than I deserve, after missing dinner.'

'Is it enough?' She came to put her hand on his shoulder. He bent his head to rub his cheek against her fingers, and saw a flicker of something bitter cross Ealasaidh's face; then Alys spoke again, and it was gone. 'What are the questions you need to ask? Can I help?'

'You can,' he admitted. 'I think you might get more from Annot than I have been able to learn, maybe even from the other woman if the Serjeant would let you near her. I've still questions for Otterburn and the men who searched Clerk's Land last night, and I want to go back there myself.'

She looked down at him in alarm.

'Take my father, or at least take a couple of Otterburn's men,' she said.

'Take me where?' asked Maistre Pierre, stepping into the hall from the courtyard. 'We have a loose tile above the drawing-loft, Alys. Ah, Gilbert, what progress do you make? What did you learn of this woman who is taken up for it?'

'She never did it,' said Ealasaidh firmly. 'I am as certain as I am of my life. My brother bade me tell you the same, before he left for Dumbarton. He is still talking of deceit and falsehood and a false face. And she spoke the truth,' she added, 'when she said she had no knowledge of the sack of money.'

'You think?' said Gil, spooning raisin sauce over the turnips on his plate. Since this had been his own conclusion he merely went on, 'And did she know the folk on the toft? Was she telling the truth when she said she was just passing through?'

'Of that I have no knowledge,' admitted Ealasaidh, her dark brows drawing together. 'Not all she spoke was truth. She is more frightened than she appears.'

'She'd be a fool otherwise,' Gil said. 'Pierre, are you busy? Could you spare me the rest of the afternoon?'

Maistre Pierre, on hearing what Gil's errand was, enlisted Luke's presence as a further bodyguard, and all three walked up the High Street, the dog at Gil's heels, past houses and pends where working people were just stepping out into the afternoon drizzle to return to whatever task earned their daily kale. At the Castle Socrates raised his head to sniff at the strong smell of boiling stock-fish which drifted from the buttery; the same air had found its way into Otterburn's chamber, where it mixed badly with the spices he had cast on the brazier.

'Put you off your supper, it would,' he complained, holding a pomander under his long nose. 'Never could stand the smell o stockfish. What did they find yestreen? Apart from the woman wi two names, you mean? See us your notes, Walter.'

His clerk searched briefly in one of the trays at his end of the table, and passed over a sheet of paper. Otterburn turned it for Gil to read.

'Three households and an extra workshop, as you can see, one house holds a single man working his lone, two wi married men though only the whitesmith keeps a journeyman. Whom my lads lifted on suspicion o theft, though we had to let him go, his maister swore he'd given the fellow the stuff himsel, no that I believed him. Also one fine for a fire too close to the thatch, same household, which got us a few curses so Andro said but at least they moved the fire down the yard a piece.'

'A fire in the open yard? What did they burn?' Maistre Pierre asked.

'Wood scraps, shavings, some old rags, a hantle kale stalks. Stink and smoke and no great heat, so Andro said.'

'And that's the lot.' Gil was studying the page of neat writing. 'They never looked at the workshop, and not at the hammermen's graith either, I suppose? What mells they have, what other kind of tools? Were they looking for coin, or silver, or the like?'

'No, it was just the usual,' said Otterburn. 'Checking there was a fire-cover to every hearth, counting the windows, frightening the weans. Here, are you thinking it was someone from Clerk's Land nailed the woman Torrance?'

'Not entirely, though it could ha been,' said Gil. 'Then again, it could ha been anyone in the burgh, by what I can make out. Has the Erschewoman been questioned again?'

'Aye, wi my own interpreter,' said Otterburn, 'no that it made any odds, she lied like the wife of Ananias, or else she claimed she couldny mind.'

'I'd like to know where she was all day,' said Gil. 'It might lead us to the missing servants.' He turned the paper round and passed it back to Otterburn. 'We'll away and question them on Clerk's Land again, see if we can find out why they assaulted me.'

'See if you can provoke an effusion of blood this time,' recommended Otterburn, 'then we can take the whole lot up.'

Chapter Seven

'I'm no right certain I can do that, mem,' said Jennet, pausing with the brush in her hand and Alys's light brown riding-dress in the other. 'I never met the lassie, how can I get talking wi her?'

'The same way you talk to any other lass you meet at the pump or the market,' Alys suggested. 'You all bring home news daily, some of it must come from folk you've never spoken wi before.' Jennet looked dubious, and applied herself to brushing the garment. After a moment Alys went on, 'But if you're not sure you can manage it, I'll take one of the other lassies with me. Nancy, maybe, or perhaps Kittock would like to get out for a bit.'

'Nancy!' repeated Jennet. 'She's never let a word past her lips she doesny need to, the soul. She'd as soon find out what you want to ken as soar to the moon!' She stopped, staring at her mistress, and began to laugh. 'Aye, you're a fly one. Very well, mem, I'll try it. But no blame to me if it doesny work, right?'

'Right,' agreed Alys, 'so you may help me into the blue broadcloth, and then we will go out to the Drygate.'

They set out shortly, Alys in the good blue broadcloth and her second-best Flemish hood, Jennet with a clean apron tied on over her striped kirtle, both of them wrapped in plaids against the chill drizzle and mounted on sturdy wooden pattens against the mud.

'I wish May Day was past,' complained Jennet, pulling her plaid over her head. 'It's no that cold for April, but the rain! We'll all get washed away.'

Alys made no answer, thinking of the May Day two years since when she had first spoken to Gil. It did not seem so long – or else, she thought, we've known one another for ever. She set off up the High Street, nodding and smiling to acquaintances. There went Maister Hamilton their neighbour, large and imposing in his Deacon's gown with the black velvet facings. How glad he must have been that Agnes his wife had seen him in it before she died. The two men with him did not seem to be his journeymen.

The wright and his two companions were still ahead of them when they turned into the Drygate. Alys was peering through the drizzle, trying to make out which pend they were making for, when Jennet broke off her account of something John had done to say,

'Mistress, here's the potyngar's wife calling after you.'

She turned, startled, to see that they had just passed the shop where the Forrest brothers purveyed apothecary goods and other items to the Upper Town. Christian Bothwell, the new wife of the younger brother, was hurrying towards her, calling her name.

'Mistress Mason! Alys! A moment, will you?'

'Christian!' She put out her hands. 'How good to see you. Are you well?'

'I'm well. And you, lassie?' Christian stopped in front of her, a stocky woman in a new gown of tawny woollen, staring earnestly at her face, and took a firm grip of her hands. 'Have you a moment? I've a thing to tell you, we think your man ought to hear of.'

Both brothers were in the shop, serving a very stout cleric whom Alys did not recognize, their manner confidential. All three paused as the women shed their pattens and went past them, and though Adam smiled at his wife he did not speak; only when Christian led the way through into the house and closed the door did the low voices start again.

'In here,' said Christian, and opened another door. 'They'll no hear us, or we them. He's come all the way fro

Paisley to consult,' she divulged. 'Little point, for he'll not listen to the first advice any potyngar will give him.'

Seated by the window of the little parlour with its view of the Drygate, she put aside a tray of wizened roots which she had obviously been sorting, gave Alys another earnest look and said,

'It's maybe no connected, but we talked o this last night, and then the day—' She paused, and visibly put her thoughts in order. 'We'd a gathering yestreen, see, all the potyngars o Glasgow.'

Alys nodded. There were three apothecary businesses in the burgh: Syme in the High Street dealt with the luxury end of the trade, selling cosmetics and spices and exotic candies, this shop sold herbs and spices and medicaments, and a hair-dye which some of Canon Cunningham's colleagues found very useful, and Christian's brother Nanty Bothwell still ran the booth by the Tolbooth which served the lower town and the suburbs across the river. The three households were close, mainly as a result of the traumatic events six months since when James Syme had inherited his business.

'And Jimmy was talking about how he'd sold a package of goods, yesterday morn,' Christian went on, 'to one of the servants of the woman that's slain, away along the Drygate here.'

'That is so,' agreed Alys. 'Our lad Luke told me he had spoken to Maister Syme of it, too.'

'Aye, and the laddie thought there were two men about the errand,' Christian said. They obviously discussed it thoroughly, thought Alys. 'And being Jimmy, he gave us a list of all what was in the package,' She looked away and enumerated on her fingers, 'Root ginger, cloves, flowers of sulphur, senna-pods, rhubarb, and anise laxative. Aye, that's right. And a wee bottle of Jimmy's restorative for the hair, she'd a done better wi ours, it works far quicker and doesny smell as bad.'

'Yes, but what—' Alys began. Further into the house a child laughed: Wat, the older brother, and his wife had one

144

child, who had survived the measles last winter. What was it like, she wondered fleetingly, to share a household, two women in a kitchen, two men overseeing the accounts?

'Wait and I'll tell you. My brother, when he heard that, he said, Was it wrapped in the ordinary white paper, or another sort? And Jimmy said, Aye, a new sort, we've just taen a delivery of paper and it's more a kind o yellowy colour.' This did not sound like Syme's phrasing, but Alys made no comment. 'And my brother, he said, So that's where she had it. It seems there was some Ersche lassie trying to return just sic a package at his booth, wrapped in this kind o yellowy paper, wanting the money back.'

'When? What did she look like?' Alys asked. Christian shrugged.

'Nanty wasny very plain about it. Nor he never said what she was like, other than being Ersche. Sometime the afternoon, I'd say. He turned her away,' she added.

'That is interesting,' said Alys. 'And useful. My thanks, Christian, and I will tell my husband when he—'

'Aye, but there's more,' said Christian bluntly. 'We talked o that, and wondered a bit, but what sent me out when I saw you passing,' she nodded at the window, 'was, we had another one in here the day wi the selfsame package, or else one gey like it.'

'In here?'

'Aye. Yellowish paper, folded the way Jimmy does, no the way my brother does, the contents being ginger, cloves, flower o sulphur, rhubarb, anise lax, senna, and a bottle o Jimmy's hair restorative.'

'Did you know her?' Alys asked. 'Was it the same lassie?'

'It was no lassie, it was Barabal Campbell fro Clerk's Land down the road here,' Christian jerked a disparaging thumb eastward, 'forty if she's a day, borne six weans, and a digestion like a washhouse boiler, never a day's trouble wi her belly says Adam though she's been here afore wi women's troubles. So we neither o us believed her tale about it being something she'd bought earlier and needed none of. We turned her away and all.'

'From Clerk's Land,' said Alys thoughtfully. 'That would fit well. My thanks, Christian, and I know Gil will be grateful for this.'

'Is that the lassie that's taken up for murder?' asked Jennet with interest. 'I wonder she never took it all back to Maister Syme, if she wanted rid o't. Or threw it in the mill-burn.'

'Aye, we wondered the same,' agreed Christian, 'but it was the man that purchased the goods, and the lassie trying to return it yesterday, so maybe he'd not told her which apothecary it was or that it was all on the slate and no paid for.'

'Or not told her right,' agreed Jennet.

'And now the people at Clerk's Land have it,' said Alys. 'Or did, this morning.' And where was Gil, she wondered. He should know of this. Had he reached Clerk's Land himself yet?

There was no sign of him as they passed the head of the toft. Alys paused in the drizzle, considering the muddy path past the pewterer's house, and two children at the door ceased their squabbling to watch her. No other adults were visible, though loud angry male voices were audible from beyond the buildings, including Maister Hamilton in full cry. So that was where he was bound, she thought, and moved on.

Averting her eyes modestly from the mermaid on the door of the next house and wishing she could study it, she stepped up the fore-stair of the house beyond it and rattled at the pin. Behind her Jennet drew an apprehensive breath, and she said quietly,

'Never fear, lass, it's just to get talking wi the girl. Good day to you,' she went on as the door opened, to reveal a maidservant as neat as any of her own. 'Is Maister Fleming within? Or your mistress? I'd like to talk about some blankets.'

* * *

146

An hour later, striking the bargain with Maister Fleming for a dozen blankets of new wool, with a further half-dozen of half size for John's planned trundle-bed, she felt that the afternoon was not wasted whatever Jennet had learned.

'And a pleasure to do business wi a lady that kens her own mind,' said Maister Fleming. 'I aye say to my wife, if the customer kens what she wants, we can weave it to her. If she canny tell me, I canny tell my weavers. You've a note o all that, Jaik?' he added to his apprentice, solemn at the tall desk with a pair of tablets in his hand.

'Very true, maister,' agreed Alys. 'And I wanted the best, so I came to you.' They smiled at one another, pleased with this exchange of compliments. 'I'm sure you must supply the whole of the Upper Town,' she went on, 'though I think that was no customer of yours that died so strangely the other day.'

'Oh! A dreadful business,' declared Maister Fleming. He was a brisk, middling-sized, competent man, stripped to his doublet for the task of showing the samples to a customer; now he cracked the last one, folded it neatly with the apprentice who hurried to help, stowed it back on the rack, and lifted his short gown. 'And comes closer to home than I'd care for,' he admitted. 'There's one of my lassies, a good worker and a right promising weaver, has hardly thrown a pick these two days, for she's taken it into her head it was some laddie she's a notion to that slew the old woman. And I don't have to tell you, mistress, if one lassie's dowy, the rest's sure to be infected. I hardly dare step into the weaving-shed the now.'

'Oh!' said Alys, unable to believe her good fortune. 'Maister Fleming, is that by any chance a girl called Bess Wilkie?'

'Aye, it is, that's her name,' he said, holding the door open for her.

'If I might have a word wi her,' she said hopefully, 'I may be able to cheer her, and I think she might be able to tell me something useful as well.' She saw his blank look.

'My husband is investigating the death,' she pointed out, 'as the Archbishop's quaestor.'

'Oh, aye, I'd forgot that,' he said, preceding her to the stairs. 'Come away up to the hall, mistress, and we'll send for the lass. No, I was thinking you're ordering all this for your father's household, I wasny thinking o your man at all.'

Alys forbore to comment, but followed the weaver up to the comfortable hall where Fleming's wife Barbara Graham, whom she knew slightly, was instructing her two older daughters in needlework. Alys admired the wobbly seams and settled down to chat about the weather and the wool crop while Bess was sent for. When the girl appeared, Jennet arrived with her.

'I thought maybe you'd want me soon, mem,' she said, bobbing a curtsy from the door.

'Aye, very like,' said Mistress Graham, 'and if you'll can counsel this silly lassie to dry her eyes and get back to her work, I'll want you too. Here, Bess, go over by the other window, speak to Mistress Mason and answer what she asks you like a good girl.'

'I'll try, mem,' said Bess shyly. She was a pretty girl, with a quantity of fair curling hair and hazel eyes red with weeping. The sleeves of her shift and woollen kirtle were rolled up to show bare sturdy forearms, and scraps of thread clung to the folds of her skirt.

'Tell my mistress what you were telling me the now,' said Jennet encouragingly. 'About the laddie at the back yett. Attie, did you cry him?'

'Was it Attie indeed?' said Alys, leading the way across the hall, out of earshot of the two little seamstresses.

'It was, mem,' said Jennet, 'and she talked wi him till his fellow cam back for him.'

'Let Bess tell me herself,' said Alys, and Bess nodded.

'That's right, what she says, mem,' she admitted. 'I was talking to the laddie all the while his fellow was up the town, and then he cam back, and the two o them went away, and the next I heard was, the old dame at Canon

Aiken's was slain by one o her servants, and, and,' she wiped at her eyes, 'I'm fearing it was Attie, and he seemed like such a nice laddie.'

'What was the other fellow called?' Alys asked.

Bess paused, the new question steadying her a little.

'Alan, I think. That's what Attie called him.'

'What was his errand, did you learn?'

Another pause. The girl clearly had not thought about these details before.

'I think they said it was the 'pothecary on the High Street. That's right,' she said more confidently, 'they'd a great list o messages from there, ginger and cloves and sulphur and that. Why they'd no gone to our own 'pothecary here on the Drygate they never said.'

'What made you think it was Attie had killed their mistress?' Alys asked gently. Bess bent her head, wiping at her eyes again, and Jennet said,

'Och, that was what one o the other lassies tellt her. She was down the drying-shed, this other one, see, where the blankets go when they come back fro the fuller's, right at the foot o the yard next the back gate.' Alys nodded. It made sense for the damp fulled wool to stay where it came onto the property, rather than be carried up the slope to where it might make other items musty. 'And she heard some folk arguing on the path, just through the wall, see, that were running away from their employ because their mistress was dead.'

'I need to speak to that lassie myself,' said Alys.

The second girl was a rather different proposition, something which was obvious as soon as Mistress Graham, hearing her name, announced that Alys would be very welcome to go out to the weaving-shed to speak to Ibbot. Called from her loom in the busy shed, the girl bounced over to the door, shaking back dark elf-locks and smirking at Bess in a way Alys disliked immediately.

'Oh, aye, mem, I heard them,' she averred. 'Talking all kind o treason, they were, and plotting how to be rid of what they'd stole.'

149

'What did you hear?' Alys asked. 'How many were they?'

'Two,' she said. 'Oh, and a woman and all.'

'And they spoke in Scots?'

'What else would they speak?' Ibbot retorted.

'You be civil to my mistress,' said Jennet at Alys's elbow. 'Tell her what they were saying, what you heard.'

'I'm telling her, am I no? So there was two o them, and a woman, and they stopped just by the drying-shed, and I could hear as clear as day through the cracks in the planks, see, and they were arguing what they should do next. One said, *Why are we running*, and another said, *The old witch is dead, or so she says, are you wanting the blame for it?* Then he says, *We must be rid o* – something, and the other said, *Aye and* something else *and all*, I never learned what it was,' she said with regret, 'and the woman says, *They'll seek for us, where will we go?*'

The nearest weaver rested her shuttle a moment and said,

'She's been on about that these two days, mem, never heed her.'

'You keep out o this, Mamie Elliott!' retorted Ibbot. 'Just in cause you never heard anything like.'

'Aye, well, she's aye making trouble, mem,' said the weaver, and kicked at the treadle of her loom. A heddle lifted, the threads parted, and she took up her work again.

'Did you hear any names?' Alys asked, before Ibbot could continue the argument.

'Oh, aye, that's how I kent it for her sweetheart,' said Ibbot, jerking her thumb at Bess with an unpleasant air of triumph. 'The woman had some heathen name, Ersche or the like I dare say, and one o the men was Alan, so who would the other ha been but his fellow that she was speaking to? Attie, or whatever she cried him.'

'You never heard his name used?' said Alys.

'No, but who could it ha been else?' repeated the girl.

'You never keeked through the cracks?' Jennet said in faint disbelief.

150

'Aye, but they must ha heard me, for they went away,' said Ibbot. 'I got naught but a glimp of their backs. Blue velvet livery, they wore.'

'So you heard,' said Alys, 'two men in blue velvet, one called Alan, and a woman with an Ersche name, running away because their mistress was dead, and speaking of how they must be rid of something.'

'Two things. Maybe more. One o them said *these* and the other one said *this and all*. Likely they'd stole her purse or her jewel-box.' Ibbot smirked again. What lay between the two girls, Alys wondered.

'Is that all you heard?' she asked. 'Did they say where they were going?'

'Oh, aye. Am I no telling you? For the one man said to the woman, *Here, you take that back*, and she said, *Where to?* and he said, *The potyngar away down the High Street*, and she said, *Where will I get you after?* Then they argued a bit more, and it fell out she was to get them somewhere they said was handy for the potyngar's, and then the other man said, *We need to be rid of these first, I'm no walking through the town in it*, and then they went away.'

'Ah,' said Alys. 'Thank you, Ibbot.'

'So I'm right, am I no? Him that she's a fancy to has slain his mistress and run off, and the Serjeant's seeking him now?'

'No,' said Alys. 'Attie is still wi Maister Livingstone, who trusts him.' I won't say just how well, she thought, anything to wipe that smirk off this girl's face. 'It must be two of the other men you heard.'

Ibbot snorted, tossed the black elf-locks like a refractory pony, and flounced away. Beside Alys, Bess put out a hand to grasp the doorpost and said faintly,

'Oh, is that true, mem? Is he really safe?'

'Aye it's true!' said Jennet stoutly. 'If my mistress says it, you can be sure it's right.' She lent a sturdy arm as the other girl swayed, and helped her to the nearest weaver's stool, hurriedly vacated, as work halted and whispers spread across the shed.

'There, lass,' said the woman whose seat she occupied, seizing a limp hand to chafe it with sympathy, 'all's well after all, you were right to be sure o him. You'll see your laddie again, never doubt it.'

'And what you've told me will help indeed,' Alys said. 'Thank you, Bess.'

'More questions, is it?' said Forveleth, staring through the shadows of the cell.

'More questions,' said Alys. 'And some food. I think you may not have eaten today.'

'That's a true word.' The woman laughed rather bitterly. 'At least they fed me last night at the Castle. This great lump of a man would be sparing no food for his prisoners, I think.'

Alys made no reply, but drew the loaf and the meat pasty from her basket and set them on Forveleth's folded plaid. She had pursued the woman from the Castle to the Tolbooth with some misgivings, knowing that the Serjeant would be far less likely to allow her to speak to the prisoner than either the Provost or his captain, and had hit on this as a means of access. To her surprise it had worked.

'She'll be wi us a day or two yet,' the Serjeant had said, 'I'm no wanting her to fade away afore she can be tried. Shout when you're done, mistress. Oh, and you can tell your man,' he added, 'I've had no word o the other servants yet, but we'll track them down, never fear.'

'When you left the house on the Drygate,' she said now, as Forveleth broke off a piece of the pasty, 'where did the men go?'

'Men?'

'No, we'll not play games.' Alys sat down on the narrow plank bed, hoping her gown would not suffer too much. 'Listen, Forveleth, the Serjeant reckons you are guilty in Dame Isabella's death.'

'So he is telling me. He would have me sign a paper about it, but I told him, no, I will sign nothing.'

152

'Aye, very wise,' put in Jennet from her post by the door. She was clearly dismayed by the condition of both the cell and its occupant, holding her skirts up away from the dirty straw on the floor and casting sympathetic glances at Forveleth's bruises, which showed up even in the dim light. 'Put your mark on nothing, that's the way.'

'So if you will tell me the truth,' persisted Alys, 'it will help you.'

'Will it?' Forveleth chewed cautiously, as if her mouth hurt.

'You went out by the back gate,' Alys said, 'and along the path by the mill-burn. Two of the men were with you, I think Alan and Nicol. They are brothers, am I right?'

'Yes, brothers, those two.' The woman peered at Alys, then down at the pasty. 'What did I do then? I'd maybe not remember,' she said, and broke off another fragment.

'You argued, on the path,' said Alys. Forveleth looked up sharply, and made the horns against the evil eye. 'One of them, Alan I think, gave you the package from the potyngar, that he still had on him, and told you to take it back.'

'Aye, and the surly grollop wouldny – How do you know all this? Who's been spying on me?'

'What else did they want rid of? They were saying they had to be rid of something.'

'It was someone listening. We thought there was someone listening!'

'What was it they had to be rid of? Was it the livery? They could hardly go through the town in livery without being seen and recalled later.'

'How would I be remembering?'

'And then where did you go?' Alys pressed. 'You tried to take the package back to the potyngar, and had no fortune there. When did you go back to Clerk's Land? Where were you in between the times?'

'You mean you don't know?' Was that a note of relief? Her hand was still clenched in the ancient sign of protection.

153

'Why Clerk's Land, anyway? Is one of them your kin? Which is it, the woman Campbell?'

'There is no Campbells that is my kin!' she said sharply. 'If you must know, it is Bethag nic Donuill, that is cousin to my brother's wife, is married on the whitesmith, more's the pity for her and all. So it was her I went to, and they let me in, but when the laddie came running to say there was the Provost's men at the close-mouth they were quick as the wind to push me out the door.'

'Did Alan and Nicol not go with you to Clerk's Land? Where are they now, Forveleth? '

'She's maybe lost them,' said Jennet. 'Likely they went another way. Maybe they're not wanting her wi them.'

Forveleth looked round at that, but did not answer.

'The purse your mistress had in her jewel-kist,' said Alys. 'What was it like?'

'Blue velvet and gold braid.' There was puzzlement in her voice now, at the change of subject.

'What was in it, do you know? Her body-servants would know that, surely?' Jennet stirred at the doorway, but Forveleth accepted the idea.

'Coin, I suppose. I never looked, but Annot said she did. It felt like coin in my hand.'

'And you gave it to her, the last you saw her alive.'

'That iss so.' Suddenly the accent was marked.

'Why did she ask you for it, do you think, at such a moment? Who had she seen coming down the Drygate?'

The prisoner exclaimed in Gaelic and scrambled backwards into the corner of her cell, making the horns again with one hand, crossing herself with the other.

'How do you *know* all this?' she repeated. 'Where was you watching me?'

'So who was it? Why would she give money to such a person?' Alys leaned forward, to put a hand on Forveleth's wrist, but the woman snatched her arm away. 'Whoever it was, they may really have been the last to see her alive. Is it someone you need to protect, or is it a stranger? Why are you letting yourself be suspected?' There was a silence,

154

broken by Forveleth's panting breath. 'My dear, Alan and Nicol were both out about your mistress's errands. Attie can speak for Alan at least. They were elsewhere when she died.'

'Is it Alan she fancies?' Jennet asked.

'Mary mild protect me,' burst out Forveleth, 'you know too much!'

'So tell me the rest,' invited Alys.

Another panting silence. Then Forveleth gave an incoherent wail and buried her face in her hands. Jennet stepped away from the door and put a hand on her shoulder, saying,

'There, now, you tell my mistress all, she'll help you the best she can.'

'Who came to her window?' Alys asked.

'It was a man Campbell, so she said,' admitted Forveleth eventually, raising her head. 'She said, *Here's that Campbell coming down the street, and another wi him*, and then she said, *Hand me the blue purse out my kist and get out o here.*'

'Which man Campbell?' Alys asked. 'The one from Clerk's Land, or the one who was to come home soon, or another?'

'I was never seeing him. I tried to look past her, over her shoulder, to see was it Bethag's man or another, and she struck me away. But when I went to another part of the house, to overlook her window, all I was seeing was a stranger, and the back of him at that.'

'Where was the stranger?' Alys asked. 'Was he at the window?'

She shook her head.

'Walking out at the gate, he was, as if he'd been within on an errand.'

'What did he look like? What way did he turn from the gate?'

'He was turning up the hill,' said Forveleth after a moment, gesturing with her left hand. 'I never saw him, I told you that.' Alys waited, watching her. 'He was tall, I suppose. Wrapped in a great gown or cloak or the like. Just

155

a – a black figure.' She shivered, and crossed herself. 'Like as if it was Death himself come for the old carline.'

Jennet, mouth open in amazement, crossed herself likewise.

'I'm no surprised you ran off!' she declared. 'But you'd ha been better to stay and tell your maister what you seen?'

'What, and be taken up for theft of the blue purse?'

'If you had stayed where you were,' said Alys, 'and the purse could not be found in your possession, you would have been safe enough from that charge. As it is, there's this matter of the leather bag of coin. Do you know anything about that at all? Did you know it was all false coin?'

Forveleth shook her head in the gloom.

'The first I ever saw of it was when they showed it me afore the Provost. What have I to do wi false coin?'

'What had your mistress to do wi false coin?' countered Alys. No answer. 'How did it get into your bundle, then?'

'If it was in my bundle,' said Forveleth sourly. She paused to think. 'When I – I had the package from the—'

'The package from the apothecary,' said Alys helpfully.

'Aye. I had my linen and my spare kirtle rowed in my good plaid, and I put the, the package in wi them when I,' she swallowed, 'went back to Clerk's Land. It was not there when I saw my things laid out afore the Provost, and the bag o coin was, so they said. Whether it was them that put it there, or some other, I canny tell.'

The rain had stopped. Emerging blinking into the afternoon sun, Alys considered the length of the shadows and thought about what to do next.

'Who else have we to question?' Jennet asked at her elbow. 'Is this what Maister Gil does all day and all? I'd like fine to get my living like that, just talking to folk. Only maybe no in a cell, the next one, mem?'

'Not in a cell, no,' said Alys. 'We will go up the hill again and call on Lady Magdalen Boyd. I should have offered sympathy before now.'

156

She set a brisk enough pace up the High Street to silence Jennet, which gave her space to think. The death of Dame Isabella made little sense in any way, and the random inclusion of the counterfeit coins seemed to make even less sense. Finding the man, or men, who had spoken to Dame Isabella at her window might be the next step, but how do we do that? she wondered. Is there anyone on the Drygate who might have seen them? Who dwells opposite? Has Gil spoken to the neighbours? Where was Forveleth between speaking to Nanty Bothwell by the Tolbooth and escaping from Clerk's Land? And where have the men gone to? Alan and Nicol, and the third one, what was his name?

'Who was that, mem?' asked Jennet. Alys paused and looked about her. They were near the top of the High Street, within sight of the high pink sandstone walls of the Castle, with smaller cottages on either side. A few people were moving about, and some of the boys from the grammar school on Rottenrow were just starting a battle with their book-bags for possession of the Girth Cross. She could see nobody she knew.

'Who?' she asked.

'Was a man that looked as if he kent your face,' said Jennet, staring at one of the low houses. 'He dodged down the path yonder, atween that house and the next. Tall fellow wi a padded jack.'

'Was he wearing a badge?' She could think of nobody she knew who wore a padded jack about the burgh.

'None that I saw. No, he's away, I canny see him. Just it was odd the way he went off, as if he'd avoid us.'

'Maybe you imagined it,' said Alys, and walked on.

Magdalen Boyd was not what she had expected. Gil's rather sparse description had conjured up a pale, chilly, spiritless creature, but she was greeted with warmth and her promise to pray for Dame Isabella was met with genuine gratitude.

'And you've come all the way up here just to tell me that?' marvelled Lady Magdalen. 'That's right kind in you, madam. Come away up and be seated in my chamber,' she offered, 'we'll have a cup of ale and talk a wee while. Maybe you can tell me where your man's at wi this business? He was here earlier, but he'd only questions, no information.'

'It's always like that at the beginning,' Alys said, following her up a wheel stair into a light bedchamber. 'If we're kin by marriage, may we not name names between us?'

'I'd like nothing better. But Alys,' she waved her to a seat by the window, beyond a box bed with hangings of worn verdure tapestry, 'has my kinsman learned nothing, wi all his questions?'

'He asks questions,' Alys said, 'till he has all the answers. Then he fits the answers together, and that's when he's sure of who is the criminal.'

'Criminal,' repeated Lady Magdalen sadly. She drew up another backstool and sat down. 'Aye, I'd like best to see whoever killed my godmother given time to repent, and amend his life, but I suppose the law must be involved.'

'That is truly forbearing,' said Alys.

'Vengeance is to the Lord,' said Lady Magdalen, 'we must give place to wrath. So Maister Gil is still asking questions? How long does it take?'

'Until it's finished.'

A servant entered with ale and small cakes on a tray, and they paused to deal with this. When the man withdrew Lady Magdalen said,

'Alys, I'm right glad you're here, for I wished to say something to you.' She hesitated, then went on, 'I'll not speak ill of anyone, but it was others made the decision. I wouldny ha tried to conceal what we were offering to, to the bairn you care for. It's maybe no a gift you'd want to accept, now you ken who the tenant is.'

'I'm more concerned wi the tenants of the other toft,' Alys admitted. 'But tenants move on, Magdalen, you ken that, and the value of the land remains. Does the offer still stand, even though Dame Isabella is dead?'

'It was nothing to do wi her,' said Lady Magdalen in her gentle voice. 'It's my offer, wi my husband's consent, and it still stands.'

'I'm not certain of this, you'll appreciate,' said Alys, and the other woman nodded, 'but I think my father and my husband are minded to accept it on the boy's behalf. They'll speak to you in good time, I'm sure of that.'

'We'll drink to a thanksome outcome o that,' said Lady Magdalen, and they raised their beakers. 'And then there's the matter of your good-sister's gift.'

'So there is,' said Alys, who had not forgotten this. 'I wonder what will happen about that now?'

'I hope my godmother made a will,' admitted Lady Magdalen. 'She'd planned that Lady Isobel would have the land out by Carluke, and I'd as soon see that happen, for I'd not wish to lose the land in Strathblane that she promised me. John sets great store by it and what wi the confusion over which piece was mine already he's right owerset wi the matter.'

'I expect he is,' said Alys with sympathy, wondering just how the newly tamed Sempill would express this. A snatch of an alchemical treatise rose in her mind: *Take a red man and a whyet woman and wede them together, and let them go to chambour*. What sort of philosophers' stone would these two beget? Had it already come into being, and begun to transmute Sempill? 'Land is important, after all.'

'Oh, aye, and this piece seems to have a great attraction for John. Indeed he's away out there the now, him and his cousin, they rode out afore dinner. It brought John and my godmother together,' she said, smiling sadly, 'they were aye discussing what must be done wi one tenant or another.'

That did not make sense, Alys thought, though she kept her face sympathetic. Tenants had names, and so did their holdings; surely Dame Isabella must have been aware that they were talking of different parcels of land. Unless she nourished the confusion on purpose?

'Did you know your godmother well?' she asked. 'I only met her the once. I thought she was a,' she hesitated, seeking for the right word in Scots, 'a lady of very strong mind, and very concerned for you and my good-sister.'

Lady Magdalen bent her head, dabbing at her eyes, and agreed.

'She was aye concerned for those she felt needed her help,' she said. 'Lady Tib, and me, and Lowrie, she'd a plan in her head for Lowrie though the Livingstones disagreed, to get Maister Gil to take him on as assistant and train him up as notary.' She bit her lip and half laughed. 'There, I meant no to repeat that, I'm all tapsalteerie the day, Alys.'

'I don't think Gil needs an assistant,' said Alys in some annoyance. 'And he's well able to choose his own when he does.'

'There was to be a sum o money to help. I've made you cross, I'm right sorry.' She sighed. 'I never knew her till after my mother died, my brother wrote to tell her of it, seeing they'd been good friends at one time, and next thing we kent she'd arrived at the gate wi a match for me all ready, and after that she was aye there wi advice when she thought I needed it, though her and William never got on after we were wedded. My first man,' she elucidated, 'he was a Chalmers. Chalmers of Glenouthock.' She sighed again. 'It seemed a right good match, but – anyway, after my godmother and me were both widows she would have me come and stay wi her, seeing my brother was away about his own dealings, and she took right care of me, aye concerned for my health and my reputation. I'll miss her sore.'

'And then you were wedded to Sempill,' said Alys. 'Gil tells me you are happy with the match.'

'Oh, indeed!' The smile was genuine. 'John's as kind to me!'

'And it pleased your brother?'

The smile remained, though it seemed to lose its light somewhat.

'I've not seen my brother these six months. He came to see me wedded to John, but he's been out o sight, I hope it's no down to any misliking between the two o them.'

'You've not heard from him? Does he know about – about—'

'About this?' Lady Magdalen looked down at her still-flat waist. 'Likely no.'

'And you've no idea where he is?' Alys persisted, her mind working. The other woman shook her head, and reached for the ale-jug.

'He's got his own dealings,' she said again. 'Likely he'll turn up.' She turned her head sharply as a door banged and voices rose in the hall below them. 'Is that John come home?'

'Maidie?'

Lady Magdalen put out a restraining hand as Ays prepared to rise, and called,

'I'm here, John. Here in my chamber.'

'Maidie?' The loud voice again, heavy feet on the stair. 'No, Philip, I'll no have him brought in on it, it's my business and none o his! Maidie, are you here?'

'I'm here,' she said. His boots sounded on the landing and then on the broad pine floorboards as he entered the chamber, still hidden from them by the great bed, saying,

'Here's a bit trouble out yonder, and Philip wanting to get Gil Cunningham in–' He stopped, staring at Alys. '–volved, of all the daft things,' he finished.

Chapter Eight

'So what's it to do wi us, if some auld wife got hersel killed?' demanded Adkin Saunders the pewterer. He lifted a small hammer from his workbench and went on, 'I've work to do, maisters, I'll thank ye to get away and let me get on, and no stand about asking me questions I canny answer.'

His wife, tall and deep-bosomed in her checked gown, two children clinging to her skirts and another in her arms, scowled at them from the hearth. Outside, the lorimer's dog barked from the door of his workshop. Gil said patiently,

'The dead woman's servant was taken up from this toft last night. Was she in this house?'

'I've seen no woman's servant,' said Saunders, 'nor do I want to. I've enough trouble wi her,' he jerked his head, 'without taking to do wi any more *banasgaleann*.'

'So you knew she's an Ersche speaker,' said Gil quickly. Maistre Pierre frowned at this, and Saunders' wife drew a sharp breath.

'It's a word I'd use o many women,' said Saunders.

'And the sack of coin,' said Gil. 'Did that come from this house too?'

'They neither of them were coming out of this house,' said the woman. 'We knew nothing of any stranger here, nor of any sack of coin.' She freed one hand to gesture about her, with expressive grace. 'Do you think we have coins to keep in a sack?'

The house was not so bare as she implied; the bed was

well furnished, the draw-bed under it seemed to have plenty of blankets, and a handsome assemblage of crocks was arranged on the sideboard next the wall. An iron cooking-pot hung over the hearth, probably her dowry, Gil surmised.

'Never mind that, woman,' growled her husband. 'And you, maisters, if you want to know about some Ersche trollop, you can ask at Campbell the whitesmith down the toft a bittie, no at my door—'

'My brother would be having nothing to do with it!' began his wife indignantly.

'Will you mind your tongue, woman, and no contradict me under my own roof!'

Gil drew breath to point out that it was not Saunders' roof but his landlord's, whoever that might be, and then thought better of it. His caution was repaid.

'Is that you trying to get my brother into trouble, then? When he's no more and no less in it than—'

'Mind your tongue!'

The smallest child began wailing, and the next took up the note.

'As for him across the way wi his leather scraps and his—'

Saunders flung the hammer down on the bench and took two strides across the room. The children screamed in unison, his wife flung up an arm to protect herself, Maistre Pierre seized the man by the shoulder. Gil stepped quietly away from the melee and inspected the bench closely. Rounds of pewter ready cast for shaping, moulds of differing sizes for cups and platters and bowls, hammers with heads of metal, of wood, of padded leather, a handful of metal dies with which to strike a pattern into the metal. He lifted these, but none of them bore the image of James Third, and in fact none was broad enough to strike a coin.

'Here, leave my graith be!' Saunders was at his elbow. 'And away and let a man earn his bread in peace, will you?'

Gil stepped away from the bench, and nodded to Maistre Pierre.

'I think we can leave you for now,' he said. 'But I'll likely see you again. Maister Mason and I will be taking over the toft.' He lifted his hat, with the caution it still required. 'We'll be your landlords.'

Out on the muddy path, Socrates and Luke were equally relieved to see them.

'There's been all sorts going on down there,' Luke said, nodding down the toft, while the dog nudged Gil's knees. 'I seen a bairn run down from this house, and a woman came running up and into yon workshop,' he indicated the lorimer's ramshackle premises, where the dog still barked at Socrates, 'and away again, and Danny Sproat came by and gave me a look, he'll ken me again, and away down to the donkey's shed. And then the man out that workshop went away down the toft as well, and hasny come back yet.'

'Good lad,' said Gil. So they were alarmed by his presence, were they? But Dod Muir the image-maker, whom the girl Cleone had seen strike him down, had not been mentioned.

This turned out to be because the image-maker was still not at home. Repeated rattling of the cast-iron ring on its twisted pin on the doorjamb had no result. After a pause, Maistre Pierre stepped to the window and peered in through a crack in the shutter.

'No movement,' he reported. 'Dod Muir! Are you within?'

'I could ask across the way, maybe,' suggested Luke. His master hammered on the shutters, which rattled wildly under his big fist.

'You might as well,' he was saying, when there was a shout behind them.

'There they are! Breaking in at Dod's window, and all!'

Socrates growled. Gil turned, to see the whitesmith and the lorimer, all indignant eyes and pointing fingers, hurrying down the path from the Drygate. Behind them, large

164

and important, strode not the Serjeant but Maister Andrew Hamilton, a neighbour from the High Street and present Dean of the Guild of Hammermen, wearing his Dean's robe of office over his working clothes and shedding curls of shaved wood as he went.

'You, Peter!' he said. 'I'd thought better of you! What's afoot here, anyway? These two,' he indicated his fellow guildsmen, 'cam running to me saying they're being harassed unlawful, and here I find you forcing Dod Muir's shutters? That's no like you!'

'Nothing of the kind, Andrew,' retorted Maistre Pierre, reddening. 'We are here about two errands, one of them to find out why my good-son was assaulted on this toft yesterday morning.'

'Nothing to do wi me,' said the lorimer quickly. 'I wasny on the toft!' His dog, more courageous in his presence, snarled at Socrates from behind his knee.

'Aye, I heard about that,' said Maister Hamilton. 'Was it on this toft then? Now that's serious, lads,' he said to his guildsmen. 'Which of them was it struck you, maister? Was there any effusion of blood?'

'No,' said Gil, wondering why the whole of Glasgow wished to see his blood let. 'It was this fellow Dod Muir that struck me,' he nodded at the shutter still rattling faintly, and turned back towards Hamilton in time to catch a startled expression crossing Campbell's face. 'I've witnesses,' he concluded. 'He had help throwing me in the burn, and all.'

'Oh, you have, have you?' said Maister Hamilton grimly. 'And who was the help, then?'

'No me!' said the whitesmith quickly, and the lorimer shook his head.

'Aye, well,' said their Dean, eyeing them, 'I'll see you right when you're doing right, lads, but assault wi witnesses is a different matter. What had you done to provoke it, maister?'

'Poking his nose in here, thieving in Danny Sproat's stable,' began the lorimer.

'You know a deal about it for one that wasny here,' Gil said. And you were here, he recalled, eyeing the bright red hair which hung below the lorimer's blue bonnet. 'Maister Hamilton, if the offer we've had still stands, Pierre and I will shortly be landlords here on wee John's behalf. I was inspecting the place, trying to decide if it was worth taking on, and I was struck down all unsuspecting.'

'Asking questions!' said the whitesmith.

'There's no law agin asking questions,' said Hamilton. He hitched up his black gown, stroked its velvet facings and braced his elbows importantly. 'We'll have to have this out, lads. Go and summon the other fellows, Saunders and the donkey man and all I suppose, and we'll hear all here and now. And where might Dod be, d'ye ken?'

'Never seen him the day,' admitted the lorimer. 'Nor yesterday neither, when I think on it.' Danny Bell, that was his name, Gil recalled, and the whitesmith was a Campbell. And the pewterer's brother-in-law. He stepped sideways, head cocked to hear Campbell banging on the pewterer's door. The woman answered it, with a spate of anxious Ersche which got a 'Wheesht, Vari!' from her brother. Then there was a half-whispered exchange among the three adults, almost inaudible through the wailing of another of the children, in which he caught Dod Muir's name, and then suddenly, clearly, the phrase *Alan agus Nicol*.

Next to him, the lorimer's dog suddenly got its courage up and went for Socrates. Kicking it away Gil restrained his own dog, his mind working furiously.

He knew only a few words of Ersche, unlike Alys, but he could recognize that: Alan and Nicol. Two of Dame Isabella's missing servants.

'From Madam Xanthe?' repeated Gil.

'Aye, from my mistress,' agreed the boy Cato.

'What does she want?' Alys asked, coming forward from the hearth. The boy gave her an ingratiating grin and bobbed nervously, scattering raindrops from his plaid. Gil turned the note over in his hand, broke the seal, and held the orange-scented paper to the light from the candle she held.

'She wants to see me,' he said after a moment. 'About the false coin.'

'When?' said Alys.

'Maybe now?' said Cato hopefully. 'She bade me say, if you'd see your way to calling on us the night, she'd be right glad of it.'

'But I'm not,' Gil began, and bit that off.

'She bade me say and all,' Cato assured him, 'she kens you're no charged wi it, but she'd like fine to talk wi you just the same.'

'Did she say anything else?' And how did she know that much? he wondered.

'No, no, that's all, excepting it was about Strathblane, she said. The coin, I mean.'

'Strathblane?' Gil looked at the boy, then at Alys. 'I think I must go,' he said in French.

'I think you must,' she acknowledged, eyebrows raised, 'but not alone, surely. Maybe you could take Luke with you again. And the dog.' She glanced over her shoulder at the group by the hearth; Maistre Pierre and the two McIans were still engrossed in a debate on the merits of different styles of harp. Socrates, recognizing *chien*, raised his head and looked at her.

'No,' he agreed, 'I won't take your father out again tonight. Warn Luke, then, if you will, and I'll put on my boots. And a cloak.'

'Aye, you'll want a cloak, maister,' agreed Cato. 'It's right wet out there, we'll ha a quiet time o it in the house. Keeps the customers away, so it does, the rain,' he informed Alys, nodding wisely.

Sending Cato to the kitchen to alert Luke, Alys lit a lantern and followed Gil out into the rain and across the yard to their apartment, Socrates on her heels.

'It's curious she mentioned Strathblane,' she said as they picked their way past the tubs of flowers.

'Very curious.'

'Sempill was out there today.'

'Was he now?' Gil looked down at her, and opened the heavy door to their stair. 'What was he doing?'

'I don't know,' she said regretfully, 'but he came home in a great temper, saying there was some trouble, and that Philip wanted to involve you. Then he saw me, and would say no more.'

'Did you ask?'

'Of course I did,' she said indignantly, 'but he was rude to me, so Lady Magdalen rebuked him, and he went off in a sulk.' She followed him into their outer chamber, put the lantern on a kist and sat down to watch him pull on his boots. 'I learned some useful things today,' she added. 'I was waiting to tell you when we were alone.'

'Go on.' He straightened the heels of his hose, folded the wide leg of each boot about his calf, the soft leather waxy under his fingers, and buckled the straps while Alys recounted the visits she had made and the information she had gathered. He did not ask why she had not told him this before; supper had been a lively meal, with a sparkling conversation about the power of music and little opportunity to discuss the case.

'This is all useful, sweetheart,' he agreed at last, stamping to settle his feet in the boots. 'It confirms all the servants' stories, so far as it goes. I wonder what the bag of coin was doing in Clerk's Land?'

'Maybe Madam Xanthe will know,' she suggested, with an odd emphasis on the name. Their eyes met in the lantern-light, and he nodded slightly, then looked about him for his plaid. She rose to fetch it from its nail in the inmost chamber, taking the light with her. He stood quietly in the dark, wondering what the reference to Strathblane might mean, while the dog nudged his knee.

The House of the Mermaiden was lit and humming with conversation behind its shutters, but Cato led them round

168

the side of the house and in at the back door. Madam Xanthe, gorgeously dressed and turbaned, was alone in the room where Gil had been dried off the previous day, seated by a branch of candles with a ledger open on the table before her. When they entered she looked up, smiled, and pushed the heavy volume away.

'Maister Cunningham! In a good hour,' she declared. 'Oh, and a wee lapdog wi you!' She stretched a long white hand to Socrates, who paced forward to inspect it, then on to thrust his nose into her lap. She fended him off. 'Cato, take Maister Cunningham's man out to the kitchen and see him dried off, and then bring us some of the good wine.'

'And the wee cakes, madam? Ste– Strephon's made some of his wee cakes, they're right good this time—'

'Aye, you daft laddie, some o the wee cakes! Now get off wi the two o ye, till I get talking to my guest.'

Luke departed hopefully with Cato, and Madam Xanthe turned to Gil, her hand still busy about the dog's ears.

'You're recovered from your wetting, then?' she observed. 'And the dunt on the head?'

'I'm fine,' he said politely. 'I hope I see you well, madam?'

'Oh, if we're to be formal!' She rose and swept him a magnificent curtsy, the wide folds of her dark blue taffeta gown rustling in a great pool round her, the gold turban gleaming in the candlelight. Gil responded, and she took his arm and drew him to a seat by the brazier in the centre of the chamber. Socrates padded about, inspecting the place.

'And madam your wife's in good health? Your good-father? Right, now that's seen to,' she went on without waiting for a reply, 'will you tell me what you ken o these false coins, or will I go first?'

'What was the reference to Strathblane about?' he countered, watching the painted face, which was now partly shadowed. The paint and the turban combined to remind him suddenly of one of the players in a student play two years since, a repellent boy playing Dame

169

Fortuna in fluent Latin, who met his death within the hour. With an effort he brought his mind back to the present. What was the purpose of this summons? How much information did this pretentious individual hold, and where had it come from?

'Och, that was just to fetch you out.' There was a burst of loud laughter from the hall above them; Socrates growled quietly, and Gil snapped his fingers to bring the dog to his side. 'Mind you Danny Sproat and his donkey seems to have been out that way, which is likely what put it into my mind, for as I recall Isabella Torrance had some land there. Or claimed she had.'

'*Claimed* is nearer it,' Gil agreed. 'So now you've fetched me, what can you tell me? I was warned off the false coin by Robert Blacader,' he said, keeping his voice neutral, 'but it seems to be involved in the matter of the old woman's death, or at least there are more false coins floating about her than seems reasonable, so if you ken aught of any use, I'd be glad to hear it.'

'I've no doubt of it.' Madam Xanthe paused as Cato entered with two glasses, followed by Luke with a jug in one hand and a platter of little cakes in the other. Socrates cocked one hopeful ear, but did not move. 'Good laddie, leave them there and we'll serve ourselves. Away out to the kitchen now, do you hear me? Aye, that's what I hear,' she went on as the two young men left. 'A great sack o the stuff found on the lassie that went missing, for a start, and did I hear there was another purse gone as well?'

'You're well informed.'

There was another burst of laughter from the hall, and a scattering of notes from a lute. Two voices rose entwined in sweet and inappropriate harmony; Gil identified the song about the hurcheon.

'I have my sources,' said Madam Xanthe, pouring wine. The light from the candles struck matching dark red glints from the brocade under-sleeve within the wide folds of taffeta. She handed him a glass. 'So what else have you got?'

170

'Very little,' Gil admitted. 'We've had coin from the market, one or two from the Gorbals, none from anyone that kent who he'd got it from. Or was willing to say,' he qualified scrupulously, thinking of Ysonde's tale. 'I've spoken to the Provost about it, and I'd a talk wi Eckie Livingstone about coining and how it's done. That's it.'

'And you'd nothing useful fro this afternoon on Clerk's Land.' Madam Xanthe was watching him under the long painted eyelids. 'It didny seem like a peaceable gathering.'

'It wasny.' He shut his mouth firmly on that. The pale eyes did not move from his face. He sat still, thinking about the long argument on the drying-green, with Maister Hamilton exerting all his authority and his considerable voice to keep order while he questioned the three hammermen about the assault on Gil, questioned Gil and Pierre about their presence on the toft, refused to listen to complaints about the fine for a fire which nobody would admit to having set too close to the thatch, and finally directed his fellow-guildsmen to be civil to the Archbishop's man.

'And you'll tell Dod I want a word wi him,' he said ominously. 'This is all a storm in a chopin, I hope I willny have to come out to it again, or there'll be more than the one fine to pay.'

'But he'll no need to be searching our houses,' said Campbell the whitesmith.

'No, I wouldny say he'd any need to search your houses,' agreed Maister Hamilton. 'Right, Maister Cunningham?'

'What are they hiding, then?' speculated Madam Xanthe now. 'Something the Provost's men missed.'

'Or wereny looking for,' he said, and tasted the wine. It was more of the stuff she had offered them the other morning, smooth and heavy with a dark taste of apricots. 'They were hiding the woman Forveleth, until Campbell put her out to fend for herself, I'm reasonably sure of that. It's Campbell's wife is her kin, by what she says, no doubt he feels less responsible for her. They had the big sack of false coin, and exchanged it for a parcel of potyngary she

171

had on her, I assume in the hope of getting it off the place and at least off their hands, and I'd dearly like to ken why they had that much in their possession, but of course they denied all knowledge of it.'

'Of course.'

'They mentioned two of Dame Isabella's men, two of the ones that are missing—'

'Missing?'

'Alan and Nicol, brothers I think.' He shook his head, and took another sip of the wine. 'The Serjeant was to cry them abroad, but there's been no word of them. I think they're not on the toft, there's little enough room to hide two men, so where they can have gone—'

'Plenty places to hide in Glasgow,' remarked Madam Xanthe. 'They're not here, at least, maister.'

'You disappoint me. Then there's the matter of the fire that nobody admits having set, and the prentice that Campbell claims he doesny have, though two others have mentioned him.'

'Prentice?' Madam Xanthe looked at him, eyes narrowed. 'Who told you that? I've never seen any sign o one.'

'John Sempill told me he kept a prentice,' Gil recalled, 'and I think – aye, the Provost's men arrested him on suspicion of theft, and had to release him when his master swore it was something he'd given him.'

'Theft of what?'

'No idea. This was yestreen, I wasny at my best.' He eyed her across the heavy glow of his wine. 'And what do you know? Have you other information?'

'Some.' She offered him the platter of cakes. He took one and nibbled it. 'Have you had aught from the Gallowgate? Any coin I mean?'

'The Gallowgate?' He shook his head. 'We've no trade down there that I'm aware of. I'd say,' he added, thinking of the children again, 'there are more false coins found at the foot of the town than up here, but that's all I ken.'

'Aye.' She drank some of the wine, then suddenly set her glass down on the table and sat up straight. 'The deil fly away wi this, I'm sick o playing Tarocco. Come away up, maister.'

'Up?' he repeated, startled.

'Aye. Up to my chamber.' The arch expression surfaced, for the first time this evening; she put a long white finger to her painted lips and looked at him sideways. 'I've that to show you, will make you right astonished.'

'Will it, now?' he said, raising his eyebrows.

She lifted her glass again. 'Bring the wine.'

Warily, he followed her from the chamber, through another where shadows jumped from her candle, to a narrow stair at its far corner. The dog was at his heels, claws clicking on the waxed boards.

'This was what I liked about this house,' she said, setting foot on the lowest step. 'The second stair, completely separate from the hall. Come away up,' she said again, holding the candle high. 'I'll tell you, once we've left, you should move in here wi your wee wife, set up your own household. A man should be maister under his own roof.'

'You think?'

'I know.'

She stepped off the stair into another darkened chamber, opened a door which was barely noticeable in the candle-light, set off upwards again. This time they emerged in a bedchamber, sparsely furnished, the box bed curtained with plain linen. Socrates set off to explore the room.

'You don't bring clients here,' Gil recognized, looking about him. Madam Xanthe did not answer; setting down glass and candle on a stool she delved under her dark blue taffeta to produce a key, crossed the chamber, and unlocked another half-hidden door.

'My closet. Come in, maister. Bring the candle, and come and unlace me.'

Gil paused in the doorway of the small place. It held even less furniture than the outer room: a desk, a couple of kists, two stools. A shelf with books, a lute in an open case. Its owner, staring challengingly in the candlelight.

'Can you not unlace yourself?' he suggested.

'Oh, now!' The pale eyes glinted, the husky voice was mocking. 'You don't want to disrobe me, reveal my white flesh and soft—'

'I think,' said Gil deliberately, 'you're about as soft as tempered steel. Sandy.'

Sandy Boyd gave a crack of laughter.

'I wondered!' he said. 'I wondered if you'd jaloused me.' He dragged off the gold turban, and ran his fingers through pale hair. 'Christ aid, how can women wear these tight things all day? What gave me away?'

Gil shook his head.

'Nothing particular, I think. You're gey like your sister, and Madam Xanthe's too good to be true.'

'Oh, never!' Boyd put a hand to his cheek, with Madam Xanthe's simper. 'How can you say so? Maybe true, but *good*, maister?'

Gil grinned. 'What's it in aid of?'

'Aye, well.' Boyd flung off the blue taffeta. 'I wasny joking when I asked if you'd unlace me, Agnes has a strong arm and I'll never reach the knot she's used.' He turned his back and Gil obediently began work on the knot in the lacing of the dark brocade kirtle. 'As for what it's in aid of, what but this false coin? I'm put in here by Robert Blacader to get at the source. See, it's good stuff. Good silver. The Treasury wants to ken where it's coming from.'

'Oh, you are, are you?' He took in the rest of the utterance. 'What, you mean it's purer silver than the coin of the realm?'

'That's just what I mean. Thanks.' Boyd wriggled the kirtle loose, and began to work one arm out of the tight sleeve. Socrates clicked into the room and over to thrust his nose against the brocade skirt. Boyd pushed him away with his free hand. 'Blacader said,' another short laugh, 'they could buy it all up at face value, coin it new and still make a good profit at the Mint, save that we'd not want word to get round.'

'I can see that.' Gil turned to the jug of wine where he had set it on one of the kists, and refilled his glass. 'Does

174

the old woman's death fit in here, do you suppose? That's my prime concern the now, particularly if you're after the coin.'

'You'd do better to look in other directions. Though as you say, there's a lot of the stuff floating about her. It's taken me the six month I've been here to get this far, Gil. Pour me some more o that wine and all, will you?' He extracted his hand from the second sleeve and began easing the kirtle down over narrow hips. Beneath it he wore a woman's shift, the neck elaborately worked and pleated. Stepping free of the heap of brocade he caught it up, threw it on top of the blue taffeta gown, and delved in the other kist.

'Boots,' he muttered, 'hose, drawers, what the deil has Agnes done wi my – aye, there they are.' He closed the lid, kicked off Madam Xanthe's large but dainty Morocco leather shoes, and began dressing. 'How is Maidie, anyhow?' he asked. 'You've seen her lately? And the charming John, a course.'

'Just the day. Your sister looks well, and seems happy,' Gil said. 'I'd say she's dealing uncommon well wi the charming John.' He sat down beside the wine-jug, and went on, 'So how far is that, you've got? Where does the stuff come from?'

'If I'd jaloused that, I wouldny be here.' Boyd tucked the shift into his hose. 'It comes into Glasgow from some-where, I'm assuming as bars o silver rather than lumps o rock, and gets struck into coin and then carried out to the Isles. We're sure enough o the other end, it's this end we want to track down, the workshop in Glasgow and the mine the stuff comes from.'

'We?'

'Those I work for.' He was tying the points of his hose to a dark jerkin now and did not look up.

'So that's more than Blacader.'

'I'm surprised they've no recruited you,' said Boyd obliquely. 'Mind you, a married man.'

'And that's how far you've got in six month?'

'That and some other matters unrelated.' He fastened a dark doublet and reached for his replenished glass. 'Ah, that's good. The barrel's near finished, be time to move on soon, I canny contemplate Glasgow without a decent drink.'

'So why am I here?' Gil asked bluntly. 'What do you want of me?'

'I need a look at Dod Muir's place, and I thought you'd like to come along.'

'What?'

'Wheesht! Are you wanting half Glasgow to ken you're in my chamber? No that I'd mind, you understand, but—'

'Why Dod Muir's house, and why now?' Gil asked, lowering his voice obediently. 'There's plenty folk about that toft, do you reckon they'll all be asleep? Where's Muir himsel sleep anyway?'

'He dwells in the house, but he's no been back there the day, at least no by the time it was dark.'

'And how about the dog?' Gil added, as Socrates nudged his elbow. 'There was one there this afternoon.'

'It's Bell the lorimer's. He takes the brute home wi him at night along wi the takings. The rest'll be asleep. No, I think Dod Muir might ha been the source o the dies they're using, and seeing it was him put you in the mill-burn . . .' He let the sentence die away. Gil sipped wine and looked at the other man. The dark clothes he now wore receded into the shadows, leaving Madam Xanthe's painted face floating in the candlelight surrounded by wild pale hair.

'And if we're heard,' he said. 'What will you do if we're taken up for theft and rookery?'

Boyd gave him Madam Xanthe's arch painted smile.

'How fast can you run?'

This was madness.

Moving quietly after Boyd, the dog at his knee, Gil wondered how he had agreed to what was, in effect, housebreaking. The moon, he recalled, was a day or two

176

past the full; it could not be seen, but the clouds gleamed faintly silver here and there. Clerk's Land was asleep in the rainy night, snores sounding from behind the shutters of the pewterer's house as they slipped past. Boyd's shut-lantern gave them just enough light to see the path before them and threw a wet sparkle on the flagstones and on the doorway of the lorimer's workshop. Beyond it, the image-maker's house was black against the sky.

Boyd paused, held out the lantern. He was wrapped in a huge black cloak, his head covered by a felt coif, and his face and hands floated eerily, isolated in the night, as Gil directed the light at the fastening of Muir's door. The handle for the latch had been drawn into the house, as if the man was at home; Gil said softly,

'Are you sure he's no here?'

'Nothing's sure,' returned Boyd, equally softly. He produced a latch-lifter, inserted it into the hole in the door and turned it cautiously, seeking the point where the hook on the end would raise the bar of the latch, while Gil held the lantern steady and wondered whether the door had been barred from the inside as well. Socrates, perhaps catching his mood, leaned hard against his leg.

There was a click as the latch rose. Boyd exhaled, pushed gently, and the door moved under his hand. Not barred then, thought Gil, as the hinges creaked. They stood frozen on the threshold, listening for any movement within. Nothing stirred, and at length Boyd took the lantern from Gil and stepped inside the house. Gil followed, and pushed the door to behind the dog.

'What are we looking for?'

'Aught out o place.' The lantern's narrow beam moved slowly round the place. One small room, a workbench at one end, a hearth at the other. The light glinted on a rack of tools, raising a glow from blades of chisel and gouge, casting darkness beyond a mell on the bench, its head as big as Gil's two fists. Two kists, a rack with papers, a table and two stools, another rack of shelves with kitchen stuff on them, a ladder in the corner leading to a dark loft. The place smelled of damp, of cold ashes, of something else. Socrates left Gil's side and padded round, sniffing in corners, his paws rasping on the beaten earth floor. The lantern, in Boyd's hand, moved towards the workbench, the light skimming over a clutter of wood shavings, several gouges, two small-bladed knives. The hearth, when Gil stepped over to it, was cold, though the two crocks washed out and set to drip beside it still had damp patches beneath them. He frowned. Something did not quite fit there.

'Where's the work-piece?' he asked quietly. They were both using the voice a little above a whisper, the pitch least likely to disturb the sleeping neighbours. The light swung across the bench, round the room, dipped to the floor.

'Here.' Boyd stooped and came up with a piece of wood, set it among the shavings, held the lantern close. A figure emerged from the cross-lit surface like a corpse out of water, St Paul with book and sword, six inches high.

'He's been interrupted,' Gil said. 'A craftsman doesny leave his work like that, he makes all tidy and stows his tools. And yet he's had time to wash the crocks, and not so long since at that.'

'So where is he?' wondered Boyd. He was inspecting the bench, and now bent to peer under it, the light showing a shelf with baskets ranged along it. 'What have we here? Aye, different work, a couple wax medallions, an alabaster waiting to be mended.' He was pulling the baskets towards him one by one, peering into each. 'No metal-work. Where does he do his metalwork?'

'He doesny,' said Gil. 'He's a carver, a maker of figures and pictures.'

'He does engraving. I've seen him. I'd wager it was him made the dies for the coiners. I hoped there might be something in the house to prove it.' The other man straightened up, and the beam of light flitted round the room again, the shadows dancing away from it. Outside, a child wailed, an adult spoke, and Boyd snapped the shutter of the lantern closed. Darkness choked the little house, and they waited, listening, while the dog snuffled at something. Both mother and child spoke again. Gil, ears at the stretch, breathing quietly, realized that muffled in darkness as he was his other senses were heightened; he was aware of Boyd moving away from the bench, of air stirring past his face, of the smells of damp earth and new timber, ashes and cold meat. Socrates' strong claws scraped at wood. The child had fallen silent; the strapping of a bed creaked. Sweet St Giles, he thought, you might as well live on the Tolbooth steps.

The lantern opened again, startlingly bright after the thick darkness, and showed Socrates, his nose pressed intently at the lid of one of the kists. Gil, wishing he had a light himself, moved past his dog to the second kist, while Boyd turned his attention to the papers in the rack.

'Contracts,' he said after a moment. 'A St Francis for the Greyfriars, a Philip and James for St Thomas's. He's doing well enow.'

'Clothes in here,' said Gil. He dug cautiously among the folded garments. 'Couple of medals, a purse wi a few coins. No metalworking tools that I can feel.'

'See us the coins,' requested Boyd. Gil obediently drew the purse out, and his companion took it to the workbench and tipped the contents out into the beam of the lantern. Gil moved to the other kist, elbowed Socrates out of the way and lifted the lid. 'Two, no, three false ones,' Boyd reported. Gil grunted, peering at what lay inside, something light and dark in patches which filled the kist to its top –

The lid fell with a bang as he recoiled with a shudder, fell over Socrates, and went down, taking one of the stools with him.

'You great juffler—' began Boyd. Outside, the child wailed again, and someone shouted. 'Quick, bar the door, they'll be out like a spilled byke—'

Gil scrambled to his feet and collected himself, pulling his doublet straight, patting his apologetic dog. Boyd was making for the door, but he put out a hand and seized the other man's arm.

'A moment,' he said, and drew a slightly shaky breath. 'I think I've found Dod Muir.'

'*What?*'

There were loud voices in the house across the toft. Someone shouted about a light.

'In the kist. He's cold, and softened. I found his face.' He wiped the other hand on his hose, trying to eliminate the feeling of the clammy flesh. 'Let's have some light on him.'

The body in the kist was folded up, knees on chest, head tilted sideways. The face was pale in the thin light, the features flattened by the lid of the chest. The eyes stared at them pleadingly. Socrates inserted his long nose under Gil's elbow and sniffed curiously at the dead man's ear, and Boyd said with reluctance,

'Aye, it's Muir right enough. How did he die, I wonder?'

'I can smell blood,' said Gil, 'though it's not fresh.'

'*Dhia!*' said a voice above them in horror.

The lantern jerked convulsively, but Socrates looked upwards, ears pricked. Gil followed the dog's gaze. At the top of the ladder, against the darkness of the loft, a dark-browed face stared back at them, appalled.

'Christ aid!' said Boyd. 'Who the devil are you?'

'Dod!' shouted someone outside, and there was a hammering at the door. Socrates scrambled to his feet, head down, growling. 'Is that you, man? What's befallen ye? Are ye scaithed?'

'Euan Campbell,' said Gil with resignation. 'Come down out o there.'

'It iss mysel, no my brother,' said the man in the loft. 'I will just be putting my boots on, maybe.'

'Who's in there?' demanded the voice outside.

'Niall, *an tu a tha'ann?*' A woman's voice, shrill with anxiety. The child was screaming now. Sandy Boyd calmly handed Gil the lantern and drew his cloak about him in an elaborate gesture. Suddenly, Madam Xanthe was back, simpering in the dimness.

'I'll let you deal wi't, seeing you found him,' she said archly.

'My gratitude,' said Gil with feeling, 'knows no bounds.' He opened another shutter on the lantern. The hammering on the door was growing more urgent, and Socrates was growling insistently. 'Neil! Get down here, man!'

'You were just wanting somewhere to sleep,' repeated Otterburn. He stared at Neil Campbell, his expression baffled. Gil sympathized; conversation with the Campbell brothers often left him feeling the same way. 'So why did you pick Dod Muir's loft?'

'My cousin was saying he was from home.'

'Your cousin being,' Otterburn referred to his notes, 'Noll Campbell the whitesmith. Christ on a handcart, I think the whole of Scotland must be kin to the folk on this toft. And how did he ken the man Muir was from home?'

'But he was not from home,' the gallowglass pointed out earnestly.

'What,' said Otterburn with thinning patience, 'made your kinsman think Muir was from home?'

'Well, he was never seeing him all day. And nor was the women.'

'Hmm,' said Otterburn, gazing at Campbell in the candlelight. 'What are you doing here anyway? Why are you in Glasgow the now?'

'Visiting my cousin,' said Campbell, innocence shining in his face.

'So why were you not lodged wi him?' Gil asked.

When he had opened the door of Dod Muir's house, Saunders the pewterer, clad in shirt and boots, had almost fallen into the chamber clutching one of his bigger mells. Behind him his wife held her plaid about her over her shift, a lantern in her free hand, her gaze going past Gil into the dark corners, to Neil Campbell on the ladder.

'You!' said Saunders. 'What are you at here? What have ye done wi Dod?'

181

'The man Muir is dead,' said the gallowglass, as the whitesmith appeared out of the rainy darkness.

Saunders' wife screamed, and crossed herself. The whitesmith pushed past her into the house, staring round in the leaping shadows.

'What are you about?' demanded Saunders, raising the mell. 'Seize the man, Noll, we've got him red hand!'

'He's been slain and hidden here,' said Gil, 'I'd say yesterday some time.'

Both householders began shouting, ably assisted by Saunders' wife. The resulting broil had attracted the attention of the Watch; during it, somehow, Madam Xanthe slipped out and away without being noticed.

The Watch, five stalwart indwellers of the burgh in a mixed set of ill-fitting armour, had been deeply dismayed to find they had a murder on their hands.

'Is it Dod Muir right enough?' said their leader, peering into the kist in the lantern-light. 'His face is all sideways, it's no that like him.' He felt respectfully at the folded corpse, and shook his head. 'Whoever it is, he's caulder than charity, and he's stiff and softened again, he's been gone a while.'

'Who else would it be?' said his neighbour scornfully, hitching at a breastplate which Gil estimated had been made forty years since for a thinner man. 'Hid here in the man's own kist, in his own house?'

'It might be someone he's slew himsel,' said one of the other watchmen.

'You need,' said Gil, exerting authority, 'to send to the Castle. Get them to wake the Provost, and fetch a couple of his men back wi you.'

'Wake the Provost?' repeated the leader doubtfully.

'Aye, and take up this nosy—' began Saunders. Gil stared him down, but his wife said shrilly,

'Ach, indeed, nothing but trouble, he is, always poking round here, uncovering what he ought not, high time he was taken up and locked away!' She fell silent as her

182

brother hissed something threatening in Ersche, and Gil said to the leader of the Watch,

'It's none of your duty to deal wi murder, man. Send one of your lads to the Castle, tell them there's been a murder, bid them come and take over from you here.'

'Aye, you're right there,' agreed the man, grasping at this idea with relief. 'Wee Rab, away up to the Castle, d'ye hear? And the rest o us will just stay here,' he said, with more courage now he knew the task was limited, 'mak sure nobody moves aught they shouldny.'

'Aye, well,' said one of his henchmen. 'It's out the rain, and all. But how did ye come to discover him, hid away like this?'

'I'll ask the questions, Tam Bowster,' said the leader. 'How did ye find him, then?'

'The dog led me to him,' said Gil, having anticipated this question. The men looked askance at Socrates, who was now sitting politely at Gil's side, his teeth gleaming in the light. The child was still screaming in the near house; Saunders sent his wife away with a mutter and a jerk of the head, and Noll Campbell the whitesmith said,

'For one that claims to be our landlord, maister, you do a rare lot o spying and creeping about. What was bringing you in here, that the dog could sniff out a death? Did you ken he was there to be found?'

'When did you last see him?' Gil countered.

'I'll ask the questions,' said the leader of the Watch. 'When was deceased last seen, then? Was he at his work the day?'

'He couldny ha been,' objected the man in the antique breastplate, 'he's been deid since yestreen by the look o him.'

'I'd an encounter wi him yesterday morning,' said Gil rather wryly. 'I've been looking for a word wi him ever since.'

'And you!' said the watchman to Neil Campbell, not waiting for an answer from the householders. 'What are you doing here? You're a stranger, are ye no? Was it you slew the man and hid him in his own kist?'

'I never knew the man was there,' protested Neil.

He said the same now to the Provost. Otterburn snorted.

'Answer Maister Cunningham,' he ordered. 'Why were ye no lodged wi your cousin? What made him bed ye down in Muir's house?'

'I was sleeping there before,' said the gallowglass. Otterburn snorted again, and set his tablets down with a bang on the table.

'Take him away, Andro,' he ordered. 'Shut him away wi the rest o them, we'll get a right word wi them all the morn's morn. And yoursel, Maister Cunningham,' he added as his man-at-arms removed the startled Campbell, 'what's all this about, anyway? Respected burgess like yoursel, creeping about the back-lands in the night? Don't think I haveny noticed what ye were about.'

'I found Dod Muir,' Gil pointed out, aware that his face was burning. Otterburn glared at him. 'I was in pursuit of a matter concerning Dame Isabella's death,' he continued.

'And did you find it?'

'No,' he admitted. Otterburn grunted, and pushed his chair back with a scraping noise, very loud in the quiet tower.

'Get away hame to yir bed,' he said, 'and be back here betimes, if you would, Maister Cunningham.' It was not a request. 'I'll want a good word wi you and all afore the old dame's quest, and I'll want you wi me when we get a look at Dod Muir. He'll keep in his box till daylight.'

'Very well,' Gil said, rising when the older man did.

'And next time you're taken up by the Watch,' said Otterburn, 'I'll have you arrested same as the lave o them.'

Chapter Nine

'I'm right flattered,' said Lowrie, 'that Maister Gil trusts me to keep you safe, but I thought bringing a couple of our lads along as well might be wiser.'

Alys gave him an enigmatic smile, and pressed her horse to a faster walk. She had left Gil still asleep. He had returned some time before dawn, rousing her long enough to give her a confusing account of Sandy Boyd, Archbishop Blacader and a body in a kist, before they had both become distracted; when she woke again at the more usual time and slid out of his embrace he hardly stirred.

It had taken her an hour to organize horses and escort for this outing, while contriving to give both Catherine and Ealasaidh the impression that she was acting on Gil's instructions. She hoped one of them would wake him in time for the quest on Dame Isabella; meanwhile she preferred to leave Glasgow behind as soon as possible.

'I was certain you would know the road out to Strathblane,' she said. 'I have never ridden that way.'

'Where are we headed, anyways, mem?' asked Luke suspiciously from her other side. 'It's a bonnie day for a ride, but there's work to do. The maister wasny best pleased at your message.'

'Strathblane? Is that to Balgrochan?' asked one of Lowrie's men hopefully. 'Willie Logan that's grieve there's got a generous hand wi the ale-jug. Good ale his wife brews and all.'

'That and Ballencleroch,' said Alys. Luke frowned, and

Canon Cunningham's groom Tam turned in his saddle and looked hard at her.

'Is that these two feus the row was about?' he asked. 'When yon auld wife was at our house, that asked the maister—' He broke off what he was about to say.

'I think so,' said Alys.

'Asked him had he had his bowels open, did she?' said the other of Lowrie's men, and guffawed. 'She'd ha asked the Pope himsel the same question, I can tell you, good riddance to her!'

'Sim,' said Lowrie repressively, and the man ducked his head and muttered an apology. 'Mistress Alys, it's twelve mile. Are you ready for such a ride, and the ride back and all? And the dog,' he added, as Socrates loped back from his inspection of a milestone.

'Oh, yes,' she said confidently, assessing the state of the road. 'Shall we canter?'

The first part of the journey passed quickly enough. As Luke had said, it was a good day for a ride, dry and fine for April, though with enough cloud moving on the brisk wind to prevent the horses overheating. The road from Glasgow to Stirling went by Cadder and Kirkintilloch, small towns which Alys had heard of but never seen, each with its group of thatched cottages scattered round a little stone church. At Kirkintilloch they paused to admire the vestiges of the wall built by the Romans to keep the savages out, and to let the horses drink and rest briefly. Lowrie, claiming to be thirsty, procured ale for all of them to drink, standing on the grass beside one of the cottages, while the hens clucked round the horses' hooves and several children gathered to stare at them. Alys relaxed in her saddle and looked at the traffic on the road. One or two people went by on foot, dusty to the waist, bound on who knew what errand. Wagons grumbled past in twos and threes, pulled by oxen or small sturdy ponies, shifting the merchandise of Scotland. Barrels of wine, barrels of fish, barrels of dry goods from the ports of the Low Countries, moving around the kingdom –

'That's a soil-cart coming,' said Lowrie. 'Drink up, lads. Are you about finished, mistress? We'd best be on the road afore that passes us.'

'Yes, indeed,' agreed Alys, handing her beaker down to him. 'Thank you, Maister Lowrie, I was glad of that. Do we continue on this road?'

'We turn off in a mile or so.' Lowrie mounted, checked that all the men were in the saddle, and urged his horse into the roadway. The soil-cart was already making its presence felt; in this wind direction they would be aware of it until they left the road, but if they got behind it they would be aware of it for a lot longer. Alys had seen the soil-carts rumbling out of Glasgow, their unsavoury contents dripping in the mud behind them, and splashing on the legs of people and horses who followed. And attracting the burgh dogs to roll in the residue, she realized, and looked round hastily for Socrates, who grinned at her from under the belly of Luke's horse.

'Tell me of Dame Isabella,' she said to Lowrie, nudging her horse alongside his. 'Did you know her well? Was she always so – so—'

'So individual,' he supplied tactfully. 'All the time I've kent her, aye. But I was away at college most of the year, you'll mind, so I never got the worst of it. My mother had a few tales of her doings.'

'Lady Magdalen thinks well of her,' Alys observed.

'The old dame was fond of the lady, by what she said,' Lowrie said. 'We turn off here, mistress, up the Glazert water.'

'So she could be good to those she thought well of.' Alys obediently turned her steed onto the new track, a broad stony trail through the low ground beside another river.

'I'd say so.' Lowrie laughed shortly. 'Whether they wanted it or no.'

'Had she plans for you?' she asked innocently.

'She had. Our Lady be thanked she never got putting them into play.'

'What, was it not something you would want?'

'It wasny that,' Lowrie said, going scarlet, 'so much as the way she'd have gone about it, ordering Mai – ordering people to do her bidding and handing over a great lump o coin to sweeten the bargain. I'd as soon get a post for friendship or kinship, or even on my own merits.'

'I can see you'd not want a place bought for you in that way,' Alys agreed. 'And yet she meant well.' She looked about her, taking in the lie of the new river valley. The Glazert rattled in its wide bed, wriggling down the valley floor; flat meadow-lands on either side were full of cattle grazing the new spring grass, herd-laddies from different ferm-touns watching each other warily from the dykes. At a distance, the valley sides sloped sharply. *A grete forest that was named the Countrey of Straunge Auentures*, she thought. 'How different this country is from Lanarkshire.'

'It's got fields and dykes and houses,' objected Luke, 'same as any other.'

'No, but,' she gestured with one hand, trying to describe what she could see. 'The fall of the land, the way that burn has cut into its bank, the slope opposite that, all these. The stone is not the same colour, it must have its own properties, so it makes different shapes of the ground.'

'I know what you mean,' agreed Lowrie, looking curiously at her. 'It changes even more when you get closer to the Campsies yonder.' He nodded at the hills to the north. 'They go up in layers like a stack o girdle-cakes, a thing you never see in Lanarkshire.'

'And yourself, Maister Lowrie,' she went on. The track was less well maintained than the Stirling road, so they could not hurry. That meant it was much easier to talk, and she was determined to learn what she could. 'Have you brothers and sisters?'

'Three brothers living, all older than me,' said Lowrie, 'and two sisters much younger, still unwed – though Annabella's been betrothed since she was four. But my faither's well able to provide for me,' he added, 'whatever the old – lady said.'

'Indeed, yes,' Alys agreed. 'He put you to the college, after all. What are his plans for you? Maister Michael, who will be my good-brother, is to take on management of his father's coalheugh once he is wed, a great responsibility.'

'Aye, so he wrote me. We'd thought of the law,' said Lowrie, his head turned away. 'Anything but Holy Kirk. I've no notion to be a priest, and my faither says he'll not make me, not when my brother Alec's doing well at Dunblane.'

'Nor did my husband wish for the priesthood,' she said, and thought for a moment of Gil as she had left him asleep in their curtained bed, warm and satisfied, his jaw dark with stubble. No, not a suitable priest, despite all his learning. And this young man, though of course he was not Gil, seemed more estimable the more she talked to him, *a clene knyght withoute vylony and of a gentil strene of fader syde and moder syde.* 'The law is a good trade.'

'It's a way to win a living,' said Lowrie.

They rode in silence for half a mile or so, during which Socrates started an argument with a cow-herd's dog and discovered it had friends; Tam beat them off with his whip, and Socrates made a dignified retreat to his previous position under Luke's horse's girth.

'So why are we out here, mistress?' Lowrie asked suddenly. 'Maister Gil never said aught about inspecting these two properties. Does it relate to the old dame's death?'

'It does,' she answered, hoping this was true. 'It – it arose from something John Sempill said, when I visited his wife.'

'Him again.' Lowrie frowned. 'That was right odd, him having the wrong property in mind. He and the old dame must have been taking in one another's rents for months.'

'It is strange,' she agreed. 'Where are the two properties? Can we see them from here?'

'The road-end for Balgrochan's just yonder,' said Lowrie's man Sim. He pointed to a track which led up the hillside towards a group of low cottages. 'And the other's no more than a couple o mile further, at the foot o yonder glen, see? We'll get a good mouthful o Balgrochan ale within half an hour.'

'So what is it we want?' Lowrie persisted. 'Willie Logan the grieve can tell us most things, I've no doubt, but is there anyone else we should bid him send for?'

'Likely not.' She took a moment to arrange her thoughts into Scots. 'Principally I wish to find out about where the Ballencleroch rents go, as you say, and what they are, and who is in charge, and what—' She bit her lip, and then went on, 'what trouble there might be on the property. But it seems foolish to come all the way out here and not check the other place as well.'

Lowrie looked warily at her.

'Ride onto the place and ask what the rents are?' he said. 'What – where will that get you, apart from hunted off the ground wi a pitchfork? Why does he need to ken the rents?'

She shook her head.

'We're looking for anything out of place. I'm – my husband suspects that—'

'If Sempill of Muirend's involved,' said Tam over his shoulder, 'I'd say aught Maister Gil suspects is right.'

It was less simple than that, of course. For one, she had not thought of the tenants being Ersche speakers.

'Aye, the whole pack o them,' said the grieve, refilling her beaker. 'Seat yoursels, mistress, Maister Lowrie. This bench here's a good seat, you get a pleasant view o the best land in the shire o Stirling. Aye, there's one or two has enough Scots to get by at the market in Kirkie, but for the most part you'll ha to make do wi me. So ask away, mistress, I'll answer if I can. If ye're a friend o Maister Lowrie's that's enough for me.'

'But is it my faither holds the feu?' Lowrie asked bluntly before Alys could speak. Maister Logan attended to his beaker too, delaying his answer in a way which told Alys the man spent most of his time among his Ersche tenants, and then placed himself at the end of the bench beside them, by the door of his house where hens wandered in and out crooning.

Balgrochan lay some way up the slope of the Campsie hills, so the view was indeed pleasant. The Glazert wound its way down a flat valley, the cattle they had seen grazing were now smaller than John's toy horse, and a lark tossed on the wind above them, its song reaching them in gusts. A man walked purposefully on the track by the river. The far skyline seemed to be the hills of Renfrew and Lanarkshire. Could that be Tinto Hill away to the south-east, Alys wondered? Nearer, two of the Ersche speakers were dragging a broad wooden rake along the ridges of the infield, small birds chirped in the dyke, and several women in loose checked gowns like Ealasaidh's were gossiping by another house door, with covert glances at Alys's riding-dress.

'I'd say no,' the grieve pronounced finally. 'That is, I'd say he does and he doesny.'

'Talk sense, Willie,' invited Lowrie. 'Where do the rents go?'

'Oh, the rents?' repeated Logan. 'If it's the rents you're asking me about, that's easy. They go to the old dame, the widow of your uncle Thomas, maister, your grandsire's brother.'

'So it's her holds the feu?'

'Oh, that I wouldny ken,' Logan peered into the jug of ale, 'for it was your faither let me know I'd to send her the rents and no argument. Three year since, that was, when your uncle Thomas was yet alive.'

Alys glanced at Lowrie, who shook his head, looking blank. Socrates returned triumphant from somewhere, scattering the hens, and sat down at her side.

'And then,' Logan went on, 'I'd a word from the old dame hersel, brought me by the lad that came to fetch the rents, that they were to go to a Lady Magdalen somebody. But since it's still the same fellow that fetches them away, I made no mind. So that's how the rents are, maister. As to the feu, I suppose Livingstone o Craigannet thinks he holds it, since he's gied me instruction on it, but maybe the lady thinks she holds it and all.'

'Was there no taking of sasines?' Alys asked. 'That is why it happens, after all, so that everyone may see who holds the land.'

Logan shrugged.

'No that I recall, mistress. No since the heriot fee was paid, when Maister Lowrie's faither came into the property. Ten year syne, that'd be.'

'And who is it fetches the rents?' she asked. Logan grinned.

'No doubt o that, at least. It's a great long dark fellow, name o Campbell, that turns up just afore the quarter-days.' Alys closed her eyes a moment in resignation. Of course it would be that pair, she thought. 'Mind, times he answers to Euan, times to Neil, but it's aye the same man.'

'Do you know aught of a man called John Sempill?' asked Lowrie. 'Aye, I'll ha more of that ale. It's uncommon good.'

'Sempill?' The grieve considered briefly, then refilled the beaker. 'Is that the man, a cordiner down at Kirkie? No, he's cried Stenhouse. Canny say I've heard of a Sempill, maister.'

'Perhaps at Ballencleroch?' Alys suggested, scratching the dog's ears.

'There's no cordiner at Ballencleroch.' The name sounded different in this man's pronunciation from her own. 'In fact,' Logan divulged, 'there's no as many of any trade at Ballencleroch as there was. The Clachan's like to be deserted if any more folk leaves it.'

'Leaves it?' repeated Lowrie. 'Why? Why are folk leaving?'

'They're saying the Deil's taken up residence in the glen,' Logan said, 'wi smoke and thunder and foul airs, and hellfire flickering at night. There's folk has seen it.'

'What, in Campsie Glen?' said Lowrie incredulously.

'Aye, you may laugh, Maister Lowrie, but my boy Billy and a hantle of friends went to hae a look, you ken what

192

laddies are like, and that's what they seen and all. And one o the deils took a run at them wi a pitchfork, he said, so they fled, the whole pack o them, never stopped running till they came to our house and fell in ahint the door.'

'They had a bad fright, then,' said Alys seriously. 'How old is Billy?'

'Eleven past at Candlemas, and a sensible laddie for the maist part,' said Logan, a little defensively. 'I'd an idea to go mysel by daylight and see what it was that frighted them, but it's been ower busy, what wi lambin-time, and getting the ground ready for the oats, I've never gone yet.'

'When was that?' Lowrie asked. Logan glanced at the sky, and counted on his fingers.

'Six days syne. But whatever it is, it's still there, for the word is, there's another family left the Clachan yesterday, feart to dwell that close to Hell's mouth.'

'Is it really Hell's mouth, mistress?' said Luke.

'What do you think?' asked Alys. He rolled his eyes at her, and after a moment said,

'I think it might no be.'

'Good.'

'But I'm no wanting to take the chance,' he said obstinately.

'Very well. What will you tell the maister, or Maister Gil?'

'What do you plan to do, mistress?' Lowrie asked while Luke digested this.

'What would you do?' she countered. *The Countrey of Straunge Auentures*, she was thinking.

'Go away and get a Trained Band from Stirling. I'm none so sure the five o us can take on what we're like to find up the glen.'

'Six,' she corrected. 'And the dog.'

'Five,' said Lowrie firmly, and Tam echoed the word. Alys nudged her horse to a faster walk and did not reply. 'I wish you'd taken Willie Logan's advice and waited

193

there,' he went on. 'His wife's a decent body, you'd have been fine wi her.'

'She fed us well,' said Alys. 'And the laddie seems truthful enough.'

'I'd agree he gave us the truth as he recalls it,' said Lowrie cautiously, 'but I'd say he's recalling more than maybe happened at the time.'

'Oh, yes, for certain,' agreed Alys.

'You mean there's maybe no a giant?' said Luke, between hope and disappointment.

'I would discount,' said Alys, gathering her reins into one hand to enumerate with the other, 'the flames reaching to the sky, the green devils, the pitchforks.' She paused to recall what else Billy had told them in hesitant Scots as he stood before the company, wriggling in embarrassment at all the attention while his father looked on proudly, ready to cuff him if he thought the boy was being impertinent. Lowrie had questioned him carefully, but some of the details he had extracted were more credible than others.

'The giant's breathing,' Lowrie said now. 'As Luke here says, that's never likely.'

'It isn't a giant,' agreed Alys. He looked at her, startled.

'They heard screaming,' Tam offered. 'And there was black things flying all about like bats by daylight. I heard the laddie say it mysel.'

'Crows,' said Alys firmly. 'Or is it jackdaws which have a cry like that?'

'Oh, is that why you asked about the trees?' Lowrie said.

The track from Balgrochan came round a slight shoulder of the hillside and found itself suddenly in the midst of another huddle of cottages, the usual low structures of field stones and turf. To their left a burn hurried down towards the main valley floor, and on its far bank a bigger house of dressed stone, with several shuttered windows and a wooden door, suggested the property was a wealthy one; up the hill to their right, beyond the cottages, stood a small stone church. A few hens scratched round a gable,

194

and a goat bleated somewhere. A trickle of smoke rose against the hillside from the thatched roof of the kirk, but otherwise the place appeared deserted. Alys sat her horse and looked about her, while the servants drew together and Luke crossed himself. Socrates raised his head, sniffing.

'The kirk?' Lowrie suggested. 'Sir Richie would likely stay longer than the rest.'

'But where have they all gone?' wondered Alys. 'I am surprised none of them have taken refuge at Balgrochan.'

Sim had dismounted, giving his reins to his companion, and now ducked past the leather curtain at the nearest house door and peered inside.

'Taken the cooking pot and the blankets,' he reported, emerging, 'but no the bench or the creepie-stools. I'd say they was hoping to come back. They've never taken the roof-trees, after all.'

Alys nodded. It still seemed odd to her, though it was completely natural to Gil, that the tenant of such a place by custom supplied his own roof-timbers; if the little house still had its roof, the tenant hoped to return.

'Let us seek out the priest,' she said. 'Perhaps he can tell us what he knows.'

Like the biggest house, the kirk was constructed of dressed stone, in this case a grey and fawn coloured free-stone with prominent chisel-marks. She studied it carefully as they walked round to the low west door, but could not recognize any work-hand she knew. Little surprise in that, she reflected, the building seemed fifty years old or more. Narrow unglazed windows gave no view of the interior. Lowrie tried the door as she reached it, but it did not budge.

'Barred,' he said, and hammered on the planks with the pommel of his dagger. 'Sir Richie! Are you within? It's Lowrie Livingstone here!'

There was a long pause. Then a faint, quavering voice floated out to them.

'Come here till I see you first, maister.'

Lowrie, raising his eyebrows, stepped round the corner of the little building, to where he might be seen from the nearest window.

'I'm no alone,' he said. 'I've a lady wi me, and four men and a dog. What's amiss here, Sir Richie?'

'A lady?' There was another pause, and then the bar behind the door thumped and rattled into its corner. The door opened a crack, and a wary eye peered out at them. 'What sort o a lady? Where are ye, Maister Lowrie?'

'A Christian lady,' said Alys reassuringly. She bent to find her purse, under the skirts of her riding-dress, and drew out her beads. Clasping the cross on the end of the string, she smiled at the eye. 'We're no threat, sir priest.'

'Aye.' The door opened further, and the priest stepped back. He was a small man, spare and elderly, one hand at his pectoral cross, a stout cudgel dangling from the other wrist. 'Come away in, then, till I bar the door again,' he ordered them, in that quavering voice.

The little building was shadowy inside, the narrow windows admitting little light and the glow of the peat fire against the north wall helping little. Seated on the wall-bench, Alys said with sympathy,

'Your parish is near empty, Sir Richie. What's amiss, then?'

'Oh, Mistress Mason.' Sir Richie shook his head. 'Sic a thing as you never heard o. My folk are all feared the Bad Yin himsel has taken up residence in the glen.' He waved the cudgel northward. Socrates looked up briefly, his eyes catching the light, and returned to his inspection of a distant corner. The men drew closer together. 'They've all run off to stay wi kin in one place or another down Strathblane.'

'It's true, then?' said Luke, crossing himself. The old man shook his head.

'I couldny say for sure, my son, but it's awfy like it, and what's worse, this very day hardly an hour since there was another great howling, like wild beasts it was, away up the glen, I could hear it from here. So I barred myself within the kirk, and I've been asking Our Lady and St Machan for their protection. Maybe that's who sent you,' he added, brightening.

'Have you never been to look yoursel?' Lowrie asked. 'Tell us what's happening. When did it begin?'

It had begun in early December, when a shepherd on the hillside had reported hearing noises from one of the offshoots of the main glen, half a mile upstream from the church.

'Digging, he said, and scraping. And when he went closer, and called to find out who was at work, he heard a groaning and a howling like wild beasts, just the same as the day.'

'Did he not speak to the folk at the House?' Lowrie demanded. 'Surely he got a hunt up to deal wi beasts? Was it a wolf, or a wildcat?'

'There's nobody dwells in the House the now,' protested Sir Richie, defensive of his parishioner, 'and though they got a hunt thegither about St Lucy's Day they came back, saying they'd all heard the sounds and it was like no canny sort of beast whatever, and they'd never gone close enough to see it.'

Lowrie grunted. Alys said,

'And then what happened?'

Another man, pursuing a strayed goat about Epiphany, had followed it up the burn and into the foot of the same side valley.

'And there he smelled smoke, and then he saw flames, and two fiends, and they were making the groaning and howling,' Sir Richie assured them, 'so the hunt was right to turn back, maister, you can see.'

'Aye,' said Lowrie, unconvinced.

'That was near four months ago,' said Alys. 'Has there been nothing more?'

Sir Richie shook his head.

'There's been all sorts, mistress. Times we've all heard the cries they make. Why, at Candlemas itself, when Jockie Clerk and I opened up the kirk to say Prime afore the first

Mass, we both heard the fiends howling and groaning, and so did the folk that turned out for the Mass and all.' He swallowed hard. 'I took the cross from the altar, and we brought that and the candles to the door, and I, I bade them begone in the name o the Blessed Trinity, and there was sic a laughing and shrieking as you never did hear, and, and, well, it never worked, for they were there again a day or two after.'

'But have you told nobody?' Lowrie demanded. 'Your bishop, your landlord? Who's the feu superior?'

'Where do the rents go?' Alys asked. Socrates padded back to put his chin on her knee, and she scratched his ears.

The rents, it seemed, were collected by the same man as visited Balgrochan, every quarter for the last year or two; but only yesterday, said Sir Richie earnestly, the feu superior had paid them a call.

'Sempill of Muirend?' she said. Lowrie glanced sharply at her, but the priest nodded.

'Aye, aye, that's the man. And I tellt him the tale entire, and showed him how the Clachan's deserted, and he rode off, swearing to put matters right.' Did he so? thought Alys sceptically. 'Indeed I thought when I heard your horses it was to be him returning, maybe wi the Archbishop or the like.'

'So what's to do, maister?' asked one of Lowrie's men from the shadows.

'We go up the glen to see what's what,' said Alys promptly.

'Oh, no, we don't, mistress!' said Lowrie. 'We'll go. You'll stay here, if you please, wi Sir Richie.'

'Nonsense,' she said. 'This is my adventure, I don't expect you to—'

'We'll ha enough to do facing fiends frae Hell,' said Tam rather nervously, 'let alone worrying over keeping you safe.'

'I can keep myself safe,' she said.

'No, no, madam,' protested the old priest, 'much better you stay here. Indeed I'd as soon you all stayed here, or else left me and went to bring back a greater number and a great retinue of clerks as well—'

Alys stood by the door of the little kirk, Socrates at her side, and watched the men out of sight. Sir Richie had insisted on blessing each of them with holy water and a tremulous prayer, which had done very little for Luke's spirits; she had considered asking for the boy to stay with her, and discarded the idea. He would be little help for her next move.

'I am concerned for the horses,' she said to the old man. 'I'll just go as far as the gate and make sure of them.'

'But, daughter,' he began from inside the church, but she slipped away, round the corner of the building towards the gate, the dog almost glued to her skirts. The men had scrambled over the tumbledown drystone wall of the kirkyard, but she was not certain she could do the same in her riding-dress before Sir Richie could catch up with her. Through the gate she cast a cursory glance towards the horses, which were standing peacefully enough in the shade of one of the cottages. The taller beasts were making inroads on the edge of its turf roof. Turning right, bending low, she scurried along the wall and then down into the hollow of the burn where it chattered and bubbled among dark smooth stones. Crossing it by the plank bridge she had seen from the door of the kirk, she set off up the glen after the men, Socrates at her heel, oblivious to the faint cries from behind her.

It was a lovely setting, she thought, looking warily around, with the spring just beginning to breathe across it. On this side of the burn a grassy path led upstream, with occasional tall trees to shade it. On the other, above the church, was a patch of well-tended woodland. Beyond, on both sides, the flanks of the Campsies rose, smooth and grassy, dotted with sheep and lambs. Some of the trees showed green buds, a few small flowers gleamed in the grass, and birds chirped and flitted busily among the branches. Sir Richie had stopped calling after her, and apart from the sheep bleating to their young any other sound was swamped by the noise of the water. There was certainly no sound of fiendish laughter or wild activity.

She went carefully, paying attention all about her, relishing this moment of freedom. Now she was married she rarely went unattended anywhere, and it was good to have no complaining servant at her back, though perhaps, she thought, one might be glad of company in a few minutes. Whatever had been happening further upstream?

The dark stones in the burn had been smoothed by the water, but were the same colour as the jagged rocks of a miniature cliff beneath the clasping roots of a hawthorn bush, where a thick vein of some lighter mineral showed gleams of green and rust. The path under her feet had been much trampled, with sign which went both ways. When did it last rain here? she wondered, studying the prints. The dog, sniffing where she looked, raised his head and stared up the glen, his ears pricked.

The little valley narrowed, curved to the right, then to the left. She paused by a scatter of rougher stones, and bent to lift one which caught her eye, turning it this way and that in the light. Socrates came to see what she was looking at. Satisfied, she pushed his nose out of the way and found her purse again, tucked the scrap of stone into it, and drew out the dagger she had extracted from Gil's kist last night. Leaving its sheath in the purse she shook her skirts straight and moved cautiously onward, the haft of the little weapon comforting in her hand. She was fairly sure now of what they would find, but if it came to an argument with the occupiers, it might help to be armed.

The burn beside her widened into a pool with a noisy waterfall at its head. The bank they followed rose, and the path swung away from the pool to skirt the waterfall. Beyond it she could see a wall of dark jagged rock, overhung with ivy and leaning bushes. Moving carefully, she climbed to the crest of the fall and paused warily in the shadow of some trees, studying the land. Socrates waited beside her, looking up at her face.

This was where the valley forked; the main burn swung to her right, a smaller burn tumbled in from the other side. There was no sign of flames, only a thread of smoke rising up somewhere on her left, but there was a sense of threat, the feeling of being watched, although nothing stirred but some black birds sailing against the brisk clouds, croaking in annoyance, and smaller singing birds hopping in the trees above her. She drew breath, told herself firmly not to be foolish, and moved forward to go and explore the new valley.

'Both dead when we found them,' said Lowrie.

'The poor souls.' Alys crossed herself, gazing at the scene, then knelt to close the remaining eye of the body nearest her. 'What can have happened? I think this one must have fallen into the furnace, but the other?'

'Stabbed,' said Tam. 'He was the luckier, I'd say.'

She nodded without looking up, biting her lips to keep the tears back, and touched the undamaged portion of the dead man's face and neck with care, silently promising him her prayers.

Across the hollow the little furnace was still smoking, occasional flames leaping from the charcoal which was exposed where the clay and stones had crumbled. There was what looked like a crucible tilted among the debris, with crushed rock sintered into a lump; the big leather bellows were scorched beyond repair, a pair of tongs lay where they had been flung down, a patch of clay had been smoothed and grooved for pouring whatever should have run from the crucible. The other dead man lay on his face, sprawled, his hands out before him. A narrow slit in the back of his hooded leather sark told of his end. There was a smell, of blood, of burnt flesh and hair, of mud.

Her escort stood bareheaded and awkward in the presence of death. Luke was now openly weeping. Socrates sat at her elbow, subdued by the mood of the group.

'But what has happened here?' she asked, sitting back on her heels. 'Have they fought one another? Was there a third man? I think,' she tested the rigid neck again, 'he is dead perhaps three hours or a little more.'

'I've made out four men a'thegither,' said Lowrie's man Frank, gesturing at the trampled earth. 'It's no that clear, you'll understand, but I've saw both their marks, and two others. Three o them's all over the place here, one above the other, they've been here days I'd say or even longer. The last one's just on the top o the rest, and him, well, it's like he's been fighting, the marks go all ways and the heels is right dug in, you can see where he jumped aside to get this fellow.'

'Is this what you expected, mistress?' Lowrie was trying for a normal tone of voice. 'The mining? I take it they're getting silver?'

'I – yes,' she admitted. 'I wasn't certain, you understand, but it seemed the best explanation. When I saw the rocks in the burn I thought it more likely. I saw a silver mine once before,' she explained, 'in France, in just such rock as this.'

'A siller mine?' said Sim hopefully. 'Is there like to be siller lying about for the taking?'

'We should check,' said Lowrie. 'But mind it belongs to the Crown, man, keep your light fingers off it if you see anything. And keep back from that furnace, it may no be yellow any longer but it's still ower warm.'

'Yes, we must check,' said Alys, getting resolutely to her feet and looking round. Sim unwound his plaid and laid it over the dead man with care, hiding the ruined face. Frank followed his example to cover the other corpse. 'Show me these marks,' she said to him.

With an indulgent air he pointed out the traces of the different footprints, not easy to see in the rough broken stone underfoot, more readily picked out in the muddy patches near the burn. When she found another set of marks near the shelter he looked at her with more respect.

'Aye, that's number fower,' he agreed, 'he's got a narrower heel than these ithers, and his toes is more like the shape o Tam's or Luke's and all. These ither three all had their shoon frae the same place, and it wasny hereabouts, I'd say.'

Alys nodded, gazing about her.

'So these two were about their work,' she said, 'and this man with the different feet came and fought with them. One fell in the fire, and the stranger stabbed the other.'

'Aye, or they fought among the three o them,' the man offered. 'Then he made off.'

'I wonder how far he has gone,' she said. 'And where is the other man with these shoes? Could they be out there?'

They were only a few yards from the main valley, but because of the way this smaller burn twisted, they could neither see nor hear the other watercourse. The dell where they stood must once have been pretty, with little white flowers and hawthorn bushes under a ring of taller trees in which jackdaws commented busily on the strangers below them. Now it was scarred by the industry of the dead men and their companion; there was their small shelter of bent branches and hides, a stack of green wood cut for burning, the broken furnace now cooling rapidly, its spoil mixed with broken and crushed rock all about. Not far upstream a bigger spoil heap was smothering the aconites, and a low dark hole in the rocky bank spoke of a mine adit. What did the folk at the mine by Carluke call it? Oh, yes, an *ingaun ee*.

'What were they doing here?' Luke wondered, sniffing. 'Why would you break the stone so small, mistress?'

'To get the silver out,' Lowric said before she could answer. He bent and lifted a scrap of rock, turning it to the light as Alys had done on the path. There was a small gleam from one angle.

'Oh, I see!' said his man Sim. 'And then they melt it in the furnace, and catch it in thon dish in its midst. That's right clever. I never kent that was how you got siller.'

'Was that the flames they all seen?'asked Tam, who was poking about the little shelter. 'How about the howling and the fiends?'

'Could two men work and two pretend to be fiends?' Alys wondered. And this poor soul's injuries, she realized grimly, would explain the howling Sir Richie heard this morning.

'That's what I thought,' admitted Tam. He straightened up. 'But there wasny four o them, mistress. There was three, for there's three scrips here, and three bedrolls, and no sign there's ever been a fourth dwelling here, the neat way it's all fitted thegither.'

'So where is the third?' Lowrie looked about.

'There's four sets o prints,' said Frank.

'Aye, and what do we do wi these two, maister?' asked Sim. He clapped Luke on the shoulder. 'Here, laddie, it comes to all o us soon or late. No sense in grieving for a man you never met.'

'I never kent eyes would do that,' Luke said, wiping his nose on his sleeve, and sniffed again.

'Take your dagger,' Alys said in some sympathy, 'and go cut some hazels to make hurdles, then we may carry them down to the kirk. Maybe Frank would go with you?' She raised her eyebrows at Lowrie, who nodded briefly. 'Tam, what else have you found?' She crossed to the shelter, and bent to peer in. Above their heads the jackdaws rose and swirled, commenting indignantly on the extra movements.

'Aye, well, they've been snug enough in here. Their blankets, a kettle for cooking, a couple lanterns—'

'They would need the lanterns in the mine,' Lowrie suggested. 'No tools?'

'How neat it all is. Is there nothing to tell us who sent them?'

'No that I can see.' Tam straightened up to look at Alys,

but his gaze went beyond her. 'Here, where's the dog away to?'

She turned, in time to see the lean grey shape hurtling up the eastward slope away from the burn. Alarmed, she called him but he continued, and vanished among the bushes. Around her the men drew their weapons and scanned the valley sides, all three poised for action. Luke and Frank had gone the other way, she realized, westward, and as the thought reached her there was a terrified yell from the crest of the slope, and an outbreak of snarling.

'Socrates! Hold!' she shouted, and picked up her skirts, intending to follow the dog.

'Wait here!' ordered Lowrie, running past her. Tam and Sim were already part way up the slope, moving cautiously, peering through the branches for the sources of the snarling argument above them. Lowrie, whinger drawn, caught up and passed them. She stood anxiously staring as they worked their way up among the new leaves, trying to make out what Socrates was doing. His low, continuous growl told her he had trapped someone or something, but she thought he was uncertain what to do with his catch. A wolf? Surely not, this close to Glasgow, she told herself. A man? Is this who was watching earlier?

'Stand still,' said Lowrie sharply. A man, then. 'I said stand still! Tam, Sim, get his arms, if he'll not listen to me. Mistress, will you call the dog?'

It was less simple than that, of course. In the end Alys had to climb the slope to adjudicate between the dog and the three men. Socrates gave up his prisoner with reluctance, and watched jealously while the newcomer was escorted back down to the dell.

He was no more than a boy, she realized as she slithered after them, younger than Luke. He was dressed in shabby clothing of strange cut, jerkin and hose and a jack with holes at the elbows, and must have been hunting for the pot; a sling hung at his belt, and he had two coneys in a bag on his back. His boots were broad and round of heel and toe. He looked terrified, but when he saw the two

205

silent forms in the hollow he checked in horror, and then flung himself forward with a cry. Lowrie dived after him, but was not in time to prevent him pulling back the checked folds of Sim's plaid and revealing what the intense heat of the furnace had done to the dead man's face.

'*Vati!*' he said, and choked, and heaved drily. '*Ah, mein vati!*'

'High Dutch, I think,' said Alys, overwhelmed with pity. 'He says that is his father.'

'I've no tongues other than Latin,' said Lowrie, 'and I doubt this laddie – *loquerisne latine*?' There was no reaction; the boy had staggered back a few steps, and was staring at his father's corpse, still gagging. 'Either of you speak High Dutch?'

'No me, maister,' said Sim, and Tam shook his head. Alys mustered the few words of Low Dutch she knew, and put a hand on the prisoner's wrist.

'*Ik* Alys,' she said, pointing at herself. '*Du?*'

He stared at her, as if returning from a great distance, then looked round at the men in fear. Lowrie shook his head and made a calming gesture with one hand, but the boy shivered.

'*Du?*' Alys repeated.

It took some time, during which Luke and Frank returned with armfuls of withies and began to construct a couple of hurdles, looking askance at the boy. His name was Berthold Holtzmann, the same as his father. Numbly, he identified the man under the other plaid, stroking the cold brow: his uncle Heini. They were here to mine silver, but he could not or would not understand Alys's attempts to ask who had brought them here. He was clearly terrified about his own fate, and she could not find the words to reassure him.

'When did he leave here?' Lowrie asked. That took a lot of sign language and pointing, but eventually the boy pointed at the sun and tracked it back to where it had been when he left. 'Five, maybe six hours,' Lowrie estimated.

'And you thought these two were dead three or four hours. This laddie's been fortunate.'

'You think it was not him who slew his uncle,' Alys stated. He looked at her.

'I think he's the third man living in the shelter,' he said. 'There's been another here the day, by what Frank sees, and this one touched both corps without a qualm. And their shoon came from the same soutar, all three pair. I think we seek the fourth man.' He looked again at the sky. 'We should leave here. We've to ride back to Glasgow, after all, wi an extra—'

'Glasgow?' repeated the prisoner. He was sitting shivering on the ground now, one of the blankets from the shelter wrapped about him, clutching his beads like a lifeline.

'Aye, Glasgow. You know that word, do you?' Lowrie said. The boy looked up at him, apparently trying to read his expression; then he looked at his father's body again, bent his head meekly and nodded. Tears fell on the rough wool of the blanket.

Chapter Ten

'So give me the tale again,' said Otterburn. 'Were you alone? I find that hard to believe.'

'I've no doubt of that,' said Gil politely. The clerk Walter glanced up briefly, and down again at his work. Gil thought the man was smiling. Himself, he had little to smile at. It was nearing Sext, and the day was going much too fast.

On last leaving the Castle, not really that long since, he had found Luke sound asleep beside Cato in the kitchen behind the House of the Mermaiden, the pair of them curled up on a straw mat like a pair of puppies. Helped by a disapproving dog he had roused the boy, steered him homeward, and eventually fallen into his own bed. By the time he woke, the sun was pouring in at the windows, Alys's side of the mattress was cold, and no one in the household appeared to know where she was. Ealasaidh McIan seemed to want to talk to him, but he had excused himself to his duties.

'You and – one other? decided in the midnight that you'd find Dod Muir in his own kist,' said Otterburn. 'Then you set up a shouting match wi the rest o the folk on Clerk's Land, and bade the Watch rouse me. Have I that right?'

Gil bit back the first reply that rose to his lips, and after a moment said, with formality,

'As I told you last night, Provost, I searched Dod Muir's premises in pursuit of information concerning the person who killed Dame Isabella. I found Muir himself while I was doing that, and dropped the lid o the kist from surprise. That was what roused the neighbours.'

Otterburn glared at him, but rose, lifting his tablets from the table before him.

'Come and we'll look at Muir,' he said. 'Assuming it wasny you put him in there, you need to see what we found when we got him out his kist.'

'I'm grateful,' said Gil, following the man down the forestair from his lodging. 'Provost,' he added quietly, as they reached the centre of the courtyard, far enough from the various passing servants to go unheard. Otterburn swung round to stare at him. 'How well are you acquaint wi Madam Xanthe?'

The narrow gaze sharpened. Then the other man nodded briefly and moved on, but when he next spoke his manner was less curt.

'It's as well I seen the man last night,' he said. 'It's clear enough he'd had time to set and soften again, he'd been dead since some time on,' he counted, 'this is Saturday, must ha been Thursday. We took him out as soon as it was light, for I want to get on and get the quest on him dealt wi as soon as we've sorted the old dame this morning, and here he is.' He stepped into the shelter where both corpses were laid out, nodding to the man on guard, and pulled one of the linen cloths back from the form it shrouded.

Muir was a small man, dark-haired and spare of build. He had been stripped and washed, and the greenish tinge of decomposition could clearly be seen spreading across his hairy belly. There was no mark on his chest or abdomen; Gil bent and peered the length of the body, holding his breath, but could recognize nothing like a death-wound. Conscious of Otterburn's gaze, he walked round the bier, lifted the scarred and calloused hands to study them, turned the head to search for a wound.

'Ah,' he said, as the bones of the skull shifted like gravel under his fingers. 'That's it. Was there any mark on his hands? Had he fought? Was there aught under his nails?'

'Nothing,' said Otterburn. 'I looked.'

No huntsman, Gil thought, liked to take another's word for the sign he found, but in this case he had no choice.

'He's been struck down,' he said slowly, 'likely from behind, by a man he knew.' He felt again at the crushed bones of the head, and ruffled through the short locks to expose the scalp. 'The weapon must ha been a heavy thing, but maybe padded, for the skin's not broken.' He grimaced. 'The man's workshop has any number o mells. Indeed, there was one laid on the bench, a monstrous great thing.' He demonstrated the size of the mell head as he recalled it, and Otterburn nodded.

'I sent a couple o the lads round to take a look,' he said, 'and they cam back wi one like that. They'd a look round, found the other fellow's scrip that was lying in the loft, nothing else untoward. You're welcome to take one o them and get a look yoursel,' he added, 'but I wanted the place checked afore the neighbours stripped it.'

'I'd sooner question the neighbours themselves,' Gil admitted. 'What about this fellow's clothes? Was there aught useful on him?'

'You could say so.' Otterburn looked modestly triumphant. 'Nothing to speak of in his purse, but in the bottom o the kist – well, come and see.'

Back in his lodging, he made for the great kist by the wall. Walter looked up again as he unlocked it, but did not speak.

'We need a stronger place to keep the likes o this,' Otterburn pronounced, delving under the lid. Gil repressed a shudder, thinking of the way he had put his hand on Dod Muir's cold face doing the same thing. 'Aye, here it is. Now what d'ye make o that, maister?'

It was a small column of brass, as long as Gil's thumb, surprisingly heavy. One end was splayed like the top of a fence-post, as if from repeated blows of a hammer; the other –

'Ah!' he said, as James Third leapt briefly in the light. 'This is what we were – this is one of the dies they've been using.' He tilted it against the light, so that the image came and went. 'Is it the first one, the worn one? The king has no ringlets that I can see.'

'So I thought,' agreed the Provost. 'And it was in the bottom o the kist, like I said.'

'What, just lying there? Had it fallen out of his clothing or his purse, maybe?'

'I wouldny ha said so,' Otterburn considered. 'Maybe as if he'd been holding it, or the like, when he was struck down.'

'He'd ha dropped it, surely.' Gil looked at the object. 'I'd think it's been hidden on purpose along wi the corp, or – no, for it would be found when the corp was found, and that wouldny ha been much longer.'

'He's a bit ripe already,' Otterburn agreed. 'So's the old dame.'

'So why was it in there? I wonder what the man kept in that kist for usual? Was there anything under him?'

'A blanket wi the moth. And no, nothing under the blanket, we looked.' He glanced at the window. 'Here, I've the quest on the two o them called as soon as dinner's done wi. If you're wanting to question any of the neighbours afore that you'd best get about it. They're down in the cells, you'd best speak to Andro about it.'

Gil nodded, hefting the brass die in his hand. 'I'll take this with me, if I may. I'll not lose it.'

Locating the captain of the guard, who was wrestling in his chamber with accounts overdue for the last quarter-day and very glad to be interrupted, Gil requested time with the prisoners, separately.

'What, one at a time?' Andro said, frowning. 'Aye, well, I suppose it can be done. You can get them up here, if you want, it's secure enough.' He glanced out into the guard-room, where several men were sitting about playing dice or arguing about football. 'Who d'ye want first? Jack! Jimmy! Away down and fetch that Neil Campbell up here to Maister Cunningham.'

'Are they held separately?' Gil asked. 'They've had no time to agree their tale, have they?'

'No on my watch,' said Andro, pushing his papers unceremoniously aside. He tramped out into the guard-room, returning with a jug of ale and two beakers. 'Hae a seat, maister. Jack, you gomeril, I tellt ye *Neil* Campbell, no *Noll* Campbell.'

'I tellt ye,' said one of the men escorting the whitesmith.

'Well, it sounds the same,' argued the other, propelling the prisoner into the chamber. 'Right, you, stand there and behave.'

'I'll take this one for now,' said Gil, rearranging his thoughts. 'I'll see Neil Campbell next.' He looked up at the surly face of Noll Campbell, and held up the brass die. 'Where's the other one, Campbell?'

The man's gaze went to the bright thing, and he frowned briefly, and then said,

'What other? What is it?'

'Oh, I think you know well enough,' said Gil. He turned the die over, making it appear and disappear between his fingers as if it was a coin. 'There should be two. In fact I think there are four, because the first pair wore out. When did you cast this one? Does Maister Hamilton and the rest of the guild ken you're working in brass as well as white metals? I'm sure they'll be interested, since it means you're at default in the guild fees.'

'I don't know what you're talking about,' said the prisoner, scowling, trying to pretend he was not watching the brass pillar slithering through Gil's fingers. 'Nor I don't know why I was flung in the jail last night, it was never me found Dod Muir dead in his own kist. I had nothing to do with it.'

'So you say,' said Gil agreeably, and set the die on the table. 'No, I'd sooner hear why you put your cousin Neil to sleep in Dod Muir's loft. Why should he not sleep in your house?'

The whitesmith shrugged.

212

'He never has. He has aye slept at Dod Muir's, him or Euan, when they are in Glasgow.'

'Why?' Gil asked, curious.

'We have but the one bed, it's ower narrow, and,' with a flash of wry humour, 'he would not be fitting in the cradle.'

'Where does your prentice sleep?'

'Prentice? I've no prentice. I can barely support mysel, I've no work to spare for a daft laddie.'

'And your sister has no room either?' Gil suggested.

'What has our kin's arrangements to do wi you?'

'You speak civil to Maister Cunningham,' said Andro, pouring ale for himself and Gil. 'Or we'll learn you some manners.'

'What brings Neil to Glasgow, anyway?' Gil continued, ignoring this as much as the prisoner did. 'Who is he working for?'

'How would I be knowing that? He runs errands for one or another, so far as I can tell, there is no pride in him. You can ask at him for yoursel.'

'Oh, I will, be sure of it. So if you've no prentice,' Gil said, twirling the little column of brass round a forefinger, 'who was it was taken up for theft the evening the Provost's men searched the toft?'

'No idea,' said Campbell firmly. 'It was just someone was passing, it was them decided he was my prentice, I never said a—'

'Oh, you did so, you sliddery leear!' exclaimed the man on his right. 'For I was there, it was me took up the fellow when he would ha run off, and I heard all you said!'

'Did you now?' said Gil with interest. 'Tell me more, man.' And why did the tale not reach me before this, he wondered. I suppose because none of us asked.

'Aye, speak up, Jack,' said Andro, sitting forward. 'Taken up for theft, wasn't he? What like was the fellow, and what had he thieved?'

'Aye but he hadny,' objected the other man. 'Thieved anything, I mean. Sir.'

213

'You be quiet, Jimmy,' ordered Andro. 'Jack, let's ha the tale from you. Start at the beginning. Where was this thief?'

'Wasny a thief,' muttered Jimmy. Jack kicked him on the ankle behind the prisoner's back, and said diffidently,

'He was in this fellow's forge.' Gil nodded encouragement. 'See, this fellow and his wife was at their meat, and we'd about got to their door when we spied a man in the shadows in the forge. Right by the house, sir,' he elucidated in Andro's direction. His officer nodded. 'So I shouted, and he started to run off, and we laid a hold o him, and he had a bundle on him he wasny keen we should see, and when we shook it out, well—' He paused for effect.

'Well?' said Andro irritably. 'Get on wi't, man!'

'Naught but a heap o scrap metal,' said Jack. The prisoner scowled at him. Gil lifted the brass die from the table.

'Metal like this?' he asked. 'Was it brass, or pewter, or what?'

'Well, it was all kind o yellow-like,' said Jack doubtfully. 'But maybe no so yellow as that. But,' he went on, regaining his narrative, 'I ken even wee bits o metal is valuable, for they can melt it down and cast it all again like new, so we tellt him he was charged wi theft, at which he said, No he never, his maister gave him it. And when we asked who was his maister, he said this man here that was eating his supper in his own house. Save that he wasny by then,' he admitted, 'for he was out at his door wanting to ken what was afoot, were you no, you?' He kicked the prisoner, who mumbled some sort of agreement to this statement.

'So it was the other fellow said he was the prentice,' said Gil thoughtfully. 'Who is he, then, Noll Campbell? You don't earn enough to keep a prentice, but you let this man claim that's what he was, and agreed you'd given him the scrap brass. Who is he? If you're dealing honestly, man, you've nothing to hide.'

'He's no dealing honestly,' said Jimmy derisively. 'He wouldny ken honest dealing if it kicked him in the cods.'

214

'What's the fellow's name?' Gil repeated, watching Campbell's face.

'I've never a notion,' the prisoner said. 'It's just some chiel I was selling the scrap metal to. My wee furnace will not be hot enough to melt brass, see, it needs a bigger fire than I can raise.'

'What did he gie you for it?' Gil asked, as something wriggled at the back of his mind. What had been said just now? The man before him hesitated. 'A leather sack o false coin, maybe?'

'Nothing o the sort!'

'So you just let him away. And you never got his name,' said Andro rather grimly to his minions. They looked sideways at one another, and shook their heads. 'Aye, well, the garderobe's needing cleared again. Did ye at the least get a description?'

A little argument, and some harsh words from Andro, produced an account of a man of more than average height, between twenty and twenty-five, wearing a blue bonnet and a jerkin of green, brown or possibly dark red, boots or shoes, and no plaid. Oddly, they were agreed on that point. Gil frowned at them, still trying to get hold of the elusive idea at the back of his mind. Something else he needed to ask about, something reported along with the apprentice who was no apprentice.

'The fire,' he said, as it suddenly emerged. 'There was a fire in the yard, I think.'

'Aye, that's right,' agreed Jack. 'Away too close to the thatch.'

'Which I never set,' said Campbell resentfully. 'None of my doing it was.'

'What was in the fire?' Gil asked. Jack shrugged.

'Kale stalks, making a rare stink, a few scraps o wood and shavings. Some rags. Someone burning a bit rubbish, but away too close to the thatch, so we fined the lot of them.'

'Aye, you did,' said the prisoner sourly.

'What kind of rags?' Gil asked.

'Bits o blue velvet?' The two men looked at one another again, and Jimmy nodded. 'Looked like someone's old livery, by what you could still see,' Jack went on. 'There'd been a fair bit o stuff, there was quite a heap of ashes. I'm surprised this lot hadny taken it down the rag market, the way they complained about a wee bit fine that deserved them well.'

'So where did Alan and Nicol go?' Gil said to Campbell. The man's eyes widened in shock, but he made no reply. 'Are they staying wi the man Miller?'

'Are they, then?' demanded Jack, and shook Campbell's arm so that his chains clanked. 'Come on, speak up, answer when ye're asked!'

'No! No, I—' Campbell began. 'I don't know – I don't know what you're talking about,' he finished as the shaking stopped. 'I never – I've no notion who you're on about.'

'The men who wore the blue velvet livery,' said Gil. 'Whose kin are they? The Provost is right, I think, half Scotland is kin to someone on Clerk's Land. There were three of them when they left Dame Isabella's household. Where are they now, Campbell? Why did they come to your toft for help?'

'I don't know who you're on about,' repeated Campbell. Gil eyed him, and changed the subject.

'What happened when you had words wi Dame Isabella at her window on Thursday morning?'

'Eh?' The prisoner stepped back, crossing himself, his manacles clanking, and was hauled forward by his guards. 'What are you – I never – it wasny me!' he stammered.

'It wasny you what?' Gil studied him. 'Wasny you spoke wi her? Wasny you slew her? Wasny you at her window? You were seen,' he said, stretching the point a little. 'What happened to the velvet purse of money? The leather one you hid in Forveleth's plaid, but there's a velvet purse wi gold braid missing, and it was last heard of just before you reached that window, Campbell.'

'I never laid a finger on any sic thing!' protested the prisoner. 'I never saw any purse o blue velvet!'

'So how d'ye ken it was blue?' demanded Andro.

'Who was the other man?' Gil asked. 'Was it you stepped into the old woman's chamber and slew her, or was it you kept her talking while he took a mell to her?'

The manacles clanked again as Campbell first crossed himself and then made the horns against the evil eye, staring wildly at Gil.

'I never,' he said hoarsely. 'It wasny me, I never!'

They got no further answers from the man, only continued denials, and after a few more attempts Gil ordered him back down to the cells. He thought a look of surprised relief crossed the prisoner's face as he turned away with his escort, as if he had expected other questions which had not been put, but it was too fleeting to be certain.

'And bring up the right Campbell this time,' recommended Andro.

Neil Campbell was a great deal more civil and more forthcoming, but provided little useful information at first.

'Any time I am in Glasgow,' he said earnestly. 'There is room for two in that loft, and little enough in my cousin's house.'

'And when are you in Glasgow?' Gil asked. 'I've not seen you that often.'

The gallowglass shrugged. He had not been manacled, perhaps having been a more biddable prisoner, and stood easily now between the two men of his escort, lanky and dark-haired, innocence shining on his high cheekbones.

'Now and then, just,' he said.

'On what errands?'

'Any I can find. It is my calling, Maister Gil, you ken that, my sword is at anyone's service that will pay me for it.'

'So what errand are you about now?' Gil asked. Neil looked wary.

'I am thinking maybe it is not—' he began. 'Maybe I will not be completing it.'

217

'Why?' Gil asked bluntly.

'Och, it is not possible.'

'Because? What's changed, Neil?'

'Because of all that is happening.'

'Dame Isabella's death, you mean?'

The gallowglass considered this question.

'No,' he said at length. 'I would not say so.'

'Were you working for her? Or was your brother?' Gil added quickly, recalling previous attempts to interrogate these two. 'Philip Sempill thinks you were.'

'Strange, it is, the way these ideas gets about.'

'So what was this errand that you might not complete?'

Neil appeared to make a decision.

'It was for McIan,' he explained. 'McIan of Ardna-murchan, that is, that dwells in Mingary Castle and is lord over all the West.' This was not wholly accurate, Gil knew, but he let it pass. 'I was to take a leather sack of money to him, but it is not in the hands of those that—'

'The leather sack of coin that the Provost holds?' Gil interrupted. 'That was taken from one of Dame Isabella's servants the other night?'

'I would not be knowing of that,' said Neil. 'But it is certain it is no longer with those that were to give it to me.'

'And those were?'

'My cousin,' admitted the gallowglass. 'Or maybe my other cousin, that is Barabal, the wife of the man Saunders.'

'Likely they had it in the house, one or other,' said Andro, 'and planked it in the woman's bundle when they saw our lot coming.'

Gil, who had long since concluded the same thing, merely nodded.

'Have you done this before, you or your brother?' he asked. 'Taken money from here to Mingary, I mean.'

'Maybe,' said Neil cautiously.

'How many times? Last month? The month before?'

'I was carrying a good sum last month,' admitted the gallowglass. 'And before that at the New Year, which was a great trouble, as you might know, what with the weather we were having at that time.'

'I can imagine,' said Gil. 'So who ordered you to fetch this coin to McIan? Was it the man himself, or another?'

'Och, no, it was my kinsman who called me in,' said Neil easily, 'saying he was to send it to Mingary and I would be well paid for the journey. And I was well paid indeed,' he added. 'Sword, helm and hauberk I've had from McIan's own hands, one time or another.'

Gil rubbed at his eyes, considering what he had learned.

'Do you know aught about Dame Isabella's death?' he asked.

'Who?'

'This old dame that's slain on the Drygate,' said Andro. 'You must ha heard o't, the whole of Glasgow's buzzing wi the tale.'

'Has your cousin mentioned it?' Gil asked. Neil shook his head.

'No, no,' he said. 'They would never mention the like in front of me.'

'Why not?' Gil asked casually. The gallowglass opened his mouth to answer, and closed it again, visibly thinking better of his reply. 'So they are involved? Did your kinsman slay her, or was it another man?'

'I would have no knowledge of that,' said the prisoner flatly. 'Why would my kinsman slay her, that was—' he stopped again.

'That was what?'

'That was a stranger to him, so far as I ken,' said the prisoner. Gil did not think this was what he had started to say. He studied the lean dark face before him, wondering how to get past the man's practised evasion.

'Did they say aught about Dod Muir?' he asked.

'No, I – only that they had not seen him yesterday or the day before since.'

'Were you no blate about lying in the man's house, if he was away?' demanded Andro.

219

'I had lain there afore. My kinsman said he had spoken to Dod.'

'Had he, now?' said Gil. 'When was that?'

Neil shrugged.

'He was not saying. I wondered, mind you,' he admitted, 'when I saw that all his gear was lying out, and he had never washed his porridge-pot.'

'Ah, was it you cleaned the crocks?' Gil asked.

Neil nodded. 'Though I would not be touching another man's working graith,' he said earnestly, 'so I never moved any of his knives and that.'

'How tall was Dod Muir, would you say?'

'How tall?' The gallowglass looked startled. 'A wee sprout of a fellow. Well shorter than me.' He looked at his two guards, who were showing signs of boredom. 'No taller than your man here, maybe even a handsbreadth less.'

'As short as that?' Gil considered Jimmy, fully half a head shorter than the gallowglass. 'An easy enough target then, for a bigger man.'

'It was him that was in the kist right enough?' asked Neil. Gil nodded, and the man crossed himself and bent his head briefly, muttering something in Ersche. 'He was quick tempered, so my kinsman said, but he was aye friendly enough to me, and hospitable,' he said after a moment.

As epitaphs go, thought Gil, you could do worse. 'What does your kinsman say about the man Miller?' he asked. 'Does he call him Dusty to his face?'

'To his face? No him!' said the gallowglass, and stopped, mouth open, looking dismayed. There was a short pause, into which Andro said,

'What Miller is that? You're no talking o Maister Millar at St Serf's, are you?'

'No,' said Gil, without taking his eyes off Neil Campbell. 'It's another man entirely, isn't it, Neil? Have you met him?'

'Never,' said Neil firmly.

220

'Don't you want to? How is he involved in all this?'

'How would I be knowing that?'

'Does he strike the coin? Is that where it all comes from?'

'I have no knowledge of that,' said the gallowglass. 'All I did was carry the coin, Maister Gil. There is no knowledge at me of where it came from nor how my kinsman is in the matter.'

'Is that right?' said Gil sceptically. 'He never speaks of it in front of you, he and his wife never discuss it in your hearing?' He considered the man's blank expression. 'Neil, you ken the penalty for making counterfeit coin. It's treason, because it's falsifying the King's image. False coiners are condemned to be hanged, drawn and quartered, and by the time that happens they're like to be glad of it. Better to tell me what you ken, so I can speak for you.'

The narrow face was intent, as some inward battle was fought. Finally the blue glance slid sideways to meet Gil's gaze and the gallowglass said,

'There is little enough that I know.'

'Ah!' said Andro. 'Now we're getting somewhere!'

'Tell me it,' Gil encouraged, ignoring him.

It was little enough, indeed. Neither Neil nor his brother had set eyes on the elusive Miller, though both had heard him named about the toft.

'Feart for him, they are,' said Neil. 'The least wee word fro him, they act on it immediate.'

'Why?' Gil asked. 'What hold does he have over them?'

'I would not be knowing that. But my cousin and his woman were arguing when I came to the house yesterday,' expanded Neil, unstoppable now he had decided to talk, 'and Bethag was saying the same, asking at Noll why was he bound to the man, and Noll bade her close her mouth, she knew nothing of it. He is dwelling down the Gallowgate, I am thinking, maybe outside the port, and they were saying he had been in Clerk's Land on,' he paused to count on his fingers, 'Thursday, would it be? and he was enraged for something, carrying on like Herod so Bethag was saying, and frighted the Saunders' bairns, and wanting Dod Muir to see to something for him, that Dod wouldny, so he . . . killed . . . him,' he said, grinding to a halt as he realized what he had given away. Gil eyed him steadily, and he swallowed in some alarm. 'There was only what the woman was saying,' he protested, 'I never saw it, nor spoke of it with my kinsman! And she never said no more than that, for they saw me at the door and left off their arguing.'

'So you kent he was dead,' said Gil.

'I see why they might be feart for this Miller,' said Andro drily. 'We never lifted the two women, maister, seeing there was all those weans. Will I send out and fetch them in?'

'I'll go out there, I think,' said Gil. 'Likely they'll talk better in their own place. And Neil may come with me to translate if it's needed,' he added kindly. Neil threw him a hunted look.

'Maybe I should staying here,' he said, without much hope. 'No doubt that the captain here would be wishing me still under his eye.'

'Will you no wait for the quest on the old dame?' Andro asked, ignoring this. 'The women will have been cited for the second quest, they might come out to see the whole show, bring the weans and all. We'll ha folk selling hot pies and gingerbread in the court here afore we know where we are.'

'Send one of your men round the crowd wi a hat,' recommended Gil. 'That ought to keep the numbers down. I'll go now, then I might be back in time for the quest.'

Clerk's Land was oddly silent. Even the screaming children were absent, the lorimer's workshop was shuttered, there was no smoke rising through the thatch of Saunders' house. Two passing apprentices stopped when they saw Gil at the top of the muddy track.

'They're all away,' said one, a spotty youth with a scar on his brow. 'Up at the Castle.'

222

'Getting put to the question, maybe,' said the other gleefully, 'getting all their fingernails pullt out and their teeth broke. There's nob'dy there.'

Gil thanked them and looked about him, waiting until they had gone reluctantly on downhill.

'Maybe they've all went elsewhere,' said Neil hopefully.

'Maybe,' agreed Gil. He moved forward, alert for anything stirring. Beyond the lorimer's shack where the path opened out the place was still quiet. Dod Muir's house was understandably deserted, and rats scurried away from his woodstore as they approached.

'They're all away, maybe,' said Neil. 'Will we just be going back to the Castle now?'

'Quiet,' said Gil. He stood still, listening, and after a moment heard it again, the low murmur of women's voices. It came from the whitesmith's house.

It took some persuasion before the gallowglass would step up to the door. Gil watched from a little way behind the man, as he rattled at the tirling-pin on the doorpost and then stood looking uncomfortable while the voices inside turned to hissing whispers.

'They're maybe not—' he began, half turning from the door, just as it opened. The woman on the threshold gave him one quick glance, and Gil another, and said in Scots,

'It's yourself is it then, Neil Campbell? And what are you doing here? How is it you that's lowsed, and no my man or my brother? And you,' she said, with another hard look at Gil, 'prowling about here again. What are you after?'

'A word wi yourself, mistress,' said Gil politely, raising his hat to her. 'And wi Mistress Bethag and all.'

'Well, we are wanting no words with you,' she retorted, 'so you may take yourself away, whether to your wife or the hoors next door I carena!'

'It's talk wi me now, or talk wi the Provost's men at the Castle,' Gil suggested, 'and I think you'll find I'm more civil than they are.'

223

The younger woman appeared at the door behind her sister-in-law's muscular shoulder, her baby clasped tightly to her.

'*An caisteal?*' she repeated in alarm. 'Let them in, sister, we not – we never—'

The other children were not visible. Barabal, when asked, said sulkily that they were with her man's sister.

'And where does she dwell?' Gil enquired, seating himself in the whitesmith's chair.

'Yonder.' She jerked her head vaguely northwards.

'Is that where Alan and Nicol are lodged and all?'

Her eyes widened, but she said nothing. The younger woman, laying the sleeping baby in its cradle, began to move about the hearth, finding oatcakes and cheese and a bottle of something, clearly taking comfort from obedience to the laws of hospitality. Gil, hoping it would not be usquebae, said,

'I've heard a bit about Thursday morning.' Barabal scowled at him. 'How come Miller was here? He dwells down the Gallowgate, does he no?'

'He was discussing matters,' said Barabal, while the other woman crossed herself at the sound of the name.

'What was he so angry about? Frightened your weans, I think, mistress?'

'There is no knowledge at me of that,' she said. 'The man was in a great rage, but it was not my business what angered him.'

'I hope the weans never saw him killing Muir.'

'No, they were down the back, thanks be to Our Lady,' she said, 'I was keeping them there out his way, and I waited till he had hid the—'

'You kent he was in there?' demanded Neil Campbell. 'You kent he was in the kist, and you never said?'

'You would never jaloused it,' she retorted, 'if this lang drink o watter was not powterin where it was none o his business!'

'Where did Miller go after he hid the body?' Gil asked.

She shook her head, the ends of her linen veil swinging against her massive bosom.

'Off down the burn, likely, to his own place. He is not one that welcomes being spied on, you will understand.'

'And after that the three men came looking for help. They're kin of yours, are they?'

'On her mother's side,' said Neil hastily. She threw him a very ugly look.

'That Billy is no kin of mine,' she objected, 'you will never say so.'

'He must be kin to somebody,' Gil said. 'So far as I can make out everyone in this is related. How is the man Miller your kin?'

She checked, staring, then shook her head again, looking alarmed.

'No kin to any of us, that one!' she said. 'They are all in the guild thegither, just.'

Her sister-in-law came forward with a beaker in one hand and a platter in the other, and offered them to Gil with the graceful curtsy he had seen other Ersche women make. He accepted, concealing reluctance, and sipped at the beaker. It was usquebae, and new stuff at that, the raw, fiery spirit biting at his throat. Neil said something in Ersche, and the young woman tightened her lips and set about preparing food for him too.

'Then later,' said Gil, 'the woman Forveleth was here. I think she's your cousin, Mistress Bethag?' She looked round, and nodded shyly. 'So it was hardly friendly of your man when he exchanged the bag of coin for the package of apothecary goods in her bundle, and gave it to Mistress Barabal.'

Barabal made the sign against the evil eye.

'You are knowing too much a'thegither!' she said, glowering. He smiled, and raised the horrible usquebae in a toast to her.

'And where is the purse of blue velvet?'

She shook her head. 'I have seen no purse of blue velvet, and so I was telling the soldiers when they were here.'

Neil translated the question at Gil's nod, but the other woman made the same answer. No purse of blue velvet had been on the toft since the day they moved in, no matter how hard the Provost's men had searched.

Gil paused to eat one of the oatcakes. It had been smeared with green cheese, and was rather tough. He had heard Maggie say that the cook's mood affected the baking. Small wonder, then, he reflected, and took another sip of usquebae, hoping the one would cancel out the other. The combination was even less palatable.

'What brought Miller back that evening?' he asked. 'The Provost's men found him in the forge out here wi a parcel of scrap metal on him. What was he looking for?'

'Old metal, I am supposing,' said Barabal before the other woman could speak. 'He takes the old stuff, the broken pieces—'

'The scrap,' he supplied. 'What, you mean he buys it in from other hammermen?'

'Hah!' she said bitterly, and Bethag in the shadows shook her head.

'Not buying,' she said softly.

'Does Maister Hamilton ken this?' he asked.

'What are you thinking?' retorted Barabal.

Opening his purse he fetched out the brass die, and held it out on his palm.

'You ken what this is, mistress?' he said.

'Not me!' said Barabal boldly, though her eyes had narrowed at the sight. 'Good enough brass, but someone is hammering at it, by the look of it.'

'Was Miller looking for this, maybe?'

'I would not be knowing. I never spoke wi the man, I had the bairns to keep from him. They fear him.'

'There should be two of these. Is the other one about the toft, would you say?'

Her sister-in-law said something emphatic in Ersche, which Neil translated:

'There is nothing the like on this toft. She is sure of that.'

226

Gil frowned, trying to pull all this into one tale. It would not fit. Something was still missing, something he had not asked.

'How much have you had to do wi Dame Isabella?' he ventured.

'Who?' said Barabal blankly, at the same time as the younger woman said,

'Is mistress to Forveleth, is so?'

'And to Alan and Nicol,' agreed Gil. 'What has she done for you?'

'Nothing good,' said Barabal, 'causing them turn up here and ask our aid, and us wi troubles enough!'

'But before that?' Gil suggested. 'Had she no part in the other troubles?'

'No,' said Barabal firmly. Her sister-in law shook her head, though whether in agreement or disagreement Gil was not certain.

'Has Miller been here the day?' he asked.

'Why would he do that?' returned Barabal. 'He has ears, the same as the rest of Glasgow, he will be hearing of what has happened. Why do you think we are shut in here, instead of about the toft as we should be? Half the Drygate was running about the place this morning, wanting to question us, nothing for it but to pretend we are not here. None of their mind it is, whatever happens on Clerk's Land.'

'She here yestreen,' said Bethag reluctantly. 'Miller.'

Gil, familiar with the Ersche confusion with the Scots *he* and *she*, simply looked questioningly at her. She gazed back at him, spread her hands, and spoke rapidly to Neil.

'She is saying,' he relayed, 'The man was here yesterday. After you was here and before I came to the door, she is saying.'

'And what did he want then?' Gil asked.

'They were shouting,' he relayed. 'She was not understanding it all. Her Scots is not so good as mine,' he said disparagingly. 'Were you hearing what they said, Barabal?'

'I was not,' she said firmly, 'and nor was Bethag if she has any sense.'

'He wanted her man to do something,' the gallowglass went on, 'and he would not. And he wanted him to go somewhere with him the day.'

'Where?'

The answer to that was clear enough: Strathblane.

'Why?' Gil asked. 'What did he want there?'

She shook her head blankly. 'Important,' she said. 'No ken why.'

Chapter Eleven

Alys was still not to be seen, and nobody seemed to know where she had gone.

Leaving the two women to be escorted up to the Castle by Neil Campbell, Gil had made for home by the path along the mill-burn, pausing to look into the donkey-shed at the foot of Clerk's Land. It was empty, and the cart was absent as well; presumably Sproat had some work somewhere.

At the house he was greeted with faint hostility by the women in the kitchen.

'The dinner-hour's long over, Maister Gil,' said Kittock pointedly when he appeared in the doorway. 'I might find you some bread and cold meat, but. No, I've no idea where the mistress is, but if that one up the stair thinks she can tell me how to run my kitchen,' she went on, as much to the loaf she was hacking as to Gil, 'she can go and bile her heid.'

'John's growing fine,' said Nancy from her seat by the hearth, where she was mending one of the boy's little shirts; John himself was rosily asleep on someone's straw pallet in the corner. Kittock turned and gave the nurse-maid a harried smile.

'I ken that, and you're a good lass, Nancy. But I'll no have one wi no authority coming about my door wi orders like that.'

'What's to do?' Gil asked, aware that this was unwise. Jennet, chopping leeks at the other side of the great wooden table, snorted grimly. Kittock shook her head, laid a generous slice of cold meat on the wedge of bread, and looked about her.

'I'll not tell tales,' she said improbably, reaching for one of a neat row of bowls at her side. 'But there's Annis weeping her heart out over the crocks in the scullery, and Jennet here all put out and all, I'll not have it, and so I'll let the maister hear.' She spooned thick dollops of amber-coloured onion sauce over the meat, clapped another wedge of bread on top, and swept the knife through the stack, once, twice. Arranging the four little towers on a wooden platter, she stuck a scrap of parsley in the bailey at their centre. 'There you go, Maister Gil. That'll no spoil your supper, but it should keep you on yir feet till then.'

'But the mistress is not back?' he persisted, accepting the food. She had turned away to draw him a beaker of ale from the barrel in the corner, and did not hear him. Nancy looked up from her mending and nodded.

'Never been home,' she admitted. This was probably as many words as she ever uttered at one time.

'She's got the dog wi her,' Kittock observed, returning with the beaker. Gil took it from her and set it down on the table long enough to put the leaf of parsley in his mouth. 'The wee one was fair missing his Ocketie.' She added another generous pinch of parsley leaves to the platter, lifted the ale again and put it in his hand. 'Now away out my kitchen, Maister Gil, till I get my feet clear for the supper.'

'What was she wearing?' he asked. Jennet looked up, narrowing her eyes.

'I got her up in her blue linen,' she said. 'That was afore you was awake, maister.'

The everyday gown, for the market and for calling on close friends, he thought. She would have been home before now, and if not the dog would have become bored and come to find him.

'She took Luke,' offered Nancy.

Upstairs in the hall he found Luke's master and Ealasaidh McIan, seated together on the great settle admiring the jug of flowers in the empty hearth. Questioned, Maistre Pierre agreed with Nancy.

'I had work for the boy,' he complained. 'Did she tell you where she went, mistress?'

Ealasaidh shook her head.

'She was never saying, that I heard,' she said reluctantly. 'Was it no some errand you had set her, Maister Gil?'

'No.' Gil scraped oozing onion sauce off the side of one of the little towers and licked his finger, trying to recall whether Alys had said anything yesterday. No, there was nothing. And better not to mention the state the kitchen was in.

He moved to sit in one of the window-seats and stared out over the garden, unseeing, trying to order what he knew about Dame Isabella's death. He needed to locate the serving-men, but two of them were certainly in the clear and it was possible the other two could speak for one another likewise. One of the waiting-women was still suspect, the other was not. Who else could have approached the old woman at such a moment without causing her alarm? Some kin, perhaps. The two Livingstone men spoke for one another, though he had not asked them to investigate their own household. What about Sempill? he thought, chewing. The man was capable of killing the old woman, for certain, and was good enough with his hands to achieve the skilful way she had been killed, but his amazement at hearing of her death had seemed genuine. Could he dissemble that well?

'Perhaps she is gone to a friend's house?' suggested Ealasaidh, breaking into his thoughts. 'Or to your sister's house, maybe?'

'She would take John if she went there,' objected Maistre Pierre. 'And she would not need Luke. Even Catherine does not know where she is,' he grumbled.

Gil nodded vague agreement, and put another sprig of parsley in his mouth. Lady Magdalen, now, was she capable of the deed? It hardly seemed like a woman's method of killing, despite what it said in Holy Writ, and she was a slender creature, but all things were possible. It should be easy enough to check whether she had been out of the house that morning. I should have done all this yesterday, he realized irritably, what was I thinking?

What reason was there for killing the old woman? Was she killed because she was an objectionable old beldam, or for another reason? How was her death connected to the matter of the false coin? I ought to get a longer word with Sandy Boyd, he thought, frowning, and absently lifted the last of the onion sauce with the final crust of bread. And I should never have let Neil Campbell out of my grasp just now. I wonder where his brother is?

'Perhaps she went to the tailor,' Ealasaidh offered. 'That might take the whole day.'

In fact, Gil thought, I have spent two days allowing others to direct me. I need to take charge of my own investigation. Confound this blow on the head, it has addled my wits more than I realized.

He set the platter down on the cushion beside him and swallowed the last of the ale.

'I'm going out again,' he said. 'If Alys comes back, send to let me know, will you? I'll be about the Drygate or Rottenrow.'

Canon Aiken's house was quieter than when he was last there; the black hangings were still at the door and windows of the wing where Dame Isabella had died, and Maister Livingstone was seated glumly in the upper hall, reading in a small worn book. He rose when Gil was shown in, setting the book aside, and exclaimed,

'In a good hour, maister! You had my message, then?'

'No,' said Gil blankly. 'Message?'

'Jock Russell's back from Craigannet, man. You mind he was to ride out to ask Archie about some of these properties? Lucky it was we waited till the next day to send him, and he took word o the auld beldam's death as well as the other questions we had, and now he's back, wi word from

232

my brother and a note of her will that they found in her kist. Fetch wine and cakes, Tammas,' he added to the retreating servant. 'Come and get a seat, and look at this, likely you could do wi a look at it, for it concerns your sister.'

'Does it now?' said Gil, raising his eyebrows.

'Aye. Lady Tib will get the land in Lanarkshire after all, the other would go to Lady Magdalen if it wasny part o the Livingstone heriot right enough. The auld ettercap's been stirring it.'

The note was in fact a full copy in a set of wax tablets. The document was clearly enough drawn up, and had been signed only a few days ago. Gil studied it carefully, not entirely sure what to expect, though after this disclosure he hoped there would be no unpleasant surprises; what startled him was the direct bequest to John Sempill, the size of another to Lowrie, and the final destination of the residue.

'Did she have so much to leave?' he asked. Livingstone grimaced.

'She did not, though she thought she did, that's clear. Archie reckons the land at Gargunnock that she's left the lad was part of the heriot and all, same as both the plots in Strathblane. Just the way Lowrie's luck falls, that. And I'd say Archie'll be in for a fine battle wi John of the Isles for most of the rest. Stirling men of law will eat well this winter. Aye, set it there, Tammas, we'll serve oursels.'

'Why John of the Isles? He's dispossessed, he's landless and forfeit and living on the King's pension, why would a woman like Dame Isabella leave him near all she had?' A woman who *couldny stand these heathen names*, who abused her Ersche servants for thieving fools, he was thinking.

'Christ and His saints alone ken, but she thinks the world o him. She made a right tirravee when he was brought to Stirling last year,' Livingstone said sourly, handing him a glass of Malvoisie, 'wanting Archie to offer to keep the man, or offer him funds, or the like. The names she called him when he wouldny oblige her, you'd wonder she wasny struck down by a thunderbolt on the spot.'

Gil sipped the wine and considered the words incised in the greenish wax. The copy was cramped but the original had been carefully composed; Maister Edward Cults of Stirling, whose name was in the colophon, was clearly a qualified notary. It assigned the familiar parcels of land to each of her goddaughters and another *to my nephew Lowrence Livinston for that his faither will not see to his providing*, with further gifts of some value to all three, and conventional if paltry sums to the testatrix's own household. To *Jhone Sempil of Muirende, spous of my gude-dochter Magdalen Boidd* went another piece of land in Renfrewshire, along with *my smal kiste of norowa dele with al held therin*, and then the final sentence: *Al uthir gudes, chattils and londes of which I dye invest or infeft I leve to the use of Jhon Macdonneld sumtyme erle of Ross callit Lord of the Yles for his lifetyme.*

'You'd get them back eventually,' he said. 'John of the Isles is, how old? Sixty? Can't be far short of it.'

'Aye, but that's no the point, is it?' said Livingstone indignantly. 'He'll get how many years' worth o rents off that, if it's hers to leave, and we reckon it isny.'

'Have you found the Norway deal kist she leaves to Sempill? I wonder what's in it?'

'So did we,' said Livingstone. 'It's not in her baggage. Some earnest o good behaviour, or the like, I've no doubt, that she extorted from him afore she wedded her goddaughter to the man.'

It would fit, thought Gil, but did not comment. 'She gives no reason for the bequest of land.'

'She's entitled to assign what's hers where she wishes,' said Livingstone, 'and that's hers – or at least, it isny ours – but I agree, you wonder why, more particular when her servants, that she owes a duty to, get no more than five merks each. Though I suppose wi the way they've run off, she's no that much of a duty to them. And Archie's full able to see to the lad's providing,' he added.

'I never doubted it,' Gil said, still studying the will. 'I'll not mention this to Sempill.'

'I'd be grateful,' said Livingstone. 'There's enough to see to, without him underfoot demanding his rights afore they're due.' He heaved a sigh. 'At least we can see the auld ettercap into the ground now, Christ be praised. Were you at the quest? I never saw you.'

'I was elsewhere. What did it conclude?'

'Oh, clear enough, clear enough, murder by an unknown felon, though I did think for a while they'd bring it in against the woman Marion, or whatever she's cried. But Otterburn can steer an assize, he's no so daft as he's made out, and they returned that after a bit.'

'Did you wait for the second one?'

'I did not. Naught to do wi us, and I'd to speak wi Andro Hamilton to get Dame Isabella in her kist and received at Greyfriars. We'll put her in the ground the morn's morn.'

'Did Lowrie stay? If he's not back it's maybe not over yet—'

'Lowrie?' said Livingstone, in surprise. 'He's away out the town wi your good lady, maister. Out to Strathblane.'

Leaving Maister Livingstone to establish belatedly whether any of his own household had been anywhere near Dame Isabella's quarters on the fatal morning, Gil strode up the Drygate to the Castle, turning this news over in his mind. He knew his wife well enough to be sure she had some purpose in the journey, and she had made certain of her escort – Lowrie and two men, Luke, the dog, and whoever had accompanied his uncle's horses made a good retinue. She ought to be safe, he thought, and Lowrie has a good head on his shoulders. But what will she ask, and who will she ask it of? What will she find? Will she ask the right questions?

What are the right questions? he wondered, and had to admit he was not certain of the answer. And when will they be back? He glanced at the sky. It was not more than four in the afternoon, there were four or five hours of daylight left, and it was a good dry day. They might be back for supper.

Otterburn was not in a good mood.

'I could ha done wi your presence,' he said grimly, 'as the finder o the man Muir. No to mention as one that can contradict the Serjeant. He's fine when it's a matter o forestalling or avoiding the mercat fee, John Anderson is, but gie him a trail to follow and he'll cross it as sure as winking. I'd the deil's own job to keep them from naming that woman in the Tolbooth for the old dame.'

'No, it was never her,' Gil said absently. 'What did they resolve about Dod Muir? And where did that pair of gallowglasses get to?'

'Oh, we're putting some fellow Miller to the horn. Mind, it would help if I kent his forename, Dusty willny do for the paperwork, but the two women you sent up here wi that sly fellow made the tale clear enough, and spoke up to it. Eventually. Even an assize couldny mistake the matter. Is that who you're wanting, the man Campbell? I thought he was about the place, maybe talking wi Andro. You could try at the guardhouse.'

'Have you searched for Miller?'

Otterburn gave him a look which his mother would have called old-fashioned.

'My faith, I never thought o that. What do you think we've been doing? Andro's no long back, in fact, he was down the Gallowgate wi four men asking the fellow's whereabouts, but turns out nobody kens him. Must be invisible.'

'The missing servants from Dame Isabella's household,' Gil said, without apology, 'are likely with Barabal Campbell's good-sister, somewhere by the Stablegreen Port. One o them at least she sent to Miller just before she was murdered, so they should be able to take you to the man's workshop.'

'Ah!' Otterburn rang the little bell on his desk. 'Walter, get Andro to me, and that Neil Campbell wi him if he's still underfoot.'

236

'And Miller was talking about going out of Glasgow the day,' Gil added, 'to Strathblane.' Where Alys had gone, he realized. Would they encounter the man? Would Lowrie be able to defend her? It was a wide valley, but they would all be looking for the same people, the same spot.

'All the better,' Otterburn was saying. 'If we can find his premises and search them, then put a watch on the ports for him, we'll maybe no need to horn him.'

The tramp of booted feet announced Andro, with a reluctant Neil Campbell at his back. The gallowglass was dismayed to be ordered to find the missing servants.

'I have never set eyes on my cousin's good-sister,' he protested. 'You would be wanting my brother for that.'

'And where is your brother?' demanded Otterburn. Neil shook his head.

'I am not knowing that. He was in Glasgow yestreen, but—'

'If you went down Clerk's Land,' Gil recommended, 'you could ask Saunders to take you and some men to his sister's house.'

'Aye,' said Andro, grinning. 'And he's still that grateful no to be hung for Dod Muir, he's bound to help us.'

'Is he?' said Gil.

'He will be when I'm done wi him.' Andro grinned again, touched his helm to the Provost, and left, shouting for his men. Gil laid a hand on Neil Campbell's shoulder as he turned to follow him.

'Not so fast, man. I need a word.'

'Maister Cunningham iss aye welcome to a word,' said Neil courteously, though his eyes rolled in alarm, 'but—'

'Several words, in fact,' said Gil. 'Tell me more about the coin you're carrying to Ardnamurchan. To Mingary, was it?'

'Och, no, I am knowing little of that,' protested the gallowglass. 'All I have done is carry the stuff, I have no knowing where it is from or who makes it—'

'So it's not this man Miller?' Gil suggested.

237

'I would not be knowing. Just my cousin gave me the leather bag and I was taking it to McIan.'

'And never helped yoursel from the contents?' said Otterburn sceptically.

'I am an honest man,' said Neil indignantly. 'I would not be thieving from those that employ me. Besides that, it was sealed,' he added, 'the sack I mean.'

'Whose seal?' Gil asked. He shook his head.

'The old woman's, I am thinking.'

'Old woman?' Gil repeated. 'What old woman?'

'Some old woman that was paying them to—'

'Was it Dame Isabella? Isabella Torrance?'

'Maybe.' The man backed away from Gil, looking anxiously at the Provost. 'It wass not Sempill's, for certain.'

'Sempill's? What does he have to do with it?'

'He had the seal,' said Neil, as if it was obvious. 'He was there to seal the bag, wass he not, and pay my kinsman for his work, and me and my brother for our time. Like the other morning,' he said helpfully.

'What other morning?' Gil felt he was floundering, but this seemed like a support to clutch at. 'Do you mean Thursday morning? The day Dame Isabella died?'

'The day you wass rescued in the – yes,' finished the gallowglass, changing his mind about what he had been about to say.

Does the entire town know I was rescued by the bawdy-house? Gil wondered. 'What time was he there?' he asked.

'Och, early on, maybe about Prime. No, it was later, for I heard the bells, but it was not so late as Terce.'

'So he was on Clerk's Land before Terce, sealing the bag of coin,' Gil began.

'No, he wass not, for it wass not there to be sealed, the man Miller only came by with it after he had gone away.'

'And then what happened?' Gil was trying to fit the sequence of the morning together. And you said you didn't know the man Miller, he thought.

'Miller and my kinsman were going off to speak with the old woman.'

'Why?' asked Otterburn. 'Was that usual? No, it couldny be, she didny dwell here in Glasgow. Why did they want to speak wi her?'

'I would not be knowing,' said Neil politely. 'But maybe it wass because of what Sempill of Muirend was saying.'

'Christ aid, it's like drawing teeth!' said Otterburn. 'So what was Sempill saying, and who did he say it to?'

'Oh, I wass not listening,' declared the gallowglass. 'He wass not talking to me, you understand, so it wass not right to be listening.'

'Neil,' said Gil levelly, 'tell me what he said.'

The gallowglass gave him a reproachful look.

'Only that there was to be no more silver,' he said. 'He was in a great rage, I thought, and the whole of the Drygate likely heard him, but that was all he was saying. No more silver, and no more coin.'

'No more siller,' the Provost repeated. 'And where was there to be no more siller from?'

Neil shrugged his broad shoulders.

'He was never saying that.'

'Did your kinsman argue with him?' Gil asked.

'Who argues with Sempill of Muirend?'

True, Gil thought.

'And then your kinsman told the man Miller,' said Otterburn, thinking about it, 'and the two o them went away down the Drygate to speak to Isabella Torrance. To complain to her? To clype on Sempill?'

'To kill her?' Gil supplied. Neil Campbell stepped back in alarm.

'I have not said it!' he exclaimed. 'I have no idea who was killing her! They have said nothing of it when they came back to Clerk's Land, only that she was telling how it would certainly go on, she would see more silver into Glasgow if it was to kill her. . .' His voice trailed off, and he stared at Gil. 'I think it was not them,' he finished.

'Hah!' said Otterburn, rubbing his hands together. 'Looks as if we'll sort that killing as well as Dod Muir's if we take the man Miller, Maister Cunningham.'

'Maybe,' said Gil.

It was nearly an hour before Andro returned, with the three missing serving-men. There had clearly been some dissent about whether they accompanied the Provost's men or not; two had puffy eyes, one was dabbing at a split lip, and all three were covered in the mud of the Stablegreen. Andro's men were hardly unblemished either; the Provost, surveying them, said drily,

'Well, well, we'll ha some repairs to put on the bill, I can see. Right, you three.' He stared at the row of men. 'It'll likely save time if I tell you what we ken already. You left your mistress's house when you kent she was dead by violence, along wi the woman,' he turned his tablets to read the name, 'Forveleth nic Iain nic Muirteach. She went to hand a package back to the potyngar, while you three went by the back lane to Clerk's Land and there burnt your livery,' all three men gaped at him and two crossed themselves, 'and then I think you went to the place where my men just found ye. No?'

They looked at one another in dismay. Gil, seated by the window, identified the two who were brothers, dark of hair like the gallowglass. They must be Nicol and Alan, he thought, and the third was called Billy, a short, round-headed man with a ginger beard.

'Aye,' said Billy now. 'Small point in denying it, maister. What,' he swallowed, 'what d'ye want of us now?'

'Ye'll have heard,' said Otterburn, 'the quest on yir mistress brought in a verdict o murder.' His tone was pleasant, so pleasant that the men took a moment to realize their danger. 'So what can you three tell me o that?'

'Persons unknown,' said Billy nervously. 'We're no, no what ye'd say unknown, maister, ye can see us clear in front o ye.'

'Aye,' said Otterburn in that pleasant tone.

'She was slain while we were out about her errands,' said one of the other two. 'We cam back all about the same time, and waited in the outer chamber, see, and then Annot cam out screeching that the old dame was, was—'

240

'I still think it was an apoplexy,' muttered his brother.

'So where did you go?' Gil asked. 'It was Alan went to the potyngary, I think, Maister Syme gave me a good description.' One of the brothers looked even more dismayed by this. 'Where did Nicol and Billy get to?'

'To the Campbells,' said Billy promptly.

'And?' Gil encouraged. Billy and the remaining man eyed each other sideways, and Gil said, 'Now I ken fine you went your separate ways. What I want to know is what those ways were.'

The two exchanged another glance, and Billy said reluctantly,

'I gaed to Clerk's Land. To ask about that pair o Campbells. Euan or Neil or whatever they're cried. And then I waited on Nicol meeting me,' he admitted when Gil prompted him further.

'Was it a long wait?' Gil asked, and bit his lip, thinking of the prentice joke. 'How far had Nicol gone?'

'Long enough,' admitted Billy. 'How long was ye, Nicol? Best part an hour, I'd say.'

Nicol nodded reluctantly.

'All the way down the Gallowgate and back,' Gil said. 'It's shorter by the back way, of course, down the Molendinar. Down the mill-burn,' he translated, as they looked blankly, unfamiliar with the Sunday name. 'And was Miller at home?'

Nicol's jaw dropped. Recovering it, he said, 'No, he wasny, nor his woman didny ken where he was, save that a laddie came to fetch him an hour afore I was there.'

Gil and Otterburn exchanged a glance. The Provost nodded at his captain, who left the chamber, and Gil said carefully,

'What kind of time was that, then? When were you down the Gallowgate, Nicol?'

Nicol looked blankly at him, and then at Billy.

'They'd done wi Terce,' Billy said helpfully, 'afore ever we set out. You could hear the bells ringing.'

'Och, it was long after that,' said Nicol.

241

'Is that no what I'm saying? Half an hour after eight it would be, likely, when we left the lodging, and getting on for Sext when we got back.'

'And there was nobody about Canon Aiken's house other than the folk o the two households,' said Otterburn. Billy nodded, the brothers shook their dark heads. All seemed to be agreeing with him.

Andro returned, with four men, rather fresher than the last set.

'Right,' said the Provost, and rubbed his hands together again. 'Seeing you ken the way to this Miller's house, my lad, you'll take us there now. And to make certain you behave yoursel, we'll just keep your brother and your friend here waiting for you. Any fun and games, laddie, and your brother's the one that pays for it. Right?'

Out past the Gallowgate Port, past Little St Mungo's, Nicol led them hesitantly down an alleyway among tumbledown hovels, little huts of wattle and clay with balding thatch and sagging walls. Women paused in their gossip and turned to stare as they went, a gaggle of children gathered in their wake, but as it became obvious where they were heading, somehow the interest evaporated. The children hesitated and turned back, the women ceased to watch them directly, though Gil suspected that by the time they stopped outside a shack no different from any of the others he could have obtained a detailed description of every member of the party from anyone within fifty yards.

Andro, following the plan the Provost had outlined before they left the Gallowgate, led two of the men quietly round the back of the little structure. Gil drew Nicol to one side, and Otterburn stepped up to the door and hammered on it with the hilt of his sword.

'Miller!' he shouted. 'Open up, there! Open up for the law!'

A child in a nearby house began screaming, and a few heads popped out of doorways and as quickly popped

242

back in. Like rabbits with a ferret in the warren, thought Gil.

'What's he done, maister?' asked Nicol softly. 'Why's the law after him? Is he put to the horn, maybe?'

'If he's not here,' said Gil, 'he will be at the horn, for the murder of Dod Muir at the least.' Otterburn, tiring of shouting at the door, had lifted the latch and flung it open. 'I'd say he's not here, would you?'

'It's deserted,' said Andro, appearing in the open doorway. 'We got in the back. There's a workshop ahint the house, sir, you'll want a right look at.'

The house was very small, and with eight men in it uncomfortably crowded. There was another doorway immediately opposite the one they had entered by, with a leather curtain; to the left was a single dwelling-space, to the right a couple of stalls where a goat bleated in alarm. Otterburn, ordering the men-at-arms out to watch front and back, cast a glance round the place and stepped through to the workshop Andro had mentioned. Gil stayed where he was, Nicol at his side, studying the sparse furnishings.

'You said he had a woman,' he remarked.

'Aye.' Nicol was looking about him too. 'And there was a cooking-pot and two-three platters at the hearth, and a couple more stools, when I was here afore. And a better blanket on the bed.' He grinned nervously. 'He's no a – no a good-heartit man, maister. Likely he beats her. She's maybe took her chance when he's away, and went somewhere kinder.'

'Aye.' Gil lifted the lid of the one kist in the place, with caution. It held some worn garments and a pair of down-at-heel boots; there were several choicer garments hanging on nails on one end wall of the box bed, and a pair of sturdy shoes set neatly below them. 'He's come into some better living lately,' he observed. 'Been here many times?'

'Twice or thrice,' admitted the man. 'An errand for the old dame, ilka time.'

'What was your message this time?'

'To let him ken she was here in Glasgow,' he said readily enough, 'and wanting a word wi him.'

'Was that how she put it?' Gil asked, amused.

'Well. Maybe no. Maybe it was more like, *Tell the man Miller I'll get a word wi him as soon as he pleases, and no to wait about.*'

There was nothing under the bed, and nothing on its roof save some dust. The ledge at the top of the wall, below the rafters, yielded some oddments of broken crocks, a plain wooden comb, a few other fragments of domestic life. He prodded the bed, but found nothing stowed in it. Above the goat's stall a bucket hung in the rafters proved to be empty.

'If he'd anything worth it, his woman's likely taken it with her,' offered Nicol.

'Maister Cunningham!' Otterburn called from outside. Gil followed the sound across a small yard of beaten earth well-sprinkled with goat droppings, past a turf-banked furnace to a substantial shed whose door stood wide.

'The man thinks more of his work than his dwelling,' he observed, ducking under the lintel.

'Aye, very like. See what we've found here,' said Otterburn, gesturing largely. Gil looked about the dark interior. There was a shuttered window, and a bench below it, the sort of low structure a man could sit astride with his workpiece on a raised portion before him. A rack of small hammers and mells was fixed to the wall below the window. Two wooden bins held scrap metal of different qualities, other tools and materials were neatly stowed.

'A hammerman's workshop,' said Gil.

'There's more.' Otterburn was grinning in the shadows. 'There's more. Show him, Andro.'

Part of the back wall of the shed swung open, and Andro stepped through.

'There's no air in there!' he complained, fanning himself with one hand. 'Aye, sir, it's all there, all Maister Livingstone described, so far's I saw afore you shut the door on me. A bar o siller, a sack o blanks waiting to be struck, a sack o powder I suppose could be dried argol. And here's the dies.'

'It's no that secret,' said Otterburn disparagingly, 'but you'd no spot it unless you were right next it, in this light, and it's a right neat wee press when you get inside, all well stowed. It's a false back wall to the shed, see, you'd no guess unless you paced it out. See us the dies, then, man.'

There were three of them, identical in size and heft to the one which had been hidden with Dod Muir's body. Gil moved to the door to inspect them. Two showed the cross and four mullets, with no balls as Madam Xanthe had said. One of these was badly worn. The third should be the king's head, he thought, turning it to the light.

'Here's a thing,' he said. 'Could this be why Dod Muir was slain?'

'Eh?' said Otterburn from the hidden press.

'The die we found wi him was a worn head, right? Livingstone reckoned there were two heads and two crosses, one of each worn out, so we ought to have a good head here.'

'Aye?'

'This one's damaged. There's a great scratch across it, maybe from a chisel or the like, right across the king's jaw.'

'You mean Miller wanted him to make another and he refused?' Otterburn came to look. 'Why would he refuse? He was in it up to his neck any road.'

'Maybe he hoped to get out of it.' Gil admired the three dies where they lay in a row on his palm. 'Maister Otterburn, I think we've found our counterfeiter.'

'Well, we've named him, any road,' said Otterburn, prodding the dies with a long forefinger. 'We've no found him yet, Maister Cunningham.'

'No,' said Gil, with a sudden rush of anxiety. 'No, we haveny, and he's out the same side of Glasgow as my wife.'

Chapter Twelve

Sir Richie was astonished by their story. He was already out at the corner of his little church, staring up the glen, and when the little procession came in sight he vanished, to reappear shortly round the kirkyard wall, stole about his neck, a little box clasped carefully in one hand. Bearing this he made his way down to cross the burn by the plank bridge Alys had used, and came hurrying towards them.

'Who's hurt? Is there time to shrive them?' he demanded as soon as he came within earshot. 'Who is it? You're all hale – who is it?'

Leaving Lowrie to direct his men and keep an eye on young Berthold, Alys came forward to explain. He listened attentively, crossing himself, then inspected the two dead men, flinching away from the burnt face of the boy's father, exclaiming over and over.

'And these were the demons? So they were flesh and blood after all! Bring them within the kirkyard at least. Were they Christian souls?'

'I think it,' said Alys. 'The boy has a set of beads, I think he was praying for his father. Or perhaps for himself,' she added thoughtfully.

'Bring them in, then, bring them in. But what can we do, maister? If they've been murdered as you say, we should raise the hue and cry, but there's never a soul to hear it in the Clachan, and none wi the authority to command the pursuit neither.'

'Kirkintilloch would be the nearest,' agreed Lowrie, lending a hand to steady one of the hurdles as Sim and

246

Frank made their way down towards the burn. 'Who would take charge in the usual way?'

Socrates' ears pricked, and he growled. Alys turned her head, trying to hear over Sir Richie's rambling answer. Was that more horses? Voices? She moved a little upstream and jumped across the burn, leaving the bridge to the bearers, then hurried up the rough grassy bank and, bending low, picked her way along the kirkyard wall with the dog at her heel. At the corner she paused, listening. Yes, there were voices, they had been heard, there was shouting about *Someone's down yonder by the burn*. She moved forward to peer cautiously round the corner of the wall, and found herself almost nose to nose with Philip Sempill.

She sprang back quickly enough to take her beyond the reach of his aborted sword-thrust, and said, over the dog's snarling,

'Maister Sempill! What—?'

'Mistress Mason!' He lowered his whinger, gaping at her as she grasped Socrates' collar. 'Of all the people to meet here! What are you doing?'

'Catching demons,' she said, and indicated the procession behind her. 'We have found silver miners in the glen, which I am *quite certain* your kinsman did not know of, and two of them are dead.'

'Dead!' he repeated, staring. 'Who – who are they? How did you come to—'

'Philip?' John Sempill appeared behind his kinsman. 'Who the deil are you speaking to? *You?*' he said incredulously. 'Deil's bollocks, woman, can you no keep out of what doesny concern you? You're worse than that man o yours.'

'Good day to you, sir,' she said, tightening her grip on the dog's collar, and dropped him a curtsy. 'I hope you left Lady Magdalen well?'

'And who's yonder?' he demanded, ignoring this. 'Philip, what's going on here? Is that that fool o a priest down there and all?'

247

'Mistress Mason says they have found two dead men in the glen,' said Philip, with care. 'They were mining silver. Is that not amazing?'

'What do you—' His cousin stared at him, pale blue eyes narrowed in suspicion. 'Oh,' he said after a moment. 'Aye, that's amazing. Right enough. Who's dead? I mean, who are they? Is there just the two? Who killed them, anyways? What are you doing here? And him!' he added, as Lowrie approached up the bank.

'There's one still living,' said Alys.

'Lowrie Livingstone, is that you poking about on my land where you're no wanted? Was it you killed these two? Why?'

'It was not,' said Lowrie levelly, 'and I don't see why you assume it was. And it's no your land, Muirend, it's either my faither's or Dame Isabella's.'

'It's my land,' Sempill began, and bit the words off as his cousin kicked him on the ankle. Lowrie gave him a small tight smile and stepped round him, guiding the men with the two hurdles up towards the kirkyard gate, the boy Berthold keeping somehow on the further side of the group.

Inside the little church, the boy made straight for the small bright figure of the Virgin and dropped on his knees before her, and Sir Richie, much reassured by this, directed the bearers where to set the hurdles down and began doing what was required for the dead. Alys took time for a brief word with St Machan in his brown robes, but she had trouble concentrating. Yesterday John Sempill had said there was trouble in Strathblane, and today here he was, presumably to deal with it. But had he already taken some action? He must have known the miners were there; did he also know about their deaths? Had Berthold recognized him just now?

Emerging from the building she found the two sets of servants eyeing each other warily from different corners of the kirkyard, and a stiff, chilly discussion going on across a table-tomb near the east end.

'It's still part o the heriot,' Lowrie was saying as she approached. 'My faither has the original disposition, it was never Thomas's to alienate, let alone Dame Isabella's.'

'She was very clear about it,' Philip Sempill observed.

'Maidie's no going to be pleased,' said his cousin grimly. 'I don't know why you had to come meddling out here. Or you!' he added to Alys, with hostility. 'Who is it that's dead, anyway? Who did kill them, if it wasny you? Was it that ill-conditioned laddie that's in there the now?'

'The laddie was away hunting for the pot,' said Lowrie, 'came back while we were debating what had happened, and he seems right grieved by the deaths.' Sempill snorted in disbelief. 'My man Frank, that's a good huntsman, found the traces of four men in the clearing, three of them wi footwear they never got hereabouts, the other wi a narrower heel than any of us. If we can get this laddie somewhere there's a speaker o High Dutch we can learn more from him.'

Sempill snorted again, and gave the younger man a hard stare, but Alys thought the words *good huntsman* had their effect. No landowner was likely to argue with an experienced huntsman's reading of the ground.

'And where was all this siller they've been winning?' he demanded. 'Stacked waiting to be carried off, I suppose!'

'There was no sign of it,' said Alys. 'Perhaps someone had collected it quite recently.'

He grunted, scowling at her.

'You'd know all about that, I suppose,' he said, 'creeping about Glasgow asking questions. You and Gil Cunningham, you're well matched.'

'Why, thank you sir,' she said, and dropped him another curtsy.

'What brought you out here?' asked Philip Sempill. 'You came here for a purpose, it's well out the way for a casual ride for pleasure.'

'Unless you were here *for* pleasure,' said his cousin, with an unpleasant grin. Alys found her face burning, but Lowrie said calmly,

249

'Maister Cunningham asked my escort here for madam his wife, since I ken the road.'

'Aye, but why?'

She had foreseen this question.

'I came to see the two properties out here,' she offered, hoping she did not sound glib, 'because of the confusion over what my good-sister was to have. After all, Dame Isabella's will is yet to be found, one of these might yet go to Tib, and we thought it wiser to—'

'In other words, you were poking that long nose into what doesny concern you,' said Sempill. 'Life 'ud be a lot easier if you and your man wereny aye nosing about. Philip, I want a word.'

He flung away across the kirkyard, and Philip, with a resigned look, followed him. Alys turned to Lowrie.

'What do you wish to do now?' he asked her. 'There's the boy Berthold to think of, and two men to bury, and the murder to cry forth. It all needs seen to. What would Maister Gil do?'

'He'd do what's right,' she said without hesitating.

'Aye, he would,' Lowrie agreed. 'The trouble is to discern what's right here.'

She bit her lip. 'I had it in mind to take that boy to my father. He speaks High Dutch, he has been in Cologne and places like that, and he can question him kindly.' Lowrie smiled, and nodded. 'As to burying the men, that's for Sir Richie to think on in the first place. If he'll not have them, we have to think again, but he's our first road.'

'I agree,' said Lowrie. 'But the murder. It's remarkable how those two,' he glanced at the Sempill cousins, whose word was becoming an argument, 'turned up so prompt after it.'

'It is,' Alys agreed slowly.

'How do you read this, anyway, mistress? What's afoot? If it was Sempill sent someone to kill those men, then he kent they were there and what they were at. So why kill them?'

'And who did he send?' She stared up at the trees

250

beyond the kirkyard wall. 'I think, though I've no proof yet, the silver from here is the silver being coined in Glasgow.'

'It's more economical to believe that,' said Lowrie, watching her, 'than that there's another silver mine within reach. The stuff's scarce enough, Christ kens.'

'But at whose behest? Dame Isabella, or Sempill, or Lady Magdalen? What will your father do about it, maister?'

'Report it to the Crown. I'd not think Lady Magdalen would act against the Crown, either. I reckon more like it was the old dame who caused the coin to be struck, seeing it was her making use of it.'

'Was it?'

'I thought it was,' he said after a moment, 'but I'm no so certain now.'

'No, I think you are right,' she agreed, 'though I also think we have no proof yet. What is John Sempill coming to say to us?'

'Here's what we'll do,' began Sempill when he was still several graves away. '*You*,' he nodded at Lowrie, 'and Philip can go and see what's all this about narrow heels. You can take your *good huntsman* wi you, and one o our lads and all, and you'll be quick about it, for I want to get home for supper.'

'But Mistress Mason—' Lowrie began.

'I'm sure I'll be safe in Sempill of Muirend's keeping,' Alys said sweetly. Sempill of Muirend scowled at her, but Lowrie bowed, and said politely to Philip,

'My pleasure, then.'

'And I'll go and take a look at these dead men, and see what I think they dee'd from,' Sempill went on with emphasis, 'and get a word wi the priest about getting them in the ground. You can come too if you must, I suppose,' he added disagreeably to Alys. 'And there's never a word o use trying to talk to that boy, either, he's got no more Scots than your dog there.'

Possibly less, thought Alys, considering the number of words Socrates understands, but how do you know that?

251

She paused to speak to her own men about watering the horses and allowing them to graze a little, and followed Sempill into the little church.

Sir Richie, having dealt with the matter of conditional absolution and said a charitable Mass for the dead, was much more willing to talk to his visitors now. Exclaiming over the flesh-and-blood nature of the demons, thanking Sempill repeatedly for returning to take care of the problem, he displayed the corpses and their wounds as if he had discovered them himself, shooing Socrates away.

'Terrible injuries, terrible,' he said as he uncovered the older Berthold's burns. 'Only see how dreadful! Get away, away wi you!'

Alys stepped back from Sempill's unmoved consideration of the sight, snapping her fingers to call the dog, and looked at the younger Berthold. He had turned from his intent conversation with the Virgin, and was watching anxiously. What must it be like, she wondered, to be trapped in a strange country, where you spoke none of the language, and you had just lost your kinsfolk. She moved quietly to his side and put a hand on his arm, making him jump.

'Berthold,' she said gently. He touched his brow to her, and bobbed a shy bow. She drew him to the stone bench at the wall-foot, and launched again into the mixture of language and gesture which she had used before. With difficulty, she established that he was fourteen, that his hunting had taken him further up onto the hills, that he had seen nobody, or perhaps that nobody had seen him. He seemed dubious about that. She raised questioning eyebrows, and he mimed someone peering from cover, watching something. She nodded understanding and looked cautiously over one shoulder and then the other, and he said, '*Ja, ja, ich fühlt' überwacht,*' and shivered. He pointed at the two dead men, and turned his face away.

Was it the man with the narrow heels, she wondered. And had he been watching as she picked her way up the burn? If the dog had not been with her – She put a hand on the rough hairy head at her elbow and shivered as Berthold had done.

She was about to assemble another question when the church door was flung wide and Luke tumbled in.

'Mistress, are you here? Here's Maister Livingstone coming back, and all them wi him, and he's got someone prisoner, so he has!'

'Prisoner?' John Sempill swung round, staring. 'What prisoner? What's going on?'

'I wouldny ken what prisoner, maister, but you can see for yoursel,' Luke said, gesturing at the door. 'You've only to look! They're having a right time of it, Tam's gone to gie them a hand.'

Alys was already hurrying out into the sunlight, shading her eyes to stare across the little burn. The party on the far bank was having some trouble, as Luke said, the figure in its midst writhing in the grasp of all four men. As she watched someone tired of the battle and clouted the struggling man across the head. It made little difference, but a second blow and then a third had more effect, and brought an approving grunt from John Sempill behind her, though Sir Richie protested faintly.

'Aye, that's the way to deal wi him,' said Sempill. 'Who is it, anyway? What were you no telling us, Mistress Mason? Have they found someone else at the mine?'

'I've no more notion than you, sir,' she said politely. The returning party hoisted their limp captive across the burn, and Lowrie, leaving Tam to take his share of the burden, hurried up the bank towards the kirkyard wall.

'He was searching the place,' he said, scrambling over the mossy stones. 'Frank was in the lead, and took the huntsman's approach, and saw him before he saw us, so we got him by surprise.' He paused to acknowledge Socrates' greeting.

'Searching the place?' repeated Sempill. 'What was there to find?'

'Little enough,' said Lowrie, 'though he obviously thought there was more.' He nodded to the group now

253

carrying the prisoner in on the easier path by the gate. 'One thing, though. Frank reckons his heels fit the tracks he found, and the rest of us are agreed.'

'So what does that tell you?' demanded Sempill. 'Are you saying this is who slew the two fellows in there?'

'He was certainly at the mine earlier today,' Alys amended. Sempill threw her a surly look and said to his cousin, approaching over the rough grass,

'Better tie him up, Philip, in case he gets away. The priest might have some rope. If you're all agreed he's guilty we could string him up here, there's plenty trees. I've not had a good hanging in months.'

'Oh, surely no, he must have a trial, maister,' protested Sir Richie. 'We should see if the boy recognizes him, maybe, or question him, aye, we should question him!'

'Who is he?' Alys asked. The prisoner was dropped on the ground, where he bounced slightly, groaning. She seized the dog's collar before he could investigate the newcomer. 'Did you question him?'

'He drew his dagger on us,' said Frank, twisting to look at a gash in the side of his leather doublet. 'Near enough got me, and he's nicked Harry there's ear.' Harry, standing beside him in John Sempill's livery, grinned self-consciously and mopped at the dripping blood. 'So no, mem, we didny take the time to question him ower much.'

'I can see you wouldny,' she said, looking down at the man. He seemed to be of more than middling height, aged perhaps twenty or twenty-five, with well-barbered dark hair. His jerkin was dark red broadcloth, his boots were good but very dusty. 'We must search him. Had he taken anything from the miners' shelter?'

'No that I saw, he was just poking about,' Frank said, 'looking amongst their graith and the like.' He bent to turn the prisoner onto his back, and the limp figure convulsed like a mantrap Alys had once seen, came up snarling, a knife in his hand from nowhere in a sweeping gesture which had Frank flung sideways and crying out.

It all seemed to happen very slowly next. Lowrie dived forward, shouting, Harry grabbed at the man's wrist, which slipped from his grasp, Alys leapt away from the action wishing she had not put Gil's dagger back in her purse, and caught her heel in a tussock of grass and went down. The same dark lightning movement seemed to happen above her, and she was dragged to her feet, painfully by one arm, and hauled against a panting chest. A hoarse voice spoke over her shoulder.

'Keep aff me. Keep aff me or the lassie gets it. And if that dog comes here I'll knife it and all.'

'*Down!*' she ordered, almost on a reflex, and relief swept over her as the dog obeyed, reluctantly, quivering with eagerness to attack.

There was a knife sharp against her ribs. A small part of her mind recognized that it must have found one of the gaps in the whalebone bodice of her riding-dress. There were not many.

'My son, consider what you are doing!' protested Sir Richie. Behind him Philip Sempill emerged from the church carrying a hank of rope, and stopped, staring in horror. His cousin looked grim. Lowrie was standing poised, hands twitching, trying to work out what to do, staring at her with almost exactly the same expression as Socrates. The hoarse voice spoke again next to her ear.

'Just stay nice and quiet where you are, and I'll walk her down to the horses.'

Yes, and what then? Her mind raced, the whalebone forgotten. This man would never let her go alive, he used a knife too readily. This had happened to her before, perhaps there was a sign written on her brow, *Take this lassie hostage at knifepoint*, but since that time Gil had taught her one or two tricks to use against a man with a knife.

'Right, lassie. You be quiet, the way you're doing, and I'll no hurt ye. We're going to take a wee walk, see? Nice and gentle, to see the bonnie horses.'

She collected herself as the pressure of his arm tried to turn her slightly, to move backwards down to the gate. She caught Lowrie's eye, indicated her dangling right hand as well as she could without moving. His gaze dropped, and she counted off ostentatiously with her fingers. One. Two. Three.

She went limp, so that her entire weight fell on the arm which restrained her, then as her captor braced himself against the sudden burden she dug in her heels and thrust backward. They both went over and down, hard, and she heard the wind go out of the man.

She rolled frantically aside, seized the fallen knife, scrambled up out of the way of the rushing feet and the snarling.

'Mistress!' It was Lowrie at her elbow. 'That was well done! You're no hurt, are you?'

'I'm hale.' She found she was grinning in relief. 'Gil taught me it.'

'He has a good pupil.' He gave her an admiring look, and returned to the fray. Socrates was poised on the man's chest, snarling into his face, white teeth snapping, and as earlier today was reluctant to give up his catch. Trying to persuade herself it had been perfectly safe, that the blade at her breast would never have got through the whale-bones, she went forward to congratulate the dog and haul him off, ignoring John Sempill's muttered comments about taking a stick to the ill-nurtured brute.

The prisoner was reclaimed, without gentleness. Of course, thought Alys, observing the way even Lowrie, even Luke, went out of their way to handle him roughly; eight men stood by, watched me taken at knifepoint, watched me save myself. The dog's reaction was exactly the same.

Stripped to his linen, his arms tied, held kneeling at the point of several whingers on the cobbles before the door of St Machan's Kirk, the man was rather less impressive, but he still managed a snarl the equal of Socrates' when John Sempill demanded his name.

'You're asking me, are you?' was all the answer he got.

'Aye, I'm asking. And what were you doing up the

glen?' Sempill nudged him under the ribs with the toe of his boot. 'Back to strip the place o siller, were ye? No content wi slaying unarmed men about their lawful work, were ye? Can ye tell me good reason why I canny hang you for murder fro yon tree?' Each question was marked by another nudge.

'Lawful!' The prisoner spat.

'And what d'you mean by that?' Another nudge from the boot, powerful enough to wind the man. 'Show him the two corps, lads. And that worthless laddie, see if he kens him.'

Alys rose from the table-tomb where she had seated herself in the hope that her knees would stop trembling, intending to follow the group into the church. She was distracted by Lowrie, who was making an inventory in his tablets of the prisoner's possessions.

'Mistress Mason, look at this.'

'What is it?' She crossed to where he sat on the grass, and he held out the man's purse.

'I've just the now opened it, I was writing down his clothes and boots. Look what was in his *spoirean*.'

The purse was in fact a sturdy leather bag, almost a scrip, as big as her two hands and made to be slung from a belt. She took it, finding it heavy, lifted the flap, peered in. Something gleamed in the shadow within. Coin? Not loose, surely, it would fall to the bottom. She tilted the thing to see better, and blue velvet and gold braid caught the light.

'*Ah, mon Dieu!*' she said in amazement, and drew out a fat purse. A purse of blue velvet, trimmed with gold braid. 'Where did he have this?'

'Are you thinking what I'm thinking, mistress?'

'There can hardly be two of the things,' she said, her mind working. 'It must be Dame Isabella's, the one that is missing. But how did he – Unless he was the stranger, that morning!'

'You mean she gave him it?' Lowrie said. 'But in that case, was it him killed her?'

257

'Forveleth said,' she recalled slowly, 'the old dame said to her, *Here's that Campbell coming down the street and another wi him,* and then she said, *Hand me the blue purse out my kist and get out o here.* So it would fit. But why did he kill her? Who is he?' She knelt beside Lowrie, looking at his tablets without seeing them. 'Who is involved in this anyway? Your man Attie, the other servants, I take it he's none of those.' He nodded agreement, a gleam of humour in his expression. 'The folk from Clerk's Land. Madam Xanthe and her girls. Forgive me,' she said briefly as a wave of scarlet swept up his brow. 'Useless to pretend such places don't exist. What other names do we have?'

'Dusty,' said Lowrie suddenly. 'The man Miller, the one the little girls saw.'

'Of course, the one who dwells down the Gallowgate. Have you set eyes on him?' He shook his head. 'Nor has Gil. I can think of no others, apart from folk like yourself, or Maister Syme, or Kate's lassies.' She sat back on her heels and looked triumphantly at him. 'Well, I think we have a surname and a by-name for this man, though we still do not know why he killed Dame Isabella.'

'Sempill of Muirend will be disappointed,' he said after a moment. 'I think he's looking forward to a hanging.'

By the time they rode back into Glasgow in the twilight, Alys was bone-weary.

Sempill of Muirend had indeed been disappointed. His reaction, in fact, put her in mind of small John denied a sweetmeat, involving as it did red-faced shouting, stamping and finally a prolonged sulk. She found herself wondering how Lady Magdalen dealt with these episodes: did she use one of the remedies which were so effective with a small boy? The adult was less easily distracted, could not be smacked and put to bed, and would not be reasoned with. Finally Philip Sempill took his cousin on one side and talked to him quietly and forcefully, then returned with a curt,

'Get him on a horse, then.'

There was still some delay. Decisions had to be made, and Frank's slashed arm to be bound up. Sir Richie was persuaded to allow the two dead miners to lie in St Machan's overnight, arrangements made for their burial on Monday, for the boy Berthold to be present ('My father will see to that,' said Alys confidently) and for one of Sempill's men to ride down Strathblane to spread the word that the demons were vanquished and proved to be no more than flesh and blood.

'Though whether they'll believe it,' said Sir Richie dubiously, 'I couldny say. They're fond o a good story, see, and demons make a better tale than miners.'

The remaining horses were untied and led out to graze and find water before the ride back, and at Lowrie's suggestion, several of the men went up the glen to dismantle the miners' shelter and pack their belongings into the hides which had covered it, bringing them back to stow in St Machan's safe from further pilfering.

'It belongs to the boy,' he said, 'and if he gets away after all this, he'll ha need of it.'

Alys, who had been hoping nobody else would recognize Berthold's criminal status, said nothing and Berthold himself, shown the bundles as they were hoisted into the loft, merely nodded. He seemed to have retreated into a distant, silent place; Alys thought he was probably hungry, but she did not wish to mention it in front of Sir Richie, who could hardly feed all of them.

The prisoner himself, tethered to the great ring handle of the church door, watched all with a sour expression. He still denied everything, refused to account for his presence in the glen, and claimed he had never seen the two dead men before.

'He touched them willingly enough,' said Lowrie. 'It might be true.'

'Not everyone holds by the belief,' Alys said.

'Aye, but it's more often scholars, folk that's been to college, that accept that the dead are dead. This fellow looks far more like to believe they'll sit up and accuse him, or bleed when he touches them, or the like.'

'He reacted to the name,' she said, snapping her fingers for the dog.

'Maybe.'

Addressed as *Miller* from across the little church, the prisoner had frozen briefly, but made no other sign, and refused to answer when asked if that was his name, even when encouraged by Sempill's boot and fist. Since the man was obviously a quick thinker, Alys was inclined to take this as proof; the others were less convinced. The blue velvet purse had elicited even less response, although John Sempill had exploded in righteous indignation when he understood what it was, and had to be restrained.

Finally, the prisoner tied on Alys's horse, Alys herself put up behind Lowrie, the boy Berthold perched in front of Tam, they set off. They made a good pace down the valley, hoping to reach the better road before the light began to fade. John Sempill was still deep in his sulk, but Philip brought his horse alongside Lowrie's and said,

'Do we take him to the Tolbooth, or to the Castle?'

'The Castle,' said Alys promptly. 'The Provost is more like to accept him without arguing. He has the better instruments of interrogation, too,' she added, glancing at John Sempill's hunched back. Philip followed her look, and grinned.

'A good argument,' he agreed. 'Do you think we've found the man that killed Dame Isabella?'

'He denies it,' said Lowrie. 'He denies knowing her.'

'Otterburn will sort that,' said Philip confidently.

'I don't see why else he would have the purse,' said Alys. 'We know,' she paused, assembling an accurate statement, 'we know that Dame Isabella saw two men from her window, one called Campbell and another, and asked for the blue purse and dismissed her waiting-woman. Now we have the purse, and a man she might not have known. It fits, but not inarguably, I suppose.'

260

'He might have stolen it from someone else,' Lowrie agreed, as Philip looked surprised. 'Or been given it, or even had it from the miners before he killed them.'

'I never thought of that,' said Alys.

They pressed on, passing little knots of cattle being driven home for the night, sleepy herd-laddies trudging behind them. Socrates ignored their dogs with a lofty air. Alys clung to Lowrie's waist and considered the day. It seemed to her to have been extremely successful; she had achieved what she set out to do in this country of strange adventures, and more besides. But where had the blue purse come from? Why would Miller, if he was Miller, kill Dame Isabella?

Where the Glazert met the Kelvin, turning towards Glasgow, Lowrie and Philip Sempill consulted briefly and ordered more speed. There was little more traffic than there had been in Strathblane. The carts had found their destination or settled down somewhere for the night; they passed a few groups of riders, occasional people on foot, most with curious looks for the cavalcade. Ten riders at a fast trot through the spring twilight, thought Alys, one of them stripped to his shirt, can hardly be an everyday sight. She clung tighter to Lowrie, her teeth rattling.

At the Stablegreen Port the guards had heard them coming, and were waiting to swing the heavy gate across the way behind them in the very last of the light. Lowrie called his thanks, but John Sempill suddenly roused himself to say,

'Right, Livingstone, you can tell the Provost I'll be at home if he wants me, and you two wi me,' he flung over his shoulder at his two men. 'Philip, what are you doing?'

'I'm for the Castle,' said his cousin. 'They'll be glad of the extra hands, I'd think, to get this fellow into custody.'

'Aye, well, if you'd let me put him on a rope you'd ha no need to worry,' retorted Sempill, and clattered off into the night towards Rottenrow, his men behind him. Lowrie watched him go, lit by the lanterns on successive house-corners, and said to Philip, 'Likely we'll deal better without

261

him, but we might need his witness about the property and the silver mine.'

'He might prefer not to give it,' said Alys. Philip made no comment. 'Luke, leave your horse with Tam and go on home, and you can tell them where we are.'

'What, here on the Stablegreen?' said Luke blankly, and she realized the boy was nearly asleep, and Berthold was completely comatose in Tam's grasp.

'We'll be at the Castle,' she said. 'Go on now, and tell them in the kitchen to put some food aside for me.'

Andrew Otterburn, roused from a domestic evening by his own fireside, was at first startled to be presented with a half-naked prisoner, but when he grasped who the man might be he was delighted.

'We'll get someone to identify him,' he said, as Miller was manhandled away across the courtyard, struggling as fiercely as he had done outside St Machan's. 'The trouble the Clerk's Land folk have caused me the day, it's no pain to me to get one o them out to put a name to this fellow. Walter, see to it, will you, and see these beasts baited. And find someone that speaks High Dutch and all, maybe speir at the College if there's none o the men.'

'Or send to my father,' suggested Alys. Walter nodded and hurried off.

'And who's the laddie, anyway?' asked the Provost.

'It's a long tale,' said Lowrie. 'May we sit down? And might we beg a bite to eat? The laddie's likely fasting since this morning, and the rest of us, well, it's long while since dinner.'

'Aye, come up, come up to my chamber and we'll see to it,' said Otterburn, but Alys was not listening. Socrates had pricked his ears and rushed away across the courtyard. Light shifted under the arch of the gatehouse, hasty feet echoed, and a tall figure with a lantern emerged into the torchlight, paused to look about, and made straight for where she stood, the dog dancing round him. Gil had come for her.

Neither of them spoke. A quick smile, a searching look

262

exchanged in the torchlight, and they turned to follow Otterburn, hands brushing lightly back to back. But suddenly she felt she could go on for as long again.

The tale took a while. Food appeared, bread and cold meat and the remains of an onion tart, with a huge jug of ale; she ate, the jug went round, and Lowrie embarked on a competent and precise account of what had passed that day. Otterburn listened well, she thought. He asked a few pertinent questions, called Frank in to explain his part. That was when she realized that she and Gil, Lowrie and Philip Sempill, were the only ones in the Provost's chamber; the servants and the boy Berthold had been left in the antechamber.

'Have the men something to eat?' she asked, interrupting Frank's account of the capture of their prisoner. A grin spread across his face.

'Our Lady love you, mistress, aye, we have. Much what you have here,' he nodded at the laden tray, 'so long as that greedy Sim hasny finished it afore I'm done here.'

'Get on wi your tale, then,' said the Provost, 'and you'll catch up wi him the sooner.'

'Aye well, it's soon ended,' admitted Frank, 'for that's about all. Save for the man getting loose again, and Mistress Mason here capturing him. And then—'

'I did not!' she protested. Gil leaned away to look down at her, concern in his face. Socrates, sprawled across their feet, raised his head, then went back to sleep. 'It was all of you took and bound him.'

'Aye, once you'd fell on him and winded him,' said Frank admiringly. 'A neat trick that, mistress, I'd like to ken who taught you it.'

'The drop-dead trick,' she explained to Gil. He nodded, and she saw she would not get to sleep tonight without giving him a complete tale.

'Then we stripped the man Miller, while he was in his swound,' said Lowrie, 'and while Sempill of Muirend set to questioning him I made an inventory of his goods, and found this in his *spoirean*.' He drew the blue velvet purse from the breast of his doublet, and leaned to set it on the desk before Otterburn. The Provost looked at it gloomily for a long moment.

'Well, well,' he said finally to Gil. 'Here's us searching Glasgow and the Gallowgate, putting a watch on the ports, crying the fellow at the Cross, and your lassie falls on him out the sky and fetches him home.'

Gil's arm was round her again. 'I'd expect no less.'

Otterburn looked at them both with the hint of a smile, but all he said was,

'And John Sempill questioned him, did he? What did he learn fro the man?'

'Little,' said Lowrie. 'He denies all, or answers nothing.'

'It's a great pity John isny here to tell us himself,' observed Gil.

'He went home,' said Alys. 'I thought,' she said slowly, assembling her recollections, 'I thought he knew the man. When he asked his name, the man said, *You're asking me?* As if he was surprised. And even before that, Sempill was very determined to hang him out of hand. He was very angry when we insisted on bringing him here to justice.'

Otterburn's gaze went from her to Gil, and then to Philip Sempill, while Lowrie said,

'You could be right at that, mistress.'

Philip said nothing, but his face darkened in the candle-light under Otterburn's steady stare. After a moment the Provost said, raising his voice a little,

'Right, Walter, how're you getting on wi those tasks I set you?'

His clerk stepped in from the antechamber, looking smug.

'It's the man Miller right enough, maister,' he said, 'named afore witnesses and writ down on oath. As for what he swore he'd do to the woman that named him, well, it's as well her Scots isny that good.'

'She understood what she swore to?' said Gil sharply.

'I'm no caring,' said Otterburn over Walter's assurances. 'She's sworn and that's that. And the interpreter?'

264

The interpreter proved to be one of the men-at-arms, a sturdy fairish man introduced as Lappy, which surely must be a nickname. He claimed he had spent time at the wars in High Germany and learned some of the language. Alys had doubts about the man's vocabulary, but Berthold, roused and brought through, understood the first questions put to him clearly enough. The boy seemed so stunned by the events of the day that he did not react with surprise, but nor did he answer. A spate of words tumbled out, clearly a question of his own, and another.

'Haud on!' said the interpreter. 'I'm no that fast.' He paused, putting the words into Scots. 'He's asking, maister, what o his faither and his uncle, when are they to be buried, will he can get to the burial? Is that right, they're dead?'

'Tell him,' said Otterburn, before Alys could speak, 'if he answers my questions, I'll see about it. Then ask him again why he's in Scotland and what they were doing.'

The boy's eyes turned to Otterburn, then to Alys. He spoke to Lappy, sounding surprised.

'He says, did the other man no tell you? It was him called them here, he thinks, and him that gave them orders.'

'Other man,' said Otterburn flatly. 'Does he mean the man Miller? The prisoner?'

'*Nein, nein!*' said Berthold as Lappy translated. '*Der böse Mann!*' He pulled an angry, sulky face.

'John Sempill!' said Alys and Lowrie together.

'I'm feart he's right,' said Philip.

Chapter Thirteen

'This is a right tirravee,' said John Sempill of Muirend
angrily. 'Why did you have to rout Maidie out her bed and
all? It's none o her mind, any o this.'

'John,' said his wife, putting a hand on his arm. 'If it's a
matter for the law, I've no complaint, though I'll not deny
the time could be better chosen. Is it about my godmother,
sir? Have you discerned who it was,' she bit her lip, 'that
killed her?'

The servants had been sent home, Lowrie and Philip
Sempill had made signed depositions and left reluctantly,
the boy Berthold, asleep on his feet, had been tucked in a
corner of the guardroom despite Alys's objections. Otterburn wanted him handy, he said. And four men-at-arms
had been despatched to escort Sempill of Muirend and his
wife to the Castle, and not to take any refusal.

Gil, watching from the window space, could not decide
how much either of them understood of Sempill's position.
Three candles in the pricket-stand beside Otterburn's desk
did not show their expressions clearly, but Lady Magdalen
certainly seemed ignorant of wrongdoing, merely puzzled.
He looked down at Alys, and found her watching intently
despite her weariness. Socrates was sprawled across her
feet, snoring.

'Aye, well,' said Otterburn. 'I'm tellt you'd likely prefer
to be turned out your bed the night rather than the morn,
what wi the morn being the Sabbath.'

Ah ah! thought Gil. So Otterburn has got there too,
has he?

'What's that supposed to mean?' Sempill said quickly.

'John.' Lady Magdalen turned to the Provost. 'Any day's right for God's work, and surely finding the truth is aye God's work? May we no sit down, sir?'

'Aye, get on wi't,' said Sempill. 'I want my bed. I've had a long ride the day.'

'So has my wife, John,' said Gil, 'and a fight wi a dangerous man forbye, while you stood and watched.'

'You can keep out o this,' snarled Sempill over his wife's shocked exclamation. 'If the pair o ye'd kept yir noses out fro the start it would ha been easier!'

'Very likely,' said Gil, 'but would it ha been honest?'

Otterburn cleared his throat significantly.

'We'll all be seated, if you please,' he said firmly, 'and we've a few things to discuss. Maister Cunningham, will you begin?'

Gil drew his stool forward so he could see all four faces in the candlelight. Sempill was scowling, Lady Magdalen wore her usual calm smile, Otterburn and Alys were both watching him with care. He marshalled the facts in his head and began.

'On Wednesday evening, John, you had a word wi Dame Isabella at her window. You were heard,' he forestalled interruption, 'after she'd kept you waiting, and then refused to see you. What was it she ordered you to do?'

'None o your mind,' retorted Sempill.

'On Wednesday evening?' queried Lady Magdalen. 'No, no, you said you never had a word wi her, John.'

'Aye, well,' he said uncomfortably, 'she wouldny see me alone, dismissed me like a groom, and after I'd waited as long. Was it those sleekit servants?' he demanded of Gil. 'Sneaking about listening in corners?'

'By what I'm tellt,' said Gil, amused, 'there was no need for that. The whole of the Drygate might ha heard you. She gave you an order, and you said you'd see her in Hell afore you did that. What did she say then, John? Will we hear it?'

Sempill opened his mouth to answer, closed it and stared at him, cornered and baffled.

'Did she bid you,' Gil chose his words with care, 'have no more to do wi the Ballencleroch toft? The one that holds Clachan of Campsie and the glen?'

'Aye,' said Sempill in relief. 'That was it.'

'The one you thought was mine, John?' said Lady Magdalen. 'Well, that was right. There was no need for you to be concerned wi that toft, unless she was to give it to me.'

'That's true,' agreed Gil. 'So what were you doing out there?'

'That's my business,' said Sempill, with more confidence.

'No, John, let us know,' prompted Lady Magdalen. 'Were you dealing wi the factor and so forth? Was that it?'

'There's no factor,' said Gil. 'He's been collecting the rents, and taking an interest, haven't you, John.'

'Aye.'

'Well, if that's all—'

'And he put the miners into the glen.'

'Miners?' Lady Magdalen looked from Gil to her husband, the dark woollen veil sliding over her shoulders as she turned her head. 'Surely no, maister, there's no mining in Strathblane. It's no coal country.'

'Not coal,' said Gil, watching Sempill. 'It's silver, as my wife worked out, and there were three men working it. A nice wee vein, the boy tells us, and should last another year or so.'

'Silver?' Lady Magdalen repeated in astonishment.

'Nothing to do wi me,' said Sempill defiantly.

I never met so many liars in the one case, Gil thought. All along, folk have not merely concealed things, they've lied outright.

'Silver,' repeated Lady Magdalen. 'I canny believe it, sir. Has it gone to the Crown, as it ought? You'd see to that, would you no, John?'

'Well, I would have done,' said Sempill unconvincingly, 'but I never had the chance.'

268

'How was that?' Gil asked. 'What prevented you?'

'Surely, all you had to do was send to the Treasurer,' Lady Magdalen said. 'That's no hard task, John. I could have writ the letter, if you wanted.'

'The old – the old – Dame Isabella,' Sempill burst out. 'She wouldny let me! She insisted – she's been buying it off me! It was all to come down here, and I never had the least notion what she was doing wi't.'

And if you believe that, thought Gil, you'll believe anything. Aloud he said,

'So the silver was worked up in Strathblane, and run into ingots, or bars, or what you call them, and brought down to Glasgow. Was it Neil Campbell and his brother that fetched it?'

'Aye, damn you!' said Sempill grudgingly. His wife sat back, looking at him reproachfully. 'If you've nosed out that much, why do you need to ask me?'

Gil thought about the rest of the detail Berthold had given them. It had been the angry man who had brought his father and uncle to Scotland, and put them in that narrow valley and told them to keep the local folk away. Well, miners were used to that attitude, so they had used the tricks they always had, which had worked. The man who fetched the silver had brought them meal, which they had disliked, and onions and cheese. They had spoken to nobody else. Nothing to unsettle Sempill there.

'What happened to it next?' he asked instead. 'Where did the Campbell brothers take it to?'

'Oh, that was all the old dame's concern,' said Sempill loftily. 'None o my mind, so I got paid for it.'

'What, you just let it out o your hands?' Sempill nodded. 'Well, well. So on Wednesday evening Dame Isabella ordered you to have no more to do wi the toft that holds the mine.'

'Why would she do that?' Lady Magdalen asked in puzzlement. Sempill glowered, but Alys looked up and caught Gil's eye.

'Dame Isabella had just learned that there was a confusion,' she pointed out. 'The toft with the mine on it was hers, not Lady Magdalen's.' Or possibly Archie Livingstone's, Gil thought, but did not say. 'She had been buying silver which was her own.'

'Did she ask for her money back, John?' Gil asked in some amusement.

'Aye, she did, the auld—' Sempill bit off the next word as his wife laid a hand on his sleeve. 'I told her I'd see her in Hell first, and I meant it.'

'Did you now,' said Otterburn. Sempill looked at him in alarm, and then at Lady Magdalen's dismayed expression.

'Here – no, no, I didny mean it like that!'

'You've just said you did,' said Gil.

'Aye, but I wouldny – I didny—'

'John.'

He stopped, looked at the pale hand on his arm, and covered it with his own, met his wife's gaze. She said earnestly,

'John, tell me you didny kill my godmother.'

'I didny kill her,' he said obediently. 'I swear it on—' Her hand twitched, and he bit his lip. 'I mean, my word on it, Maidie.'

She put her other hand on top of his.

'That's enough for me. But we need to find out who did, so he gets time to repent. You'll tell Maister Gil all he needs to hear, won't you, John?'

'Aye,' he said reluctantly.

Lady Magdalen smiled at him, nodded at Gil, and sat back, one hand still on Sempill's arm. Gil, wondering whether he would know if Alys managed him in such an obvious way, said,

'So what did you do?'

'Do?' Sempill stared at him. 'Nothing. Went home to my bed.'

'About the silver,' Gil said. 'The next morning, the Thursday, you were from home when I came looking for you. You came in about Terce, I'd say. Where had you been?'

'Out looking for you,' said Sempill boldly. 'I tellt you that, I mind.'

'And I'd said I'd meet you at the house. No, by what I hear you were down at Clerk's Land, John.'

'If you ken that, why'd you ask me? You hear a curst sight too much,' Sempill added. 'I was looking for you there, thought you might be spying round the place.'

'You were speaking to Campbell and Saunders,' Gil corrected him. 'Letting them know there would be no more silver, no more of the old dame's scheme. What was the scheme, John?'

'Scheme?' Lady Magdalen asked. 'What was happening to the silver? Do you know, John?'

He threw her a hunted look.

'No,' he said. 'No, I – I wasny in it, once she'd paid me for the silver. I've no idea what she was at.'

'You knew enough to tell the Clerk's Land folk,' said Gil.

'Aye, well, I kent that was where Neil took the stuff. Seemed only civil to let them hear it was all at an end.'

Gil, setting aside the combination of John Sempill and the word 'civil' for later contemplation, looked at Otterburn and said,

'Then we come to the Clerk's Land folk.'

'Aye.' Otterburn grunted. 'All in it thegither, save for the lorimer. And maybe Danny Sproat's donkey,' he considered. 'Two hammermen and an image-maker, and their friend Miller the knife man from the Gallowgate.'

Sempill sat motionless.

'After you left the toft,' Gil resumed, 'Campbell sent one of the Saunders children down to summon Miller up there, and passed the word to him. The pair of them decided to go and have it out wi Dame Isabella, and went off down the Drygate. Dame Isabella looked out from her window and saw them approaching, and she ordered her woman to give her the purse of blue velvet and leave her.' Lady Magdalen's pale eyes were fixed on his face, her lips

271

parted. She must have been fond of the old woman, he thought, or is she feart I'll prove John killed her after all? 'The woman got no sight of the two men, she only saw a stranger leaving by the gate a few minutes later. Nobody else was seen about the place. But when they next went in to Dame Isabella she was dead.'

Lady Magdalen bent her head, and her lips moved silently. After a moment she said,

'So is it one of these men, Campbell or Miller, that killed her? Where is the blue purse, sir? Is it found?'

Straight to the point, he thought.

'We found it in Miller's possession,' said Alys. 'It seems likely she gave him it. One of them must have kept her talking while the other went round into the house and into her chamber.' She leaned forward to touch Lady Magdalen's free hand. The dog raised his head, then went back to sleep. 'I'm sorry. It's a great loss to you, I understand that.'

'My thanks,' said the other woman with a tremulous smile. 'But has neither o them confessed?'

Sempill glared at Alys, patted his wife's shoulder awkwardly, and said,

'Aye, you need to put them to the question, they'll confess soon enough if you go about it right.'

'They will the morn,' said Otterburn confidently. 'Either or both. Now, can one o you set light on a subject that's troubling me? Why in the name o Christ and all His saints would a woman in her position be sending false coin out to the Isles?'

'What?' Sempill jerked upright. 'To the Isles? Why in the Deil's name?'

'John.'

'Aye, but what's the point o that? You tellt me she was daft for John o the Isles,' he recalled, scowling at her, 'more sense surely to send it to him and let him pay for his escape if he wants to. No that he's worth it,' he added, 'a burnt stock that one if ever I seen one.'

272

Of course, thought Gil, John of the Isles is pensioned at Paisley Abbey, not so far from Muirend.

'It's changing the balance of the region,' he said. 'It's altering matters like who has more men, more ships, more importance. There's been enough arguing since Earl John was dispossessed, if it comes to war out there, no knowing who'll come out victorious.'

'She knew him,' said Lady Magdalen suddenly, in a faint voice. 'Forgive me, maisters, this has been a great shock to me.'

'You should lie down,' said Sempill. 'You should be home in your bed, no sitting here till all hours answering daft questions. We'll be away, Otterburn—'

'No yet,' said Otterburn, quite mildly, but Sempill sat down again. 'She knew him, you say, madam?'

'She once tellt me.' She put a hand to her brow. 'I canny mind right. She must ha known Thomas Livingstone, that's her last husband, sir, when they were all young, for she spoke o his sister, that was wedded to John of the Isles. They'd been good friends, I think.'

'Dame Isabella and the Livingstone lady were friends?' Gil interpreted, untangling this. She nodded.

'And ever since, she'd had a great regard for him, by the way she spoke. So maybe, maybe,' she bit her lip, 'it doesny maybe make sense, but I wonder.'

'You wonder if she wished to destabilize the Isles,' Alys supplied. 'Perhaps even hoping that John might get back to his possessions.'

'Aye,' she said gratefully. 'It sounds right daft, when you put it like that, but she was, she was, she was aye one wi her own—'

'She was a steering auld ettercap,' said Sempill forcefully, 'and I'll no forgive her for putting you through all this.'

Gil met Alys's glance, but kept his face straight.

'Well,' said Otterburn. 'I can see we've a lot to think on, all o us present. I think I'll ask you to take Lady Magdalen home to her bed, Sempill, but first,' he went on, ignoring

273

Sempill's expostulations, 'I'll have you swear, and I'll have your word, madam, no to depart fro Glasgow till I give you leave.'

'I'll come and go as I please!' exploded Sempill, 'and no Archbishop's placeman's going to—'

'John.' Lady Magdalen turned her weary face to Otterburn. 'Sir, you may have my word on that, and gladly, but why?'

Could she possibly be as obtuse as she appeared, Gil wondered. Otterburn appeared to think the same, for he looked hard at her, and then said,

'I need your man where I can put my hand on him. There's been silver mining without informing the Crown, there's been shipping the metal about the realm, there's been supplying counterfeit coiners, there's been offering comfort to the King's enemies—'

'I never!' burst out Sempill. 'I never did any o that, all I did was let the old dame have the stuff, it's none o my blame what she did wi it!'

'John.'

'You might,' continued Otterburn, 'get off wi a great fine, but that's no for me to decide. So I need you where the justiciars can see you, man. Will you swear, or will you spend the night below here along wi the man Miller?'

'Your word, John,' Lady Magdalen prompted gently. He threw her a sulky look and mumbled something. Otterburn, clearly deciding to make do with what he could get, nodded and rose to his feet.

'I'll get a couple o the men to see you home,' he said. 'And my thanks, madam.'

'I'm feared I canny return the compliment, Provost,' she said. 'You've left me wi a deal to think about, and the most o it unwelcome. But I'm grateful that you've uncovered the reasons for my godmother's death, you can believe that.' She held out her hand to Sempill, and he leapt up hastily to assist her to her feet. 'Bid you good night, Alys, maisters.'

At the foot of the stair, watching the other couple disappear under the gatehouse arch with two sleepy men-at-arms behind them, Gil remarked,

'D'you think they'll sleep, either of them?'

'He's got a curtain lecture like none other waiting for him, I'd say,' said Otterburn. 'What a woman. But you're right, maister, she'll no want to come before the justiciars, they'll discern more than she'd wish for.'

'She makes no attempt to conceal it,' said Alys, leaning against Gil. He looked down at her, full of pride and a sudden compunction. Socrates yawned hugely beside her.

'I ought to take you home,' he said. 'I should never have let you stay the now.'

'I wanted to stay,' she pointed out.

'No, no, it was a good help having her here,' said Otterburn, 'but you should get her home to her bed now. I dare say the two of you have as much to talk o as that pair that's just left. I'll get a couple more men out to get you down the High Street.'

'We'll manage fine,' said Gil. 'I've the woman that took the man Miller to protect me, after all.'

Out in the silent street, making their way round to the High Cross, Alys said,

'What will you do now?'

'Do?' he said, startled. 'I've a disposition to scribe for Monday, likely I can get time at that tomorrow.'

'No, now.'

'Get you to bed, madam wife. You can tell me in the morning how you guessed it was a silver mine in Strathblane.'

'Is that all?'

He finally recognized the drift of her questions. 'Why, what do you want to do?'

'I thought,' she said diffidently, 'that Madam Xanthe might wish to know what happened today.'

'Madam Xanthe?' He stopped, and swung her round, holding the lantern higher to see her face. The dog came back from his scrutiny of the Girth Cross, looking up at them curiously. 'Are you sending me out to the whore-house, after a day like this?'

Her quick smile flickered.

'Not sending,' she said. He waited. 'I thought you might take me?'

He suppressed a crack of laughter, and hugged her close, thinking yet again how fortunate he was in this woman.

'I see what it is,' he said. 'You want to inspect these naughty paintings.'

'That too,' she said against his chest. 'But I should borrow your plaid, this riding-dress is all too conspicuous.'

He unfolded it and shook it out, swinging it round her. It was a full-sized man's plaid, two ells long by the full one-and-a-half wide; the pattern was a dark check in the natural greys and browns of the wool, and in this light it disappeared altogether, making her nearly invisible, a patch of shadow crowned by a jaunty hat like a man's.

'If anyone sees us, they'll just think I'm selling you into the place,' he said, and she giggled.

The House of the Mermaiden was quieter than Gil expected. It could hardly be midnight, but the hall windows were dark. He held the lantern low so they could pick their way round the side of the house, past the kitchen where snores issued through the shutters, to the back door. The window beside it showed light, and quiet voices spoke inside. Gil tapped on the shutter, and they stopped.

'Who's there?' said someone sharply.

He spoke his name. There was an exclamation, quick footsteps, a heavy rattle and thump as the door was unbarred. Light spilled out past the plant-tubs, over the cobbles. Socrates padded forward, tail waving.

'Gil? No, who's that wi you? We're closed this evening, sir—'

'No matter,' said Alys in French. 'I've wanted to meet you.' She curtsied full in the candlelight, and Madam Xanthe laughed, and replied in the same language.

276

'And I to meet you, madame. Come away in! You'll take a glass of wine?'

The wine was the same rich, fruit-tasting stuff as before, but everything else was different. The little panelled chamber where he had been dried and fed cordial and soup was almost bare, the padded bench and a few stools standing forlornly amid a sea of kists and boxes, and the woman Agrippina was kneeling before another, trying to fasten the straps.

'You're packing,' Gil stated.

'Such penetrating observation, I see how you're made Blacader's quaestor,' said Madam Xanthe. 'Your health, madame. You can see, you've caught us just in time. The wagons are ordered for first light.'

'A moonlight flitting?' Gil challenged.

'Oh, I've paid the rent to the end of the quarter, no doubt o that. But we're done here in Glasgow. Anyway this is the last o this barrel, I could never stay longer.' She lifted the jug and topped up their glasses again.

'Where are you off to?'

She gave him that arch smile.

'Who can say, maister? Where my fancy takes me, wherever the oxen stop like St Serf's wagon, somewhere there's need of my talents?'

'I can't imagine where that could be. And the lassies?'

'Nor can I, sir. Oh, the lassies? The most of them's bound for Edinburgh, for their talents are certainly wasted here, but Cleone and Cato are going to her granny's house in Renfrew.'

'Are they left yet?' Alys asked quickly. 'There was something I wished to ask Cleone.'

Madam Xanthe tilted her head to look at her. 'Did you so? Is that what brings you visiting?'

'No, merely a distraction. I wished to thank you for your help to my husband,' said Alys, smiling into the painted face. 'And we have just come from the Castle, and a long talk with John Sempill and his wife.'

277

'A pleasant evening that would be, certainly,' said Madam Xanthe, her gaze sharpening. 'As to the other, you thanked us well enough with the basket of sweetmeats. That was a kind thought, and well received. Agrippina, would you go up and see if Cleone is still awake? And how is the charming John?' she went on as the woman rose, lifted a candle and left quietly.

'Chastened,' said Gil. The fine eyebrows rose.

'What, by your doing?'

'Mostly Alys's, I should say. She and young Lowrie found the source of the silver today, out in Strathblane, and the surviving miner claims it was Sempill brought them over to Scotland. Then they captured the man Miller, who seems to have killed the other two miners, and found the renowned blue velvet purse on him.'

Madam Xanthe's gaze dropped to her fingernails.

'Dame Isabella's purse?'

'The same,' agreed Alys, 'or so we assume. The Provost will get it identified in the morning.'

'Well, well. And what does he conclude from that?'

'That the man Miller killed Dame Isabella,' said Gil.

'Ah!' She sat back, then turned her head as Agrippina returned, with a blinking Cleone in her wake. 'Och, you silly lassie, could you not have covered yourself decent?'

'She's perfectly decent,' said Alys quickly, switching to Scots as Madam Xanthe had done. 'Cleone, I am Maister Cunningham's wife.'

Cleone took this in, smiled broadly, and curtsied as well as she might in her abbreviated shift.

'You sent us the sweetmeats, mem! Thank you, they were right good! C-cato was sick twice wi eating them. And the ribbons was that bonnie!'

Alys accepted this as it seemed to be intended, and said earnestly,

'I wished to ask you something, Cleone. Do you mind how you saw Maister Cunningham struck on the head?'

A wary expression came into the blue eyes.

'Aye.'

'Who was it struck him?'

'Dod Muir, like I said.'

Alys looked steadily at the other girl, while Gil considered that he had wondered about the same point. After a few moments Cleone looked down at the floor.

'Dod Muir was shorter than my husband,' Alys observed, 'by a good span. He'd have had trouble reaching up to hit him on the crown of the head. And in any case, lassie, he was dead by then.'

'Aye,' said Cleone, 'but I didny know that, did I?'

'Did he shout at you?' Alys asked with sympathy.

'No at me, at Col. Cato,' she corrected herself. 'He's no, he's no – he's a bit daft, Col, but he's a good laddie, there was no need to give him a swearing just acause he got in the man's way.'

'I understand that,' said Alys. 'So who was it struck my husband?' Cleone looked sideways at her. 'Did you ken him? Was it a stranger, or one of the other men on the toft?'

'It was that stranger,' she said after a moment. 'That one that's aye coming about the place, and they're all feart for.'

'The one called Miller?' Alys asked. Cleone shrugged, and the short shift bounced. 'Can you tell me what the man looked like?'

Another shrug.

'Taller than Dod Muir,' she offered. 'He'd a red doublet and good boots, and a blue bonnet.'

'What colour was his plaid?' Gil asked. Cleone smiled at him.

'Our Lady love you, maister, he wasny wearing one.'

'Thank you, lassie.' Alys sat back, nodding to Madam Xanthe. 'I'm sorry to have brought you out your bed, but that's a useful thing you've told me.'

'And more useful if you'd tellt the truth in the first place,' said Madam Xanthe crisply. 'Away back up the stair afore you freeze to death, you silly lassie.' She watched the girl go, and as Agrippina settled to her packing again said, 'And you're saying this man Miller's been taken? After you searched his workshop today, you've likely put a stop to the coining. So all's at an end?'

'All's at an end,' agreed Gil.

'Tell me about it, my dears. You won't mind Agrippina coming and going, will you?'

They kept the tale short, though Gil had to hear the full account of Miller's capture, guiltily aware of a wish to display his wife's talents before someone who could appreciate them. Madam Xanthe listened attentively, and was suitably impressed by the drop-dead trick.

'I must keep that in mind,' she said, and tittered. 'Though nobody's likely to take me hostage at knifepoint, I imagine. Well done, madame.'

She laughed aloud at their account of John Sempill's crushed demeanour, but heard about the promises Otterburn had exacted without comment or expression.

'Do you think Sempill will get away with a fine?' Alys asked when they had finished. 'He has broken the law, after all.'

'Oh, my dear, how can I say?' said Madam Xanthe, waving a long white hand in front of her face. 'I'm a simple woman, I've no idea how the justiciars will act.' She paused, looked from one to the other, and tittered again. 'Do you know, you are looking at me with the same expression, both of you! Positively eerie, I assure you!'

'Can you wonder?' Gil said. 'I believe no part of that statement was true.'

'Do three negatives make a negative?' she speculated absently. 'So you think your case is ended, maister? The matter of Dame Isabella's death is concluded?'

'I think so,' said Gil deliberately. Alys nodded.

'So why did she die?' The painted face altered somehow and Gil found he was looking at Sandy Boyd's pale gaze, direct and challenging in the candlelight. Not *Who killed her?* he thought, but *Why did she die?*

'A number of reasons,' said Alys, 'though the ones Maister Otterburn saw will do for the justiciars.'

'You think so? Both of you?'

Gil exchanged a glance with his wife.

'I think so,' he said at length. 'It's clear enough how and when the old woman was killed, and Miller had reason enough and was seen approaching just afore she died. Even if he continues to deny that one he'll certainly hang for Dod Muir, St Giles be thanked, we have witnesses enough for that.'

'I'm right glad to hear it,' said Boyd. 'And you, my dear?'

Alys set down her wineglass and gathered up her skirts to rise.

'*Mon mari a raison*,' she said. 'Madame, I must beg your forgiveness. It is late and I am very weary. I wish you good fortune wherever you are next, and whatever occupies you.'

'Why, thank you.' Madam Xanthe was back, taking Alys's cue, rising in a crackle of taffeta. 'And I wish you the same.'

'And I hope,' said Gil deliberately, 'that you will be able to separate personal business from professional next time.'

'But *monsieur*!' The pale blue eyes met his direct, but the arch manner was more exaggerated than ever. 'It's so convenient when they overlap, you must see that!'

'Oh!' Alys paused, turning away from the door. 'Before we go, might we look at this painted hall? I've heard great things of it.'

'Oh, and so you should.' The light laugh, the hand on Alys's arm. 'Come away up now, we'll find candles and let you inspect it at your leisure. It's caused a lot of comment among our guests,' she confided. 'I believe there's nothing like it in Glasgow.'

'Very likely,' said Gil with emphasis.

Walking slowly down through the silent burgh, the plaid wrapped round both of them against a light drizzle which had begun while they were admiring the paintings, Alys leaned her head against Gil's shoulder and said,

'I should like a longer look at that house by daylight.'

281

He had been thinking how good it would be to fall into bed. 'Hmm?' he said.

'The paintings are very good. One could put a plate-cupboard in front of the naked lady, though it would be a shame to hide the golden hair. It has how many chambers?'

'Seven chambers, three closets, four hearths under the main roof,' he recounted. 'Or so Sandy said, the first time we were there.'

'Yes,' she said thoughtfully, as they turned in at the pend which led to her father's house. 'Smaller than this, but a good size.'

'A good size for what?' he asked, with a faint feeling of alarm.

'For us.' She paused under the pend, the beams of his small closet over their heads. 'This is my father's house, Gil. You should have your own roof, and when you take an assistant you need to have room to house him.'

'An assistant?' he repeated in surprise, his voice rising.

'Hush, you will wake John. Yes, you need an assistant. I'd suggest Lowrie, after today, but you will make your own decision of course.'

'Will I?' he said. And what was I thinking earlier about being managed? 'He made a good impression, did he?'

'He did. Oh, he is not you, but if you teach him he could be nearly as good as you. His manners are good, he is well read. Socrates likes him.'

'An infallible sign of merit,' he said, amused. She pushed him lightly.

'No, but think how difficult it would be if you took someone the dog disliked. Where is he, anyway?'

'Waiting for us at the door.'

The house door opened at that, and as Socrates whisked inside out of the rain Maistre Pierre's voice, lowered in deference to the hour, said,

'Are you to stand out there till the dawn, or are you coming in?'

Chapter Fourteen

'I'd not expected you so early,' said Otterburn with faint irony. 'How's Mistress Mason the day?'

'Weary.' Gil grimaced.

He had not slept well, despite fatigue and the late night; conversations of the day had replayed themselves over and over in his head, while Alys breathed slowly beside him. This morning she was tired, stiff and cross, and dealing with a crisis in the kitchen. She had shown no interest in explaining to her father and Ealasaidh, who were agog to hear them, any of the details of her day in Strathblane. It had been left to Gil to convey the gist of her adventures and their results, with an account of the midnight interview with Sempill and Lady Magdalen. Ealasaidh had been first amused and then shocked, crying out in disapproval of Dame Isabella's behaviour. Maistre Pierre had listened more carefully, taking particular note of one or two points, and then frowned at Gil.

'Better this way,' he said.

'Och, yes, better indeed. But to be stirring trouble in the Isles!' said Ealasaidh. 'And her no kin to any of the folk there! That is simple badness, though I suppose,' she added darkly, 'it would be all you would expect of an immodest woman like that.'

Gil nodded.

'I wish McIan was still here,' he said. 'He might make me understand how things are out to the West.'

'No, no,' said Ealasaidh seriously, 'there is no understanding it, for as soon as it is settled, they are changing what they ask for.'

'But do you think the old woman's scheme will have had any success?'

'No knowing at all,' she said. 'Money is not a thing they are using much, it might have made no difference at all.'

He had called briefly on his uncle, to give him the end of the tale, though he had skimmed over Alys's *Straunge Aduenture*. Canon Cunningham's reaction had been similar to Maistre Pierre's.

'We would certainly have had to question everyone in the matter,' he agreed. 'Better this way, without letting the light of day into everyone's inmost thoughts. Indeed, Gilbert, almost one might say the old – dame had been executed ahead of her trial, it comes so convenient for the Crown.'

'So one might,' agreed Gil. His uncle shot him a sharp look.

'As to this mad scheme of hers, to destabilize the Isles, I never heard of such a thing. Rank treason, at least in intent. I very much doubt whether it would have succeeded,' he pronounced.

Now Otterburn was saying much the same thing.

'No saying it would have worked. It's a barter market out there, little enough coin changes hands.'

'Aye, but the whole chain leaked,' Gil said. 'It was the coin getting away every time a purse moved that worried Blacader and the Treasury. It seems as if they kent it was going out to the Isles, but not where it was coming from, till we started digging here in Glasgow.'

'Did they now?' Otterburn was shuffling papers on his desk. 'Aye, here we are. You might like a sight o my report, and then you can have a read at the man Miller's deposition. Oh, and his Christian name, maister, you'll never guess, I might as well tell you straight, is Hilary. What were his parents thinking on? No wonder he stuck wi his surname or his by-name! We got a confession off him for Dod Muir, seeing we had witnesses a plenty, and he's admitted to the two miners wi a bit persuasion, well, one o them, he swears the other was an accident, but him and

Noll Campbell both are determined neither of them slew Dame Isabella. How did ye get the blue velvet purse then, I asked him, and he says, *She gied me it hersel*. For all his hard work, he says. Can you credit it?'

Well, yes, I can, thought Gil, skimming Walter's neatly scribed copy of the report to the Archbishop. It was a masterpiece of suppression and suggestion, and would fit neatly with his own; he was glad to see that Alys's adventure and her part in the arrest of Miller was one of the items suppressed here too. Pride in her achievements was one thing, bringing these to the attention of senior churchmen was another. As for Dame Isabella, better to have her murdered by a passing counterfeiter than to put what really happened onto paper where anyone might read it.

'And I've a couple o the lads down the Gallowgate now wi one o the clerks,' Otterburn continued, 'asking about among the neighbours to see if they can find out why they were all so feart for the man. We might clear up a couple more matters while we're about it.'

'So how many have you held, in the end?' Gil asked.

'It's in there.'

'What, no others? Miller, Saunders and Noll Campbell. You've let the women go? And the miners' laddie?'

'Oh, him!' said Otterburn. 'Aye, young Livingstone came by afore Sext, wi a tale of escorting the laddie out to see his kin put in the ground, so I released him into his hands, for there's no reasonable charge I could bring against him. The deil kens what Livingstone will do wi him, but he's no my problem any more. As for the women in the case! Sic a weeping and wailing as you never heard, and that bairn screaming and all, I bade them begone. Likely they were in the conspiracy and all, but it was their men did the work and broke the laws o Scotland.'

'And the gallowglass?'

'Could talk his way out o a locked kist,' said Otterburn. 'No, no, I'm happy wi what I've got, maister, and so will the justiciars be when the time comes. Save only that I've to hold them and feed them till then,' he added gloomily, 'but I might get that past wi the other expenses. Oh, that Ersche leear woman that was in the Tolbooth, I've sent to the Serjeant to set her free and all.'

Gil compressed his lips, reluctant to say what he was thinking. After a moment he said instead,

'I see the House of the Mermaiden is empty again.'

'Is that right?' Otterburn's close-set gaze was expressionless. 'Walter did say he'd seen wagons loading at the door. I dare say their prices was too dear for Glasgow. Make someone a handsome dwelling, that would, save for the price of getting a new door put on.'

'Easy enough to turn that one, hang it the other way. What about John Sempill?'

'What about him? That wife o his, she minds you o an alabaster weeper on a tomb, but she's fair got him muzzled. How does she do it? He was feart to answer our questions for what she'd think o him.'

'Will you charge him, do you think?'

'That's a matter for the Crown,' said Otterburn regretfully. 'But I'll tell you, whether they fine him or charge him wi treason, if the land the mine's on really does belong to Livingstone o Craigannet, then by what his son was telling me when he fetched young Berthold away, Sempill's got more to worry him than what his wife thinks about it. Archie Livingstone's no one to let another man get credit for what's his. I'd say the Stirling men of law will eat well this winter.'

Dissatisfied, but unable to work out why, Gil went out into the busy Sunday morning of the burgh. Families passed him coming from hearing Mass at St Mungo's, apprentices, journeymen and maidservants were setting out to enjoy a day off, even the weather seemed on holiday with bright sunshine broken only by a few clouds. He drifted down the Drygate among the crowds, past the two silent tofts to Canon Aiken's house.

Here he found Lowrie absent but the young man's uncle present, with plenty to say and a jug of Malvoisie to say it over.

'I tell you, I'm sorry I ever ordered a coffin for the auld carline,' the older Livingstone admitted, filling Gil's glass. 'If I'd kent all she's been at, she could ha gone into the ground in her shift for all I cared, never mind her shroud! But it's ordered and paid for, so she might as well make use o't. So it was your bonnie lass jaloused it was a mine out at Ballencleroch? My, she's an accomplished one. Does she keep a good household and all?'

'Oh, she does,' said Gil, with a fleeting thought of this morning's discordant breakfast. 'A generous kitchen, and rarely a cross word.'

'She's no sisters, I suppose?' said Livingstone hopefully. 'No, the best ones never do. Some more o this wine, maister. And it seems it was the counterfeiter that slew Isabella when she put an end to the scheme? Aye, well, he'd have the eye and the hand to strike the nail home, I can believe it right enough, for all young Lowrie says the man's denying it.'

'He'll hang for Dod Muir,' said Gil as he had done before.

'Fortunate for us, though,' said Livingstone thoughtfully, 'that he slew her when he did, for if the matter had got out and she'd gone to trial at the Justice Ayre, everyone round her would ha been drawn in, me and my brother questioned as to whether we'd kent what she was at and whether we'd benefited from the coin she was having struck. And me a past moneyer and all! I'd never ha lived it down.'

'Fortunate indeed,' agreed Gil, and took another sip of the wine.

'And her household back here yestreen, all but that Marion or Forveleth or whatever she's cried. I don't know what to do wi them, they'll follow her coffin all in black to make a decent show, but once she's in the ground they'll have to take what she's left them and go. I'd send them to

287

Lady Magdalen, but she'll likely no be hiring new people for a while, by what you say. Quite the contrary, indeed.'

'Indeed,' Gil agreed. He set the glass down and leaned forward. 'Maister Livingstone, I've another matter to consult you on.'

The hall of the White Castle was surprisingly crowded. It contained Lowrie, studiously conversing with Socrates, and Maistre Pierre speaking High Dutch with the boy Berthold; but it also contained the woman Forveleth, standing near the kitchen door in her stained and filthy clothing, her bundle at her feet, and Ealasaidh, tall and threatening in front of her. These two were hissing at one another in venomous Ersche while Alys attempted to reason with both in Scots. Gil took all this in, nodded to Lowrie, and went quietly to join Catherine where she sat at the hearth, her fingers busy at her eternal handwork while her black eyes flicked from one group to another.

'*Que passe, madame?*' he asked, sitting down beside her. She greeted him formally, and said, choosing her words carefully,

'There is some objection to the presence of that woman in our kitchen.'

'Objection?' Gil was used to the level of charity exercised under Maistre Pierre's roof. This did not appear to match it. 'Why?'

'I think she may have caused offence previously. It is hardly a guest's place to order her out, but the matter ought to be resolved. Since our *maistre* will not intervene, it would be proper for you to do so.'

'Do you think so?'

She nodded significantly. 'Someone should support *la jeune madame*.'

Maistre Pierre was still as studiously intent on his conversation with Berthold as Lowrie was on his with the dog. Clearly, though he might not support Ealasaidh, he was not going to support his daughter. A sudden uneasy suspicion struck Gil, and he looked at Catherine in dismay. She nodded again.

'She will need your help, *maistre l'avocat.*'

She certainly will, he thought, bracing himself. Catherine gave him an approving smile and returned her attention to the long trail of lace, or braid, or whatever it was, which hung from her twisted hands. He rose and crossed the room to join the argument.

It was easier than he had feared it might be to soothe matters for the moment. The Ersche argument ceased as he approached, both women looking warily at him.

'Good day to you, Forveleth,' he said casually. 'The Provost told me he had ordered you set free. Have they fed you in the kitchen? Is that what brought you here?'

'They would have fed me,' said Forveleth resentfully, 'but this one was ordering them to throw me in the street, and not listen to their mistress, though I said I had a word for her, and now she will not let me speak.'

'I don't know why she would do that,' Gil said, raising his eyebrows at Ealasaidh. 'It's my wife runs this house, it's her kitchen, she is well able to decide for herself who'll be fed there and who she'll speak to.'

'This one is a fool and a false speaker,' said Ealasaidh, her rich Scots vocabulary deserting her for the moment. 'I was wishing only to protect the lassie from her, the way she would be taking advantage.'

'I'm grateful for your consideration, I've told you that,' said Alys, her exasperation well concealed, 'but I can use my own judgement, you've no need to protect me.'

'I meant for the best.'

'I'm certain of that,' agreed Gil, 'but you've no need to concern yourself. Go down to the kitchen, Forveleth, and see if they can let you clean yourself up, and then maybe we can all dine soon.' He looked hopefully at Alys. She smiled rather too brightly and said,

'We'd all be glad to eat. Go and wash, Forveleth, as my husband says, and bid them come up to set the table if you would.'

'And after dinner,' Gil went on as the woman slipped away down the kitchen stair, 'you and I and Lowrie will go down to visit Kate. Lowrie promised to tell the wee girls if there was news of the false coiners.'

'Well, it was the younger one I promised,' Lowrie said over dinner. 'Ysonde, is that her name? A strong-minded lassie. She was very insistent I came back,' he explained to Alys.

'She would be,' Alys said.

'Now, this boy Berthold,' said Maistre Pierre. He glanced at Ealasaidh, eating her dinner in a haughty silence, and went on, 'He tells me he has no kin left in Germany, and no wish to go home for now. He seems a good laddie, though not of the cleverest, but I think he knows little about stone, for a miner's son, and he is clumsy with his hands.'

'So not a mason's prentice, then,' said Gil.

'No. I did think of it, when you told me of the boy this morning, but he would not do. He may stay here till he learns enough Scots to get by,' he offered, 'but then you have to find him a position. He makes a good servant, perhaps. He likes horses. I help you to some of this mould, madame,' he added to Ealasaidh, who accepted the gesture without speaking.

Gil glanced past Forveleth who was talking to Jennet, to Berthold seated at the foot of the board, apparently asking Luke for the names of one item after another on the table. Near them, on Nancy's lap, John shouted the words after them.

'A resilient laddie,' he said. 'He should do well wherever he settles.'

'I'd thought much the same,' said Lowrie. 'But someone needs to have a care to him for now.' He held out his wooden trencher for Maistre Pierre to transfer a slice of the kale mould with powdered ginger, and added reflectively, 'He might teach me High Dutch. It's clear to me it's a good thing for a man to speak more tongues than his own.'

290

'Cloth,' said Luke at the foot of the table.
'C-lof?' essayed Berthold. 'Coff!' echoed John.
'Quite so,' said Gil.

Lady Kate's stepdaughters were not at home. John and
Lowrie were probably equally disappointed, Gil thought
as he introduced Lowrie to Kate's husband, but John was
the more vociferous about it.

'Onnyanny?' he demanded. '*Where* Onnyanny?'

'Hush, John,' said Nancy without effect. 'Don't wake the
wee baba.'

'They've gone for a walk,' Kate explained across
Edward's cradle. 'They won't be long. They've gone to put
flowers on their own mammy's grave,' she added for
Lowrie's benefit. 'It's a pleasant walk on a fine day and
Nan has kin in the Greyfriars yard as well.'

'Come and sit down,' Augie Morison invited, waving at
the wide, sunny window space where Kate's great chair
was set, 'and tell us the truth of what we're hearing. There
surely canny be a silver mine in the Gallowgate!'

'It's yersel, Mistress Alys, Maister Gil.' Kate's gigantic
maidservant Babb appeared from the kitchen stair, a tray
in her hands. 'And what's this I'm hearing?' She hooked a
stool into place with her ankle and set the tray on it, nodding at Lowrie who had leapt to help. Alys expertly distracted John, who had appeared at her knee reaching for
the cakes, by breaking one in half and putting a portion in
each little hand, then lifted the platter to put it out of the
boy's reach. Babb looked down at her. 'Did I hear you
might be flitting, mistress?'

'What?' said Kate, astonished.

'Cake John. *Two* cake, John!'

'Where will you go?' Augie looked from Gil to Alys.
'When did you think of it?'

'This morning,' said Gil. 'No more than thought on, and
we've never mentioned it aloud, have we, Alys?'

'Oh,' said Babb in disappointment. 'Your Jennet was saying when I saw her at the Greyfriars, when I went to hear Mass, she thought you'd be out o there soon.'

'I must have a word with Jennet,' said Alys. 'No, we have no plans to leave soon, only I have thought of a bigger house and our own household.'

'Aye, you'd be well to,' agreed Babb. 'Your own roof, and that.'

'Thank you, Babb,' said Kate. 'Hand the cakes and ale, and you can go back to talk to Ursel.'

'Do I no get to hear all the news?' Babb asked, offended. 'I want to hear how Mistress Alys fought wi the man that slew that old woman in the Drygate!'

She listened better than some of their hearers had done, Gil thought, with a few exclamations and muttered words of praise, but no interruptions. Kate and her husband also heard their tale with attention, much amused by the midnight interview, but Kate grew more puzzled as the account lengthened.

'Aye, you're a warrior, lassie, right enough!' said Babb at the end, taking her leave to convey the news all hot to the kitchen. It seemed to be a compliment. 'What a tale, is it no, mem!'

'What an adventure!' said Augie. 'So the mine's in Strathblane, is it? You never think of such a thing in a place like that.'

'It doesn't make sense,' said Kate.

'Onnyanny!' announced John, waving his toy horse. 'Onnyanny have cake.'

Out across the yard the smaller leaf of the great gates swung open and the two little girls came through with their nurse.

'He must have heard them, mem,' said Nancy proudly. The girls tumbled into the house, stopped at the sight of the guests, made their curtsies when prompted by Nan. Ysonde sprang up from hers and launched herself in glee at Lowrie.

292

'You came back!' she said, while her sister went shyly to her father's side. 'You said you'd come to tell us about the dusty man. Is it all made right now? Is he in prison for making the false pennies?'

'He is,' agreed Lowrie. 'He's a very bad man, so he deserves to be put in prison.'

She leaned against his knee, ignoring John's cries of 'Have cake!'

'Tell me! Tell Wynliane too,' she added generously.

Under cover of the distribution of cakes and Lowrie's restricted version of the tale, Kate said again,

'It doesny make sense. Why would the man Miller kill Dame Isabella?'

'No,' agreed Gil. 'But he was quick to kill at other times. The man Muir, the miners. He clearly has a reputation for violence.'

'No, Gil,' she said. 'That's a good story to send Blacader and to tell the justiciars, but what really happened?'

'Kate's right,' said Augie. 'What did he gain?'

'What did he gain by killing Dod Muir?' Gil countered.

'That was in anger, surely,' objected Kate. 'Did you no tell us Dame Isabella was killed in cold blood, by someone who went in to her ready armed? Why would Miller plan to do that?'

'Miller,' said Alys thoughtfully, 'never wore a plaid, in any of the accounts we have heard.' She looked at Kate. 'There was a sighting of someone leaving the courtyard of the house, *wrapped in a great durk cloak or gown or the like,*' she quoted. 'That's hardly how I would describe Miller as I saw him either.'

'So does either of you believe it?' Kate demanded. Gil looked at her in exasperation.

'It's what I'll report,' he said firmly. 'As for your question, consider who else she was a danger to if she'd carried on as she was.'

'Sempill?' Kate said. 'He was our aunt Margaret's stepson, I mind him from her wedding.'

'I've dealt wi him,' said Augie unexpectedly. 'I'd not think it was him. If he saw a threat coming I'd be gey surprised, though he wouldny want the Treasury looking closely into his affairs.'

'Which of us would?' Gil said. Lowrie was now entertaining the little girls with riddles. I hope he'll teach them nothing unseemly, he thought.

'Sempill was elsewhere when she died,' said Alys.

'The Crown?' said Kate. 'Was she executed for her treason? Without a trial?'

'I suspect she was executed to prevent her coming to trial,' Gil said. 'Everyone connected to her and her scheme would have been drawn in.' As Otterburn said, as my uncle said. How close was he working with Blacader's agent? Did everyone in Glasgow know about it but me?

'Which reminds me,' said Alys improbably. 'I have seen the painted chamber in the bawdy-house.'

'What?' said Kate. 'How did you – no, no, I won't ask. What like are they? He wouldny tell me,' she jerked her head at Gil. 'Are they as naughty as they say?'

'No, nothing like that. I thought they were bonnie,' said Alys, 'very well painted and cheerful subjects, love and the muses and springtime and the like. I can't believe that Lady Magdalen wanted us to whitewash over them.'

Kate laughed.

'Gil told me that. She was aye a serious one, very pious as a lassie, by what my mother once said o her.' She stopped, looking from Alys to Gil. 'Ah. Oh! Is that it? No, she wouldny want to come to the law's attention if that's the case, would she?' Gil nodded. 'But Otterburn gave her no grief?'

'He seemed sympathetic,' Gil said cautiously.

Augie was looking puzzled; he always had trouble with the allusive nature of Cunningham exchanges, and this one must not be brought out in the open. Kate could tell him later, Gil thought. Magdalen Boyd would be safe enough, so long as her religious beliefs stayed outside the scrutiny of the law. Lollards, who preached against Holy

Kirk, who believed that the saints were no more than idols and ordinary people could speak direct to God, were harmless enough provided they kept themselves to themselves. But they all had an unfortunate tendency to make their ideas public when questioned, and that could only end in tears and torture, and probably in flames as well.

I would kill to protect those I love, he thought. But I hope I would be less detached about it than Sandy Boyd.

'You could always come with me to see the house by daylight,' Alys was saying. 'Now it's empty, I want a longer look.'

'So you are thinking of moving?' Kate allowed herself to be diverted from the other topic. 'I thought you were comfortable enough here in the High Street.'

'Gil is to take an assistant,' Alys announced. 'We will need more room, if we are to have our own household.'

'An assistant? What, an apprentice? Who will it be?'

'An apprentice quaestor,' Gil said thoughtfully. 'I hate to think what we'd put in the indentures. *Promise to teach the aforesaid all the mysteries of the craft, as, inspecting bodies, detecting poisons, studying wounds.*'

'*Asking impertinent questions,*' Kate supplied, laughing.

'*Nosing about,*' said Alys, obviously quoting somebody.

'And all the other ways of clearing innocent names,' said Augie with feeling. Kate sobered, and put out her hand to him, and Gil said,

'No, merely an assistant, to help me with the work and to train as a notary forbye. It's Lowrie here. That's why I brought him down the now, to introduce him.'

Lowrie looked up, smiled, accepted their good wishes. Augie poured more ale, and they drank a toast to the future and the signing of the contract. John and his wooden horse had galloped off across the wide hall, but Wynliane and Ysonde watched with interest.

'What's it for?' Ysonde asked Lowrie, tugging at his sleeve.

'I'm to serve Maister Gil,' he explained, 'and learn to be a man of law.'

'Is it a good potition?'

'A good position? One of the best,' he assured her seriously.

'That's good. Then when I'm old enough, you can marry me, and I can help to catch bad men too. Will we do that?'

Her parents and nurse exclaimed at her forwardness; Gil covered a grin and avoided Alys's eye; but Lowrie, flying scarlet at the ears, sat down again and held out his hand.

'If your parents permit, and you're still of the same mind, when you are old enough I'll wed you.'

She put her hand in his.

'I won't change my mind,' she said. 'So they'd better.' She leaned against his knee and smiled at the company. 'That's all right, then.'